PROFESSOR MORIARTY
The Napoleon of Crime, unstoppable, unkillable, unutterably evil, as he puts his evil imagination to work battling his greatest rival...

SHERLOCK HOLMES
The World's Greatest Sleuth, responding to his greatest challenge, as his arch-rival returns "from the dead" in two exciting new adventures to challenge his powers!

"EXCITING!" —*St. Louis Globe-Democrat*

"GOOD NEWS FOR THOSE OF US WHO STILL REVERE HOLMES AND WATSON!"
—*Nashville Banner*

"LITERATE AND INTELLIGENT, AS WELL AS WITTY...LONG MAY PROFESSOR MORIARTY RUN!"
—*West Coast Review of Books*

Berkley books by John Gardner

THE RETURN OF MORIARTY
THE REVENGE OF MORIARTY

THE RETURN OF MORIARTY

JOHN GARDNER

B

BERKLEY BOOKS, NEW YORK

FOR
TONY GOULD-DAVIES

This Berkley book contains the complete
text of the original hardcover edition.
It has been completely reset in a typeface
designed for easy reading, and was printed
from new film.

THE RETURN OF MORIARTY

A Berkley Book / published by arrangement with
G. P. Putnam's Sons

PRINTING HISTORY
Berkley Medallion edition / April 1976
Berkley edition / February 1988

ISBN: 0-425-05093-9

A BERKLEY BOOK ® TM 757,375
Berkley Books are published by The Berkley Publishing Group,
200 Madison Avenue, New York, New York 10016.
The name "BERKLEY" and the "B" logo
are trademarks belonging to Berkley Publishing Corporation.

PRINTED IN THE UNITED STATES OF AMERICA

10   9   8   7   6   5   4

Contents

Preface

LONDON: *Thursday, April 5, 1894*   1
   (RETURN TO LIMEHOUSE)

Friday, April 6, 1894   32
   (FANNY INVESTIGATED AND MORIARTY'S MEMORIES OF
   THE AUTUMN OF 1888)

Friday, April 6, 1894   70
   (THE REAL MORIARTY)

Friday, April 6, 1894   97
   (A DAY IN THE COUNTRY)

Sunday, April 8, 1894   112
   (TAKING STOCK)

Monday, April 9, 1894, 1:00 A.M. to 9:00 P.M.   134
   (THE ENEMY AND THE TRUTH CONCERNING MORIARTY
   AT THE REICHENBACH FALLS)

Monday April 9, 1894, 9:00 P.M. onward   152
   (THE NIGHT OF THE PUNISHERS)

Tuesday, April 10, to Thursday, April 12, 1894   166
   (CROW AMONG THE PIGEONS)

Thursday, April 12, 1894   189
   (THE MANNER IN WHICH MORIARTY PROCURED
   FREEDOM FOR THE JACOBS BROTHERS)

Friday, April 13, 1894   199
   (THE CONTINENTAL ALLIANCE)

Saturday, April 14, 1894   212
    (AN ASSASSINATION IS ARRANGED)

Sunday, April 15, to Wednesday, April 18, 1894   218
    (THE WEDDING)

Saturday, April 21, 1894   248
    (THE HARROW ROBBERY)

Sunday, April 22, to Friday, April 27, 1894   260
    (THE REALMS OF NIGHT)

Friday, April 27, 1894   276
    (THE LAST TRICK)

Saturday, April 28, 1894   285
    (THE SECOND EXILE)

Glossary   287

Preface

There is need for some explanation regarding this volume and how it came into being. Therefore certain facts should be made clear at the outset.

In the summer of 1969 I was engaged in research concerning the current problems and operational methods of both the Metropolitan Police and the sprawling criminal underworld of London and its environs. During this period I was introduced to a man known to both the police and his associates as Albert George Spear.

Spear was at that time in his late fifties: a large well-built man with a sharp sense of humor and lively intelligence. He was also an authority on Criminal London—not only of his time but also of the previous century.

Spear was not without problems, being well-known to the police, with a record of many arrests and two convictions—the last carrying with it a sentence of fifteen years for armed bank robbery. In spite of this he was a thoroughly likable man, whose favorite pastime was reading any book that came to hand. On our first meeting he told me that he had read all my Boysie Oakes books, which he found amusing and entertaining rubbish—a criticism not far removed from my own view.

One night toward the end of August I received a telephone call from Spear saying that he wished to see me urgently. At the time I was living in London, and within the hour Spear was sitting opposite me in my Kensington house. He brought with him a heavy briefcase, which contained three thick leather-bound books. It is as well to say here that the bindings and paper of these books have since been subjected to the usual tests and indisputably date back to the second half of the nineteenth century. The writing contained in them, however, cannot with absolute certainty be dated, the results of chromatographic analysis and further tests being inconclusive.

Spear's story concerning the books was intriguing, the volumes having come into his possession via his grandfather, Albert William Spear (1858-1919), and in turn his father, William Albert Spear (1895-1940).

My informant told me that he had not really examined the books until recently. All three generations of Spears seem to have been involved in criminal activities of one kind or another, and Spear remembers his grandfather talking of a Professor Moriarty. He also claims that his father spoke much about the Professor, who was apparently a legendary figure in the lore of the Spear family.

It was on his deathbed that William Spear first spoke to Albert about the books, which were kept locked in a strongbox at the family home in Stepney. They were, he claimed, the private and secret journals of Moriarty, though at the time of his father's death the younger Spear was more concerned with the activities of one Adolf Hitler than with the family legend.

Although Spear was an avid reader, he had not really read or studied the works of Sir Arthur Conan Doyle until the late 1960's— a strange omission, but one that did not worry me since I was also a latecomer to Dr. Watson's chronicles concerning the great detective.

However, when Spear eventually began to read the saga, he quickly came across the few references concerning Holmes' archenemy, Professor James Moriarty, and was immediately struck by the descriptions in the Holmes books which had bearings on some of the things his father had told him.

One night he became so intrigued by both the similarities and paradoxical inconsistencies that he began to examine the books he had brought for me to see.

The pages were in good condition, and all three books were crammed with careful, rather sloping, copperplate handwriting. One could make out certain dates and street plans, but the remaining script was at first sight unintelligible. Spear was convinced that his father had told him the truth and what he possessed were the real Professor Moriarty's private journals, written in cipher.

I cannot deny that my first sight of those books gave me an immense thrill, though I remained on guard, expecting the sharp Spear to put in a plea for hard cash. But money was not mentioned. It would please him, he told me, if someone could decipher the journals and perhaps use them to good advantage. His interest was purely academic.

In the days that followed I came across a number of immediate inconsistencies, not least of which was the fact that the journals continued for many years after the spring of 1891—the year in which, according to Watson, Holmes disappeared at the Reichenback Falls, presumed dead after a fight with Moriarty, only to reappear in 1894 with the story that it was Moriarty who had perished.

If these journals were those of the same Moriarty, then obviously someone was either glossing fact with fiction or there was some strange case of mistaken identity.

My own knowledge of ciphers being small, I eventually took the books to my good friends and publishers Robin Denniston (who has had much experience with codes and ciphers) and Christopher Falkus. After many long hours of arduous trial and error, coupled with applied science, the cipher was broken. The result is that at the time of writing, some one and a half books have been decoded.

Quite early in this operation we realized that the documents could not be published as they stood. Even in these permissive times there is little doubt that Moriarty's inherent evil—which lurks on every page—could cause concern. Also, the memories of too many revered and famous personalities would be subjected to wanton rumor and scandal.

We decided, therefore, that it would be best for me to publish Professor Moriarty's story in the form of a novel, or novels. This is why some of the locations and events have been slightly altered—though in some cases, such as Moriarty's involvement in the Ripper murders and the so-called de Goncourt scandal, there is no point in concealing the facts.

As further reason for this form of treatment is that Spear disappeared shortly after handing the journals to me. As I have already stated, we cannot positively date the writings, so it is just possible, though I do not believe this, that Albert Spear, with a mischievous sense of humor, has taken some pains to perpetrate the second largest literary hoax of the century. Or maybe his grandfather, who is much mentioned in the journals, was a man of imagination? Perhaps the publication of this first volume may bring us some of the answers.

I must, however, add one final acknowledgment, which is, I believe, of interest. I am deeply indebted to Miss Bernice Crow, of Cairndow, Argyllshire, great-granddaughter of the late Superintendent Angus McCready Crow, for the use of her great-grandfather's journals, notebooks, correspondence and jottings—papers which have been invaluable in writing this first volume.

JOHN GARDNER

Rowledge,
Surrey

For three long years . . . Watson and the world thought that Holmes also lay dead beneath the dark and swirling waters of the Reichenbach; but Holmes in 1894 was very much alive. . . . Why not Moriarty? . . . Anyone familiar with the history of evil in the world since 1894 has little difficulty in seeing that Professor James Moriarty was taking advantage of a long period of social unrest to consolidate and expand his undisputed position as the Napoleon of crime. . . .

—WILLIAM S. BARING-GOULD

LONDON: *Thursday, April 5, 1894*

(RETURN TO LIMEHOUSE)

"So THE TRUCE is to be tested at last." The man behind the desk allowed himself a grim smile of satisfaction. "You're in no doubt?" His questing eyes searched the face of the small, whippet-like figure standing before him.

"No doubt at all, Professor. I'd know, so would Parker."

"It's Parker you've had in Baker Street then?"

"No other."

"Suitably disguised, I trust?"

"Been his beat for the past month, acting as a lurker."

"Performing on his Jew's harp, I suppose."

"It's his best side."

"Mmmm. That and the thread." The man behind the desk was familiar with Parke's skill as a garroter. There had been cause to use him many times in the past.

The room was pleasant, a high ceiling, two windows looking out onto the river, and not overcluttered with furnishings.

The furnishings, in fact, looked relatively new, as they indeed were, the redecoration of the room having been carried out in a safe, private manner by Godfrey Giles & Company of 19 Old Cavendish Street.

The carpet was a knotted-pile Persian; one of the famous "Sir Walter Raleigh" smoking chairs stood angled to the fireplace where, because of the unseasonal early spring chill outside, a cheerful fire crackled in the grate. Behind the smoking chair was a bookcase lined with leather-bound tomes, among the spines of which, the discerning could have observed such works as Bosanquet's *Essentials of Logic* or *The Morphology of Thought* and Emile Faguet's *Politiques et moralistes français du XIX siècle* nestling cheek-by-jowl with Lagrange's *Analytical Mechanics*, a beautiful copy of *Principia Philosophiae* and Moriarty's *The Dynamics of an Asteroid.*

Apart from the large desk—the central feature of the furnishings, a kidney-shaped Regency-style piece with a leather top—there were a pair of Chippendale tables in dark mahogany and two Morocco-covered easy chairs, the latest design from Hampton's of Pall Mall. There was no bric-a-brac, no attempt to overlay the utilitarian, stern interior with fripperies. There was, however, one painting, which occupied a central place on the wall opposite the desk, so that it could be seen by the man who sat there: a haunting work showing a young woman, head on hands, peeping out of the canvas with a coy, sideways look. To the expert it was undoubtedly the work of Jean-Baptiste Greuze, that unusually successful French artist of the 1700's, popular for his paintings of young girls like this one, and scenes depicting family virtue.

The man behind the desk lowered his head, as though in thought, while the whippet person shuffled his feet.

There was a third occupant in the room, sprawled in one of the easy chairs. A man in late middle age, with a high, deep-lined brow, aggressive nose and cruel blue eyes, the lids of which drooped cynically. He shifted purposefully.

"Is he still in Baker Street?" the third man asked.

The one who stood before the desk flicked his eyes from his interlocutor in the easy chair to the man behind the desk.

The first speaker, seated behind the desk, slowly raised his head, the face moving from side to side in a manner reminiscent of an iguana.

"That is for me to ask, I think, Moran." His speech was quiet but with a great sense of authority. "You have done well in my absence, apart from one or two stupid and unnecessary bunglings, such as this foolish business of Adair, but I would be grateful if you would remember that I am now back in full command."

Moran grunted, his eyes narrowing.

"Is Mr. Holmes still at the Baker Street house, Ember?" continued the Professor.

"He has gone to Kensington, to visit his friend Watson."

Moran made another irritable, grunting noise from the depths of his chair.

"Ah, the physician." The Professor allowed himself a thin smile. "That means . . ."

"It means he will begin meddling with the Adair business," cracked Moran sharply. "Watson is already interested."

"So you informed me. Moran, you are a fool to have become involved with Adair. With Holmes and Watson interested we will have to take steps I could have done without at this stage. I have much to do, a great deal to organize now that I am back at the helm: the business in France, the general progress of anarchy throughout the world, not to mention the day-to-day work here. You saw how many people were waiting downstairs, all wanting to see me, all wanting favors." He raised his right hand, flicking it toward the door in a peremptory gesture. "Leave us, Ember."

The whippet, Ember, nodded sharply and backed toward the door after the manner of one leaving the presence of some Eastern potentate. When the door had closed behind Ember, the man they called the Professor rose from his chair.

"Let me deal with Holmes." There was venom in Moran's tone. "If I do it, he'll be out of your way once and for all, Moriarty."

An unseen observer would have been surprised to hear the Professor being referred to as Moriarty. Apart from the habit of oscillating his head like a reptile, the man who stood behind the desk bore little resemblance to the only recorded description of Professor James Moriarty.*

This man was not unusually tall, around five feet ten inches, one supposed, in his stocking feet. True, he was not of bulky build, but you would call him slim rather than thin, and his head was topped by a generous mane of well-barbered hair, graying at the temples in a distinguished fashion. His posture was upright, shoulders square and not rounded as Holmes' description leads us to believe. As for his face, the complexion was certainly not pale; rather it was that of a man who has spent a generous amount of time in the sun, not deeply brown, but certainly tanned. He was clean-shaven and there was indeed a certain asceticism about him, but the eyes were bright, far from being sunken. In all he appeared to be a man of much younger age than that suggested by the Holmes description, which until now has been taken as historical fact.

Moran—Colonel Sebastian Moran, Chief of Staff to Moriarty, for that is who he was—repeated, "Let me deal with Holmes."

"I have to think. This is not the time for any quick decisions, as you should well know. There is too much at stake in the future. If

---

*The description referred to is, of course, Sherlock Holmes' famous word picture, documented by Dr. Watson in *The Final Problem.* "He is extremely tall and thin, his forehead domes out in a white curve, and his two eyes are deeply sunken in his head. He is clean-shaven, pale, and ascetic-looking, retaining something of the professor in his features. His shoulders are rounded from much study, and his face protrudes forward, and is forever oscillating from side to side in a curiously reptilian fashion. He peered at me with great curiosity in his puckered eyes" *(the Final Problem,* Sir Arthur Conan Doyle.)

Holmes has only just returned to London and is seeing his friend Watson for the first time, twenty-four hours will make little difference. Watson has believed his friend dead for the past three years; there will be some emotional shock. Following that, they will have a great deal to talk about.''

"I would rather complete the matter now. Today." Moran sounded peppery.

Moriarty looked hard at his lieutenant, the eyes, like those of a mesmerist, reaching grimly into Moran's mind. People often noted the chilling power of Moran's blue eyes, but they were no match for the austere and commanding stare Moriarty was able to summon.

"I would prefer you to set certain other business in motion." Moriarty seldom raised his voice, but the tone he could produce, and the authority with which he spoke, generated obedience from all but the most foolhardy and willful among those who followed him.

Moran gave a grudging nod of acquiescence.

"Good. There are matters I wish you to arrange. If I am to resume control, then it will be necessary for me to meet with all our leading captains in Europe. The meeting can be here or in Paris, I do not mind either way, but I wish a date to be set within the next ten days. Arrange the date and place. And on your way out would you tell Ember that I am ready to see those who have come for help or favors?''

Moran hesitated, his mouth half open as though he wished to make another appeal to the Professor, then, thinking better of it, he gave a curt movement of his head, turned on his heel and left the room.

Professor Moriarty's chambers, however pleasant and well appointed, were not set in the most salubrious of neighborhoods. London in the 1890's was still a city of great contrast, the glitter of the West End having little in common with the relatively dark and dangerous East End. Moriarty lived hard down by the river, close to the docks and the Chinese quarter of Limehouse, in paradoxical luxury, above an unused warehouse, the bleak and dingy front of which could be reached only by walking through a narrow maze of alleys, courts and streets; the houses, drinking dens and grubby shops squeezed tightly in on one another, by day active and noisy with their cosmopolitan population, by night an area in which a stranger would have to be nothing short of lunatic to walk alone through the ill-lit passages.

The façade of the warehouse would never arouse suspicion, even in the most observant; it gave the impression of a place uninhabited, except perhaps by rats or vagrants seeking shelter for the night. Cracked windows and scarred brickwork bore testimony to a state of decay. Yet the warehouse was known to a horde of villains, footpads, murderers, pickpockets, forgers, scoundrels, prostitutes, garroters—male and female—thugs, burglars, tricksters and the like, as a place of importance.

Several hundred of such people were acquainted with the method of obtaining access to the interior of the building—a series of sharp raps, in sequence, on the small door inset in the large, boarded, wooden gates, through which, at one time or another, cargoes ranging from grain to silk had been driven and stored until ship or other transport had dispatched them.

Immediately inside the doors, the impression of a storehouse, long inactive, remained. It was only when one crossed to the far end of the grubby expanse of floor and passed through the small door, which, to even the keenest eye appeared to be rotten, insubstantial and flaking, that you entered a different world.

On the far side of the door was a long narrow room set about with bare wooden tables and benches. To the right a fat, ruddy-complexioned man and a thin woman in her late thirties stood behind a wooden counter over which they dispensed hot tea, soup, beer, spirits and bread. At the far left a wooden stairway led to a solid doorway behind which Professor Moriarty lived in quarters that vied for comfort with some of the best bachelor chambers to be found in the more fashionable West End.

Colonel Sebastian Moran descended the stairway with mixed feelings. Below him some twenty or so men and women were seated at the tables, eating, drinking and talking in low tones. During the three years of Moriarty's absence, and presumed death, it had been Moran who greeted the twice-weekly deputations of people such as these. But he was now all too aware that during his interregnum the gatherings in the "waiting room," as it was known, had not been as quiet and apprehensive as the one upon which he now looked. Moran knew why, and it irritated him. The same officers were present: Ember; the tall muscular Paget; Spear, with his broken nose and heavy features, which might have passed for good looks had it not been for the scar, which, like a lightning fork, ran down the right side of his face, narrowly missing the eye but unhappily connecting with the corner of his mouth; and Lee Chow, the agile, dangerous Chinese. Yet today there was an orderly calm, a sense of reverence almost, which had been lacking during the three years in which Moran had taken care of matters.

The irritation was a mixture of elements; jealousy, of course, played a large role. Moran had known, during the time since

Moriarty's disappearance following the Reichenbach Falls affray, that his leader was still alive. Indeed, he had met with him on a number of occasions, in small, unsuspected villages and hamlets in different parts of Europe, in order to discuss strategy, tactics and other complex matters concerning the Professor's interests. But as far as the general, run-of-the-mill members of Europe's criminal element were concerned, the Professor was dead and Colonel Moran had become the man to whom they turned.

Even though Moriarty himself had only just praised Moran's leadership and organizational ability, the older man was all too conscious that he lacked the extraordinary powers of the Professor, who seemed to exude an authority and confidence that demanded an almost supernatural obedience. Now that Moriarty had returned, as though from the dead, Moran knew that his own power was considerably reduced. But it was not simply the fact of natural jealousy that disturbed the Colonel. With Moriarty's return, and that of the meddling Sherlock Holmes, his own position was in jeopardy. It had been in jeopardy only recently through the folly of young Ronald Adair, but Moran had concluded that business with deadly efficiency.

Colonel Moran was a man with a good background, a man who had every chance to make a way for himself in the world. As with so many criminals, his life had at one time been balanced on a watershed between good and evil; that he had eventually toppled toward the criminal tendencies that beset all men is established fact. Moran was born into a family of some note, his father being Sir Augustus Moran, C.B., at one time British Minister to Persia; he was educated at Eton and Oxford, served with some distinction with the Indian Army and was the author of two books, *Heavy Game of the Western Himalayas* and *Three Months in the Jungle*, but his passions were undoubtedly shooting (he was a crack shot and big-game hunter) and gambling: obsessions that inevitably led him toward the criminal life in which he finally indulged himself, working under the influence and direction of James Moriarty. It was the latter passion, gambling, that had led him into the situation in which he now, on this April evening, found himself.

Sebastian Moran in many senses lived for gambling, because, apart from the monies paid to him and gained from his association with James Moriarty, his present income was supplemented to a very high degree by the large sums of cash that came his way across the card tables in London's gaming clubs. Moran was a skilled gambler who only rarely lost, a fact that to any knowledgeable student of human nature and the ways of the world means one thing only—that Moran was a cheat.

Indeed, Moran was a profession cheat, a sharper of more than ordinary dimensions—a *macer*, in criminal parlance. He had made card sharping a life's work—second only to shooting—and knew such men as Kepplinger, the San Francisco sharp; Ah Sin, the so-called Heathen Chinee; Lambri Pasha; and the Spaniard, Bianco.

Yet Moran could outwit all the great names, being an expert in every department of his trade, from the more automatic devices like card marking,* reflectors† and holdouts, as well as the more sophisticated methods of manipulating cards while a game was in progress. He was exceptionally skilled in bottom dealing, crimping, bridging, false shuffling and knocking.

It is a matter of record that early in the year Moran had been a constant whist partner of the Honorable Ronald Adair, the second son of the Earl of Maynooth, Governor of one of the Australian colonies. Young Adair had returned to London with his mother and sister, Hilda, and was living with them at 427 Park Lane, the mother having come to England for an eye operation.

On the evening of March 30 Ronald Adair was found shot—his head horribly mutilated by an expanded revolver bullet—in his locked room at 427 Park Lane. The murder had caused widespread shock and concern, there being no evidence of any weapon inside the room and no signs of any killer having climbed the twenty feet to Adair's window, or indeed of having made an escape from thence.

The true and hidden facts tumbled through Colonel Moran's mind as he made his way through the dingy thoroughfares to pick up a hansom and return to his rooms in Conduit Street. At the moment only two people in London knew of the truth surrounding Adair's

---

*It is plain, from letters now in the author's possession, that Colonel Moran was familiar with such refinements as marking by dot or puncture during a game, shading and tint-making, and the intricacies of marking through line and scrollwork.

†From the above-mentioned letters it is clear that Moran consistently used a briar-root pipe reflector, this being a device whereby a "shiner" (as the reflector was known in gaming circles of the time), a small convex mirror cemented to a piece of cork, was shaped to fit inside the bowl of a briar pipe. The sharper carries the "shiner" separately from the pipe. At the required moment, he knocks the ashes from his pipe and inserts the reflector, placing the pipe on the table with the bowl facing toward him. In this position the mirror is visible to nobody but the sharp, who, with practice, can align himself so that cards dealt or passed over the table are reflected and so glimpsed. From the few facts available, the author feels that Ronald Adair's discovery of Moran's cheating at the Bagatelle Card Club (see below) was not unconnected with the pipe shiner.

inexplicable murder: Sebastian Moran, who had perpetrated the crime, and Professor James Moriarty, in whom Moran had been forced to confide. As he sat back in the hansom, Moran was well aware that if someone did not act quickly, it would only be a matter of time before others would know the facts. Watson was already interested in the case, though that worried him as little as the knowledge that Inspector Lestrade of Scotland Yard was investigating Adair's murder. Neither Watson nor Lestrade, thought Moran, would ever hit on the truth, but Holmes' return to London put an entirely new complexion on the matter. The anxiety of these facts combined with the gall of jealousy and the necessity of carrying out Moriarty's instructions, made Moran more peppery and edgy than usual.

He stopped the hansom in the Strand in order to send four telegraphs: one to Moriarty's man in Paris, another to Rome, a third to Berlin and a fourth to Madrid. The messages were in simple prearranged code. Each telegraph read:

> IMPORTANT THAT BUSINESS IS CONCLUDED IN
> LONDON BY THE TWELFTH INSTANT. SEBMORE.

Moran then returned to Conduit Street, exchanging a few words with an elderly road sweeper near his house. He then prepared to bathe and dress for dinner. Outside, the chill day was overtaken by a night which became bleak and blustery.

Inside the "waiting room" at the rear of the warehouse, Ember, Paget, Spear and Lee Chow watched Moran's departure in silence. A stillness had fallen over those who waited, ate and drank at the long tables. An expectancy was in the air from the knowledge that the Professor was now alone in his chambers up the stairs. Eyes were turned toward Ember, Paget, Spear and Lee Chow, for these four were in some ways an élite, having occupied positions of close proximity to the Professor from a time dating back before his supposed death at the Reichenbach Falls.*

*It is interesting to note here that this fact, together with one or two other points, appears to be inconsistent with Sherlock Holmes' own statements as recorded by Dr. Watson. In *The Final Problem* Holmes categorically states to Watson that ". . . the London police . . . have secured the whole gang with the exception of him [Moriarty]." From later evidence we know this was not the case. On his return from "the grave," in *The Empty House*, Holmes mentions Parker, the garroter who was watching 221B Baker Street and, of course, Moran himself. It is possible that Holmes was under the

There was a slight hesitation before Paget, the tallest and most muscular of the men, moved with extraordinary grace and silence, bounding up the stairs and softly knocking at the door.

Moriarty stood by the windows, looking out into the night gathering about the river, the low mist creeping up the waters to seep over the embankments and flow into the lanes and alleyways. At Paget's knock, he called gently:

"Come."

Paget closed the door behind him.

"There are many waiting, Professor."

"I know. There is much on my mind, Paget. It is a strange feeling to have, shall we say, risen from the dead."

Paget inclined his head toward the door.

"To them down there, guv'nor, and to us for that matter it is nothing short of a miracle. But they're patient. They'll wait."

Moriarty sighed.

"No, we must go on as before. They have come for help, favors, to supply ideas and to show their respect for my position. I would not be facing my responsibilities if I did not see them. After all, they are family men and women. Who are the most important?"

Paget was silent for a moment.

"There's Hetty Jacobs, whose two sons have been taken in custody and her left with little, with no help and none to bring in a ha'penny. Millie Hubbard, whose husband, Jack, got hisself done in last month. It's a matter that should be set to rights. And there's Rosie McNiel whose daughter, Mary, got took by Sally Hodges' girls—against her will Rosie claims. I got Sal here with the girl."

"Are there none but women?"

"No, Bill Fisher's here, with Bert Clark and Dick Gay. They've a case they want to work. It's in the monkery and sounds worthy."

"Good."

"And old Solly Abrahams is here with a load of ream swag. Then there's a dozen or so more."

"I will see Hetty Jacobs," Moriarty allowed one of his rare smiles. "She has always been reliable and deserves some justice."

Paget nodded.

---

impression that all Moriarty's agents had been secured in April, 1891; but it is clear that this was far from being the case. Certainly his European network was left intact, and a large number of close associates, including Ember, Paget, Spear and Lee Chow, whom Moriarty referred to collectively as the "Praetorian Guard." As we shall see, this quartet undeniably acted as the close bodyguards and what present-day gang leaders would call "muscle."

"It would be best if you and Lee Chow remained with me during the meetings."

Paget looked pleased.

"Very well, Professor."

"That will be a regular situation," said Moriarty. "There are certain alterations I wish to make in our daily and weekly routine. When I am advising or giving favors, I shall have you, Paget, and Lee Chow present. Inform Chow before we start."

Paget left the room, and Moriarty turned again to the window. Over the past three years his life had been free of trouble. True, he had not completely kept to the terms of his bargain. He had seen Moran, advised him, and remained in touch. He also tightened up certain matters on the Continent, as he traveled from town to town and city to city. The European side of his operation had been in need of consolidation, and the time spent there was already paying off handsomely.

Through Moran he had been able to make up his mind about other important matters, particularly the role he would have to play, together with his agents and those who worked for him, in the political arena. Moriarty had long been aware that large-scale crime, organized crime, would never be a total end in itself. Early in his career he came to the conclusion that if the organization was smoothly run, efficient, covering all departments, there would inevitably be a saturation point, a time when the whole machinery would run with a minimum effort from himself. Therefore, fresh fields, new pastures, would constantly be needed.

For many years now there had been wealth, indeed riches undreamed of, the end product of burglaries, murder for profit, blackmail, forgery and the like, prostitution, profits from dens that existed to supply strong drink or the necessary substances to dope fiends, from the simple pressures of supply and demand, ranging from special sexual services that could not be satisfied through normal prostitution, to making arrangements for some wanted man to escape from the country. A large proportion of this money was already being ploughed back into more profitable ventures within the field of Moriarty's criminal influence, and also into financing quite legitimate ventures: few people knew, for instance, that James Moriarty was the controlling financial backer behind half a dozen music halls and a dozen restaurants in London, some of them in the glittering West End, others in the smug areas of suburbia.

Lee Chow came quietly into the room, bowing low and grinning pleasure. He was a second-generation immigrant, in his mid-twenties, who had never seen China, and there was nothing inscrutable about his flat, jaundiced face, as he so obviously showed delight at both Moriarty's sudden return to London and the new status he had acquired together with Paget.

Paget followed, one great hand resting on the shoulder of a plump little middle-aged woman, whose naturally ruddy moon face was filled with anxiety.

"Mrs. Hetty Jacobs," announced Paget after the manner of the grand majordomos of the upper classes.

Moriarty's face visibly softened and he stretched out his arms toward the small woman, who now appeared to be on the verge of tears. She came forward with a look of wonder and adulation spreading over her face.

"Oh, Professor . . . you've come back to us . . . it's really you."

She took the Professor's hand and kissed it with the reverence of the faithful paying homage to a relic of the True Cross.*

Moriarty, with some dignity, allowed the woman to kiss his hand, giving the appearance that the respect shown by the action was his due. At last he withdrew his hand and allowed the woman to unbend. As she did so, Moriarty placed both his hands on her shoulders in a fatherly manner.

"Hetty, it is good to see you," he said.

"Sir, we never thought to have you amongst us again. There will be dancing in the streets tonight."

Moriarty did not smile.

"And whoring and drunkenness, too, I'll be bound. But come,

---

*At this point we should pause and reflect on a further inconsistency. Before his description of Moriarty in *The Final Problem*, Holmes says to Watson, "His appearance was quite familiar to me." We are then given the description quoted in the footnote on page 19. As we have already seen, that description does not tally with Moriarty's appearance in his chambers above the warehouse on the evening of April 5, 1894. Holmes is convinced that the man he knew as Moriarty was the one he described to Watson, and the one whom Watson himself glimpsed at Victoria and on a later occasion. Yet Moran, the four members of the "Praetorian Guard," Mrs. Hetty Jacobs and, as we shall see, a large number of friends and criminal associates, immediately recognize the younger, shorter man as the real Moriarty. At this stage we must assume that the Moriarty Holmes knew and recognized is either another man or that the Moriarty of this manuscript, known and recognized by the criminal element, is as great a master of disguise as Holmes himself. The true facts regarding this and the puzzling questions of Moriarty's age and background, will, in due course, be revealed. This footnote is appended simply to point out the inconsistency, and assure any skeptic that the facts are fully documented later in the manuscript.

Hetty. Paget has told me that you have a severe problem. Sit and tell me about it.''

Mrs. Jacobs retreated to one of the easy chairs and seated herself on it.

"It's justice I want, Professor. Justice for my boys."

Moriarty nodded, a wealth of understanding passing between him and the dumpy woman.

"That would be young William and . . . what's the name of your elder boy?"

"Bertram, after his father, God rest his soul."

"Amen to that." Moriarty remembered Bert Jacobs, Sr., who had died in prison six or seven years previously—a forger of great talent. "So what happened to your boys, Hetty?"

"They were taken, six months ago, with old Bland."

"Bland, the fence who lives near Wapping Old Stairs?"

Hetty Jacobs nodded in a resigned manner.

"They just went over there to see the old man, he was a friend of their father's as you know and they would visit him once a month, sometimes more often. Just friendly visits, Professor. They're good boys, I never ask them questions, but I know they're good boys and they've never been in trouble."

More by luck than judgment, thought Moriarty, for both Bill and Bert Jacobs were artful pickpockets who worked the West End crowds, and had done since they were quite small. The young men were well set up and on their excursions to the theaters, music halls, and parks in the West they looked and behaved like a pair of young gentlemen on a night out. Moriarty himself had seen to their training, and they would have passed as upper-class bucks anywhere. Moriarty well knew that if the boys had been operating some forty or fifty years previously, they would have been part of the Swell Mob, though now they were in a class of their own with techniques well adapted to the modern conditions.

"What happened?" he asked gently.

"They was there with old Bland, taking a glass, listening to the old man talk. He was a great talker, remembered times long gone. They always enjoyed his company."

Moriarty understood. Bland was a man with an extraordinary memory who recalled events and people, thieves, villains, murderers from his youth. Lads like the Jacobs brothers could have done worse than listen to him, for they could learn a great deal.

"They were there when the pigs came.* It seems that Bland had

*While we in the 1970's fondly imagine that ''pig'' is a recent uncomplimentary term for a policeman, derived from American police officers'

been careless. He'd got all the swag from the Maidenhead Manor break right there, in his drum. Nibbed proper.''

"And they took your boys along for good measure."

"The bastards took 'em all right, not that they didn't put up a fight."

Moriarty sighed. After all, those two boys had been trained at his personal expense and he had been getting a fair share of what they earned. They should have known better than to resist arrest. That neither of the Jacobs boys could possibly have been involved in the Maidenhead Manor robbery went without saying. They knew their place, expert dippers as they were; nothing could have persuaded them to take on anything like a robbery of those proportions.

"So they were taken for being accomplices of Bland's . . . ?"

"They're all in lumber now."

"Yes, Bland for the swag, and the boys for accomplices and resisting arrest?"

"But they weren't accomplices, sir. Never on my life would they have been involved in that."

"I know, Hetty, I know that, but English justice is a strange thing."

"There ain't no justice."

"There will be. How did the boys fare?"

"Three years each. They're both in the 'Steel. Vile place, that is."†

"They tell me it's better now, better than it used to be, they're not strictly separated anymore."

"Don't you believe it, sir. They've still got those cells there, and the turnkeys are brutal."

"I know about the turnkeys, Hetty." His voice became sharp. "Who was the judge?"

"Hawkins."

Moriarty smiled. So Hawkins was still sitting on the bench. One would have thought he would have retired by now. Sir Henry Hawkins was a renowned judge, the man who, sixteen years previously, had sentenced Charlie Peace to life imprisonment only to find that Peace was shortly afterward arraigned on another charge,

---

gas masks during student or race riots in the late 1960's, "pig" was a common term for police and detectives during the second half of the nineteenth century.

†The 'Steel: The dreaded Middlesex House of Correction, Coldbath Fields, which, during the mid-century, was the experimental site on the "Silent System."

that of the willful murder of Arthur Dyson at Banner Cross, Shef-
field.

"And they are now in the 'Steel, Hetty?"

"Yes."

"You will get justice. I'll see to it."

"But how . . . ?"

"Hetty, have I ever failed any of my people? Did I ever fail your
husband? Or any of your friends, my friends, your family, my
family?"

She cast her eyes downward, shamed by his soft statements.

"No, Professor. No, you have never failed any family people."

"Then trust me, Hetty. When I tell you that you will get justice,
then believe that you will get justice. Wait and be thankful that I
have returned."

"Thank you, Professor."

She fell to kissing his hand again, and Moriarty had to look
severely toward Paget so that the bodyguard moved in behind Mrs.
Jacobs, took her by the shoulders and gently moved her away.

Paget returned a few moments later,

"Parker's here, Professor."

Moriarty was again sitting behind his desk.

"He looks worried?"

"Very."

"It will keep. Paget, tell me about the Maidenhead Manor break.
Are we involved?"

"Not directly, sir, no."

"Do we know who?"

"The word is that it's Michael the Peg and a con-head called
Peter the Butler."

Moriarty rose again, looking toward the window. He knew
Michael the Peg (so called because one of his favorite disguises was
that of a one-legged tinker, or sailor), and there was little love lost
between them.

"Peter the Butler, otherwise Lord Peter, eh?"

"The same."

"I would not have thought either of those gentlemen would have
used Bland; after all they come from the other side of the river."

Paget nodded sagely.

"Did they get much from Maidenhead?"

"A lot of silver, jewels; they do say there was coin and paper
worth one thousandpound also."

"And it was recovered by the police at Bland's swagshop?"

"The lot. When the case came up, it only took an hour or so from
start to finish."

"It does not smell right, Paget, not right at all. It smacks of someone blowing on Bland."

"Yea, blowing to the peelers?"

"Precisely. We have had occasion, I seem to recall, to warn off our wooden-legged friend before this."

"I was there when it was done."

"When we have finished here, I would be grateful if you would nose around for me, Paget. Old Bland is my man, as are the Jacobs boys. Michael the Peg may well have to be taught a lesson. It could just possibly be that Maidenhead was done for more devious reasons."

It worried Moriarty that Bland was in prison; the old man had fenced for the Professor and his people for a long time. His removal was a serious inconvenience and, what was worse, Moran had omitted to mention the case. It was almost certain that he would have to mete out justice to Michael the Peg, but there was also the problem of Bill and Bert Jacobs. Their mother would settle for nothing less than seeing them with her around the family hearth once more.

"I shall also need you to arrange a meeting with Robert Alton," he said. "Alton is a turnkey at the 'Steel, so this will have to be performed with great stealth. You understand?"

"Understood, Professor."

"Good. I'll see Parker now."

It was difficult to tell whether Parker was naturally dirty or simply disguised as a vagrant. Certainly he smelled like one who had not seen soap or water for a lengthy stretch of time; his hair and beard were long and matted and the loose, shapeless coat he wore over stained and thin trousers and shirt was ragged and threadbare.

"You've lost him," announced Moriarty as soon as Parker was shown into the room.

"Not me, Professor. Machin lost him—or them, really, but we're certain sure that they are now back in Baker Street."

"Tell me about it."

Parker launched into the tale of how his group, all acting as lurkers (beggars), had observed Holmes, disguised as an elderly and deformed man, make contact with Dr. Watson at the Oxford Street end of Park Lane and later follow the doctor to his Kensington practice.

"I let the others do the following as I had the feeling as how Holmes had spotted me in Baker Street," he continued. "Anyhow, he was with Watson in Kensington for about an hour. When they come out, Holmes was without his disguise. They got into a hansom and Machin lost them. But since then I been back to Baker Street and Holmes is there without a doubt; you can see him sittin' in the chair in front of the window.''*

Moriarty was silent for a moment.

"The main thing," he said at last, "is that we know he is back and using his chambers in Baker Street once more. Presumably, Parker, you wish to clean yourself up and get out of your disguise."

At this, Parker looked a little surprised and hurt.

"But leave your other men on watch," Moriarty continued. "In the future it is essential that I have the best possible intelligence regarding the whereabouts of Mr. Holmes."

Paget took Parker out, returning to tell the Professor that Sweeper was downstairs. Nobody knew Sweeper's true name. He was a man in his mid-sixties, known to the criminal world as Sweeper for more years than most would like to admit. Together with several of his cronies, Sweeper was used almost exclusively by Moriarty and Moran as a messenger, carrying information and orders throughout the city, thoroughly unsuspected because of his situation as a road sweeper. It was to Sweeper that Moran had spoken in Conduit Street earlier in the evening, and he now came to tell the Professor that Colonel Moran had contacted their chief agents in Paris, Rome, Berlin and Madrid, ordering them to present themselves for a conference in London on the twelfth of the present month.

Moriarty listened patiently while Sweeper delivered his message, then, tipping the man generously, Moriarty asked him to return to Conduit Street and tell Colonel Moran that the watch was still being kept on Baker Street, where the evidence suggested Holmes and Watson were back in their old chambers at 221B. He also reinforced his previous instructions by stressing that Moran should keep well away from the vicinity of Baker Street.

Unhappily for Moran, Sweeper arrived back in Conduit Street too late. The Colonel had already left his chambers for the night and, as it turned out, forever.

*Another interesting point emerges here. Holmes, as we know from Watson's account of *The Empty House*, had observed Parker watching 221B Baker Street. He did, however, imagine that his disguise—as the elderly, deformed book collector whom Watson met in Park Lane, and who later visited the doctor in Kensington and disclosed his true identity—had not been penetrated. It is clear from the above exchange between Parker and Moriarty that Holmes was guilty of an error of judgment. He had been followed to Kensington, but, as readers of *The Empty House* know, the great detective left little to chance and took care to shake off any would-be follower once he and Watson left Kensington for the Baker Street area. In this, as in most other things, Holmes was successful.

Sebastian Moran took a final look at himself in the mirror; he was a fastidious dresser and a trifle unhappy about the set of his tie. He was clad for dinner, his opera hat ready on top of the wardrobe. Tonight he would dine alone and at the Anglo-Indian, if only because his fancy was a good curry and the Anglo-Indian was the only place in London where you could be sure of getting the real thing. After the curry he had more serious work to do, for Moran had already decided to ignore the Professor's instructions. Once satisfied with his appearance, the Colonel crossed the room to the large cabin trunk, a relic of his years in the Indian Army, took out his key chain and unlocked the trunk. Pulling back the lid, Moran revealed the contents, which appeared to be well-packed clothing, liberally spinkled with mothballs, if the aroma was to be believed. At the extreme top one could glimpse an officer's dress uniform, the lapels peeping from the protective cover.

Moran's interest lay across the clothing and was in the shape of four items: what at first sight appeared to be a heavy walking stick; a skeletal metal rifle butt, a good deal smaller than the Lee-Metford Magazine Rifle, Mark I, the standard British military rifle of the time; a small hand pump; and, lastly, a heavy card box, which, from the label, seemed to contain some kind of ammunition. Moran recrossed the room, took down his heavy overcoat from the cupboard and began to distribute the last three articles in the pockets. Finally he shrugged his shoulders into the coat, picked up the heavy walking stick, relocked the trunk, placed the opera hat on his head and left the room, descending to the street door.

Five minutes later, Moran was sitting in a hansom, on his way to the Anglo-Indian Club.

Moriarty was tired. He had seen Solly Abrahams, the wily old fence who had come to welcome the Professor back to his native haunts and, let it be said, do himself some good at the same time: he brought with him a selection of uncut gems, the proceeds of a particularly brutal murder for profit that had taken place near the docks only a few nights previously. Frederick Warner, a thirty-two-year-old mate of the cargo steamship *Royal George*, was bludgeoned to death in Dorset Street, Spitalfields, known for years before as the most evil street in London, being at the heart of Jack-the-Ripper territory.

The case had been well documented in the press, for Warner had offered the gems for sale in several public houses in the area: an act of supreme folly. Moriarty, however, was not concerned with how the gems had come into Abrahams' possession. After lengthy negotiation he secured the precious stones for a reasonable price, though the bargaining left him drained.

Before the meeting with Abrahams he had discussed a complicated issue with the three men, Fisher, Clark and Gay, who were intent on a robbery in Harrow. There were three of them and the job was obviously a four-handed affair that required certain refinements that only Moriarty could arrange. In plain language, the trio were short of cash and needed financial backing to provide a fourth man with an intimate knowledge of locks, and a wagonette or similar transport.

The three men painted a glowing picture of the riches, in silver plate, jewels, cash and other convertible goods that could be had from the house in question—the country home of a wealthy baronet who, with his wife, would be visiting relatives in the West Riding during the weekend of April 20-23, leaving only two elderly ser-'ants in charge.

Moriarty told them that he would give an answer within the next two days and, once the trio had left, sent for Ember, giving him instructions to look into the facts concerning the house, movements of the baronet and his lady, the staff, and all the intelligence that could be collected regarding amounts and values of fencible goods which could be removed.

After that the Professor dealt with six other cases. One man, Larson, a forger of exceptional ability, had come with his wife and Bostock, his partner, to pay their simple respects to Moriarty, to kiss his hand and reinforce their loyalty to the governor of their criminal family.

A father and mother, Mr. and Mrs. Dobey, came to plead for justice, not of the same kind which had brought Hetty Jacobs to the chambers behind the warehouse, for in this instance, their daughter, a girl who undoubtedly lived well within the fringe of criminal and amoral enterprise that festered in London's East End, had, a month before, had her face seamed with vitriol. John Dobey, her father, was certain about the perpetrator of this act of violence, a man called Tappit who had sought favors from the unfortunate Ann Mary Dobey, who had, until the incident, been employed as a barmaid at the Star and Garter public house near Commercial Road, now under new management since the previous owner had gone bankrupt in 1888, blaming his ill fortune on the Ripper murders, claiming that, "People aren't going out anymore. Since the killings, I hardly get a soul in here of a night."

Ann Mary had been horribly disfigured, and Moriarty promised the incensed parents that he would have the matter looked into and, if proven, would see that Tappit was brought to the same rough justice he had executed on the girl.

There was the wife of a convicted murderer who was to hang in a week and a pair of cases concerning payment—or, rather, lack of payment—for services performed on the Professor's behalf: one to a seaman who had assisted in getting a wanted man out of the country and into Holland; the other to a publican in Bishopsgate who had lodged a visiting French anarchist for a week while he made contact with some brethren of similar persuasion. The payments were made and both men left happy, swearing future loyalty to the Professor.

It had been a wearying evening, which was not over yet, for at this moment Moriarty was engaged in one of the most difficult problems, that of Rosie McNiel's daughter, Mary, and Sal Hodges.

Sal Hodges was undoubtedly one of Moriarty's many major assets. Sal ran three distinct, though linked, operations: a string of high-class prostitutes who worked out of a couple of good West End addresses—one off St. James, a night house known as Sally Hodges' House; the other more private. She also had a third string of moderately reasonable girls working from a house in the City (Sal's girls, even at the latter address, were like queens when compared with the human dregs who worked the dockland areas); she also controlled a set of well-trained young women who brought in far more in the way of money than her whores. These were the hard girls—again part of the Swell Mob—who posed as prostitutes in order to pick pockets and skin any possible client. Her methods were loosely based on those of the famous Mother Mandelbaum of Clinton Street, New York, who had, during the seventies and eighties, proved that organized women were a criminal force with which to be reckoned. These girls of Sal Hodges would work late at night around the West End, luring men into their clutches by every known ruse, from pretending to have lost their way to making blatant sexual offers; either way, if one of Sal's special girls got a man, he could say good-bye to wallet, watch and chain or any other valuables that might happen to be on his person. They were also most expert at picking the pockets of drunks and were not averse, when it was called for, to using physical violence, the most notable method being the garrotte, half, or even wholly, strangling their victims with rope or a silk scarf, looting the unconscious man, or corpse if he had put up a fight, and disappearing into the night murk like the sirens they were. As the rhyme went:

The old "Stand and deliver's" all rot.
Three to one; hit behind; with a wipe
    round the jowl, boys,
That's the ticket, and *Vive la garrotte!*

While the great garroting epidemic of the early 1860's was long
dead, Sal's girls had devised new methods, which, combined with
the old, made them into a class that rekindled the terrors of Chokee
Bill and the mid-century scourge. Indeed, in certain fashionable
areas where they worked, the wealthy and prosperous walked at
night in real dread.

Sal was in her early thirties, a woman who had known great
deprivation in the early years of her life, but who had, through
ambition and an overriding desire to better herself, traveled the
rough and steep road by way of whoring in her early teens to being a
kept woman—a situation she exploited to the full, the gentleman
concerned being a titled member of the aristocracy and extremely
rich to boot.

She endured, as she said, the situation for two years, during
which time she procured much material—letters and documents—
with which to compromise her lover. When the moment was ripe,
she simply presented the hapless man with the facts, demanded the
deeds to the house in which he had kept her, plus a not inconsiderable sum of money in return for her silence and the incriminating
papers. From that moment Sal's business thrived, the house in
which she was kept becoming the first of her more plush bordellos.
Shortly after this she came under the influence of James Moriarty
and the extent of her business grew and flourished.

She was a striking woman who dressed well and always in the
latest fashion, her hair a golden color, her frame well proportioned
and voice well modulated except in times of stress, when she had an
unfortunate tendency to lapse into the more loose speech that was
the inheritance of her youth. It was such a lapse as this under which
she was laboring in Moriarty's chambers as she faced Mary
McNiel's mother.

"You sit there as if you'd never had a pego between your thighs
and have the bloody nerve to call me a whore, you proud-arsed
cow," she shouted at Mrs. McNiel.

"Well, whore you are, Sal Hodges, and whore you'll always be,
and I'm not seeing a girl o' mine walking the streets with you and the
rest of your sisters of the abyss."

"Think your bloody daughter's too good for whoring, do you?
You'll think she doesn't shit, I suppose. Well, let me tell you a
couple of truths, Rose McNiel. Your Mary's been on the game in

her own sweet way for a good few months—long before my girls got at her—''

"You're a lyin' harlot!"

"Ask 'er, bloody arsk 'er yerself, lady bloody horse dropins."

"My Mary's a good girl—"

"Like 'er mother, I suppose? Don't think I don't remember you, Rose McNiel, because I remember you only too well. The sailors used to call you randy Rosie—"

She was cut short by Rose McNiel flinging her small body across the room, hands clawing at her face. Paget and Lee Chow moved with speed and separated the two women, dragging them—spitting and struggling—apart. Mary McNiel, a pretty, dark girl of some seventeen summers, remained seated on one of the easy chairs, her face chalk white, the blood drained from her lips.

"I will have silence."

It was the first time that day that Moriarty had raised his voice above its normal soft level.

"This is not a bar parlor, nor a meeting place for your rubsters, Sal. I ask you both to remember that."

Mary McNiel was the bone of contention. Until a few months before, she had been reasonably occupied, according to her mother, assisting the landlord of The Seven Stars in Leman Street. Then one night Mrs. McNiel had received a message that Mary would not be returning home that evening and would be staying with friends. It did not take Rose McNiel long to find out that the "friends" were Sal's girls and Mary was living in one of the West End houses. If the truth be told, Rose McNiel was more concerned about the fact that her daughter was no longer bringing in the few extra shillings a week.

"All right."

Moriarty came around to the front of his desk. Rosie McNiel had subsided into a chair, Lee Chow hovering behind her. Paget stood by Sal Hodges who was breathing heavily. (For a moment, Moriarty became fascinated with the rise and fall of her chest). Little Mary McNiel, still looking white and worried, was leaning forward in her chair. Moriarty's eyes narrowed, his face oscillating gently from side to side, the eyes moving from woman to woman.

"You have been wasting my time."

The voice was soft again, but clipped, dangerous.

"I've known Sal a long time, Rosie. A very long time. In all the time I've known her, she's only had her girls take another girl on one occasion. Eighteen eighty-eight—not a vintage year for whores, though the Ripper only touched the dregs, so none of Sal's girls need have worried. Maggie Rutter was her name, right, Sal?''

"She's still with me, Professor."

"Tall, red-haired with a skin like ivory."

Everyone had their attention fixed on the Professor.

"Maggie was working free-lance—in Sal's manor. Before that, if Sal found a dollymop on her patch, she got rid of her. One day she'd be there, the next, gone—*pouff*—like the Demon King at the pantomine. Oh, she'd turn up again, but never where Sal's girls were working. I never pry into that kind of thing. I've never asked Sal how she did it, but I knew it was done, and it is in my mind that it was not a pleasant matter for the doll concerned."

He paused, eyes flicking once more.

"Then came Maggie Rutter, and I did ask Sal about that. 'Professor,' she told me, 'Maggie looked good. I felt she deserved a chance, so I offered her a place among my own family.' You have wasted my time because I believe that is what has happened again. Is that so, Sal?"

"That's it, Professor. That's exactly it."

"So, Rosie, your precious Mary, in whose mouth butter would not melt, was taking time off from The Seven Stars public house to take a bit of trade, and I don't have to tell you that Leman Street is on Sal's ground. You suit yourselves, but I would suggest that you, Rosie, should have fair words with Sal. Come to some arrangement regarding a small portion of Mary's earnings." His head flicked toward Mary. "You, girl, I shall see you here, in these chambers at eleven o'clock tomorrow night. . . ."

"And he will not be charged, Mary, you understand?" spat Sally Hodges. "The Professor is never charged."

Moriarty's face buckled into a thin smile. "Now, get out, the lot of you."

When they had gone, Paget returned to ask if there were anything further needing to be done.

"You've enough, I think." Moriarty gave him a cold, hard look. "What with Michael the Peg and Lord Peter to be seen about, and Alton, the turnkey."

"I'll get to it, sir."

Moriarty had a lot of thinking to do. He leaned back in the smoking chair and allowed his mind to play over the many issues facing him, both here and abroad. There was an underlying thought. I fancy, Moriarty mused, a glass of port and a buttered bun. Twenty minutes later, Ember burst in with the news of Colonel Moran.

Upon leaving Conduit Street, as we have already noted, Sebastian Moran took a hansom to the Anglo-Indian Club, passing down Regent Street and through the Haymarket. Even though the night was now blustery, with a chill wind gusting the streets, the world and his wife were out, hansoms, omnibuses and carriages crowding the thoroughfares of the West End, the pavements thronged with men and women intent on a night out, some heading for the innocent pleasures of *Charley's Aunt*, still delighting audiences at the Royalty, or *Gaiety Girl* at the Prince of Wales'.

Yet Moran was pleased to observe that the more hedonist pastimes were also well catered for in the Haymarket and its adjacent alleys and streets. Those of Sally Hodges' girls who were allowed to hunt in the West End were doubtless there among the others. The individual beats of this area were not so strictly controlled as those down in the City, toward the East, so dollymops mingled easily with their harder sisters in the family of love, all of them watched by the hawkeyes of the cash carriers and the occasional rampsman.*

Moran indulged himself in the thought that when his work was done, he might well repair to one of the better night houses, perhaps Sal Hodges' best house off St. James, where he knew there was a pair of French girls, newly brought from Paris, who were particularly expert in the gamaruche. The thought was pleasing to the old soldier and hunter, whose quarry that night was very big game, the smell of which brought a thrill to his stomach and the inevitable tingle to the loins.

Moran was dressed in white tie because it was *de rigueur* in the dining rooms of the Anglo-Indian Club, and the evening found his appetite demanding the spices of Indian cooking.

He lingered in the club for some two hours, dining on a rich *Murghi Doh-Peeazah*—the aromatic chicken corbonnade; with *Phali Dum*—beans, onions and ginger served very hot; *Alu Turracarri*—the simple potato curry, much beloved of Englishmen who had served in India; a turnip dish known as *Korma Shalgam*; fried cucumbers—*Kheera Talawa*; and the hot *Mattar Paneer*—a curry of peas with Indian cheese. There were also urd lentils, lime, tomato and onion pickles, mango chutney, an onion *raita*, and crisp poppadoms together with thick, whole-wheat-flour *roti*.

The meal in itself gave the colonel fresh confidence, for it could

*The scene Moran watched from his hansom would be not unlike those we can still see in certain areas of London, where, in spite of the Street Offences Act 1959, women still manage to solicit publicly, though, in Moran's day, the open display was on a huge scale. Only recently, in March, 1973, the author had occasion to walk through Shepherd's Market on a Sunday night: The whores were much in evidence, as were the cash carriers, whom today we know as ponces, while rampsmen—tearaways— were certainly propping up the houses around Market Mews, Curzon and Down Streets.

not fail to remind him of those days he had spent, a younger man then, with the Indian Army, and the pleasures he experienced—delights, it must be said, that were laced with violent, even sadistic, overtones—in what was, to him, an enchanted country.

When he left the club, Moran was beginning to feel a tense sensation, a tightening of the muscles at the back of his neck, a prelude to the action he was about to take. Once more he hailed a hansom, this time ordering the cabbie to put him down at the crossing between George Street and Baker Street.

As he paid off the cab, Moran's heart was pounding. He knew that if luck was with him, he would, for the second time in a matter of weeks, be able to commit a perfect crime. At this moment a large force of detectives from Scotland Yard was attempting to unravel the seemingly impossible murder of the young Honorable Ronald Adair. Now Holmes was back in London, the one man whom Moran knew had the mental agility not only to understand how Adair could be shot dead by a revolver bullet in a locked room, but also penetrate the identity of his killer.

Moran walked slowly along Baker Street, his head down against the wind, moving toward the point where Blandford Street sliced through at a right angle. He could feel the bulky objects in his pockets and, as he came closer to the area that was his goal, his gnarled hand took a tighter grip on the heavy cane he carried. He was aware of one of Parker's lurkers loitering at the Blandford Street end and, as he came almost directly opposite number 221B, where Holmes had his chambers, Moran's heart almost skipped a beat.

As he looked up at the windows that undoubtedly belonged to 221B Baker Street, he could see, outlined against the luminous window blind, the sharp, black shape of a man's head and shoulders. As Moran glanced upward, the head moved, as though in a gesture of negation in midconversation. Moran knew the shape of the head and squareness of the shoulders as well as he knew his own palms. The figure behind the blind was, without question, Sherlock Holmes himself.

Moran continued to move, more slowly now, casting a glance back up the street. There were two more of Parker's men, huddled, as though sheltering in a doorway; apart from them, few people were now abroad. Moran smiled grimly to himself and plunged forward, turning right at the corner, into Blandford Street, then right again down a narrow passage, through a wooden gate and into a bare yard, the back door of a house, its windows dark and silent, facing him.

Moran slipped a key from his pocket and swiftly had the door open. He closed it softly behind him and, using all the cunning of the great hunter he had once been, stood silently in the dark passageway, allowing his eyes to adjust to the blackness. In a matter of minutes he could see almost as well as in the street and, once more with stealth, he made his way toward the stairs, creeping steadily on the balls of his feet, making little noise during his progress.

Moran knew which room he wanted on the first landing. He moved almost noiselessly into it, a front room overlooking Baker Street. Once inside his mind was filled with one thought, his eyes penetrating the darkness, moving to the window and peering out toward the casement across the street, where the silhouette of Holmes' head was still outlined. Slowly Moran inched up the window and knelt behind it. Through the opening he had a perfect view, and, as he concentrated, the colonel began to remove the items from the pockets of his overcoat.

As he worked, screwing the skeletal rifle butt onto the heavy metal cane, which was in reality the barrel and mechanism of a special high-powered air gun, made specifically for Moriarty in Germany, the pictures moved clearly, in Moran's mind—pictures of the last time he used the weapon. He saw young Adair confronting him in the private room at the Bagatelle Card Club.

"Colonel," the young prig had said, "I would rather not believe it, but now I have proof." He held out the piece of cork fitted with the "shiner," which had fallen from Moran's pipe. "I may be young and inexperienced in some of the ways of the world, but I know what this is. In Australia we have firsthand knowledge of this kind of thing. I know a "shiner" when I see one. You are a cheat, sir, and, as I have been playing with you, and winning with you, I am implicated."

Moran had stayed silent, it was better to let the young fool get it out of his system.

"I can only presume, sir," Adair had continued, "that some pressing and personal difficulty has forced you into this distressing, ungentlemanly and dishonorable act. I will not precipitate matters. You may rest easy on that score, but I cannot stay silent forever. There is, as I see it, only one course of action open to you. You must remove yourself from the temptation of resorting to this behavior again, by which I mean you will have to resign from all your clubs. A week should be more than ample time for that. I would ask you, therefore, to give me evidence of your various resignations within the week. If you have not done so in that time, then I will be forced to go at least to the secretary of this club and present him with the evidence, no matter what scandal it may bring upon me."

Moran knew the puppy was fool enough to do it. Two days later he set out for Adair's temporary home at 427 Park Lane, equipped as he was now, with the air gun and the box of soft-nosed bullets that were the weapon's deadly projectiles. While there was murder in his heart and mind, he had, on that occasion, no firm plan, as he had now. It was only when he arrived opposite the Park Lane house and saw that young Adair's window was open and the man actually in his room, visible from the street, that Moran quickly made his plan, slipped into the shadow of a convenient doorway, put the weapon together, pumped in the air, loaded it with one bullet, stepped into the street again, took fast and careful aim and noiselessly fired the fatal shot.

This business, now, was of a different mettle: calculated, cold and performed with unswerving malice. The weapon was ready, locked together, the small hand pump providing the necessary pressure of 500 pounds per square inch, and the soft bullet loaded into the breach. Moran still did not take his eyes from the quarry in the room across the street, conscious that this was possibly the most important shot of his entire life.

The black outline of Moran's target against the yellow blind was aligned with the foresight and the V of the backsight, the skeletal butt firm against his shoulder, the chill of its cold metal against the colonel's cheek.

Slowly his hand tightened as his finger squeezed the trigger. With no kick or jerk, only a slight popping sound, the air gun fired. Moran was conscious of the tinkle of glass as the bullet penetrated the window across the street.

Then all hell and chaos broke out in the dark room.*

Moriarty's face was gray. He had not taken the news of Moran's arrest well. Initially there was a reaction of rage which was quickly followed by a cold, hard, silent anger which could be felt by anyone who approached him. The lamps still burned in the main room of his chambers, though by now it was almost three in the morning. Spear had wakened Mrs. Wright—for it was Mrs. Kate Wright and her

---

*Those who are familiar with Dr. Watson's account of the incident (*The Empty House*) will know the details of what occurred. Holmes, outthinking the Moriarty gang—or what he thought was left of it—had erected a bust of himself behind the blind in the window of 221B Baker Street, and it was at this decoy that Moran fired, Holmes and Watson already being secreted in Camden House, the empty house opposite Holmes' Baker Street chambers. Inspector Lestrade and his men were nearby and, after a blow on the head from Watson's revolver, Moran was overpowered and later charged with the murder of Ronald Adair.

husband Bartholomew who ran the bar in the "waiting room" and also attended to the Professor's personal needs: his laundry, food, and the cleaning of his chambers. Kate Wright, knowing Moriarty's likes and dislikes, had prepared a glass of mulled claret, fussing about the room, hooking the mulling pan onto the grate before the fire to heat, finishing it off with the traditional warm poker and adding the cinnamon, ginger, lemon and lemon rind. Moriarty drank slowly, sipping it and staring into the fire, Spear and Lee Chow silently looking on, Ember having been sent out in an attempt to locate Paget, who had not yet returned from his commissions regarding Alton at Coldbath Fields, and the sinister Michael the Peg.

"Where's Paget got to?" Moriarty suddenly exclaimed.

"Could take all night, Professor, if he's on the lay for the Peg. Got to go easy with a man like the Peg."

"I'm not going easy with any cheap gonoph, nor anyone else. I just hope Paget isn't wasting his time in some lushery or doing a mattress jig with one of Sal's tails."

"Come on, Plofessor. Paget no faggot master or Rushington."

It was the first time Lee Chow had spoken. Moriarty allowed himself a half-chuckle at the Chinaman's short-tongued speech defect.

"Rushington, Lee Chow? Paget no Rushington? My Lord Lushington would like to hear you say that."

"True though, guv'nor," grinned Spear, glad that the Chinese had at least goaded a tip of humor from his master. "Paget'll have to work the lushing-kens for intelligence of the Peg and Peter. No other way, but I don't see him doing no mattress jigs. He's got a steady lackin of his own now."

"Oh?" Moriarty's eyebrows raised. "I wasn't told of that. So, Paget's become a family man in all senses of the name?" The Professor looked hard at Spear, realizing, for the first time, that the facial mutilation intersecting the right corner of the man's mouth gave him a permanently surprised expression.

"Well, not as how they're spliced or anything. But he has this judy. She's here in his quarters."

"Is she now?" The Professor had once more become cold. "Moran bothers me, Spear. He was supposed to keep me informed, and when I get to the bones of it, he has done little more than give me a half-finished picture. There's never been any detail, and now they have him in the lockup. I wonder how much he'll blow on us to escape being popped into the saltbox?"

"They've got the colonel square by all accounts. All the blowing in the world's not going to get him off the apple tree."

"But he can still blow, Spear. Blow on a large number of matters. I think there is no—"

The sound of boots hurrying up the stairs cut short the Professor's sentence. A second later, Paget, followed closely by Ember, was in the room.

"Ember's just told me." Paget breathed heavily. "Is it true?"

"As the dawn. You've taken time, Paget."

"I saw Alton first, at his drum in Clerkenwell. He's willing, but it will not come light on your purse."

"Our purse, Paget." Moriarty rose, stretching himself before the fire. "This is a family matter, and I am determined to have the Jacobs boys out of the 'Steel as soon as I can."

"Then it can be done. He'll meet you at any time, and you to name the place."

"And what of the Peg and Peter?"

"Whitechapel."

"Both of them?"

"Both. And more besides. They been laying out of a drum off the Commercial Road. Owns the place and four or five netherskens besides, and his bullies're carrying the cash for a couple o' dozen tails. I saw Blind Fred up the Lamb and Teazle, said he'd complained to the colonel several times over the last three months. The colonel said as how he'd do something about it, but he never did. There's some of our people been done over, and I know for sure the Peg's takin' a share of cash out of a couple of flash-houses and another dozen netherskens that he don't own. That man's a real trasseno, Professor, not a don like you."*

Moriarty ignored the intended compliment.

"How many're with him?"

"Hard to tell, but it seems he's got a lot of rampsmen in the area: bullyboys, dippers, cracksmen. A lot of rackets going."

Moriarty's face was set in a hard mask. All four members of the "Praetorian Guard" knew the look and sensed the charged atmosphere. When Moriarty was like this, it was time to look to oneself, to beware, to watch your tongue and manner. Moriarty was as dangerous as a poisonous reptile when this mood was upon him; in fact the odd oscillation of his head appeared to become more pronounced.

"That's our beat and has been for years," was all he said.

---

*While the East End of London was going through great physical changes by this time—for instance, the whole of the terrible north side of Flower and Dean Street had been demolished by 1892—many of the old doss houses, the netherskens, remained, as did the shifting criminal fraternity.

The other men nodded in agreement.

"What about the colonel, then, guv'nor?"

Paget's face betrayed his own anxiety.

"Yes." Moriarty's voice was even more soft than usual. "Indeed, yes, what about the colonel, Paget? What in hell has the colonel been up to in my absence? It would seem that Colonel Moran has been playing the shirkster at everybody's expense."

Spear shuffled his feet. It was time to display loyalty and be damned.

"At your expense to be sure, Professor."

The others mumbled assent.

"Everybody's expense," hissed Moriarty. "All our family is affected if we start to lose in any racket, any lay."

"He's spent a lot of time broading, always been a bit of a broadsman, the colonel."

"I know about the gaming, and I'll bet he's been on the randy with the winnings. Well, that's all right. We all have to have our pleasure, but when it meddles with business, that's a different matter. There's not been one report about the Peg or Peter or Whitechapel made to me. Come to that"—he looked sharply at Paget—"there's a lot of things not been mentioned to me. Like you having a lackin of your own, here in your quarters, Paget. That's something I should at least have been told of."

Paget came as near to blushing as any man of his persuasion could.

"I thought the colonel would've told you that, sir," he mumbled.

"Well, he did not. Who is she, Paget? Is she a trustworthy mollisher, a flash girl or what?"

"She's out of the monkery, name of Fanny Jones, from Warwick way. I met her in a servants' lurk a year back. She'd come into service with some swells, Sir Richard and Lady Bray. Got a mansion in Park Lane, near where that Adair was done in. They sacked her for some trifle and she was down on her luck. She knew the Bray house inside out, and I thought it might come in handy. Then I got to thinkin' she'd make a toffer, even talked to Sal Hodges about it, but . . . well, guv'nor, you know how these things are . . ."

"I know how things are, my dear Paget, and I will meet the young woman in due course. What did the Brays dismiss her for?"

"It was Lady Bray, a right dowager duchess she is. Fanny took an hour off, out of the house, one night, to go and see some friend. Well, the long and the short was that the butler discovered it, and her royal highness Lady Bray dismisses her. Into the street with bag and baggage. She's a good girl, guv'nor."

Moriarty flashed a quick look at Spear, who rightly interpreted his master and hoped Paget had missed the glance. The Professor wanted someone to ask around, making sure about Fanny's background and her story. It was something Moran had been lax about and, in a certain measure, Spear was pleased at Moriarty's thoroughness.

There was a minute or so of silence, Moriarty lost in thought. Then Paget spoke once more.

"It's true then, about the colonel, so what shall we do, Professor?"

"Why Holmes? The fool," Moriarty mused, casting his eyes first at Paget and then at Spear. "Does he not realize the damage he could have done? After all the trouble we went to, after all that happened and was said and agreed between Holmes and myself at the Reichenbach. God knows, Holmes may even believe that I have broken the truce." He paused, looking up from beneath lowered lids. "Well, the colonel is jugged by Inspector Lestrade, it seems. It's certain he'll be topped. . . ."

"Do we rescue—"

"You can ask that when you see all about you what Moran has been doing? Good Jesus, Paget, Moran is revealed as the kind of man who would not even pull a soldier off his own mother, and you talk of rescue. No, we have two problems. If Moran did not know so much, I'd say he could go to hell and pump thunder, but he knows much. Too much. He'll blow it to Lestrade, or others if he thinks it will help him."

A slow smile spread over Moriarty's face. It had all the appearance of a smile of glee, or friendship, yet somehow the face became changed, as though another visage could be seen behind, bearing all the marks of a gargoyle.

"I suppose you could call it a rescue, after a fashion," he continued. "A rescue for us. But more of a release for Colonel Moran."

Spear looked seriously at his master.

"You mean we have to do for the colonel before the Topper gets at him."

"Long before, Spear, long before. For all we know he is chaunting to the coppers at this moment; about me, this place, our family, our influence, plans, lays, rackets. He has to lose his tongue. After that we must concern ourselves with our businesses in Whitechapel."

"With the Peg," observed Ember tersely.

"You'll be needing to send the punishers in."

Paget had no doubts about the action they would have to take.

"The punishers will be only part of it. We will have to use some tact.'' Moriarty looked toward Spear. ''I want you to take over the question of Moran,'' he said. ''We have to know where he is, who is with him, which police officers, when he is being brought to trial, his routine. These things we need to know quickly. The iron is hot, so we must strike before it is cold. You, Paget''—a finger stabbed toward his other lieutenant—''round up a dozen or so punishers who've served well. Have them ready. Also see if Alton can meet me early tomorrow evening. Somewhere that people would least think we would meet. I know Alton and he can, at times, contrive to look like a gentleman, so let us say I will meet him at the Café Royal at seven. And brief him well, Paget, he must glitter. I must be in disguise. Remind him of my appearance as the older Moriarty, for that is how I shall be attired, and be certain he does not look the screw that he is.''

Paget nodded. ''We are to use the punishers on the Peg's men?''

''On some of them. Ember, get into Whitechapel; have Parker's lurkers working with you, into the lodging houses, the lush-kens and sluiceries. We need to know who the Peg's most important men are: his best half-dozen or so.''

Foxy little Ember grinned, showing a set of cracked and yellow teeth.

''I'll get to that.''

Moriarty's eyes were sparkling as they swung from one man to the other.

''If we pound his most able officers, then I think he'll listen to reason.''

''What kind of reason?'' From Spear.

''I mean to have him out of our streets and houses, away from our people. When we've punished his people, I think I will be in a position to put a suggestion to him that he will find it hard to spurn.''

All five men chuckled.

Friday, April 6, 1894

(FANNY INVESTIGATED AND MORIARTY'S MEMORIES OF THE AUTUMN OF 1888)

WHEN MORIARTY FINALLY got to his bed, in the very early hours of Friday morning, he could not sleep. The tiring events of the previous day had merged with anger upon finding that his business interests in London had been, to a large extent, neglected during his enforced stay on the Continent. With Moran in the hands of the police, the whole situation was in jeopardy, and he was particularly annoyed at the discovery that the Whitechapel area had virtually been taken over by such inferior personages as Michael the Peg and Lord Peter.

In those days Moriarty had used Whitechapel and Spitalfields as a training ground, a recruiting point and a place in which money, if only small sums, could be made. It had not been an easy matter, containing the vast and poverty-stricken, criminal-infested area, but he had done it for eight or nine years with the help of Moran—then a more agile and able man—and the abiding memory of that time was the autumn of 1888.

Whitechapel and the surrounding area were places where evil festered, stank and bloomed in a manner hideously agreeable to Moriarty's methods. It was here, in the heart of this damned area, that Moriarty was able to gather up a flock of supporters, a small criminal army, beholden to the Professor for the slightest favor, anxious to serve him with exceptional loyalty because of the many ways he could alleviate the deprivations and ills that surrounded them, willing to provide intelligence for minor amounts of cash or food. Indeed, it was well known to the floating populace of this part of London, east of the City, that Professor Moriarty's converts were better cared for and more numerous than those made by the zealous Christian Socialists, who periodically descended on the area, dispensing charitable works from places like Toynbee Hall.

Indeed, there was much high-flown talk about redevelopment plans, and renewed social work around Whitechapel and Spitalfields, but, Moriarty thanked Satan, little was actually done. Then, in the autumn of 1888, Moriarty's rich recruiting ground became a place of real terror, its lanes, streets, courts and alleys coming under the scrutiny of the police magnifying glass and the concern of the public at large.

At that time Moriarty lived in earnest comfort, nearer the West End, in a large house off the Strand. Both Paget and Spear were with him, lodged in style within the servants' quarters whence they worked with various other members of the Moriarty mob.

It was Spear who brought the first news of the trouble about to break upon them from Whitechapel. He had been out on business, as it happened, on a punitive action against some rampers who had been causing Sally Hodges a little bother and, having left on the previous evening, did not return until nearly eleven on the morning of Friday, August 31. He went straight to the Professor's office on the first floor and announced, ''Polly Nicholls has had her throat cut. They found her in Buck's Row, half-three this morning.''

The upper hierarchy of Moriarty's mob knew Polly Nicholls, a drab, sallow-complexioned, mousy woman of forty-two, who had sunk, through her predilection for alcohol, to the lowest depths of eastern London, making what little money she could on the streets and living hand to mouth in the lodging houses. But she had, on one or two occasions, been of use to Moriarty and his cohorts by passing information, mainly of a simple nature.

''We are going to have to take stronger measures with the High Rips,'' was Moriarty's first reaction. ''That is the fourth since last Christmas.''

That Moriarty himself had people working the High Rip, a bullying, sometimes violent, form of extortion from prostitutes, had no bearing on the matter. They were all aware that youthful gangs, including the Hoxton Market and Old Nichol Street mobs, had been working the High Rip in the Whitechapel and Spitalfields districts.

Moriarty's mention of Polly Nicholls being the fourth victim of fatal High Rip operations since Christmas concerned three other whores. Fairy Fay, whose real identity still remained hidden, was a woman whose body, horribly cut up, had been found near the Commercial Road on the previous Boxing Night; Emma Smith, badly assaulted by three men on Easter Monday, April 13, later died of her injuries, and Martha Tabram, found dead in almost the same spot as Emma Smith—in Osborn Street, Spitalfields—stabbed thirty-nine times in the early hours of August 7, only a little over two weeks before the discovery of the ill-fated Polly Nicholls.

Spear and Paget put the known High Rip mobs on the top of their list, but a week later things took a new turn when the body of yet another whore, Annie Chapman—Dark Annie, as she was known —was found, throat cut and stomach multilated in the backyard of 29 Hanbury Street.

It was at this point that Moriarty became badly inconvenienced, as it was soon apparent that Annie Chapman's killer and whoever had slit Polly Nicholls' throat were one and the same person, while something akin to panic began to grip the Professor's territory. But there was more—the terror that lurked behind garbled tales and newspaper insinuations brought the police out in force, and the criminal world of the area found themselves more closely observed than ever before. Uniformed police were more numerous, and plainclothes men lurked and mingled with the people of the district.

Within a few days, Moriarty, Moran and those who served close to him, were left in no doubt that for the first time since the Professor had taken the area under his wing, the authorities were beginning to ask a lot of awkward questions.

As for the horrific nature of the affair, the full weight came out late in the inquest when the coroner called the police surgeon, George B. Phillips, to give evidence for the second time in the same hearing. Even though the report of Mr. Phillips' sensational revelations was not to be found in the newspapers, and women and children were removed from the court before he appeared, the word soon got about. As well as having her throat slit, the luckless Dark Annie's intestines had been cut out and placed on her shoulder, while the uterus, part of the vagina and the bladder were removed and never found.

These grisly details were more shocking since it was generally known that Polly Nicholls' murderer had, besides slashing her throat, disemboweled her with a deep, jagged incision running from the lower left part of the abdomen almost to the diaphragm, deep and cutting through the tissue so that part of the intestines protruded. There were several other wounds on the right side and a number of gashes across the abdomen.

It was this information, together with the sense of panic, the quantities of police and local vigilantes who stalked the streets, the haunting unnamed terror, and the certain information that all clues uncovered by the police led into blind alleys,* that caused Moriarty to take his next step.

*There is no doubt, as will be seen later, that Moriarty was well furnished with information from police sources throughout his entire career.

"The police are not dealing with any ordinary flash character," he told Spear and Paget. "They are up against some kind of lunatic, a fanatic who hates whores. He could be a religious fanatic, a moral avenger, or simply a person who has been unhinged by catching the glim from one of the ladies and is out to teach all of them a lesson."

"He's goin' to have his work cut out if he reckons to chiv the lot," Paget laughed.

Students of the period will know that some thirty years previously the rough estimate of the number of prostitutes in London was about 80,000, but the true figure could have been higher. It is certain that in 1856, no fewer than 30,000 cases of venereal disease were treated at Guy's, Bart's and King's.

Moriarty was to repeat his somewhat obvious statement to a larger gathering of his most trusted men and women, including many who worked for him in the Whitechapel-Spitalfields territory. On this occasion he added some practical points:

"It would seem that the killer is likely to evade capture, just as it is certain, if he continues his trade, we will find ourselves more bitterly harrassed by the coppers."

Above all else Moriarty was worried that the criminal element would, under pressure, break with tradition and talk openly to the police: a situation he was determined to avoid at all costs. In this matter he had the whip hand. So far, the Metropolitan Police Commissioner, Sir Charles Warren, and the government had studiously avoided offering any financial reward for the capture of Leather Apron, as the unknown assassin was then tagged. True, the Member of Parliament for Whitechapel, Samuel Montagu, offered 100 pounds, to which was added a further 50 pounds from Henry White, a magistrate. But Moriarty was in a position to outbid such figures as these.

"I want the word passed," he continued, "that we are better placed to catch Leather Apron than the bobbies. Any hints, rumors or suspicions from family people must be conveyed to me, through the usual runners and not to the coppers. If intelligence reaches us and leads to the identification or capture of Leather Apron, the person or persons concerned will receive a bounty of five hundred guineas."

The amount offered was staggering to the impoverished hard-core floating element within the territory, and the certain promise of such a sum ensured both gravelike silence toward the police and renewed efforts on the part of the terrified whores, cracksmen, dippers, bullies and rampsmen. Daily, Moriarty spent several hours sifting through the fragments of rumor, accusation and gossip that passed his way, through Spear and Paget, from people on the ground.*

It came to nothing until the day before the next tragic bloodletting, the double murder of September 30. And it was after that ghoulish night's work that the killer became known by the name he chose for himself—Jack the Ripper.

On the evening of September 29, it being a Saturday, James Moriarty was giving himself a treat: a private self-indulgence to which he succumbed on an average of twice monthly. Earlier in the week he had arranged with Sal Hodges for her latest toffer, a splendidly tall, elegant girl, some twenty-four years of age, named Mildred Fenning, to attend on him at his house off the Strand.

As was his custom on such evenings, Moriarty made certain that Spear, Paget, and any other members of his dubious family, were out on business, making it clear that he did not expect to see them back until at least midday on Sunday. Those who spent much time close to the Professor were in no doubt about his habits, knowing exactly what the form was when they were ordered to spend the night away.

While none of Sal's girls who were chosen to entertain Moriarty were paid in cash, they seldom regretted an assignation. It was strange, but Moriarty was a shy man who did not rate himself as a ladies' companion, hence his consistent recourse to the better-class whores, who, in effect, found him charming, delightful company, both in bed and out, and extremely generous. Seldom did they leave without some gift of jewelry, or fripperies of the finest style; nor did they go hungry, for Moriarty delighted in good food, and his little evenings at home always began with an excellent supper.

On the evening of Miss Fenning's visit the Professor had provided an hors d'oeuvre of oysters, caviar, sardines, pickled tunny, anchovies, smoked eel, salmon, and eggs in aspic, followed by an assortment of chicken darioles, mutton cutlets in aspic, beef galantine and *zephires* of duck with tomato and artichoke salad, macédoine salad and an English salad containing lettuce, watercress, mustard and cress, radishes, spring onions and tomatoes, dressed after the French manner, the whole washed down with a fine champagne—the Royal Charter from Wachter & Co., Epernay.

While Moriarty was preparing his evening and actually enjoying

*It is fact that after the next horrific events, those of the early hours of September 30, the Lord Mayor of London added 500 pounds to the official reward, but by that time Moriarty was heading straight toward the true identity of the killer.

it, other matters were taking place in the Whitechapel area. On that Saturday night there were many among those grim streets who would not eat hors d'oeuvres, nor even cold meats and salad, neither would they quaff champagne. One among them would, however, like hundreds more, consume an overabundance of gin.

Two days earlier a couple who went by the name of Kelly returned from a strenuous month's hop picking in the fields of Kent. The man was a market porter called John Kelly; the woman, who wore a dark green print dress with a pattern of Michaelmas daisies and golden lilies, a black cloth jacket trimmed with imitation fur and three metal buttons, and a black straw bonnet decorated with black beads and velvet in green and black, was known variously as Kate Kelly and Kate Conway. She was forty-three years old, small, birdlike, an alcoholic suffering from Bright's disease, a doss-house woman who hired her body for the price of a bed. Her real name was Catherine Eddowes and she had, on and off, been cohabiting with John Kelly for the past seven years. She did not know Moriarty, even by name, though she was known by Paget and several other agents in the area. She also had a regular beat and was known to many constables as a common prostitute.

The couple had returned early from their hopping because of a chance remark Eddowes had made to Kelly a week before. There was a certain sense of safety in the country, but even there, deep among the hop fields, the talk would inevitably turn, particularly at night, to the murders and the invisible fiend who seemed to watch them all from the shadows of the doorways and alleys of Spitalfields and Whitechapel. Kelly and Eddowes had been drinking with others of that closed-ranks community when one of the company mentioned the unofficial reward of 500 guineas. Neither Kelly nor Eddowes had heard that news, and Kelly questioned the man closely.

"I can understand not telling the coppers some things," he said. "But who in hell's name are we supposed to tell about bloody Leather Apron if not the police?"

"You go to a man called Alfred Davis who is usually found at The Lamb, in Lamb Street, up Bishopsgate way. He'll fetch the big cove and you talk to him."

Later, after the events of September 29 and 30, Kelly told the police that he had returned with Eddowes "after the reward money." They took it for granted that Kelly was talking of the one hundred and fifty pounds made up by Montagu and White and did not question him further on the matter. But there is no doubt that they were after the larger sum being offered through the criminal family.

The conversation continued with various people, now becoming fuddled with drink, putting forward their own terrors and pet theories. The whole group joined in except for Catherine Eddowes who fell strangely silent. Nor did she speak much the following day, Kelly later recalling that she "seemed to be in a dream"; but on the next evening she confided in her partner that she had ". . . a fair idea of who Leather Apron is." Later she said explicitly, "I think I know who he is."

She became so adamant about the matter that Kelly finally took her up on it, suggesting that they return to London and pass on the intelligence. He also asked her continually for a name or a clue, but Eddowes, with the cunning of the alcoholic combined with the secretive closeness of a confirmed doss-house occupant, refused to tell even him.

So, they returned to London, having enough of their hopping pay left to travel on the train, drink themselves stupid on gin and obtain a bed at the 55 Flower and Dean Street doss house.

On the morning of Friday, the twenty-eighth, they both felt the pangs of depression, the gloom rising from the amount of gin they had consumed on the previous evening, coupled with the knowledge, apparent to them on all sides, that they were back among the appalling dirt and crowded conditions of the East End of London.

Catherine Eddowes did not feel too well, a not unusual state, as the Bright's disease that ravaged her body was far advanced. They were also flat broke and argued for a while about Catherine walking up to The Lamb in order to contact Alfred Davis. But she said that she felt too unwell. "After we've had a drink or two, John, I'll be fine." Like all alcoholics who have reached a chronic stage, she was unable to face true realities until the spirits had assuaged her craving.

But there was no money for drink. They quarreled violently for some time until, at last, Kelly agreed to pawn his boots. Eddowes took them from his feet, outside the pawnshop in Old Montague Street, carried them inside, popping them for an alderman.

With money in their collective pocket again, the urgency of getting to Lamb Street appeared to be reduced. Indeed, they started out in that general direction, but became lost in the small pond of gin they consumed. Time quickly loses its meaning to alcoholic vagrants. Warmed by the gin and bawdy chatter of the public houses around Old Montague and Wentworth Streets, they found themselves, suddenly, it seemed, outside, with only sixpence left and night well advanced.

Eddowes was in good humor by this time.

"I'll go up and see Davis in the morning," she told John Kelly.

"Here, you take fourpence and go back to the Flowery Dean. I'll take my chances in Mile End." Meaning that she would try to get a bed for the night in the Mile End Workhouse, something a man could not do without having to work for the night's lodgings.

By the morning of Saturday, the twenty-ninth, they both looked very much worse for wear, and once again they were broke. This time there was nothing to pawn and John Kelly was in a sullen mood. They drifted aimlessly for a few hours, and around two o'clock Eddowes, now desperate for gin, told her companion that she was going off to see her daughter.

Kelly was thoroughly out of sorts with her by now and was certain that her story about knowing the identity of Leather Apron was a figment.

"That's all right by me," he said. Then, as he turned away, "Watch out for spring-heeled Jack."

Eddowes muttered some coarse language and told him that she could take care of herself.

He did not see her alive again.

Even though she felt really ill, Catherine Eddowes was determined to get to Lamb Street. She had hoped for some opportunity such as this, because she had no intention of sharing the five-hundred-guinea reward money with him.*

Eddowes dragged herself, feeling very weak, up Houndsditch, where she and John Kelly had spent most of the morning, and into Bishopsgate, finally turning right into Lamb Street. The public house known as The Lamb stood about halfway down on the right-hand side. The taproom was crowded when she entered, and she pushed her way toward the bar.

"Hallo, ducks, you look all in. Been on the bevie?"

The barman was a fat man in his late thirties, not at all put out by

---

*Until now the facts appertaining to Catherine Eddowes' movements have left a gap of six hours unaccounted for: from two o'clock in the afternoon until eight o'clock in the evening. The information at our disposal is based on Kelly's own evidence and the police reports—particularly those from the Bishopsgate police station, where she was taken, very drunk, at eight o'clock and then released at one o'clock on the Sunday morning. Forty-five minutes later she was found dead. The missing six hours have always been of interest to criminologists and theoreticians who have asked such questions as—Did Eddowes visit her daughter? How did she provide herself with money and/or drink to be found in such an advanced state of inebriation by eight o'clock? From the coded extracts of James Moriarty's personal diaries there is little doubt about her movements during the missing six hours.

Eddowes' appearance, as they were used to all types of drunk and
vagrant at The Lamb.

"I don't feel so well," muttered Eddowes.

"Drop of spirits will soon put you right—or a drop of something."

He gave a lewd wink to a group of men who crowded near her.

"No, no. I'm just looking for someone."

But the barman knew the alcoholic look as well as anyone in his
trade. Her quick negative relaying the fact that she carried no cash.
Strangely, for few were given to offering much charity, except by
words of sympathy which cost nothing, in this part of London, the
barman felt sorry for the thin little woman, bleary eyed and dis-
reputable.

"Go on, dear, have something on me. A daffy won't harm me."

He pushed a glass containing the small measure across the
counter where Eddowes, with the voracity of her body's needs,
clutched at it, her hands shaking as she lifted the glass and sipped the
spirit.

"So who're you lookin' for, my lady?" The barman grinned
amicably.

Catherine Eddowes leaned closer, her voice dropping to a
whisper.

"I'm told I can find Albert Davis here."

The grin faded from the barman's lips and his eyes lifted quickly
from her face, his gaze darting round the room.

"Who wants him?" he asked, his face a mask.

There had been many such as Catherine Eddowes asking for
Davis in the past weeks and he knew why. The terror that had come
to this part of the City spread its tentacles wide, and not only those
living near to the murders felt the ice in their veins. Every person
who came to The Lamb asking for Davis brought the barman into all
too close a contact with the unseen, unheard beast who lurked, knife
in hand, within the imagination of all London dwellers—as well as
in truth behind corners, doors, and shadows in the East End.

"He won't know me. But I've something to tell him."

The barman watched as she swigged back all but the dregs of her
gin, then he nodded slowly.

"Wait," he cautioned, then moved away to serve three
clamoring customers before calling through to the pot boy to take
over for a moment and slipping away up the flight of stairs sealed by
a thin wooden door behind the bar.

He was back within a minute, beckoning to Eddowes, who
pushed through the throng to the right-hand corner of the bar, lifted

the flap and, passing behind the wooden counter, joined the barman at the foot of the stairs.

"Straight up there. It's the door to your right at the top," he said quietly.

Albert Davis was in his mid-thirties and had pursued a life of crime since his seventh year, when he had learned the art of dipping. By seventeen, he had grown too tall and broad to practice the true art of picking pockets, and, being something of a professional, he disliked the cruder versions of that trade, which called for jostling the plant (victim) in an obvious manner. He had served only one short term of imprisonment while picking pockets, and from that lay he finally graduated to the work of being a good cracksman. For a few years now he had worked exclusively for Paget, discovering only in the last two years that the Professor was the man who worked Paget.

Davis was a first-class family man, loyal and obedient and, like a dozen or so more, had lived most of his life in the area that divided the city from the Whitechapel-Spitalfields territory. He had been present when Moriarty himself had briefed them regarding his plans for the identification of Leather Apron and from that day had sat, without grumbling, in the small room at The Lamb, seeing anyone who came forward with rumor or accusation regarding the murderer. After all, he thought, it was not a bad way of life: a comfortable bed, as much booze as he wanted, three meals a day, a measure of respect from the landlord and his barmen and, when the occasion presented itself, sexual satisfaction from any of the informers he fancied.

"Sit down, my love," he said pleasantly to the anxious Catherine Eddowes when she entered, motioning toward a chair.

He noted that she looked nervous and ill. He also diagnosed that she was in need of drink, for he too had experienced much in his lifetime and could read the faces, twitches, shakes of people like Eddowes as skillfully as a doctor.

"Do you fancy a glass?" he asked.

She nodded vigorously, and, going to the door, Davis bawled down the stairs for Tom, (for that was the barman's name) to send up a brace of good gins. He returned to the room and remained silent until the drinks had been delivered.

"So, what's your name, dear?" he asked after watching the frail woman take a mouthful.

She told him, adding her address—which she gave as number six, Fashion Street.

"And what have you come to see me about?"

"I was told there was a reward out for Leather Apron. Not the official reward, but one from the family."

Davis nodded again. "You are a family person, so you must know that."

"I'm on the batter."

"Then you have the protection of family people. How much were you told? About the reward?"

"They said as how it was worth five hundred guineas."

"Did they now? Well, Kate, you reckon you've got five hundred guineas' worth of intelligence, then?"

"Yes."

The way she said it made Davis look at her hard. They all said they had good words when they came to him, but, as like as not, most of what they said was about as much use as a brewer's fart. Davis had, in the few concentrated weeks during which he had been dealing with the matter, developed a nose for brewer's farts. The certain manner in which Kate Eddowes had affirmed she had real intelligence was different. It was as though Albert Davis knew that he was on to something.

"You tell me then," he said as calmly as he could.

"You the one who gives the money?" she asked.

"Eventually."

But his reply did not please her.

"What I mean is, are you the prime one, the top man?"

"Well . . ." He paused, knowing that he had a cunning woman here who could probably detect uncertainty even with a skinful of gin. Whores do have that kind of sixth sense, learned through their trade, though, he quickly reflected, little good it had done for Polly Nicholls or Dark Annie. "Well, you tell me and I take it to the top man. He looks into the matter."

"I'll only tell what I have to the top man." It was a positive statement.

"Come on, girl, you can at least give me a hint. What you got? A meetin' with old Leather Apron or something?" He was to remember those words the following day.

"I know his name." Again the positive ring of truth.

"Kate, tell me, is this straight?"

"As a pound of candles."

"You know his name? You know who he is? You know where he is?"

"I know his name, or near enough. I knew where he was at a year or two ago. I know enough for him to be found."

"Then tell me, girl."

"I'll only tell the man. The governor."

Davis looked into his glass, which was, by this time, empty, only a dampness and the unmistakable odor to prove that it had ever contained the juice of the juniper. He considered Catherine Eddowes and the action he should take. At last he gave her a pleasant smile.

"I'll get the guv'nor then. I'll send for him."

By this time it was well on toward half-past three. Paget did not arrive until almost five o'clock, by which time Davis had provided Eddowes with more gin, being careful to see that she did not become intoxicated. Paget was unsmiling, for he also had faced many who had provided nothing firm in the intelligence they rushed to give.

Kate Eddowes was not drunk, but the effects of the gin were pleasant; she felt safe, at ease, and the man she now faced was tall, well built and set up. She offered him a smile, but he merely looked at her blankly as he sat down heavily on Davis' bed.

"You're Catherine Eddowes?" he asked without much expression.

"No other."

"And you have something important to tell me."

"If you're the governor."

It was at this point that Paget made his error.

"I'm as near to the governor as you'll get, gel."

The gin spoke: "Then I'll not be talking to you."

Like Davis, Paget felt something definite in the tone of voice that came from this washed out, frail, scarecrow of a whore. It was instinctive, a sense of apprehension that he was near to a truth, combined with an uncanny knowledge that the woman was almost not of this world. He was to think on that feeling the following morning.

"Look, darling," he said, in the same steady manner, so as not to betray his inner thoughts. "The guv'nor cannot come here tonight."

"Then he can come tomorrow."

"He cannot come any night."

"Then you'll take me to him."

Paget allowed himself a few seconds thought.

"I might do that, but I'll have to give him the strength of the argument."

"I've told Mr. Davis the strength."

"Then tell me."

"I know the man's name. I know where he used to be. With what I have to say you will be able to find him. And I expect the five hundred guineas for that."

"If he's found from what you tell us, you'll get the five hundred."

"Then you'll take me to the guv'nor."

"It's not as easy as that. Not as simple. I shall need some hint. We've had a great many people telling us who old Leather Apron is, and believe me, he's mostly their neighbor who they've fallen out with or some old Ikey they've popped their mother's locket to, or some innocent they don't like the look of. Kate Eddowes, I give you my word as a family man that you'll get your money if this is real strength, but I have to give the guv'nor something more definite. Tell me a little, gel, and I'll go for him at once."

Eddowes pondered on this. She was used to bargains and curb-side haggling, and her whore's intuition told her that Paget was being straight with her.

She nodded in the direction of Davis. "Nothing personal, Mr. Davis, but I'll tell Mr. Paget and nobody else, and I'll not tell all."

Paget motioned Davis toward the door.

"Speak then," he said when the man had gone.

Eddowes' eyes narrowed.

"Tell the governor that he's quite a young man, educated and that, at one of them universities. He's a professional man. A few years back he was at Toynbee Hall, that was where I first saw him. I seen him recently though, a month or so back."

"And his name?"

"He's called Drew, or Drewt, something like that."

"And how do you know this is the man, Kate?"

"Enough. I'll tell that to the guv'nor and nobody else. Nobody. I've already told you too much. You'd find him with what I've told you."

Paget nodded. "Good gel. I think the guv'nor might even see you. Maybe tonight. I'll see if I can get him. In the meantime, I want you to stay here with Mr. Davis. I'll come back as soon as I can and make the arrangements."

It was gone quarter to six by the time Paget left The Lamb. Paget hoped to reach Moriarty's house off the Strand before the Professor's lady arrived for the evening's entertainment. If he was too late, then the matter would have to be left until the morning.

There were many people on the pavements, and the traffic of hansoms and omnibuses was heavy. Paget did not get into the Strand until after half six. It was still light but Paget cursed as he looked at the house. The curtains of what the Professor called the drawing room were drawn, as were those of the best bedroom. The lady had already arrived. With a sigh of frustration, Paget began to retrace his journey, arriving back at The Lamb a little after seven. He was in many ways glad that the journey had been in vain when he saw Eddowes. Davis had found it difficult to restrain her, having foolishly ordered a bottle of gin to be brought up to the room. She was not impossibly drunk, but already three parts of the way there.

"I'll have the guv'nor here, or take you to him, at two o'clock tomorrow, Kate," Paget told her. "He's not available tonight."

Eddowes grinned and nodded. That was one appointment she would not forget.

"In the meantime, to show faith, here's a thicker for the evening."

He handed over the pound and noticed that her eyes gleamed with pleasure, as though he had given her a fortune. He was, in fact, acting on the assumption that God takes care of fools and drunks: there was more than enough for her to get dead drunk, a bed for the night and plenty of change left over.*

Paget told her that he and Davis had business to attend to and that she was not to be late for their appointment tomorrow. She promised him that she would be on time and then left, only getting as far as the taproom, where she consumed a great deal of gin.

Just before eight o'clock, she staggered out into the street, in a highly elated mood, singing and making noises. A few minutes later two policemen picked her up as she stood imitating a fire engine in the middle of Bishopsgate. They took her straight to Bishopsgate police station and left her to sober up.

From just after eight o'clock until the city police allowed her to leave the Bishopsgate police station at one in the morning—still not really sober, but long past the hour when she could lay her hands on more drink—Catherine Eddowes dozed, talked, her speech slurred, and then finally broke into song.

While she was going through these last fuddled hours of her life, Moriarty, oblivious to the fact that his people had secured substantial facts about the Whitechapel-Spitalfields killer, enjoyed himself with Miss Mildred Fenning.

In the September of 1888 James Moriarty was thirty-six years of age

---

*It is interesting to speculate about what happened to the money, for, in the time available, Eddowes could not have spent a whole pound and, when her body was found, there was no cash among her effects. One can only suspect that she was either drunken-careless or robbed, perhaps by another inmate of the Bishopsgate police station.

and had been the governor of his huge and growing criminal family for twelve years.*

While the Professor was regarded, by the ladies who served him, as entertaining, even satisfying, in bed, it was an open secret among the sisterhood of ladybirds who worked under Sally Hodges, that Moriarty, like most men, had his own sexual predilections. Be that as it may, by half-past midnight, the pair lay drowsy, exhausted by the excessive coupling, which had pleasured both of them, the Professor having quickly assumed a dominant role on the wide bed.

About twelve thirty Catherine Eddowes, who had been awake and singing for at least fifteen minutes, shouted to the jailer at Bishopsgate police station, "When can I go? I want to go out!"

"As soon as you're able to take care of yourself," the jailer replied loudly.

Just before one in the morning she was taken upstairs and told to get out.

"What time is it?" she asked, still very confused and befuddled.

The sergeant on duty laughed. "Too late for you to get any more drink. Now, off with you."

Eddowes stood outside in the relatively quiet night street and looked about her, as though not quite certain where she was. She then appeared to make up her mind and stumbled off in the direction of Houndsditch. She was not singing anymore, but the music twirled in her head; a jumbled tapestry of sounds: *I'm poor little Buttercup, sweet little Buttercup, dear little Buttercup I . . . From*

*This statement will undoubtedly confuse scholars and academics who, until now, have relied wholly upon the testimony of Sherlock Holmes as reported by his faithful chronicler, Dr. John H. Watson, plus the additional and highly specialized research of such eminent men as Mr. William S. Baring-Gould and Mr. Vincent Starrett. It appears, however, that everybody, including the great Sherlock Holmes himself, was taken in by the most dastardly and villainous act of all. Holmes, and hence his chronicler and those who have patiently sought to analyze, coordinate and annotate the evidence, accepted that Professor James Moriarty—"the Napoleon of Crime . . . organizer of half that is evil and nearly all that is undetected"— was undoubtedly the James Moriarty who was born around 1844, proved himself a singularly brilliant mathematician, writing his treatise on the Binomial Theorem in his early twenties, an academic coup that led him to be appointed to the chair of mathematics at one of the smaller universities, which he left, under a cloud, in the latter part of the 1870's. Indeed, why should Holmes doubt that the man he knew of as Moriarty was not the same fallen Professor? His eyes and ears told him that the Napoleon of Crime and the genius of mathematics were one and the same person. However, as we shall later discover, the real Professor Moriarty who left that little university town in about 1878, ceased to exist, in every sense of the word, once he set foot in London, his place being cunningly taken by the one person who knew him closely, envied him most and hated him above all men.

Greenland's icy mountains . . . From India's coral strand, . . .
Where Afric's sunny fountains . . . Roll down their golden sand.
. . . The Panjamdrum is dead . . . He died last night in bed . . . He
cut his throat on a bar of soap . . . Andthepeasranoutofhisboots-
andhedied. . . . Oh, Miss Tabitha Ticklecock, Oh-

At the corner of Aldgate High Street there was a man, though she
could not seem to focus her eyes properly and was using one hand to
assist her in walking, placing it flat against the wall. Still, drunk as
she was, Catherine Eddowes never turned down a chance.

"Hallo, darling, you're out late. How d'you fancy Miss Lay-
cock, eh?" She called out.

"Why not." The prospective customer called back.

Eddowes, still elated, drew closer to him.

"Cost you a gen. But you'll not regret it. I'll give you a good
stand-up."

"Where?"

She was now close to him.

"Come on, I'll show you." Eddowes knew where she was now.
"Real quiet. Nobody'll disturb us. Come on, darling, come with
Kate."

So she led him up Duke's Place, through the dark and narrow
Church Passage and into Mitre Square. As they entered the square
she remembered, through the fog in her head that she had to be at
The Lamb by two o'clock in the afternoon. She also remembered
why . . . and who . . . the man . . . was . . . behind . . . her. . . .

There was nothing else for Catherine Eddowes to remember.
When they discovered her, only fifteen minutes later, her throat and
face were mutilated, her right eye smashed in, the eyelids nicked, a
portion of the right ear lobe cut off. The belly was ripped open and
the intestines removed and draped over the right shoulder. Her left
kidney was missing and she was the second victim of that night, the
first being a Swedish girl, Elizabeth Stride, known as Long Liz,
whose body was discovered about half a mile from Mitre Square,
next to the International Workmen's Educational Club in Berners
Street.

Paget, full of enthusiasm, and also lurid details of the double
killing—he had, with many others, visited both the murder sites
early on Sunday morning—returned to Moriarty's house on the dot
of midday. It was hardly a convenient time, as the Professor and
Miss Fenning had decided to breakfast late and together. When
Paget went down the area steps and in through the tradesmen's door,
he could hear the sound of laughter from upstairs and had to remain
in the kitchen until a little before one o'clock when, following

prolonged farewells, Mildred Fenning was escorted to a hansom, clutching various presents.

After allowing enough time to elapse, Paget went up the stairs and, crossing the hall, tapped on Moriarty's study door. He found his employer in good humor, though looking a little tired, a state that was seemingly rectified once Paget told him, in serious tones, of Eddowes and her story.

"I knew we would find him," the Professor smiled grimly. "Get the woman and bring her here as quickly as you can. I want Spear, your man Davis, and the colonel as well. See to it."

Paget set the operation in motion, going last to The Lamb, where he waited with Davis until almost half-past-three. Rumor was rife everywhere, but the two murder victims had not yet been named, and neither Paget nor Davis even suspected that Eddowes could possibly be one of them.

"Like all the others," Paget remarked bitterly. "A cunning lush."

"I could have sworn she knew."

Davis was well aware of what they might expect from Moriarty. In the end Paget ordered Davis to stay at The Lamb until he had at least talked to the Professor about the turn of events.

Moriarty was cool, Spear and Colonel Moran having waited with him, in some expectation of their problems coming to a fruitful conclusion. By seven in the evening, Paget and Spear both had their men out in some force, making inquiries about the whereabouts of Kate Eddowes, but to no avail. Their reports were indeed depressing, for the whole Whitechapel-Spitalfields area was alive with police, uniformed and plainclothed, while local inhabitants thronged the streets—a great deal of ill feeling had been brewed by this last atrocity—and by late on Sunday evening Moriarty was conscious that things were getting out of control. Both Paget and Spear reported that they did not know how long they could really hold their own men and women, for even the closest had been emotionally roused.

Moriarty, by this time, had lapsed into anger, for he knew there was but one way of gaining his former hold on the territory—to dispose of the murderer and rid the streets of the constant patrols and lurking police officers. Thinking they were so near to success, with the news of Eddowes' seemingly firm knowledge, her swift and sudden disappearance had brought about a classic elation followed by depression. The Professor had but to sit down and think clearly to see how far and how sadly his business interests were being hindered. In many ways he now regretted having used this poverty-stricken breeding ground as a focus for much of his work. On the other hand there was no place better in London for recruitment— hunger, lack of means, degradation and filth bred a desire among the young, particularly the lads, to better themselves, and a large number of the men, operated through Paget and Spear, had been culled from the awful streets of that territory to be willingly trained in the many arts of the cracksmen, dippers, patterers, operators of Moriarty's long firms, protectors, whores' cash carriers, procurers of anything from young lithe flesh to extra amounts of laudanum, the price of which was always at a premium.

However, the world that thrived so well below the surface of high-flown morals and respectability, the thin veneer of the age, had taught even Moriarty a certain fatalist philosophy, and by Monday he had accepted the fact that Catherine Eddowes had maced both Davis and Paget.

On Tuesday the body at the mortuary in Golden Lane was identified by Eliza Gold (Eddowes' sister) and John Kelly as being that of Catherine Eddowes, alias Kate Conway, Kate Kelly, Kate Gold and Kate Thrawl.

Within an hour of the news getting out, Moriarty had Paget Spear, Davis and Colonel Moran at his Strand house, going through what little evidence Eddowes had passed on to Paget.

After much conversation, a great deal of which became mere theorizing, Moriarty said:

"It would seem that we may well be onto something more substantial after all. Our obvious course of inquiries should start at Toynbee Hall, and I think I will undertake that duty myself."

Toynbee Hall, under the aegis of the Reverend Samuel Barnett, was the focal point for missionary zeal and political ideals that set to bridge the gulf between the classes. To the hall, set in the heart of Whitechapel, came undergraduates from Oxford and men of good will from other aspects of life. So, toward the end of the first week of October in 1888, a prosperous-looking cleric arrived asking to see the Reverend Barnett. This gentleman, whose clothes and demeanor appeared to befit a man of some private means who had received the call and taken the cloth, announced himself as Canon Brewster of Bath, confiding in Samuel Barnett that he had heard much of the work which was being done by those who had been "called to the East" and, finding himself in London, had availed himself of the opportunity to see for himself.

As the good Canon's first gesture was to donate one hundred guineas to Barnett's fund, he was made most welcome, and it was only toward the end of the afternoon that Canon Brewster, whose fat and jovial manner set everyone at their ease, broached the subject of a young man, with whom he had lost touch, who had undoubtedly been of great help to Barnett.

"We have a mutual acquaintance then?" proffered Barnett.

"Indeed." The Canon smiled. "But, for the life of me I cannot remember his exact name. He came to me for advice while visiting relations in Bath and the picture he drew of your work here has remained in my mind ever since. I believe he was called Drew, or perhaps Drewt. Something of the like."

Barnett could not recall the name. He sent for the record of residents, but failed to find any similar name on it. However, one resident spoke of a Montague Druitt.

"Montague John Druitt," he said. "Why, I saw him only the other day. He was from New College and is a barrister, though at present he teaches in a school at Blackheath."

"And he has been here recently?" gasped the Canon. "How sad that I have missed him."

"Not here at Toynbee Hall," replied the resident. "I met him in Bishopsgate last week."

The Canon's head performed a strange oscillating motion while he muttered, "Oh, dear me, oh dear me, I would so have liked to see him again."

Not many minutes lapsed before the Canon announced suddenly that he would have to take his leave, and he was escorted out by Samuel Barnett himself, full of thanks for the generous gift.

An hour later, Paget was helping Moriarty out of the clerical clothes and the padding with which he had disguised himself.

"His name is Druitt," Moriarty announced with a grim, thin smile. "He is a barrister at present teaching at a school in Blackhealth. Get your people on to it. I need to know all there is to know. I want it all."

It took Paget's people the better part of a week to track down the school at which Druitt was employed at Blackheath, the area being well noted for its cramming shops. Paget reported the facts to his employer.

"He's at a school run by Mr. Valentine at Nine Eliot Place, but since quitting practice as a barrister he has still retained his chambers in the Inner Temple: Nine King's Bench Walk."

Moriarty felt the excitement of the chase coming to a close and gave orders that Druitt should be watched and followed constantly. This was done, and in the weeks that followed Druitt made three journeys to London, always shadowed by one of Paget's men. On each occasion the barrister-turned-teacher went straight to his chambers in the Inner Temple, where he appeared to stay, alone.

In the meantime the specter of Jack the Ripper—as the Whitechapel murderer had now come to be known—lowered over the dismal streets of the East End. But as week followed week and no other victim fell under the Ripper's blade, a false sense of security settled on everyone, from Paget's men to the police and vigilantes who patrolled the streets, and the loitering ladybirds who walked them.

On the evening of November 8 Montague John Druitt made a fourth sally from the school at 9 Eliot Place, Blackheath, and took the train to London. Paget's man on duty was an experienced watchdog by the name of Frederick Hawkins.

Moriarty had devised an ingenious system for Paget's watchers. They worked on a rota system, and each man had a runner—usually a young boy being trained for other work, either as a dipper or cracksman's mate: a snakesman, as they were called—who, because of his youth, build and turn of speed, could be sent to warn of any sudden change of movements by Druitt.

On this occasion Druitt took a train from Blackheath to Cannon Street, Hawkins actually traveling in the same compartment, while the runner, a lad of some ten years, was on the same train.

Druitt acted true to form, taking a hansom from Cannon Street to the Inner Temple, entering by the Gatehouse at Middle Temple Lane. Once he was in, Hawkins took up his lonely vigil, sending the lad off to report the movement to Paget, suggesting that his relief should take over from that point at eight the following morning. Paget had been uneasy during the previous three occasions when his men had followed their quarry into London itself, for he was well aware that Druitt could enter the Inner Temple by one gate and slip in and out with ease through another. He knew that he should at these times have quickly provided men to watch the other entrances, but as nothing untoward had occurred at other times he did not press Moriarty about it.

Hawkins was relatively fresh, having relieved the day man only fifteen minutes or so before Druitt left for Cannon Street. He remained awake through the night, taking what shelter he could during the bouts of rain that fell heavily in the early hours.

Dawn broke, cloudy and overcast, but at seven in the morning Hawkins was amazed to see a figure he recognized hurrying through the early light toward the Gatehouse. It was Druitt, dressed in a long rust-colored overcoat and a deerstalker hat. Hawkins was able to see that he wore a red neckerchief and that his face, adorned only by a sandy mustache, was as he put it later, "as white as death." Druitt walked quickly, though with a gait that suggested extreme fatigue. He was also carrying a package that appeared to be wrapped in American cloth.

Hawkins, in fear, realized immediately that at some point during the night Druitt must have left the Temple by either the Embankment or Tudor Street and was now returning through the normal entrance. Immediately, Hawkins sent his runner off to pass the information to Paget. At eight o'clock his relief arrived with another runner and Hawkins quickly made his way to the house off the Strand, where he found Paget.

By half-past nine Paget, Spear, Colonel Moran and Moriarty, together with Hawkins, were gathered in the drawing room. The mood was anxious and grim as it was now quite plain that Druitt had managed to evade their surveillance for some unspecified period during the night. Both Paget and Spear had sent men into the Whitechapel area so that any untoward incident could be reported as quickly as possible.

It was the morning of the Lord Mayor's show, but down in Whitechapel there were many who were disinclined to go up to the City to watch the parade. One of these was John M'Carthy, who, besides keeping a chandler's shop in Dorset Street—the most evil street in London—owned several properties in the area, including six depressing cribs in the gloomy Miller's Court. At number thirteen there lived a relatively young whore, Mary Jane Kelly, who sometimes came the Rothschild about her past, calling herself Marie Jeannette Kelly. She was twenty-five years old and her rent was overdue to the tune of thirty-five shillings.

At about ten forty-five on this Friday, November 9, M'Carthy sent his assistant, Thomas Bowyer, to 13 Miller's Court to extract what he could in the way of cash from Miss Kelly. Instead of money, Bowyer got a fright he would remember to the grave. On getting no answer to his repeated knocking, he pulled aside some sacking that covered a broken window pane and peered into the room. Mary Kelly was there, scattered all over the room. She lay dead on the bed, her head almost severed from the body, ears and nose cut off and the face slashed almost beyond recognition. There were bloodstains everywhere. On a table beside the bed were her breasts, heart and kidneys, while pieces of her intestines hung from the picture-frame nails.

It was half-past one before the police and doctors broke in the door, but Moriarty and his men had received the news, complete with gruesome details, before midday.

"So now we know," Moriarty said, in a voice as cold as the grave. "There must be no more of this."

"You want me to arrange it?" asked Paget.

"It has to have some hint of subtlety. Yes, when it has all been done, I would like you, Paget, to arrange it, but first I think Moran had better give him the stone jacket."

The men talked of the plan for the next three hours, interrupted only by the shouting of newsboys in the street below, calling, "Murder in Whitechapel. Another 'orrible murder. Terrible mutilations. Read about the Ripper's latest victim."

The watch on Druitt was doubled, but he did not make any more journeys from Blackheath to London before the term ended at Mr. Valentine's school. He did, however, have a visitor on November 30, the day before the end of term. He arrived at 9 Eliot Place just before five o'clock in the late afternoon and did not give his name, just asked if he could see Mr. Druitt on a private matter of some importance. It was, of course, Colonel Moran, and when the two men faced each other in the staff parlor on the ground floor, he had little to say.

"Mr. Druitt," he began, "I will say this once and once only. I know who you are and you do not know me. I know what you have been about in the East End and I have proof."

Druitt, who looked pale and drawn, stared about him wildly.

"Nobody else need know," Moran continued. He had made certain that his back was to the door and had one hand in his pocket, gripped around the butt of a Shattuck .32 rimfire revolver. "Today is Friday. On Monday evening at six o'clock you will meet me at the Howard Arms, which you know is not far from your chambers in the Temple. You will be alone and tell nobody. When we meet, I will hand over my evidence for the sum of sixty pounds. It is not much to ask and well within your means. I shall see you on Monday, Mr. Druitt."

With that, Moran gave a curt bow, opened the door behind him stepped back into the hall and was out of the door and away before Druitt could make any answer.

There was much rain over the weekend. On the Saturday Druitt left 9 Eliot Place and moved into 9 King's Bench Walk, his lodgings in the Temple. As before, he was shadowed by Paget's men, and this time all the Temple entrances were watched.

It is fact that Druitt was seen alive on the blustery morning of Monday, December 3, but nobody observed him making his way toward the Howard Arms off the Embankment a little before six o'clock in the evening.

Moran sat at a table in the small, pleasant, paneled taproom. There were not many people abroad on that evening because of the inclemency of the weather, but two other men sat in deep conversation at another table. The men were Paget and Spear. Moran was waiting for his guest and had in fact already ordered two glasses of brandy, one of which he sipped quietly as the time moved slowly by.

Druitt arrived a few minutes after six and went straight over to Moran.

"I have the money. A check and gold." Druitt said quietly, his hand moving toward his pocket.

Moran made a fast motion with his hand.

"Not in here. Sit down, my dear Jack, and have a little brandy. It will warm you."

Reluctantly, Druitt seated himself, looking very nervous. He drank quickly, just as Moriarty had told them he would. Nobody had seen Moran pour the white powder into the brandy as he carried the drinks to the table.

Druitt spoke only three times.

"Where is the evidence?" he asked—to which Moran replied, "In good time. I have it here," patting his pocket.

When he had almost finished the brandy, Druitt remarked, "There was good reason for it."

"I am sure," nodded the colonel.

"Those poor wretches living in filth. Someone had to draw attention to it. Perhaps they will do something good about it now."

He swigged back the remaining brandy.

Spear and Paget rose and left the bar. A few minutes later Druitt shook his head and asked if it was particularly hot in the room. He looked as though he was about to faint.

"You need some air," Moran said, getting up and helping Druitt to his feet. "Come, we'll get the business done outside."

Druitt's knees were buckling under him as they reached the door. Once outside he swooned and was caught under the arms by Spear.

The two big young men, with Moran acting as a crow, carried the Ripper across the road and laid him on the ground. Paget had already prepared a pile of stones with which they weighted Druitt's pockets, before tossing him, like a bundle of rags, into the rising waters of the Thames. Even in the bad light they observed a flurry of bubbles near to the place where he had sunk, weighed down by the heavy stones.

Montague John Druitt's body was discovered on New Year's Eve.

There were no more Ripper murders, and Moriarty smiled to himself as he recalled how he had rid the area of that terror, the memory of it strengthening his resolve to rid it also of Michael the Peg.

He slept soundly now, dreaming only of childhood as a small boy in Ireland, of the vivid green of the country, the animals and birds of his youth and then the sudden uprooting: the crowded boat tossing its way to Liverpool; his tall, thin elder brother sneering at his vomiting; his other brother offering comfort; his mother, white and red-eyed, and his father notable for his absence.

The dream whirled around through the night, throwing pictures as clear as day into his head: the new house, smaller than the farm; strange sounds and even stranger faces; the schoolroom and the master announcing that his brother, James, would go a long way in the world and his sense of hatred toward this genius who seemed to have taken his father's place in the family. There was also a boy called McCray, who taught him how to thieve small things, kerchiefs, sweetmeats and the like. He remembered the days when they were hungry and went out to "prick in the wicker for a dolphin," as they used to call thieving bread—dangerous work in those days.

In the first seconds of waking, Moriarty imagined that he was still back in 1888 at the house off the Strand. But that was only the tail end of his thoughts in the early hours and his mind quickly adjusted to the present and to the many complicated duties he now had to face—dealing with the incarcerated Colonel Moran, getting the Jacobs boys out of the 'Steel, driving Michael the Peg and his mob from Whitechapel, and a dozen more urgent assignments that skulked in the foggy patches around the narrow alleys of his mind. Today there was much to do. Tonight he would meet Alton, the turnkey from the 'Steel, then later he had the assignation with Mary McNiel, which would mix business with pleasure in a most attractive manner. From now on, life would be full for Moriarty.

Mrs. Wright had prepared the Professor's breakfast, grilled bacon, kidneys and sausages—all bought from Warwick Field & Company, Wapping High Street, and served by Lee Chow, who bustled about with the eternal smile splitting his moon face. The other members of the "Praetorian Guard" had been out since first light, getting on with the considerable work that had to be done before the Professor could reasonably claim that he was back in a position of full strength. It was important to Moriarty that his control of the capital should be reestablished. His representatives from the other major European cities would be in London by the twelfth of the month, and they had to see and believe in his strength.

Before finally going to bed, Moriarty had switched one of Ember's jobs, putting it onto Paget's shoulders. Ember had a great deal of work to accomplish: With Parker and his band of lurkers, Ember had to discover the full extent of Michael the Peg and Lord

Peter's activities; also, and most important, the names of the Peg's top lieutenants. Moriarty also instructed him to look into the matter of the proposed burglary at Harrow. This last chore he had now directed to Paget, to be carried out once the most faithful punishers had been brought to the warehouse; a wise move because bringing in the punishers aas a relatively simple job that would take little time, while the trip to Harrow could possibly take up the rest of the day, keeping Paget out of the way so that Spear, once he had reported on the condition and whereabouts of Colonel Sebastian Moran, could make his discreet inquiries regarding Fanny Jones, Paget's young woman.

Moriarty wished to clear the board, bringing all the matters in hand up to date; so when Lee Chow returned to his chambers for the breakfast crockery, the Professor motioned for him to be seated in the chair that stood opposite the large desk.

"Lee Chow, you remember last night Mr. and Mrs. Dobey came and talked about their daughter—Ann Mary?"

"Ann Maly Dobey burn bad with acid?"

"Yes. You remember?"

"I got good ear. I hear much, no speakee until asked."

"Her parents say the man Tappit threw the vitriol, the acid, in her face. I want you to go out and find the truth."

Lee Chow's face was once more slashed with the broad grin.

"I find truth. I find it good. Get all facts chop-chop."

Moriarty looked sternly at him.

"I want no errors, Lee Chow. No mistakes. If Tappit is not the man, then you find out who is, and why it was done. Understand?"

"I understan'. If Tappit no man who throw acid, then Tappit not get Tommy Lollocks crushed."

Moriarty smiled.

"Tommy Rollocks, Lee Chow," he corrected.

"I say Lollocks, Plofessor. All same Bollocks."

Moriarty chuckled.

"All right, Lee Chow. Go to it."

The grinning Chinese departed. If it does turn out to be Tappit, Moriarty thought, it won't be a simple matter of a kick in the testicles. Doing a girl's face with vitriol demanded something of a very different nature. W. S. Gilbert and Sir Arthur Sullivan had summed it up—*Let the punishment fit the crime.* Whoever had marked Ann Mary Dobey would be paid in a subtle manner. Moriarty smiled mentally, the action not passing over his face, retribution would be necessarily harsh.

By eleven o'clock the Professor had carefully gone over the last three years' accounts for five of his restaurants and a couple of the music halls. He was shrewd enough to know that the legitimate ventures were of the highest importance to him at this point in his career.

He leaned back in his chair, happy with the results of the examination. The books showed that these projects were bringing in a sizable profit. Business was exceptional, and if he added this side of things to the activities of his vast criminal network, Moriarty's position could do nothing but improve and prosper, especially since his plans to invest in the growing movement of anarchy in Europe would, in his mind, only place him in a stronger situation—the fulfillment of the first part of his ambition, absolute control of European crime.

The meeting with his Continental colleagues, arranged for April 13, was possibly the most important matter the Professor had in hand, for his whole future rested on its outcome: certainly very big things could emerge, and his plans could only solidify and move forward if the conference were successful.

Paget tapped at the door and entered.

"I've got them all downstairs."

He looked even more determined than usual.

"Our old regulars?" Moriarty smiled as Paget nodded. "I'd better come down to them. I doubt if there is room for all of us in here."

Paget gave a brief flickering grin, which reflected the hardness of the man.

"They're all there but for Fossick."

Moriarty raised his eyebrows in query.

"Fossick is past it, I'm afraid. The drink and the syphilis, I think. A shadow of his former self."

Moriarty nodded and walked toward the door.

Downstairs in the "waiting room" nine men were gathered; men who would have frightened all but the most hardened specimens of humanity. They were each over six feet in height, built broadly and muscular, with faces betraying a brutality, a cruelty even, that would have been difficult to match.

They were all former pugilists, prizefighters bearing the scars and marks of their previous profession—cauliflower ears and battered noses; one of them had his left eye askew, another's jaw was bent to the left, the result of a bad break that had been left to set on its own.

Moriarty stood at the bottom of the stairs, his eyes roving across the faces. He knew each and every one well. When he had first set eyes on them, they all had the mark of despair on their faces, now replaced by a kind of character bred of determination.

Moriarty knew that this change was, in the main, due to him.

"It's good to see you again, lads," he smiled.

There was a muttered response, almost a verbal doffing of caps and pulling of forelocks, smiles and grins lighting the hard, callous faces of the men.

"Well, Paget has probably told you already that there is work to be done," continued the Professor. "We have some troublemakers around. Eat and relax for the moment. I am waiting for our good friend Ember to return with a few names. Once he is back, I'll unleash the lot of you like a pack of avenging angels." A slow smile crossed his face. "Though it is hardly angels that I can call you."

A few of the men laughed, deep pleasurable grunts.

"Angels of destruction, if you like, Professor," one of them, a huge bullyboy called Terremant, said in a gruff voice.

"Aye, angels of destruction. Let Mrs. Wright see to your needs now." He turned to Paget. "Good work. Now get on with the Harrow business. Take your time. I will not need you back here much before tomorrow."

"I'd like to return tonight if I'm finished."

Was it anxiety in Paget's eyes?

"Ah, yes, I had forgotten that you have good reasons for being here at night. Your perfect lady. . . ."

"She's no whore," Paget bridled. To call someone a "perfect lady" was no compliment.

Moriarty allowed a pause.

"No, I'm sorry, Paget. You told me about her. Fanny Smith, was it?"

"Jones, Professor, Fanny Jones."

"Yes, Jones, again my apologies, Paget, but I am still a little upset to have learned of her at this late stage—learned that she was living under my roof. Both of you are here, so both of you are under my protection. When shall I meet the girl?"

"Whenever you like, sir."

Moriarty paused again, with brief and perfect timing.

"I have business to which I must attend today, and tonight. Maybe I will see her sometime tomorrow. Is the girl in the house?"

"Yes. She looks after my quarters and helps Mrs. Wright in the kitchen—does shopping and the like."

"All right. Go about the Harrow matter, we'll talk of her again tomorrow, Paget. It is not your fault. You are a good and trusted man."

"Thank you, Professor."

Paget nodded to the men, who were by this time engaging

themselves with tankards of ale and hot pies provided by the Wrights, and left quietly.

Moriarty went back to his chambers.

Some thirty minutes later Spear returned, flushed and nervous.

"You have found him?" Moriarty asked calmly from behind his desk. He was talking of Moran.

Spear nodded. "He's in Horsemonger Lane awaiting trial. It appears he was committed by a magistrate at Bow Street this morning, early, on a charge of murder. He will have only been at Horsemonger Lane a matter of hours."

Moriarty's brow creased, eyes narrowing.

"Awaiting trial?" He did not expect an answer. "There are certain privileges to that, are there not?"

"They can still have things taken in to them. Food and drink; clothing. Until the trial and conviction. They'll as like hang him there. They have the means in the gatehouse."

"Moran will blow long before that happens, then we will all be done for. Our friend the colonel needs to leave this planet long before the trial."

His brow creased again, and for a few moments he appeared to be lost in thought.

"Fanny Jones." He smiled. "Would the colonel recognize Fanny Jones?"

"I doubt it. I suppose he has seen the girl a dozen times, if that, and he was not much of a man for the ladies—not for their faces any road; only their mouths and thighs."

"Find out about her, Spear. Work quickly. If she is as clean as we are to believe, then there are things she can do for us. Get out and see if she did serve this Lady Bray; what she did to get so summary a dismissal. Look into her background. . . ."

"It'll take time, Professor."

"Just the outline. Feel it out. Use your instinct; I know you, Spear, you'll be certain within two hours. In any case, we will be sure once she is on her way to Horsemonger Lane."

The smile of Moriarty's face reflected true evil, that strange and rare look when a human being has touched the furthest limits of corruption. Today the psychiatrists would have a dozen names for it, but then, in 1894, Sigmund Freud was still groping in the dark toward an understanding of mental disarray, while criminal psychology, or forensic psychology, were simply words.

But the quest for power, the deliberate ambition to own— property, lives, towns, cities, souls—had flooded into James Moriarty's brain early in life. He could not have been more than ten or eleven years of age when he first knew that he was different.

He had no memory of Ireland, even though his mother, and both his elder brothers talked of the green fields, the farm and the animals. His first memories were those of the city, of Liverpool, and the quiet little house among the genteel middle classes, and the raging inferno inside telling him to break loose from his surroundings: from the faded velvet and the dead eyes of people he did not, and could not, recognize peering from the picture frames in the little parlor. They were arranged in rows along the dresser together with some plates decorated with a blue pattern.

He smiled to himself, for those days seemed far off, in a time when they had called him Jim. Three brothers named James, a foolish fancy of his father, or mother. Mam who played the pianoforte in the parlor and took in pupils while James studied and Jamie dreamed of wars and death or glory. And Jim? Jim did not dream of power, there was no time to sit and dream—James' example at least showed him that. You had to take the moment by the throat, and use it, wring every ounce of breath from it; so Jim, even at this tender age, began to look about him to see where the sources of power lay, and he found, very quickly, that they lay in various clearly aligned areas. You had to get a hold on people first, have them in thrall, exercise control over them, and that, he found, was easier than it first appeared.

Women and girls seemed to exercise great control over men, so the first step was to have some dominance over them. Jim Moriarty spent many hours wandering around at night, noting where the people who lived in their street were mostly to be found. It became relatively easy once that was discovered.

The first was the nursemaid at number fifteen. Jim had caught her, or rather seen her, with a soldier. He suspected that things were not as they should be, because the girl, age about sixteen years, spent most of her free time—one evening a week and the occasional Sunday—not with just one soldier, but several. Jim had finally discovered her behind some bushes in the old Zoological Gardens with her skirt up to her neck and a large corporal on top of her, moving as though he was trying to win a gold cup.

When it was finished, the corporal gave the nursemaid some money and left: the click of those coins remained a memorable sound. Five minutes later there was another soldier with her and the same sequence of events.

Jim Moriarty was aware of the dangers. Young boys were found dead every day in Liverpool. But that did not stop him, because he also knew that the nursemaid had a good position with a very respectable family and she had come from a favorable home; his mother had said that she was the daughter of a country schoolmaster. When Moriarty put it to her, the girl had been scornful at first.

"You dirty young beast. You don't know anything."

"Wait and see then."

"You couldn't do anything. I'd set my young men onto you."

"You'd still get caught. I wrote it all down, just as I saw it and it's in a safe place. If anything happens to me, my best friend knows what to do."

"What do you want, you little bastard?"

"Mam said you were a lady. Ladies don't talk like that."

"What?"

He told her. Half of what she made out of the soldiers. She argued and cried a little, but paid up. So did the son of his Mam's best friend, two other nursemaids, the cook at number forty-two and the prim, proper Miss Stella, who taught in Sunday school—he found out about her by accident, but she paid him like the others, just the same.

All those folk were his high-class clientele. . . . Young Moriarty had smaller fish to fry as well: the other kids at school, and it was with them that he learned the lessons of real power. But that was the beginning, and another story.

In spite of his broken nose and the disfiguring scar, Spear could well have passed as a police officer. He sat in the private bar of The Victory, close enough to Park Lane to be the haunt of those more superior servants—the butlers and valets—attached to the households of the rich, famous and influential who had their town houses in that area.

Spear did not actually tell the barman that he was from the Criminal Investigation Department of Scotland Yard. He merely hinted at the possibility. The hint worked wonders: for one thing, quite a number of plainclothesmen had been using the pub during the last weeks while looking into the murder of Ronald Adair, so it was not particularly odd for another one to turn up, especially the day after the murderer had been apprehended. The barman tipped off the landlord, who came through and actually asked Spear if he would care for a drink on the house. Spear accepted with good nature and within ten minutes was rewarded with the information that Sir Richard Bray's butler, a Mr. Halling, was in the habit of calling in at The Victory at around nine o'clock most evenings and at midday two or three times a week.

Spear was in even greater luck when, at five past the hour of noon, the door to the private bar opened to disclose a funereal-looking, tall, thin man who was indubitably in the higher echelons of service. The landlord introduced them, and Spear, speaking in low, almost hallowed tones, asked Mr. Halling if he could have a confidential word with him. He also bought the glasses of spirits.

Halling was obviously uncertain; there had been reporters from the newspapers around of late, and he did not wish to get involved.

"There's no question of you being involved, Mr. Halling." Spear's tone bordered on reverence. "We don't wish to involve anybody, but there are some side issues arising from that nasty business at four twenty-seven Park Lane."

Halling scowled, looking down his nose as though some unsavory smell had assailed his nostrils.

"Regrettable," he said rather in the manner of one commenting on the loss of a florin than on the loss of a life. "A most regrettable and unwholesome business. I would rather make no comment."

Spear sighed. He was good at impersonating the frustrated noises of authority.

"If you don't wish to talk about it, Mr. Halling, it is your affair. I simply thought it might save Sir Richard or Lady Bray the discomfort of police interrogation on a matter which I am certain is of little consequence to them. You would be called in whatever, for I'm certain that Lady Bray would need your specialized knowledge and memory to provide the facts. The matter is too trivial for her to even recall, and I'm sure very little misses your eagle eye, Mr. Halling." The damaged corner of his mouth curled in a series of small twitches.

For a second Spear wondered if he had gone too far with this last speech, but his fears were allayed the moment he caught the look in the butler's eye: It was a gleam of respect, as though Halling were mentally congratulating Spear for being so astute in recognizing the virtues that were so obviously his.

"Perhaps you would like to give me some idea." Halling actually smiled. "Some *clue*," he said heavily accenting the latter word, "to the circumstances."

"Simple." Spear took a sip of the spirits. "It concerns a young girl who worked in the Bray household at one time. Name of Jones, a housemaid or the like, came into service with Lady Bray from the country. Warwickshire, I believe. She was dismissed about a year ago. Fanny Jones."

Halling nodded, pompous and solemn. He was like a jumped-up Parish Clerk, Spear thought.

"I remember the girl." Halling's voice was totally filled with the accents of middle-class snobbery, stressing the word *girl* as though he were speaking of some useless piece of rubbish.

Spear held himself in check. He knew Fanny Jones and liked her; after all, Paget was an old mate and she was his girl, lively, bright, always laughing, a looker too, with long legs. (He knew because he had once walked into Paget's quarters and caught her undressed, by accident, and the sight of those legs had haunted him for weeks after.) But Spear was Moriarty's man first, and if the Professor had cause to look into Fanny's background, then he must remain unbiased.

"Would you tell me about her then, Mr. Halling?"

"In trouble again, is she?"

Again? Spear wondered at that.

"I'm afraid that's a police matter. I'm not at liberty to discuss it with anybody." He creased his brow, then turned to face the man as though coming to a decision. "But seeing it's you, I can say we think she's got herself mixed up with some rather fast company."

"Whores?"

Halling's head flicked toward Spear, the eyes betraying interest, while his voice suggested contempt.

Halling, my friend, thought Spear, *if Fanny is a good 'un and you had any part in seeing her out into the street, I will make it my business to see that you are undone.* The butler's look told him more in a second than he would learn in a dozen years of talk. Spear knew a regular whore's mark when he saw one, and he would put money on the somber Mr. Halling being a constant visitor to the Haymarket or Leicester Square area—he doubted the butler would venture into Soho—but one thing was certain, he would have special fancies.

"Something of the kind," Spear nodded.

"Do you know where?"

The direct question. Perhaps Mr. Halling's particular fancy was Fanny Jones herself.

"I can say no more, Mr. Halling, but we need to know something of her true background, her time in service with Sir Richard and Lady Bray. If you are interested in the young woman's salvation, I may well be able to give you information once I have spoken to my superiors."

Halling nodded knowingly, the pomposity born from generations of servility.

"A wicked and wayward girl, I fear, sir. Those are the only words I can use to describe her: wicked and wayward."

"Go on."

"She came to Lady Bray with the best of references, straight from some small place near to Warwick—Kenilworth, I think it was. We were fully staffed, but Lady Bray took the girl out of the goodness of her heart—some friend of Sir Richard's was involved, I believe. But there you are, sir, it's the old story: be good to people and they repay you ill."

"Indeed." Spear bobbed his head in agreement.

"It was one of the young footmen. I brought it to Sir Richard's attention and, characteristically, he was most lenient—had a word with the fellow—and I thought that was that. You cannot have young housemaids playing the game with footmen. Not in a household like the Brays."

Spear tutted, "Of course you cannot."

"Unhappily it was not the end."

"No?"

"I discovered, quite by accident, mark you, that Jones was in the habit of absenting herself for an hour or so in the evening—with no permission—in order to be with another young man."

"Not of the household?"

"Some young loiterer. A discharged army man, I understand. It is of no importance anyway. The girl was quite unashamed. I caught her one night, creeping back, having absented herself for some two hours. I went straight to Lady Bray and informed her. She told me to deal with the matter and dismiss her. I had the girl out within the hour."

"Out on the street? Just like that?"

"What else does one do? She would have become an evil influence on the other girls."

Spear wanted to lash out at the smug and satisfied man; he wanted to see the smooth cheek laid open, the eye cut and the teeth jolted out of place. There was little doubt in his mind as to what had really happened in the comfort of the Park Lane house. But Spear had always been a man of discipline.

"I don't think we shall have to trouble you again. Not for some time anyway, Mr. Halling. Thank you for talking to me, it has been most pleasant. I'll wish you good day, sir."

When Spear got back to the warehouse, Ember had returned, also Lee Chow, who was upstairs with Moriarty.

Ember sat in the corner, away from the nine big men, all of whom Spear knew at least by sight. They certainly knew him and showed a healthy respect in their greetings.

"They going to be used?" Spear asked, dropping his heavy body onto the wooden form next to Ember.

"Tonight." Ember glanced up from the tankard of ale. "That bastard, the Peg, has a right crowd around him, hard men, some of them known to you. . . ."

"Who?" Spear asked without emotion.

"Jonas Fray, Walter Roach—"

"Bastards. They was always the Professor's men." Spear's jagged scar twisted, transforming his face into a villainous mask.

"Well, they're the Peg's now. That's the bloody colonel for you. Wasn't doing the job, was he?"

Both Jonas Fray and Walter Roach had been men close to the "Praetorian Guard" in the old days; strong, cunning, intelligent men whom the Professor would almost certainly have promoted to positions of importance within the organization. Indeed, they had both been used, in the past, in operations that had required considerable responsibility. For them to desert Moriarty and side with someone like the Peg was, to Spear and the others, an act of gross treachery.

Spear spat on the floor, the act as violent as if he had hurled a brick through the window.

"There are others." Ember's small eyes glittered with hatred. "The Professor will doubtless tell you all—and what we are to do with them."

"Nothing can be too bad for them, and now cannot be too soon."

Upstairs, Lee Chow was reciting his evidence to the Professor, who, as usual, sat with steepled fingers, behind his desk.

There was little doubt that Tappit was the man who had burned young Ann Dobey's face with vitriol. The case was clear cut, the evidence more than enough. If the police had been involved, Tappit would already be in jail, but that was not the usual way with those who regarded themselves as part of Professor Moriarty's family. The police acted as a road to the law, and while the law was, as often as not, unmerciful, there were many cases that, for reasons known only to those who dealt justice, did escape the full weight of punishment. By the same token there were relatively innocent people—men, women and children—who suffered horrors far outweighing their small crimes. It was not unnatural, then, that those who lived in the ugly shadows of the time had a healthy mistrust of both the police and the law. It was better for them to dispense their own justice.

Ann Mary Dobey was a pleasant, pretty girl, who, as Moriarty would have been the first to admit, could have made a considerable living had she chosen to put herself in the hands of a woman like Sal Hodges. But Ann was a rarity, a girl who worked hard and arranged her own personal life, a situation made possible only by the fact that her father worked exclusively for the Professor.

As a barmaid at the Star and Garter, Ann Mary mixed freely with the cross section of humanity who patronized the house. Her wages were poor, but in the circumstances she could at least choose her men, something she did with such skill that she was never branded as a whore. Indeed, the men who were the recipients of her favors usually regarded themselves as victors even though they parted with hard cash. Ann Mary knew how to make men feel that her body was a reward, the natural result of their own charm and personality, that her gift—which was not a gift—was given out of mutual desire, having nothing to do with the more sordid business that took place with those women who plied the streets for trade or lived in the commercial hives of the night houses and brothels.

John Tappit had apparently long been an admirer of Ann Dobey—an admirer she did not encourage. Lee Chow had done his work in a thorough and speedy fashion. There were plenty of men and women who would swear to the way in which Tappit had constantly pestered the girl, who held him well at arm's length with a pleasant good humor not shared, it seemed, by Tappit. There were full descriptions of three ugly scenes in the public bar of the Star and Garter, the last of these having resulted in the landlord's forbidding Tappit entry to his house.

"Ann Maly nice girl," Lee Chow told Moriarty. "When landlord say he no come back in bar, Ann Maly take pity on Tappit and say she meet him that night a' eleven o'clock, but not able to because of many customers in bar. Tappit velly angy. Fight into bar and scream a' her: say 'I get you, you stuck-up bitch. I finish you game.' Have plenty witness of that. Then, next night, Ann Maly leaving Star an' Garter when Tappit run across road and shout a' her, then throw acid in face. Have names of three men—all good men—who see it happen. They know I come from you an' all say they try to catch him but he run ver' fast. They say you run fast an' catch him."

Moriarty did not have to question Lee Chow. The Chinese was impeccable in matters of this nature.

"Do you know where Tappit is living?" he asked.

"I find out plenty chop-chop."

Moriarty nodded.

"Find him then. After that . . . ."

He gave Lee Chow his orders in a quiet, calm and inflexible voice, sent him downstairs to get on with things and asked him to tell Spear to come up if he had returned.

Fanny Jones was twenty years of age, tall, slender and neat in appearance with an oval face framed by dark hair; she had large brown eyes, slightly flared nostrils and a mouth that suggested, even to the well-worn senses of a man like Moriarty, a paradoxical mixture of kisses as cool and sweet as cucumbers and sensuous as a honey pot.

Fanny knew that her face showed the nerves that fluttered within her. She had been more than lucky and was most aware of it, especially in the months since she had met Pip Paget. Had she not been on the verge of going on the streets when he had found her? There were plenty of other servant girls, dismissed for one reason or another, who had ended up on the streets, in the houses, or even worse, in the prisons of London.

For the last three days, since she had known that the Professor— an awesome figure to her—was back in his rightful place, Fanny Jones had been nervous about meeting him, but even that thought had been quietened by the knowledge that Pip Paget would be with her when the moment came. But Pip was away for the day, and she had been thrown into a turmoil of confusion when Bert Spear came down into the kitchen, as she helped Kate roll out the pastry for fresh pies, and told her that the Professor insisted on seeing her now.

She looked frightened, Moriarty thought, as well she might, poor child. Spear had given him the facts, briefly and clearly.

"You know where to find this Halling if we need him again?" he asked.

"I'll know where to find him, Professor, and if it is as I think, then I'd like your permission to deal with the bastard myself."

"With pleasure. If Halling was the main cause, I do not think we should involve Paget, so you can teach Halling the lesson he deserves. But, we shall see. Get the girl up here."

So it was that Fanny Jones was shown into the Professor's private chambers.

Moriarty smiled at her, holding her eyes in his, an effort to make her at ease.

"I've heard a lot about you, Fanny. Come over here and sit down," he said, indicating the chair. "There's nothing to fear."

His eyes slid quickly up to Spear, the message inherent in his look telling Spear to leave them alone.

When Spear had closed the door behind him, Moriarty leaned back.

"Please be at your ease, my dear. I only discovered last night that you were living under my roof. Paget has been in my employ for a long time and I wish you to know that anyone close to him is close to me also. Everyone who lives under my roof has my protection, and, as Paget has probably already told you, those who have my protection have to give certain allegiance to me."

The words were old to Moriarty, the pattern unchanged with the passing of the years; he had used them when still a child at school and among the Liverpool streets of his youth.

I pay you. You have allegiance to me.

You promised. You have an allegiance to me.

I saw you. So did my friends. You have a certain allegiance to me now.

You want the master to know about it? No, I think not. So you have allegiance to me.

"You understand what that means, Fanny?" he asked.

"Yes, Professor."

She understood because Pip had already told her.

"Good. We shall get along famously, Fanny, and today you can help me. But first, I have not had time to ask Paget about you. Will you answer some questions for me? Answer them truthfully?"

"I will always answer you truthfully, Professor."

There was a strange sinking sensation in her stomach.

"You are a truthful girl, Fanny?"

"I think so. Yes. Certainly with people I respect."

"Good. Before Paget found you and brought you here you worked for Sir Richard and Lady Bray, is that correct?"

"Yes, sir, as a housemaid."

"Then you know a Mr. Halling?"

He watched the color drain even further from her cheeks, forming a chalky patina, while her hands began to move, a ceaseless twisting of the fingers.

"Mr. Halling is butler to the Brays, is he not?"

She nodded quickly, little jerks of the head.

"Yes," she said in a tiny voice.

"You fear him, Fanny?"

Again the nodding.

"Was he, perhaps, responsible for your dismissal?"

Her eyes avoided his face.

"There is nothing for you to fear, Fanny, I have already told you that. If there is something you have not even told Paget, it will be safe with me. Was Mr. Halling responsible for your dismissal?"

She sat, still and stubborn. Moriarty could easily have counted up to twenty before she made any move. When she did, it was like a great gathering of strength, as though she were reaching out and drawing in invisible brigades of courage.

"Yes," she said at last, her voice trembling only slightly. "Mr. Halling was completely responsible. He tried to . . ."

Moriarty's head, which had been slowly oscillating, became still.

"Seduce you?"

"Almost from the moment I entered the Bray household. He was always trying to paw at me. I found him repellent, but I was afraid. He threatened . . ."

"Then he did have his way?"

"Once." Her eyes were cast down. "Only once."

Her face had its color again, a deep scarlet.

"He was . . . it . . ."

"I understand."

"But he kept on trying. All the time. First there were little favors. Presents. Then threats. I could not be with him again, Professor, not again."

"And the threats?"

"That if I did not . . ."

"He would see you out in the street."

"Yes."

"Which is exactly where you ended up."

The nod again, this time slow, bitter, her eyes showing the need for vengeance.

"You must not hate him too much," purred Moriarty. "If it was not for him, you would not have found Paget. But you can be certain Mr. Halling will get his gruel."

She frowned, uncertain.

"Common parlance for his punishment."

"Oh, yes. To he who waits comes nemesis."

"A very proper way of looking at it." He leaned forward across the desk. "Now, Fanny, there is a small service which you can render me."

An hour later, Moriarty had made all the arrangements. He had spoken to Mrs. Wright, and Fanny would be on her way within a short time. Spear was going to deal personally with friend Halling. Lee Chow would have the help of Terremant. And before the night was over, John Tappit would be amply repaid for Ann Doby's scarred face. Parker and his lurkers were about to report on the whereabouts of Jonas Fray and Walter Roach, the two most important Peg lieutenants; once either of them was in the open, the punishers would be out. As yet, Paget had not returned from Harrow. Moriarty hoped that he would not be back before Fanny Jones had completed her mission to Horsemonger Lane Jail. In the meantime, Moriarty himself had to prepare for his meeting with Alton, the turnkey from the 'Steel.

Friday, April 6, 1894

(THE REAL MORIARTY)

THE SURREY COUNTY Jail was known to all as Horsemonger Jail. It stood grimly in the Parish of St. Mary's, Newington, in the Borough of Lambeth, enclosed by a dirty brick wall, which almost kept it from the public eye.

Fanny Jones pushed her way through the throng of people moving up and down, happy and quarrelsome, quiet and noisy, selling, buying and loitering along Stone's End. It was a particularly busy street, a good-natured thoroughfare with undertones of roguery. The Professor had been kind but firm, and Fanny was still nervous, particularly at visiting the scene of so much pain and misery. She could not believe she was actually going to see the inside of a prison, smell its odors and taste, even for a brief moment, the horrors of incarceration. She had heard enough about it in the servants' lurk where Pip had found her. There were several men and women there who had experienced the inside of one or another of the houses of correction, and the tales they told—of the rigors, discipline, diet, restriction and brutality—were enough to make a young girl tremble her way into waking nightmares.

When Moriarty had said to her, "I need you to visit Colonel Moran in Horsemonger Lane Jail," her immediate reaction had been a vigorous negative. She had even said that she was prepared to leave the Professor's house rather than enter that place. But Moriarty had smoothly persuaded her that there was little to fear.

"It is not as though you are going to be incarcerated," he said softly. "Nor do the police want you for anything." A pause before he asked, "Or do they, Fanny?"

"No. No, Professor, of course they do not."

"Well, then. We simply wish for the colonel to have a few luxuries, which he is allowed until they take him for trial and

70

sentence. You must realize, my dear Fanny, it is important that whoever takes the basket Mrs. Wright is preparing for him should not be known to the authorities, and it is unlikely anyone will recognize you. Except perhaps the colonel himself.''

"I doubt that, sir. But the prison—will it be a terrible experience?''

Moriarty gave a short, almost gentle, laugh.

"Not as terrible as if they did not release you. It will be nothing. A short visit to another world. Be demure. A servant. Draw no attention to yourself. Dress in a manner becoming those things.''

When she left his chambers, Moriarty allowed himself the briefest fantasy. Her clothing did nothing to deny the lithe limbs and soft body beneath—at least not to a man like the Professor, who was well versed in reading the shapes and realities under outer garments. He leaned back, closing his eyes and wondering about her. The legs would be long and slender, the buttocks neat and firm, breasts as smooth and plump as ripe exotic fruit. She would enjoy the sucking of that fruit, and in her eyes he detected that deep smolder that men looked for in women. Paget, he considered, was a lucky man. Then his mind drifted off at a tangent toward the inevitable benefits of Mary McNiel, who was to visit him, there in his chambers, at eleven o'clock that very evening.

Fanny had gone to the kitchen, where Kate Wright told her to change. By the time that was done, she said, there would be a basket filled and ready to take to the colonel.

Fanny donned one of the two black dresses she had brought from her time with the Brays, set the white collar and buttoned it, then slung her cloak around her shoulders and returned to the kitchen.

Kate Wright and her husband, Bart, appeared to have been talking in low tones, stopping abruptly when she entered, standing somewhat embarrassed in the doorway.

There was a moment's hesitation before Kate smiled and touched the big basket that stood in the middle of the table, its contents covered by a starched linen napkin.

"It's ready," was all she said.

Bartholomew Wright, a large man of few words, shuffled his feet.

"One of the Professor's people is to take you by hansom cab, Fanny."

He did not smile, and she imagined she could detect a hint of concern in his eyes, but passed it off as her own nervousness.

"He will take you to Stone's End, show you the way through to the prison and then await your return. You understand, girl?''

"Of course."

There were uncanny images running through her mind: lurid pictures of criminals, convicts in the rough uniform striped with broad arrows, hideous men and women, warped in visage, shackled and dangerous. Mixed up with these fantasies were the overtones of violence, the instruments of correction, the bars and cages, the terrible treadmill (a small tweak of her own sexuality here as she remembered it was known as the cock-chaffer), the cat.

"You're trembling." Kate's hand was on her shoulder. "Come on, Fan, it'll be all right. There's nothing to worry over."

"No, I'm sorry, but I dread the whole business."

Bart said, "These places exist, Fan. It'll do you no harm to see the inside of one."

"As long—"

"As they don't keep you there, eh, gel?"

"It worries me."

Bart laughed. "The bogeyman. They won't keep you, Fan, not a lovely young girl like you."

Kate put an arm around her shoulders.

"Guilty conscience, that's what it is. You've got some terrible dark secret buried in that pretty head."

"Pip Paget, that's our Fan's dark secret," chuckled Bart. "That's what makes her feel guilty in the night, eh?"

Fanny blushed, and with some clarity, saw what he meant. Ladies and gentlemen, like the Brays and all the grand people she had seen coming in and out of the house in Park Lane, always seemed devoid of those velvet and hidden feelings she seemed to experience. They were not like the people who had surrounded her in Kenilworth—farmers and those who lived so close to nature that they knew the fleshly acts were for pleasure as well as procreation. Those superior ladies and gentlemen she saw at the Brays appeared to be part of a different order, one in which sensuality in women was equated with sin, and men were the dominant force in all things.

The driver of the hansom was a fat fellow with a red face veined with blue rivulets and deltas. Fanny Jones sat back, one hand resting on the handle of the wicker basket, her eyes restless, looking out on the changing scene as they drove down to the point where Stone's End met with Trinity Street. Once there he gave her the directions she would need to traverse Stone's End and find the alley to the jail. He would wait, he said, for one hour only, though he expected her back within half that time. He did not mention the young boy loitering nearby—a lad not quite in his teens, dressed in illfitting raggedy trousers, shirt and long jacket, the observers of better days. The boy pushed himself from the wall against which he had been leaning and began to saunter in the same direction as Fanny Jones. The Professor did not leave much to chance.

One approached Horsemonger Lane Jail through a narrow and gloomy alley turning off Stone's End and leading to the main gateway, a flat-roofed building that managed to house both the Governor and his family and the scaffold, the last meeting place of so many unfortunates.

Fanny approached the gateway and rattled the iron knocker. It was only seconds before the grille opened to reveal a face that had the appearance of being made of well-worn leather. She glimpsed the top of the high blue collar and upper buttons of the man's uniform.

"Visiting?" the warder asked, his voice devoid of feeling.

"I've come with victuals for a prisoner, sir." She made a point of stressing the *sir*.

"Name?"

"Whose name, sir?"

"The prisoner, girl."

He had taken her for a servant, which was not surprising. Apart from her mode of dress, the prison housed a large number of debtors who were the constant recipients of food, drink and clothing from friends in less constrained circumstances.

"Moran. Colonel Moran."

The warder peered at her through the grille, rather as though he were viewing some curiosity at a fairground.

"Moran the murderer, eh? And who's sending him victuals, eh?"

"A brother officer." Fanny had been well schooled by Moriarty.

The leather face crinkled into what was meant to be a smile.

"Comrade in arms. His name?"

"Colonel Fraser."

The leather face grimaced again.

"Colonel Fraser knows how to pick his servants." He began to withdraw the bolts and swing the door open. "When you've delivered the Fortnum and Mason's, perhaps you would care to take a little tipple in my quarters."

The grimace had turned into a leer.

Fanny did not have to force a blush to her cheeks, the blood rose fast, embarrassment mingled with fury. She fought back her anger.

"I am expected back. The colonel runs a strict household."

The turnkey nodded. "Your day off then?"

"I'm sorry, it's very difficult."

"It is also difficult to obtain permission to visit prisoners."

Fanny felt relieved.

"I do not have to see the prisoner," she smiled. "The basket has to be delivered, that's all."

She was inside the gatehouse by this time, the door closed and bolted behind her. Across the narrow courtyard she saw the lowering, depressing buildings, stray figures—prisoners, but not all in prison garb—interspersed with blue-uniformed turnkeys, their keys hanging from circles of metal attached to polished belts.

The gatehouse warder looked at her, a hungriness in his sharp eyes. Eventually he shrugged and nodded.

"As you wish."

There was a long, sloping wooden shelf bolted to the wall outside what she took to be his office. Three or four heavy books, or ledgers, rested on the shelf, and the leather-faced man consulted one of these before shouting across the yard to one of the turnkeys, who was intent on watching a group of shambling prisoners.

The turnkey—from the warder's shout, Fanny learned that his name was Williams—walked quickly over to the gatehouse warder, who looked up sharply, first at Fanny and then at the turnkey.

"Visitor for Moran. Men's Block A, cell seven. She's only delivering grub, so they need not be left alone—there's instructions about that anyway."

Williams nodded. "This way then, girl."

Fanny followed him across the yard, moving to the right. The solid block of the Sessions House was on one side, the main prison building on the other. The prisoners they passed were not as she had ever imagined, for those in this section of the jail were mainly debtors, tradesmen who appeared down on their luck yet in good spirits.

They turned left, through another gate, and then right. Fanny knew now that she was within the prison proper; there was a smell peculiar to it, soap and another, odd, oppressive odor she could not identify. There was also a quality of echoing awe—the sounds of a nightmare, of footsteps, the clang of doors and the hollow murmur of voices—all far away and muffled by brick and enclosed space.

Eventually they came to a long narrow passage flanked at intervals by the iron cell doors, each marked in white paint with a number.

"Men's Block A, cell seven," he intoned, taking his keys and selecting one.

The bolt was drawn back and the door swung open.

"Moran. A young woman bringing victuals," Williams barked.

Fanny did not know what to expect. There was no fully formed picture in her mind. The floor was wooden, the walls bare whitewashed brick, and light came from a small barred window set high in the far wall, though high would hardly be the word for the plain ceiling, which rose only some eight or nine feet. The furnishings were simple: a hammock, rolled and hanging from a hook on one wall, a basin and jug of water, a small table and stool.

Moran sat at the table, head in hands, the classic picture of the man incarcerated. Fanny was shocked as he raised his head. Moran had never been the most attractive of men; now, in his moment of extreme peril, the deterioration was marked—a wildness in the eyes and tremors, which, while not excessive, were undeniably present in his hands, shoulders and face.

His eyes showed no sign of recognition, the mouth half opening as though he wished to speak and was prevented by some kind of paralysis.

"Colonel Moran." Fanny approached him, her voice softly modulated. "Your old friend, Colonel Fraser, sent this basket for you and wished to know if there was anything else you needed."

"Fraser?"

His brow creased, his puzzlement so apparent that Fanny, for a fleet second, experienced consternation. Perhaps, she imagined, the Professor had made a mistake about Colonel Fraser. Then Moran's face lapsed into a bleak smile.

"Jock Fraser," he murmured. "Old Jock Fraser. Kind. Kind of him." Moran gave a throaty chuckle. "Tell him I will need his Jocks to cut me down from Ketch's tree."

Fanny moved forward and placed the basket on the table.

"He will send me with more later in the week, sir."

"Tell him that he is a good friend."

She waited for a moment, then realized the interview—if that was what one could call it—was terminated. She did not know that the basket she left on the small table of Moran's cell would be his own particular termination.

Fanny wanted to run as soon as the cell door closed behind her. The turnkey seemed to take his time with the lock and Fanny caught herself counting, a childhood and childish habit from which she could not break herself—a trick to get through nervous moments.

Eventually Williams straightened and nodded.

"We go back now, or is there anything else you would like to see?"

"I prefer to go, sir."

Once outside the prison gates, Fanny wanted to break into a run; she felt like a criminal wishing to flee the scene of a felony. In the back of her mind she also knew that she had need of a bath to erase the scents of that horrible place from her nostrils and body.

A little before six, Moriarty began to dress for his meeting with Alton at the Café Royal. At the same time the turnkeys and warders were coming on duty for the evening shift at Horsemonger Lane Jail.

The man assigned to Men's Block A started his rounds and eventually arrived at cell seven, taking the usual perfunctory squint through the Judas hole in the door. The fact of what he saw did not register for a few seconds. Then his head jerked back toward the hole. A moment later he was unlocking the door and shouting for help.

Colonel Moran lay on his side by the table, his stool overturned. He had consumed one glass of the wine that had been brought in with the basket of food, and part of the veal and ham pie had been torn away and eaten. From the remains of the pie half a hard-boiled egg started out like some grotesque accusing eye.

There was little either the turnkeys or the doctor, who came on the scene some five minutes later, could do for the colonel. He had vomited considerably and, from the attitude he had assumed on the cell floor, it was apparent that his death had been extremely painful.

"It could be *Strychnos* nux vomica or one of the other vegetable poisons."

The doctor was a somewhat pompous man who moved about the cell with exaggerated care, sniffing at the wine and food, playing the detective.

Inspector Lestrade, grave and worried, arrived an hour or so later. He talked with the doctor, made a brief examination of the food and wine, then began to interrogate the turnkeys with some care. He eventually came to the warder who had been on duty at the gatehouse when the basket was brought in, and later questioned Williams, who had accompanied the girl to Moran's cell.

Eventually, about seven o'clock, the inspector left Horsemonger Lane in a hansom, bound for the residence of Colonel Fraser in Lowndes Square.

The colonel was tall, sparse, with a yellowish complexion and brusque manner. He did not suffer fools gladly and, from the first, appeared to regard Lestrade as a simpleton.

" 'Course I knew Moran. Friend of his at one time, though I cannot say that I am proud of that now. I suppose you have to trace back his career though."

"What prompted you to send him the basket of food?" Lestrade's mouth traced a tiny, somewhat mean, smile.

The colonel's jaw dropped.

"Food? Basket? What in Hades are you talking of, man?"

"Your servant. The girl. She took a basket of foodstuffs to Colonel Moran this afternoon."

"Girl? I do not have any girl. A housekeeper, yes, but at sixty you would hardly call that lady a girl."

Fraser's color mounted to a dangerous scarlet.

Lestrade frowned, concerned. He had not considered this turn of events, as the trail seemed to have led exclusively to Fraser.

"You have not sent any victuals to Colonel Moran?" The eyebrows raised questioningly.

Fraser exploded in a welter of expletives, leaving Lestrade in little doubt as to his vehement denial.

"I would not send Sebastian Moran a rope to hang himself!" Fraser's voice seemed almost to buffet the shimmering glass ornaments in the large room. "Good God, Lestrade, the fellow's let the side down—school, regiment, family. I would not be seen in his vicinity, let alone send him anything."

"The girl said that she came from you," Lestrade bumbled, trying to grasp at straws.

"For the last time, there is no girl in my employ, nor did I send anything to the wretched man. You have my word on that as officer and gentleman. Any more of this and I will have to speak with my friend, the commissioner."

The wind had gone from Lestrade.

"I'm sorry, sir. It is a matter of some importance."

"How?"

"Whoever took the food into Moran used your name, sir. It would seem that the food was poisoned. Sebastian Moran is dead."

"And I am supposed to be an accomplice to his cheating the hangman?"

"Your name—"

"The hell with that. If you have more to say, you must say it to my legal advisers, Park, Nelson, Morgan and Gummel, Essex Street, Strand, West Central. So good day to you, sir."

On his way back to New Scotland Yard, a crestfallen Lestrade tried to clear his mind of the events surrounding Moran's undoubted murder. He had caught the colonel in the act of attempting murder—he was undoubtedly the killer of young Adair. He paused in thought, mentally adding the fact that Holmes had led him to Moran. Someone obviously wanted Moran dead. But why? Perhaps he should approach Holmes? He vaguely remembered that the great detective had made a reference to Moran's involvement with the infamous Moriarty. But he, too, was dead. Perhaps another ruler of organized crime had risen in Moriarty's place. Indeed there had been rumors of the roguish Michael the Peg in the East End, though in that morass of evil it was always difficult to penetrate to the truth. He kept coming back to the same question: Why should someone wish Moran dead? The answer was always the same: Moran had had some information. But what? Lestrade still worried at the problem as the hansom turned in through the gateway of Scotland Yard.

A private room had been booked for Moriarty and his guest, and Alton was already waiting at the Café Royal when the Professor arrived a few minutes after seven. It was early for diners and few people were in the restaurant when the two men met. Moriarty spoke only perfunctorily, to bid Alton good evening and motion him through the downstairs rooms and up the staircase.

Though only a senior turnkey at the 'Steel, Alton had the appearance of a well-dressed man-about-town, a fact owing in no small measure to his long association with Moriarty and the Professor's organization. He was a slim man of medium build, with a strangely gentle face, which he had attempted to harden with a short, graying, beard—a failure, as the beard emphasized the hint of kindness omnipresent in his large gray eyes. But the look belied the man, for Roger Alton could be ice cold, hard as granite, and at times as unfeeling as tortoiseshell.

The pair, looking as unlikely as Don Quixote and Sancho Panza, threaded through the glittering ground floor of this, the most notable London restaurant of its time, past the marble-topped tables and ornate gilt and velvet trappings, up the stairs and through into the private room, the door held open for them by a grave and bowing majordomo.

Moriarty, making no reference to Alton, ordered the meal: a relatively simple repast of mock-turtle soup, scallops of salmon and tartar sauce, ribs of beef with horseradish and potatoes, and Parisian tartlets. There were also the trimmings of French salad and cheese, a full white Burgundy with the salmon, a light red with the beef.

The two men ate in near silence, exchanging only the most necessary scraps of conversation. It was not until they were well into the beef that Moriarty rose, checked that no waiter lingered near the door, and then addressed Alton with a certain formality.

"You have two of my people under your care."

Alton allowed himself a smile.

"I'll warrant more than two."

"Two in whom I am interested. Brothers: William and Bertram Jacobs."

"William and Bertram. I know. Three years apiece. Accomplices of Bland. What do you want, Professor?"

"They have to come out. I am under an obligation to their mother."

Alton sighed, worry running small furrows across his brow, as if some invisible tiny harrow had been dragged suddenly and deeply over the flesh.

"You know the 'Steel, Professor. It will be like getting gold from a matchgirl. . . ."

"And you are under an obligation to me, Alton. In this instance we have to get gold from a matchgirl. With your help it is possible."

Alton turned down the corners of his mouth.

"They are both in the Misdemeanor Prison, what used to be the female ward. It is close there."

"And you fear the hue and cry?"

"If they can be got out at all, there will be trouble. Investigation. The governor rules the warders and turnkeys with almost the same severity as the prisoners. If two are missing . . ."

"What if they are not missing?"

"That is not possible."

"Trust me, friend Alton. All things are possible, believe me. The Jacobs boys can be out and in at the same time, with your help and some silence." He treated the turnkey to one of his rare and thin smiles. "Listen, and then give me your advice."

For a full hour the two men continued their conversation, pausing only when a waiter came into the room to replenish the brandy glasses. They spoke in low tones, an earnest urgency reflected in their faces. Alton nodded a great deal, and when their talk was over, they were both smiling.

On their way out, Moriarty and Alton had to walk through the main room downstairs. Now it was filled with diners and people meeting for an evening of convivial conversation, wit and champagne; the chandeliers threw off a sparkle and glitter that seemed almost to be reflections of the company, the elegant clothes of the women and the impeccable dress of the men complementing the furbishings of the room.

A small stir appeared to be taking place near the main doors. Moriarty could see a plump, portly man in his early forties talking to the manager. The man had a somewhat foppish appearance, made more obvious by his thick sensual lips and pasty complexion. Moriarty recognized him at once, for his name was a household word in that spring of 1894. He was accompanied by two slightly younger men, and, as Moriarty passed them, he heard the portly, affected one say to the manager, "If he does arrive, tell him that Oscar has gone to the Cadogan Hotel."

Moriarty and Alton passed through the doors and into the bustle of Piccadilly.

Jonas Fray and Walter Roach were both big men, made in the mold Moriarty liked to have around him. But they were fickle men, men who ran with hares and hunted with hounds, men whose greed outstripped fear, hoisting them to the power-ridden euphoria in which they bathed, fondly believing they were outside the law—of the criminal jungle as well as that of the land.

It was in just such a state of mind that they left The Nun's Head, on the lip of Whitechapel, just off the Commercial Road, early that evening. They had spent the late afternoon together with a number of like villains, planning, and to some extent celebrating the news concerning Colonel Moran. There had been ten of them in all, including their undisputed leader and his lieutenant—Michael Green, otherwise Michael the Peg, and Peter Butler, known as Peter the Butler or Lord Peter.

Both of these men were desperate, ambitious, ruthless and full of a guile and cunning that marked them as born leaders of the criminal fraternity. For more than a year now they had worked stealthily toward building up an organization, which they fondly believed would eventually rival Moriarty's network at the height of its powers. Yet it spoke much for the loyalty of Moriarty's family that so far not a whisper had reached them concerning the return of the Professor to his old domain. The mood during the afternoon had been jovial, luxurious even, Colonel Moran's arrest on the previous day having given all of them a sense of victory, a preliminary round won in the battle for domination.

Michael the Peg had lounged in a big, if somewhat tattered, leather armchair in the large chamber above the taproom of The Nun's Head, his heels resting on the table around which his trusted men sat, tankards and glasses in front of them.

The Peg was a small man, compact, with muscular shoulders and a face that looked as though it had been flattened by some maniac wielding a plank; the nose flared like that of a mongoloid, his skin a yellowish sallow tinge. These distinctive features could be attributed to a chance parenthood—the mating of a young dockside whore and a Chinese deckhand, on account of which Michael Green's early days had been colored by a background of poverty, lies, drunkenness, brutality and every unspeakable crime in the calendar of knavery. From the moment he could walk, Green had been forced to fight for himself, to think and act with speed, to face threat with threat, to cheat and steal until it had become second nature. His training ground centered on the streets of London, with occasional sorties into the country for the purpose of theft; and in these dealings he had, through the years, made a reputation as a skilled and vicious man—his nickname reflecting the considerable talent he had developed in the matter of disguise.

Peter Butler was of different ilk, for he had come to villainy by a more circumlocutory route. Born of countryfolk in the village of Lavenham in Suffolk—a clutch of Tudor houses whose inhabitants still lived out their time in feudal terms—Butler had entered the service of a local landowner at the age of ten and risen through the varied strata of pantry boy and scullion to second footman by the time he was seventeen.

At eighteen, Butler had gone with his employers to London for the Season, and it was there that he first met up with what was euphemistically termed ''bad company''—in this case the Swell Mob, who in turn introduced him to some of the best cracksmen in the business. They were all men who knew how to exploit a trusted servant—for Peter had certainly been that. In a few short months the young footman found himself on the periphery of robbery and violence, knowing that he was an important lynchpin, in that he was supplying information regarding the movements of fashionable society: the houses that were empty in the monkery, the jewels that were left in London houses on nights when their owners were out at soirées and balls.

By the end of that Season, the young man's whole way of life had changed; he became suspect and was forced to leave service and live among his newfound cronies in the great St. Giles Rookery—the so-called Holy Land of passages, slums and filth that was the hiding place of so many criminals in the mid-century, straddling, as it did, New Oxford Street, and stretching from Great Russell Street to St. Giles High Street.

It was there that Peter Butler's reputation grew. His slight but accurate knowledge of society and the ways of the great houses began to pay off. He could pass with ease as a trusted servant and later, as his abilities developed, as a young country gentleman in town for a spree: hence, the nicknames that came to be part of his stock-in-trade—Peter the Butler, and Lord Peter.

In the late 1880's Butler had met Green, and at the meeting, on a well-planned robbery in Hertfordshire, both men immdiately recognized each other's potential, sharing, as they did, ambitions to be leaders of an élite criminal society. It was not a unique fusion of evil, rather something that has happened many times among that antisocial element who live outside the law, and will doubtless happen many times again before Earth runs out its course.

Over a period of two and a half years Green and Butler managed to build up a ferocious if small, band of hardened criminals; yet they were not able to move into the area of power they most lusted after—the world of large pickings and large-scale manipulation that drew the best, the toughest, into its web. True, they were able to control a number of tradesmen in the East End; they ran about a hundred street women (soldiers' and sailors' girls mainly), and a couple of houses that attracted a handful of middle-class clients. But real control was denied them, for that regal land was well under the dominant heel of Professor Moriarty, and both the Peg and Lord Peter had enough sense not to cross such a dangerous path—until news spread of the Professor's untimely death.

Even then they had the prudence to bide their time for the better part of a year before taking positive action; they passed the months by sniffing out the power structure of what remained of Moriarty's family, testing its strength, gleaning every useful piece of information, examining the best strategy of infiltration.

When the moment was ripe, they started the seduction of Fray and Roach—the first pair of weak links, malcontents who, once Moriarty's iron control was removed and superseded by Moran's uncertain hand, were open to all manner of pressures, briberies and promises.

"Colonel Moran is a soak who cares only for himself and the gaming rooms," the Peg told them. "The Professor was a living lesson to us all. Nobody will see his like again."

Fray nodded, while Roach mumbled something about Moran not having the respect of those who had once counted themselves as part of Moriarty's family.

"No respect and no fear."

The Peg made no bones about the strength of fear as a weapon to gain both respect and control. He had long held a most healthy fear of Moriarty, and now that the evil genius had disappeared, his imagination roamed around the pleasant dream of replacing the Professor as the man most likely to draw out that respect and fear once accorded to Moriarty.

"You would both do better with me now," he announced boldly.

Fray looked uncertain. Roach shuffled his feet.

"There's still much loyalty among the Moriarty people." His eyes did not meet the Peg's. "Anyone who joined you now might risk much."

"And anyone who is offered a place with me now and does not take advantage might risk more."

The two men again shuffled, their eyes meeting for a moment—a flashing signal of danger. The edge of Michael Green's voice betrayed his potential: less subtle than Moriarty's overt evil, but forceful and frightening nevertheless. Greed, power and fear fused in the men's minds, and from that moment there was little doubt about their allegiance.

Fray and Roach became the hard core of Michael the Peg's organization, and during the weeks that followed he began to attract or terrorize others—not men who had been firmly planted within Moriarty's band, but fringe bullies, bludgers, mutchers (that verminous class who stole from drunks), palmers, toolers and the regular assortment of criminal dregs.

Green's and Butler's operations started in a small way, putting the age-old pressures of lusheries, which, through Moran's bad husbandry, were not being covered by Moriarty people: small burglaries, fencing, and a dozen other rackets.* They also began to control a string of whores operating on the fringes of Moriarty's area, and within the year there was at least one house in the West End catering to a better class of trade.

At the meeting during the afternoon of Colonel Moran's death, Green and Butler had both been in an ecstatic mood, for they were able to announce to their lieutenants that yet another house had been procured, this time in St. James, and after much negotiation arrangements were now complete for the shipping in of a number of country-bred girls ripe for breaking and training in the arts of select whoredom. The handful of men who were privy to Green's and Butler's methods became elated at this news. After all, they knew who would be required to do the breaking, and to men as degraded as Fray and Roach there was no better sport than separating a young, prime, country dumpling from her virginity.

There was also a pair of robberies planned, so both the former Moriarty men moved through the dingy streets with their hearts light. They did not see the beggar in the shadows near to The Nun's Head nor did they hear the soft whistle. They padded on their way, slightly fuddled with the heavy drinking, unaware that the whistle had set a small boy running hard through the streets, as though his very life were in jeopardy.

Rackets. Like so much criminal slang, it is often thought that the word "racket" (meaning a criminal dodge, swindle or particular series of illicit operations) has only come to us in recent times, and then from the United States of America. In fact the term appears to have originated in England. (See Grose, *Dictionary of the Vulgar Tongue.*) One presumes that this word, and many others, crossed the Atlantic, went out of use for a while in England and then returned, possibly in the 1920's, as a newly coined Americanism.

They had no cause for concern when they came upon the small and foxy Ember loitering at a streetcorner.

"Well, Jonas and Walter. It's been a long time. Where've you been hiding yourselves? Somewhere safe and far away from the law?"

Ember's eyes, as always, never ceased to flick back and forth as though trying to penetrate every shadow of the night.

Neither man feared Ember.

"Now, doesn't that take the Huntley." Fray grinned. "Our little old mate Ember."

"How goes it with you, Ember?" Roach towered over him in a menacing attitude.

"We heard you guv'nor got hisself removed this afternoon, Ember. Got hisself taken out of the parish."

Ember nodded and looked mournful.

"You lot're not in luck," Roach crowed. "What with the Professor leavin' you all in the lurch, and now the dear departed colonel— but then he wasn't much of a gaffer, the colonel."

"Not up to the Professor," said Ember quietly. "That's why the Professor had him done."

For a few seconds the significance of the remark did not penetrate. Fray sniggered.

"The Professor? What you bloody mean . . . ?"

They had not heard the quartet of punishers come up silently behind them.

"The Professor wishes to see you both," continued Ember, still calm.

Roach, always the quicker of the pair, sensed danger, his face registering bewilderment, like a man who has been hit hard and suddenly. He wheeled around too late, and a fist caught the side of his jaw, sending him down like a felled log.

Fray hesitated for the fast bat of an eye before trying to take to his heels. Ember simply stuck out his leg and the big man tripped, sprawling headlong, the breath knocked out of him, giving enough time for two of the punishers to lift and render him insensible with a quick blow on the back of the neck.

Ember faded into the shadows and the four punishers lurched into a broken step, half carrying and half dragging the treacherous Fray and Roach between them, singing drunkenly as they went so that any passing folk would imagine the rough-looking sextet to be out on a revel, during which a hapless pair had reached the point of no return.

For Fray and Roach there was indeed no return. In one of the many side alleys, badly lit and paved with slanting and broken cobbles, a covered cart waited, the horse docile but the driver alert. The two unconscious men were thrown unceremoniously into the rear, quickly followed by the four punishers, two of whom sat themselves heavily on top of the prone bodies. Once inside there was a soft call to the driver, and the cart moved off in the direction of Limehouse.

A little thin evening mist came in from the river, diffusing the light of the few gaslamps in the streets around the warehouse when, some twenty minutes later, the cart drew up outside the big doors.

Ember and the four punishers who had taken Roach and Fray were not the only Moriarty men abroad on the Professor's business. Lee Chow and the big punisher, Terremant, sat in the taproom of a small public house near Aldgate. The Chinese had discovered, with admirable speed, that John Tappit made a habit of calling into the place during the early evening after finishing his work as a storeman for F. & C. Osler, who had their showrooms—chandeliers, lamps, table glass, ornaments, porcelain and china—in Oxford Street.

Tappit was a thin young man with no special skills but a certain intelligence, flawed though it was by fiery emotions. The job was steady and paid little, but in these times of poverty his position was to be envied by many. On this particular evening he reached his drinking haunt a little after eight.

Lee Chow and Terremant appeared to take no particular notice of Tappit as he ordered his glass of spirits, drinking quietly and alone at the far corner of the room. Lee Chow's investigations had been thorough. He knew the young man who had so viciously burned and disfigured young Ann Mary Dobey had, for the past few weeks at least, stuck to a seemingly regular routine. Lee Chow had seen Ann Mary and even his hard upbringing failed to stave off an upsurge of revulsion over the raw burns that had clawed out the flesh in a long and irregular pattern, from hairline to jaw, down the left side of her face. He had spoken of it to Terremant on their way toward Tappit's moment of destiny, and the big punisher was as keen as the small Chinaman that Tappit should get his reward for one night's sudden and violently impetuous work. Lee Chow knew that if he did not have a change of ritual, Tappit would stay in the hostelry for only half an hour before moving back to his lodgings and a frugal meal.

They waited for some twenty minutes, the taproom becoming thick with smoke and noisy with the inconsequential and, for the most part, ignorant chatter of men and women thrown together more from desperation than friendship. Terremant eventually saw that Tappit was getting to the last drops in his glass. He nudged Lee Chow, and the unlikely pair made for the entrance, crossing the road outside and loitering with a good view of the door.

Tappit came out some eight or nine minutes later, turned left, walking at a steady, natural pace, then left again into the Minories. The Moriarty men stayed some twenty yards behind Tappit, only coming close to him as he turned once more, this time into one of the many lanes that led off that unpleasant thoroughfare.

The lane between Swan and Good Streets was deserted, as dark and menacing as that in which Ember and the four punishers had taken Roach and Fray not long before.

Lee Chow did not speak until they were hard behind their quarry.

"John Tappit. We come flom Plofessor."

Tappit stopped dead, a statue in the mist, one who had looked back upon Sodom and, like Lot's wife, had been turned to salt.

Lee Chow advanced on the still figure, moving in front of him while Terremant stepped up behind, his hands ready to pinion Tappit. In the dim light there was the glint of a knife in Lee Chow's hand. Tappit's eyes widened with a terror that rooted him to the ground. A gurgle of fear bubbled from the back of his throat, eventually emerging as a strangled, "Wha . . . Wha . . . ? W-Why?"

Terremant's arms passed around Tappit's body, holding him as though by a pair of metal clamps.

"You burn Maly Dobey's face. Now you pay."

Lee Chow was nothing if not sparse with his words, but the small yellow man's heart and mind were filled with fury. He would have liked to cut Tappit's head clean from his body and leave him dead, but his sense of vengeance was such that he knew instinctively that a quick, if painful, death was too good for any man low enough to wreak havoc on a pretty girl's face because she would not have him.

Lee Chow raised the knife, his ears deaf to the choking sobs of the petrified Tappit, who was now pressing backward against the solid muscular frame of Terremant, his head turning from side to side in a last vain effort to escape the knife blade. Lee Chow's hand swept upward, grabbing at Tappit's hair to hold the head fast.

The sobs turned into a long, shivering shriek of anguish as the point of the knife penetrated the soft flesh of his right cheek. Lee Chow's wrist performed a quick circular movement, reminiscent of an expert fishwife gutting a large and live fish. There was a slippery pat on the cobbles as Tappit's right cheek fell to the ground, but by this time the head was still for he had lapsed into unconsciousness.

Lee Chow, eyes still gleaming anger, pulled the head in the other direction and performed a similar operation on the left cheek. Terremant stepped back and the insensible body crumpled and pitched forward.

The Chinaman bent down, wiping the razor-sharp blade on the luckless man's coat, then, turning him over with the toe of his boot, picked up the two pieces of loose flesh and hurled them into the darkness.

Tappit would live, and some skillful surgeon might even patch him up, but he would become a walking lesson in the kind of retribution Moriarty meted out to anyone who took spite against those who lived under his protection—for the word would soon be out about tonight's work.

Being one of Moriarty's men did not afford any special protection from the rigors of London traffic. The cabbie, negotiating Piccadilly Circus in the hansom that contained the Professor, wished that his employer had some sway over the other cabs, private vehicles and omnibuses that pressed together in the night streets. The underground railway was still in its infancy, and, while trams had first made their appearance a few years previously, nothing seemed to ease or stem the crush of horse-drawn traffic in the streets.

Like most cabbies, Harkness—for that was the name of Moriarty's driver—was a cheery, if foul-mouthed man who had failed miserably at all other jobs and had sunk to what was considered then the low profession of a cabbie. Chance had brought him better things, and, although he still had a little deep resentment for being openly classed as the driver of a hansom, he at least had the inner knowledge that he was probably one of the best paid in London.

In the back of the cab Moriarty gazed out on the city. He felt safe and secluded here, watching the traffic and the pavements crowded with the world and his wife, bent on pleasure of one kind or another. Moriarty was content to bask in the knowledge that a good third of that passing parade would in some way be either his clients or victims.

He preferred cities—particularly the big cities of Europe—to small towns and the countryside. The lush green of country fields, the sparkle of brooks and the elegant beauty of trees and woodlands were not to the Professor's liking. They were too close to God, and he was a man who, if he feared anything, feared the power of God among men. Mammon was his safe hiding place, and cities were the natural habitat of Mammon. It pleased him to reflect on the number of thieves, pickpockets, whores, sharps and duffers who would at this moment be abroad on his business—and the number of men and women who relied on his patronage in order to practice their chosen craft.

He had been away from London for too long and now, savoring

the mixture of smells, which were ever sooty, foggy, horse-scented yet peculiar to the capital, the Professor realized how much he owed to the particular viciousness of that city's criminal fraternity. His mind also drifted back to the irredeemable action that had finally put him at the top of the underworld, making him the outstanding master of nineteenth-century crime. It was only his vanity that allowed him to take the supreme risk of keeping a private journal, which (even though he had skillfully coded the document) would, he hoped, one day present a unique record of his life and times. Moriarty, as so many had done before him, clung to the insatiable wish for immortality.

Part of that original need had come, naturally, from envy of his elder brother, the real Professor James Moriarty, whose immortality had been assured so early with the treatise on the binomial theorem, and the chair of mathematics at the small university.

It was when he had first visited James in that quiet intellectual backwater that he realized what fame his brother had already achieved. Moriarty would never forget that day: the tall and stooping boy he remembered, now transformed into a man to whom deference was shown on all sides. The letters from famous men, congratulations and flattery; the already half-finished work, *The Dynamics of an Asteroid*, lying on the smugly neat desk facing the leaded window looking out onto the quiet courtyard. It was, he supposed, at that moment, as he saw James' potential, that he knew the full flush of jealousy. His brother would undoubtedly become a great and respected man—and this at a time when he was trying desperately to build himself into a man to be feared and respected within the criminal hierarchy of first, London, and then the whole of Europe.

There had been setbacks, failures; he needed, at that point more than anything, some way of showing the underworld that he was truly a man of strength, a force to be reckoned with, a man of unique skills.

It was only after Professor James Moriarty had been acclaimed for *The Dynamics of an Asteroid* that Jim, the professor's youngest brother, saw clearly the way in which he could both further himself and remove the torment of envy from his obsessed brain. He, more than anyone else, knew his elder brother's weakness.

By the late 1870's the tall, gaunt and bent professor was fast becoming a public figure. His mind, it was claimed, bordered on genius; his star seeming to be set for a rapid rise into the academic stratosphere. The newspapers wrote of him, and there were predictions of a new appointment—for the chair of mathematics would soon be vacant at Cambridge, and it was common knowledge that

Moriarty had already turned down two similar appointments on the Continent.

The time was right for Moriarty the younger to act. And, as always, he planned as meticulously as his brother did in the world of mathematics.

Among his acquaintances, the younger Moriarty had fostered an old actor of the blood-and-thunder school, a man whose one-man performances—in which he presented a range of the great Shakespearean characters, from the hunchback Richard III to the old and embittered Lear—were still much in demand.

Hector Hasledean was by this time in his late sixties and drew freely upon a lifetime of stage experience—a flamboyant figure in private as well as public life, much given to the bottle, but still retaining the ability to move large audiences and even amaze them with his actor's craft, which included a stunning aptitude for changing his appearance in a manner at which his audiences marveled.

Moriarty, always certain of his victims' weaknesses, made himself invaluable to the old man with small gifts of spirits and cigars. He quickly won the man's confidence, and one night before Hasledean had lapsed into complete fuddlement Moriarty made his first approach. He wished to play a joke, he confided, on his famous brother by appearing before him as a replica, an imitation, of the great man.

The idea appealed to the actor, who laughed much and entered into the conspiracy with professional zest, working with Moriarty on the disguise—choosing the right kind of bald-pate wig from the greatest expert of the day; supervising the making of the boots, with lifts to give extra height; assisting in the design of the harness, which would allow the characteristic stoop to be maintained; and introducing Moriarty to the standard books of the day: Lacy's *Art of Acting, How to Make-Up, A Practical Guide to the Art of Making-Up,* by "Haresfoot and Rouge," and the more recent *Toilet and Cosmetic Arts* by A. J. Cooley.

In a matter of some four weeks, Moriarty could transform himself within an hour into an almost unbelievable likeness of his revered brother. And one week, almost to the day, after he had attained this particular skill, old Hector Hasledean was found dead in his dressing room, apparently of a seizure, which may well have been a happy accident.*

*Here one has to give the villainous Moriarty the benefit of the doubt. It is natural to suspect the worst, yet it is a fact that while the details of the various stages by which Moriarty learned the art of disguise from Hasledean are meticulously documented in the diaries, the actor's death is only briefly recorded, with no details.

Moriarty always took care when donning his disguise—changing from James Moriarty, the youngest of the three Moriarty brothers, to James Moriarty, the eldest and erstwhile professor of mathematics, author of the treatise on the Binomial Theorem and *The Dynamics of an Asteroid*.

Apart from a similar bone structure, there were so many ways in which James the youngest differed from James the eldest: height, stance, physiognomy. It was his habit to look long at himself in the buff before effecting the transformation. It was a carefully studied process, for James Moriarty was already many years ahead of his time, having evolved a system akin to that which Konstantin Sergeivich Stanislavsky was, many years later, to offer to the theater in *An Actor Prepares*.

Moriarty would stand looking at his nakedness, and it looking back at him, as he emptied his mind, filtering in the character and presence of his elder brother until, even without the aids he had yet to apply, there was a subtle alteration, as though he became another person in front of his very eyes. Or were they his eyes?

As Moriarty looked back at himself from the mirror at this moment in the ritual, there was always a deep touch of fear: For that few seconds while the complete transformation was taking place in his head he would wonder which of them he was—the killer or the victim? It had been just like that at his brother's end and his own beginning.

Once he was mentally ready, Moriarty began what had become an almost automatic rite. First the long, tight corset to pull in his flesh so that he could take on the thin, near wraithlike proportions of the other Moriarty. This was followed by what appeared to be a more restricting device, a kind of harness—a slim leather belt that passed around his waist and was buckled tight. A series of crossover straps came over his shoulders and threaded through flat loops sewn into the front of the corset; from thence they passed down to buckles on the front of the belt. When these buckles were drawn tight, the effect was to pull his shoulders forward so that he could only move with a stoop. Moriarty next donned his stockings and shirt before climbing into the long striped trousers, which had to be hitched up to mid-calf until he had put on and laced the boots, specially designed with built-up soles to add the necessary height.

All that was left now to complete the required picture was skillful alteration of the face and head, ingeniously effected by the paints and brushes used by actors and those who were expert in disguise.

First, he tucked his mane of hair under a tight-fitting skullcap and began to work on his face, using firm, deft and confident strokes so that he assumed the gaunt, hollow-cheeked look so easily identified with Dr. Watson's famous description of the arch-criminal. Even with only the skullcap covering his hair the effect was remarkable, the pallor striking and the eyes sunken unnaturally into their sockets.

Then came the final and crowning part of his disguise—a domed head covering of some pliable and thin material mounted on a solid cast. Externally the color and texture were those of a normal scalp, and, when fitted in place over the skullcap, the effect was extraordinarily realistic, giving the natural impression of the high bald forehead sweeping back and leaving only a sprinkling of hair behind the ears and at the nape of the neck. Moriarty would then make a few slight adjustments, using a small pot of flesh-colored cream, which he worked around the join between the wig and flesh. Once satisfied, he would finish dressing and, standing in front of the mirror, peer at himself from all possible angles. Moriarty looked back from the glass at Moriarty.

After wholly mastering this act of physical change, Moriarty's next step was to destroy his brother's career, a relatively easy matter for one who had so carefully observed the failings of others. He had long known that the professor was not as other men regarding the natural inclinations of the flesh. Indeed his preference lay in the company and intimacy of young men, a fact that made him particularly vulnerable as a senior don in charge of the academic progress of reasonably wealthy scions from the upper classes and county nobility.

Early in life, while still in Liverpool, Jim had foreseen the way in which that peculiar sexual hypocrisy, so rife in Victorian cities, could be exploited and used to best advantage.

Although homosexuality, in all its forms, flourished openly in all strata of life and was readily available on the streets and in bordellos, as well as being practiced in private, the mature homosexual in high office or a responsible post risked ostracism and loss of status if that deviation from the norm created any public scandal. Young Moriarty knew well how easily he could turn his elder brother's failings to advantage. He began with a whispering campaign, not simply in the university, but near to the homes of those young men in whom the professor appeared to have most interest. The results surpassed even his wildest dreams.

There were two, both students of the professor, in whom the younger Moriarty showed especial curiosity. One was the elder son of a country gentleman with large estates in Gloucestershire; the other's father was a notable London rake who had already squandered two fortunes and seemed intent on parting with a third.

The young men—Arthur Bowers and the Honorable Norman De

Frayse—were in their late teens, both already bearing the marks of early degeneracy: the languid good looks, limp hands, weak mouths, bloodshot eyes following days of overindulgence, and a style of conversation that affected a quick, if cheap, wit.

Moriarty had them both marked. They spent many evenings in the company of the professor—sometimes staying until early morning—and, in spite of their mentor's genius, appeared to have little aptitude for the kind of studies that consumed the professor of mathematics.

Through carefully cultivated friends, young Moriarty spread the word that both Bowers and De Frayse were being corrupted by the older man, the whispers quickly reaching both Squire Bowers in rural Gloucestershire and Sir Richard De Frayse in the whorehouses and gaming rooms of London.

As often happens in such cases, it was the rakehell father who reacted first—obviously stung by a sudden concern that his beloved son should not be dragged into the web of destructive pleasure and libidinous ways that were remorselessly pulling the father himself into eternal damnation. Sir Richard descended on the university, spent an hour or so with his son, and then arrived, wrathful and spleen-choked, at the vice-chancellor's lodgings.

The situation could not have been better if young Moriarty had himself maneuvered matters. First, the vice-chancellor was an elderly cleric, a man full of the paradoxical saintly hypocrisy that so often besets clerics of a Christian persuasion when they are cut off from the mainstream of life in the world. Secondly, the professor had been more of a fool than anyone would have credited.

Brilliant of mind and with incredible perception as far as mathematics and its attendant sciences were concerned, Professor Moriarty had a blind spot that even his youngest brother had not forseen: He did not understand money. During the previous year he had worked hard and been lionized, spending his spare moments of relaxation with the two young men, all three of them indulging their particular passions and whims. Yet on many occasions he had found himself low in funds, so what was more natural than to borrow from his young friends?

In all, the great Professor Moriarty was in debt to the tune of three thousand pounds to De Frayse, and, as it was later discovered, a further fifteen hundred to young Bowers. All this on top of the fact that he was an older man undoubtedly leading his students into an abnormal way of life.

The vice-chancellor, whose sanctity did not include either forbearance or understanding, was shocked and scandalized. He was also concerned for the good name of the university. Squire Bowers was summoned and rumor spread through the colleges like a raging pestilence: The professor of mathematics had stolen money; he had been caught, in flagrante delicto with a college housemaid; he had abused the vice-chancellor; he had used his academic skills to cheat at cards; he was a dope fiend; a satanist; he was involved with a gang of criminals. Inevitably Professor Moriarty resigned.

Moriarty the younger chose his time carefully, turning up, innocent and unexpected, at the professor's rooms late one afternoon, feigning surprise at the boxes and trunks open and packing in progress.

His brother was a beaten man, broken, the stoop more pronounced, the eyes sunken deep into his head. Slowly, and not without emotion, Professor James Moriarty unfolded the sad story to his brother Jim.

"I feel that you might have understanding at my plight, Jim," he said, once the terrible truth was out. "I doubt if Jamie ever will."

"No, but Jamie's in India so there's no great or immediate trouble there."

"But what will be said, Jim? Though nothing will be revealed publicly, there are already stories—many far from the mark. The world will know that I leave here under some great cloud. It is my ruin and the destruction of my work. My mind is in such a whirl I do not know where to turn."

Moriarty faced the window lest any sign of pleasure could be read on his countenance.

"Where had you planned to go?" he asked.

"To London. After that . . ." The gaunt man raised his hands in a motion of despair. "I had even thought of coming to you down at your railway station."*

The younger man smiled. "I have long given up my job with the railways."

"Then what—"

"I do many things, James. I think my visit here this afternoon was providential. I shall take you to London, there will be work for you to do there."

Later that night the professor's luggage was loaded into a cab and the brothers set out for the railway station and London.

Within the month there was talk that the famous professor's star had fallen. He was running a small establishment tutoring would-be

---

*It is, of course, still maintained by many that the professor's youngest brother ended his days as a stationmaster in the West country. Undoubtedly he did hold such a job for a time, but we have no hint of when and how he left to further his criminal activities.

army officers, for mathematics was a science that was more and more playing an important part in the arts of modern warfare.

For some six months following his resignation, the former professor of mathematics appeared to go about this dull and demanding work as an army tutor. He conducted this business from a small house in Pole Street, near its junction with Weymouth Street, on the south side of Regent's Park—a pleasant place to live, handy for skating in the winter, friendly cricket in summer, and the interest of the Zoological and Botanical Societies all year round.

Then, without any warning, the professor closed his establishment and moved, to live in some style in the house off the Strand— the place where he was still living during the Ripper murders of 1888.

Until now those were the known facts about the professor's movements after he had been driven from the high echelons of academic life. The truth was a different matter, marking the most important and ruthless move in the career of the Professor Moriarty we know as the uncrowned king of Victorian crime.

It happened some time after ten o'clock on a night in late June— an unseasonably cold night with a threat of rain and no moon.

The professor, having dined early and alone on boiled mutton with barley and carrots, was preparing for bed when there was a sudden agitated knocking at his front door. He opened up to reveal his younger brother, Jim, dressed in a long, black, old-fashioned surtout, a wide-brimmed felt hat pulled down over his eyes. In the background the professor saw a hansom drawn up at the curb, the horse nodding placidly and no cabbie in sight.

"My dear fellow, come in," began the professor.

"There's no time to waste, brother. Jamie's back in England with his regiment. There's trouble, family trouble, and we have to meet him immediately."

"But where . . .? How?"

"Get your topcoat. I've borrowed the hansom from an acquaintance, there's no time to lose."

The urgency in young Moriarty's voice spurred the professor, who was trembling with nervousness as he climbed into the cab. His brother set the horse off at a steady trot, going by unaccustomed side streets toward the river, which they crossed at Blackfriars Bridge.

Continuing along side alleys and byways, the hansom proceeded down through Lambeth, eventually turning from the streets to a piece of waste ground, bordered by a long buttress falling away into the muddy, swirling waters of the Thames, much swollen at this time of the year. The cab was drawn up some ten paces from the buttress edge, close enough to hear the river, the distant noise of laughter and singing from some tavern, and the occasional bark of a dog.

Professor Moriarty peered about him in the black murk as his brother helped him down from the hansom.

"Is Jamie here?" The tone was anxious.

"Not yet, James. Not yet."

The professor turned toward him, suddenly concerned by the soft and sinister timbre of his brother's voice. In the darkness something long and silver quivered in the younger man's hand.

"Jim. What—" he cried out, the word turning from its vocal shape and form into a long guttural rasp of pain as young brother James sealed the past and the future, the knife blade pistoning smoothly between the professor's ribs three times.

The tall thin body arched backward, a clawing hand grasping at Moriarty's surtout, the face hideously contorted with pain. For a second the eyes stared uncomprehendingly down at young James. Then, as though suddenly perceiving the truth, there was a flicker of calm acquiescence before they glazed over, passing into eternal blindness.

Moriarty shook the clutching hand free, stepped back and looked down on the body of the brother whose identity he was so cunningly to assume. It was as though all the kudos of the dead man's brilliance now passed up the blade of the knife into his own body. In the professor's death the new legend of the Professor was born.

Moriarty brought chains and padlocks from the cab, emptied the cadaver's pockets, placing the few sovereigns, the gold pocket watch and chain, and the handkerchief into a small bag made of yellow American cloth. He wound the chains around the corpse, locked them securely and then gently tipped his departed brother off the buttress into the water below.

For a few silent moments Moriarty stood looking out across the river into the blackness, savoring his moment. Then with a quick upward movement he flung the knife out in the direction of the far shore, straining his ears for the splash as it hit the water. Then, as though without a second thought, he turned on his heel, climbed into the hansom and drove away, back to the new house off the Strand.

On the following afternoon, Spear, accompanied by two men, went to the small house in Pole Street and removed all traces of its former occupant.

Now, sitting in the back of the hansom taking him from his meeting at the Café Royal, Moriarty dragged his mind back from the past and the look in his dying brother's eyes. They were almost at the warehouse. It had been a long day and, while he wanted most to refresh himself and rest, Moriarty knew there would still be work to do before Mary McNiel arrived to tend to his more personal needs.

Friday, April 6, 1894

(A DAY IN THE COUNTRY)

IT HAD ALSO been a long day for Pip Paget.

After seeing the punishers with Moriarty in the morning, he had taken the train from Limehouse station to Paddington and from thence out to Harrow. The day was cold, yet the sun bright, and the journey proved a pleasant novelty for Paget, who did not often travel by the railway—underground or surface.

At that time Harrow still retained much of its rural charm, now unhappily long departed, and when Paget finally alighted at the station, he was immediately filled with a sense of freedom. From where he stood, outside the main entrance, he could see but a few houses and the general backdrop of the vista was one of trees and rolling fields. The bustle and grime of central London had vanished with the outward thrust of the steam engine, and this feeling of space and room to move, experienced by Paget even while sitting alone in the third-class carriage, acted like a tonic. In his mind the heavy, almost cloying, burdens of Moriarty's business disappeared, replaced by an overriding image of Fanny Jones.

Paget, brought up among the teeming back streets and tenements of the city, had never experienced this kind of feeling before. For as long as he could remember, life had been one long battle for survival—a war waged with cunning and deceit, with the craft of knavery and, for much of the time, the hard and ruthless rule of fist, bludgeon, boot, razor, knife and even pistol.

There had been few moments of tenderness in Pip Paget's life; rather it was in retrospect peopled by men and women who were constantly in the front line of battle—with the authorities, poverty, each other, even with life itself. His mother had been a thin, tough and foul-mouthed woman, and his childhood had never known a steady or permanent setting. Countless uncles shared the meager and filthy two rooms occupied by his mother, two brothers and three sisters, and the nearest thing to true affection Paget had ever experienced was the occasional spilling out of lust that began in his early teens—first with his eldest sister, and later with the line of young women whose beds he had shared in return for small sums of money stolen during his daily work.

The dramatic change in Paget's life had come in the early eighties when—he was some twenty-six or -seven years old at the time, a certain vagueness surrounding his exact age—Professor Moriarty came into his life, gave him a place in his not inconsiderable household and a more tranquil, if still villainous, existence. In return he had remained loyal to Moriarty and had become possibly the most trusted of his entourage. Now a further dimension was added in the person of Fanny Jones. She had shown, to the big strong and graceful man, a new kind of respect, not born of fear, but of desire and gentle persuasion.

As Paget walked down through the main street of Harrow, he allowed his fancies to play upon a dream—impossible to realize, yet undeniably firm and disturbing—of life with Fanny Jones in the kind of world Paget now saw moving gently around him. The women, graceful, many with their children, some with their men, passed along the pavements, intent on making purchases at the many well-stocked shops that flanked the street. An errand boy cycled past, his basket heavy, a dog barking as it ran beside him. A pair of well-dressed men talked at the corner, occasionally doffing their hats to acquaintances who passed by. What was more, there was an air of contentment, people smiled, there was no crush of hansoms or omnibuses, and none of the more unpleasant odors that hung heavy in the city.

The house the three cracksmen—Fisher, Clark and Gay—had their eyes on lay a mile to the north of Harrow proper. Paget enjoyed the walk, taking an interest in the small natural things he observed around him, the dream of Fanny and himself set up in a small cottage in a place like this or even further afield in the country growing and glistening in his head. The image of himself as a man who went off to some job (as yet, naturally, indefinable) from a door surrounded by rose trellises, Fanny smiling and waving, cheeks rosy from the country air and several children clinging to her skirts, was strong, so deep rooted by the time he reached Beeches Hall that Paget had to impose an unusually strict mental discipline upon himself in order to shake the thoughts from his mind and get back to the professional work at hand.

Beeches Hall was a large Georgian mansion, which, Paget deduced, contained some eighteen or nineteen main rooms and bedrooms. It was quite visible from the road, standing as it did in some twenty acres of open lawns, flower beds and rose gardens, while a small copse could just be seen behind the house.

Access to the front of Beeches Hall was gained through large iron gates opening on a long drive that curved between bushes to end in a wide sweep before the façade. Paget ignored this, slowly working his way, first by road and then across some meadowland, to the rear, where he effected an entrance to the grounds by way of the copse. There was plenty of cover there and he lay for the best part of an hour at the edge of the trees taking in every point of interest the view afforded.

There was plenty to be noted. The rear of the house would give them a number of easy entrances; people were strange, Paget mused, they would spend a great deal on bolts and locks for a good stout front door, yet leave the back door, or tradesmen's entrance, with an old-fashioned lock and no bolts. If that door proved harder than it looked, there was a small, insecure pantry window, or an easy climb across an outhouse roof to an upstairs window, which, he judged, opened onto a landing.

He also saw that there were dogs about: two of them, big sloppy looking creatures, overfed and probably docile, but the cracksmen would have to be prepared.

Once the necessary information was firmly stored in his head, Moriarty's lieutenant carefully made his way back through the trees and over the meadow to the road, heading for a small knot of houses grouped together, at what he presumed was the furthest boundary of the estate. To his left were a farmhouse and outbuildings. Paget supposed this was also part of Sir Dudley Pinner's property. Beeches Hall, Moriarty had told him, was the second-generation home of the Pinner family.

The group of houses consisted of a dozen or so cottages, a public house—The Bird in the Hand—and a shop that bore the legend GENERAL STORES. Paget pushed open the shop door, a sprung bell jangling loudly at his entrance. An elderly man wearing wire spectacles, his trousers and shirt covered with a white apron, looked up from serving a pair of girls, cutting with a wire through the large crusted cheese that rested on his counter.

The shop was small, but it bulged with provisions and goods of all kinds. Glass jars full of boiled sweets and lollipops nudged each other on the shelves, next to jams, custard powders and tinned goods; two hams hung from the ceiling; a large side of bacon offset the cheese at the other end of the counter. Paget saw that between them stood an oval plate of homemade toffee apples. The scents of the variegated foods mingled together, producing a delicious and mysterious aroma that pervaded every corner of the shop. Around the walls signs advertised Bovril, Eiffel Tower Lemonade, and the prices of tea ("of Sterling Value"), 1/4, 1/6, 1/8. Margarine was priced at fourpence a pound, in big red letters beside the box, wherein nestled the greaseproofed drums of butter-colored fat.

"And what can I do for you?"

The man in the white apron rubbed his hands, the bell clanging once more as the girls went giggling out into the street, clutching their packet of cheese.

Paget asked for a quarter of humbugs. It was a long time since he had sucked on a humbug and, though conscious of the seriousness of today's mission, he still felt a sense of relief about the outing. His job was to make a serious appraisal of the proposed robbery but, as he had to do the job properly, Paget saw no reason why he should not indulge himself.

"Nice day," commented the shop man.

"Nice little business you've got an' all," returned Paget.

"I worked for it all me life," the man grinned.

"I tell you what"—Paget hunched himself confidentially over the counter—"do you know of any cottages for sale or to rent round here?"

"Looking, are you?"

Paget sighed. "Yeah. The wife is fed up with living down by the river. Damp and so bloody crowded."

"Well. . . ." He scratched his head. "What's your trade, mate?"

Paget smiled. He had a very open and friendly smile.

"You know. A bit of this and a bit of that."

"General." The shopman grinned, nodding.

"You might say that."

"If you can turn your hand to laboring, you might get something up the estate. Most of the cottages here have been in the same families for a long time, and they all belong to Sir Dudley. . . ."

"Sir Dudley?"

"Aye, Sir Dudley Pinner, baronet. The big house back there. Beeches Hall. This is all Sir Dudley's land round about. But there's work going—I heard one of the lads talking in The Bird last night. There could well be a cottage with it. Well-set-up man like you shouldn't have no trouble. Why don't you go down to The Bird and have a word with Mr. Mace—he's the publican. Say Jack Moore sent you." He placed the paper bag with the humbugs in it on the counter. "That'll be a ha'penny, if you please."

Mace, the landlord of The Bird in the Hand, was a large, wide-shouldered fellow, bald-headed and of some forty-five summers.

Paget propped himself against the bar and ordered a tankard of ale, and when Mace placed the foaming brew before him, Paget told him of his errand.

"Yes, I had heard there was work—up at the house and at the home farm. George!" the landlord shouted to one of his other two customers, who had been drinking at a table set in the small bow window, "there's a fellow here asking about cottages and work for Sir Dudley. George is up at the house," he confided to Paget. "Assistant groom."

"Aah." George, a sallow-faced, thin little man, nodded knowingly. "Sir Dudley's takin' on one new man for odd jobs. 'Twas goin' to be two, but old Barney's son's goin' laboring up at the farm and he's to marrying Becky Collins. . . ."

"Sly young devil," the landlord laughed. "So 'twas him that swelled her."

George cackled, and the man sitting with him gave a snort.

"They're to have the cottage up at the farm, but there's one goin' after Easter for a married man for to chop the wood and do the outside work at the house."

"And help at harvest," grunted George's companion.

"Aah." George nodded again. "You're not from these parts though, are you?"

"Stepney." Paget took a pull at his ale. "The missus wants to move out to the country. Who would I see about the job?"

"Nobody as yet." George looked at his empty tankard, and his companion tipped back the rest of his drink. They both looked at Paget, their eyes empty.

"Will you take a guzzle with me?" Paget pushed his own tankard back toward Mace. "And you, landlord."

George and his friend came across the room like a pair of chickens at the sight of an axe.

"You can see nobody as yet." George examined the depths of his ale as though looking for fish. "Nobody, because the job ain't goin' till Easter. Anyways, Sir Dudley don't do no hirin' till after he's been up north. Every year like clockwork, him and her ladyship. Up to that uncle of his. When he comes back, he'll start hirin' and grantin' the cottage. You look strong enough though. What about your wife? She done kitchen work or anything that would help?"

"She was in service once."

"Well, there you are. You could have the luck."

"When will Sir Dudley be back?"

"Let's see." It appeared to take considerable mental effort on George's part to recall dates. "Sometime after the twentieth, I think. Yes, I heard Mr. Beard talkin' of it. They goes away on the fourteenth and they're still away at the weekend. It'll be the twenty-third or twenty-fourth they'll be back.''

"So if I reutrn then?''

"If you tell me your name, I'll pass it on to old Reeves.''

"Mr. Reeves manages the estate," muttered Mace.

Paget nodded. "Name of Jones. Philip and Fanny Jones. I'd be obliged if you'd do that, and I'll return on the twenty-third. If Mr. Mace is agreeable, you could leave a message for me.''

It was all playacting, but Paget was strongly pulled toward the idea of him and Fanny working out of London, living a life untainted by fear. However, his foot was already inside the door of Beeches Hall, or, if not the door, at least the stables and outhouses.

He spent the next hour or so talking with George, Mace, and George's friend Herbert, the ale freeing their tongues so that they spoke without restraint on matters concerning Sir Dudley and Lady Pinner, about life at Beeches Hall, of the staff and the day-to-day trivial matters.

When Paget took his leave, his head was filled with facts of exceptional value. From the intelligence Paget could now furnish, the Professor would be able to make his own carefully calculated decision regarding an investment in Fisher, Clark and Gay's proposed robbery.

Paget did not hurry himself, and it was almost eight in the evening before he arrived back at Paddington. On his way to catch the train to Limehouse, he paused to purchase the latest edition of the *Evening Standard*, for a penny piece, from one of the urchin paperboys who was shouting, "Adair murderer dead in jail . . . Colonel Moran poisoned . . . Murderer murdered. . . .''

It was not until he was on the train to Limehouse that Paget read the report. It was lurid in parts but accurate:

Colonel Sebastian Moran, who was arrested by Inspector Lestrade of Scotland Yard last night and committed for trial this morning for the murder of the Honourable Ronald Adair of 427 Park Lane and the attempted murder of the detective Mr. Sherlock Holmes, has been found dead in his cell at Horsemonger Lane Jail.

The discovery was made this afternoon by one of the prison turnkeys. Moran was found on the floor of his cell, his body twisted and the face "horribly contorted," as though he had died in great anguish. It appears that he had just eaten a portion of pie and drunk some wine which was brought to him early in the afternoon by an unidentified servant girl.

Inspector Lestrade told our reporter that the matter is being treated as one of murder.

The Adair case baffled detectives for some time, but it is understood that Inspector Lestrade discovered the truth yesterday evening when Moran was arrested in the act of trying to shoot Mr. Holmes from a house in Baker Street.

The report went on to give further details of the Adair murder and to describe the various comings and going at Horsemonger Lane.

Paget smiled to himself. The Professor was certainly back with a vengeance, he thought. The man was not one to let the grass grow under his heels, and that was as well, for things had been getting out of hand for a long while.

There were a number of people in the "waiting room" when Paget got back to the warehouse. Lee Chow and Terremant were sitting in one corner, glasses of spirits in front of them. At the other end, nearest the stairway to the Professor's chambers, the other punishers were sprawled around, Spear and Ember with them, also two men, bound and gagged in upright chairs.

Paget scowled, recognizing the men as Fray and Roach.

"With the Peg?" He inquired of Spear.

"Both of the bastards."

"No others?"

"Not yet. But they'll all go down like horse droppings before long."

Ember gave a chuckle.

"Is he back yet?" Paget inclined his head toward the Professor's quarters.

"Any time now. He's out shuffling things, and we're waiting on him."

"Been busy enough anyway." Paget tapped the headlines of the newspaper.

He did not see the quick exchange of looks between Kate Wright and her husband, Bart, behind the serving counter. But something drew his eyes up toward the couple.

"Is there some food left for me?" he asked Bart Wright. "I'm so hungry it's dropping out of my nose."

"Thought you'd be well filled with country pie," leered Ember.

"A few gills of ale and bread and cheese's all I've had, Ember. And a lot of Shanks' pony."

"Fanny's in the kitchen." Mrs. Wright motioned toward the door behind the serving counter. "There's plenty in there."

Spear gave a small laugh. "Plenty enough for our Pip in there, eh?"

The others laughed and Pip Paget, usually good-natured when it came to being chaffed, felt a spring of annoyance rise inside him, but he knew better than to tangle with any other member of the "Praetorian Guard," particularly in front of the punishers and prisoners. He nodded, making his way behind the serving counter and through the door that led to the kitchen.

Fanny was sitting at the kitchen table drinking a mug of cocoa. She rose as soon as Paget entered, a blush flushing her cheeks.

"Oh, Pip, you're back. I've been so worried about you."

He held her in his arms and could feel her heart beating under his hand as she pressed close; like a frightened bird, he thought.

"There was no call for you to be worried, Fan. No cause."

"There's been dangerous things going on, Pip. I was afraid for you."

"No danger for me today, lass. None at all."

She looked up at him and he kissed her gently on the lips. She responded, wanting desperately to have him take her, to calm her fears and to act as a kind of reassurance.

"I've had an exciting day, Pip," she said at last. "I've met the Professor. Pip he was so kind and nice to me, and I ran an errand for him." She dropped her voice in exaggerated breathless excitement, like a small girl.

Paget smiled down at her. "Oh yes?"

"I've been inside a prison, Pip. I took a basket of victuals to the colonel in Horsemonger Lane."

Paget felt his heart leap and stomach turn over at one and the same time: a sickening twist of horror.

"To Horsemonger Lane, Fan. Christ."

He drew away from her, his face drained and body shaking.

"Pip? What's the matter? What's wrong?"

Paget paused for a moment, not knowing how to tell the girl. Yet she would learn soon enough if he did not speak now.

"Sit down, Fanny," he said, dry-mouthed.

"But Pip," she said, a half-smile fading on her lips. "you're not angry, are you? You're not cross with me?"

"No, Fanny, but there are things you have to know."

She slowly seated herself, erect, hands folded in her lap, still looking up at the tall, hard-faced man, adoration in her eyes.

Quietly he told her, explaining that the Professor demanded favors from all those who worked and acted for him. Sometimes those who were asked did not even understand what the favor meant or what repercussions it might have, but that the Professor always looked after his own people. He then, gently, told her about Colonel Moran.

It took a few moments for the truth to sink in. Then . . . "Oh God, Pip, I'm a murderess. I killed him."

"No, Fan. You only delivered the basket, and if it had not been you, it would have been someone else. We who serve the Professor ask no questions. Remember that."

There were tears running down Fanny's face.

"Does it always have to be so, Pip? Always?"

"Always is for long, Fanny. He made a home for me and I've served him well. I cannot give up now, and neither can you, Fanny. It is serious, and you'd be a dead woman within the week if you left—that or in the 'Steel.'"

She nodded quietly, her face gray with fear, and was about to speak when there was an increase in sound from the "waiting room," a shuffling and louder murmurs.

"He's back, Fanny. Go to our chambers and I will be with you as quickly as I can. Oh, and take me some cold meats and bread, then I'll tell you how it's been today."

Moriarty stood looking down at the bound Roach and Fray.

"Scum," he mouthed. "Evil, treacherous scum. You're only fit for a vegetable breakfast—an artichoke and caper sauce with the hangman."

Paget came through from the kitchen and joined them, Moriarty acknowledging his appearance with a curt nod.

"What are we to do with them, Professor?" asked Spear.

"Do with them? Put 'em on the everlasting staircase, that's the way. But I am a merciful man."

He turned to face Roach and Fray, squarely. Their eyes were wide with fear, for, it must be recalled, they had believed Moriarty to be long dead.

"A merciful man." The Professor laughed. "I'm willing to let the pair of you live out the remainder of your natural lives, but only in return for information. You will tell the good Spear all that you know of the vermin Michael Green and his scabrous friend the Butler—details of their haunts, their associates, their plans. If you tell the truth, then I will see you are placed somewhere safe." He turned to Spear. "And if they prove difficult, use Lee Chow. Our Chinese friend has ways of extracting truth which he claims will make the dumb talk."

Moriarty turned and began to mount the stairs. Halfway up he stopped, twisting his head down toward the assembled company.

"Lee Chow, I'll talk with you. Then Paget. After that Mrs. Wright can make things ready in my chamber. I am expecting company."

Moriarty was pleased with the way in which Lee Chow had handled John Tappit.

"He no throw acid anymore." The Chinese grinned.

"You have done well, Lee Chow, and you will be rewarded. Go now and help Spear, and you may send Paget to me."

Paget recited the information gleaned at Harrow. Moriarty, still in the guise of his dead brother, sat listening attentively.

When he had finished, the Professor said, "Then you think it is a safe crack?"

"I think it looks good."

"Mmm." Moriarty nodded. "Would you be prepared to go in with them? They are three, they want a fourth."

"I'd rather not, having already been seen there and talked to people who work at Beeches Hall. I think that would be dangerous."

"But . . . ?"

"But if you insisted, then I would go."

"We shall see. I'll take it on and we shall see." He raised his head and smiled thinly. "I have used your woman, Fanny Jones."

"I know sir."

"Ah, and does she yet know what it is about?"

"She knows Moran is dead and that she was an instrument."

"And?"

"She was upset, but I have explained the necessities of such things."

"Good man, Paget. She's a downy piece all right."

"I've done my balls on her, Professor."

Moriarty raised quizzical eyebrows.

"I had no idea you were such a romantic. But these things happen. Is it to be marriage?"

"I would like it so."

"And her?"

"I have yet to ask."

"Well, ask, and if it is to be, then I will give the breakfast, Paget. She must understand, though, that you will both go on in my service."

"She understands."

"And the high position you hold with me?"

"She knows that I respect you, sir; that you gave me my first real home."

"That you are my most trusted?"

"I am not certain of that myself, Professor."

"And why not?" The head oscillated dangerously.

"I was sent to Harrow today, and you expressly told me that you planned to meet Fanny tomorrow—that you were too busy today. I return to find that you have used her on a mission of great personal danger, of murder. Naturally I wonder if I am to be trusted."

"It was expedient, Paget, not planned. You are my most trusted. Now go and ask the wench to be your bride; it is not often the Moriarty family has a wedding."

When Paget was gone, the Professor changed, taking off the trappings of his disguise. He washed and donned a long dressing gown of dark blue silk, exotically patterned with military frogging on the cuffs and fastenings. By the time he walked back from the bedroom into his main chamber, Mrs. Wright had arranged a table with a cold collation—tongue and ham with various salads, plenty of celery and cheese and a bottle of Wachter's Royal Charter champagne.

Downstairs, as it neared eleven, the punishers, Lee Chow, Ember and Spear, removed Roach and Fray into one of the many side chambers that were cunningly built into the secret framework of the warehouse.

In their chamber at the back of the building, Paget clasped Fanny Jones tightly to him in their small bed.

"Then will you marry me, Fanny, my love? Will you be my bride?"

She smiled, her eyes glistening.

"It's a bit late to be talking of brides, Pip Paget, but yes, I love you, rogue that you are. I'll marry you, though I shouldn't doubt we'll both end up dangling from Jack Ketch's apple tree one fine morning."

Mary McNiel arrived on the dot of eleven and was escorted up to the Professor's chamber by Mrs. Wright. Moriarty smiled as he heard their footsteps on the stairs and looked at the gold pocket watch that had once been worn by the other Moriarty.

Mary looked as beautiful as she had on the previous day, and when the door was closed behind her and the Professor had removed her cloak, she allowed him to run his fingers gently through her hair. Reaching up, she took out the pins and let the tresses tumble down, shaking them out as she did so.

"You would like to sup, Mary, my dear?" he asked.

She gave him a coy smile.

"We can sup when you wish, sir. I want to sample the delights I have heard you can so readily supply for it is considered an honor among Sal's girls to be called to service here."

Moriarty threw back his head, laughing loudly.

"By God, Mary, you're the girl for me. Come then and I'll take Nebuchadnezzar out to grass with you."

Angus McCready Crow was forty-one years of age and had spent twenty-two of those years with the Metropolitan Police Force. In that time he had followed a varied and interesting career. In the late 1870's he was a constable in B Division, which at that period covered the Westminster area. And, like so many of his colleagues, he had been shocked by the events (known now as the de Goncourt case*) that shattered the small detective force of the time, sending three of its number to prison and causing a somewhat drastic reorganization.

By the 1880's the large, craggy Scot had himself become a member of the detective force, working as a sergeant, close to the famous Inspector Abberline, who goes down most unfairly in history as the man who failed to catch Jack the Ripper.

Crow was now an inspector, a very confused and concerned inspector in the early hours of Saturday, April 7, 1894. The world, together with weighty responsibilities, had fallen in on Inspector Crow.

It began a little before nine on the evening of Friday the sixth, just as he was completing his evening meal of lamb chops, potatoes and green peas, in his lodgings at number 63 King Street, off Drury Lane. The meal had been prepared for Angus Crow by his landlady, Mrs. Sylvia Cowles, a widow in her early thirties—a lady of plump and pleasant aspect, who, for the three years that Mr. Crow had been lodging with her, had done all any woman could to see that he was looked after and kept happy and contented: her motives being those of any other woman in her position.

Crow had a free evening that Friday, and, as often happened on his free evenings, he had asked Mrs. Cowles if she would partake of her meal with him. After that, they both knew the evening would be spent in polite conversation, the drinking of a little wine and then, by mutual consent, they would end the day together, either in Inspector Crow's bed or on Mrs. Cowles' large nuptial couch. On Friday, April 6, this was not to be.

Just before nine o'clock there was a loud banging at the front door of 63 King Street, and, when Mrs. Cowles opened up, she found a large police constable, shifting from foot to foot, asking to see Inspector Crow urgently.

The constable brought a summons from the commissioner, who wished to see Mr. Crow as quickly as possible in his office at Scotland Yard. Summonses from the commissioner were always matters of importance, and Crow made haste, arriving at the Yard by half-past nine. In the next twenty minutes he was invested with

*The truth about the famous de Goncourt scandal is revealed later.

the responsibilities that now weighed so heavily on his broad shoulders.

The commissioner first acquainted him with the facts surrounding the death of Colonel Moran in Horsemonger Lane Jail, and the events that had led up to the incident.

"Our file on Moran," he said, looking as grave as an undertaker, "indicates that he has for years been the chief of staff to Professor Moriarty. You know about Moriarty, of course?"

"Only that he was long considered the mastermind behind every major crime in the country and, for that matter, Europe. Yet we have never had enough sound evidence to place him under arrest, sir."

The commissioner nodded.

"Not a shred." There was an irritated nag in his tone. "We have also considered him dead for the past three years."

"Aye, I ken that also."

"Now we are not so sure."

"Indeed?"

"There are indications that he is back here in London at this very moment."

"I know Mr. Holmes is back. . . ."

"That's just it, Crow, that's it in a box. Mr. Holmes has been considered dead these three years, also. Now he has been resurrected and we nail Moran trying to murder him. Then Moran dies before Lestrade can properly question him. But Lestrade has talked to Mr. Holmes and finds that good gentleman strangely uncommunicative."

"But Lestrade's always worked well with Holmes."

"Not anymore, it seems. Something decidedly fishy, Crow. That's why I'm taking Lestrade off the case and putting you in charge. You are to select four or five men, any you wish, and your brief will be to nail Moran's murderer and discover if Moriarty is alive and back in the country. We have further intelligence though. He is reported to have been seen getting out of a hansom tonight, near the Café Royal. The report is uncorroborated, yet it is a strong whisper. The case is yours, Crow, and the glory also if you uncover the truth. I would suggest that you talk with Lestrade first. You must use tact, for he is, not surprisingly, somewhat out of sorts with me." The commissioner smiled pleasantly. "I should imagine your next step will be to speak with Mr. Holmes, but you are experienced enough to follow your own line of inquiry."

Crow spent the next two hours with Lestrade, and the bulky files that would need to be fully assimilated before he took the next step.

Lestrade was glum and reticent, telling Crow of his most recent conversation with Holmes. "It's there in my report," he said, "but I cannot put my true feelings into words. It was as though Holmes was holding back; as though there was something not quite right. If I did not know Holmes as well as I do, I would say that he has come to some arrangement with . . . I do not know. It is the first time that I have known Holmes avoid my eye."

"Your eye and your questions, then?"

Lestrade had thought for a moment or two. "He has a knack of changing the subject and you do not realize that he has avoided the question until it is too late. When I asked him why Moran should want him dead, he replied that many people would probably prefer him dead. There was a strange arrogance about that."

Crow seemed about to interrupt, then changed his mind and nodded as Lestrade resumed. "I put it to him that there might be wider issues involved. He said that wider issues were always involved in criminal action. I recall his words exactly. He said, 'Every crime emits ripples, Lestrade. Some crimes can be likened to tossing a pebble into a pool: the ripples move outward in widening circles. With others the reverse is true, as if the crime itself becomes the focal point, where the ripples decrease, moving inward, sucked toward it.' "

In the early hours Crow chose to walk back to King Street, and it was with very mixed feelings that he finally took to his lonely bed.

Saturday, April 7, passed without any notable incident. In the Limehouse headquarters few people set eyes on the Professor. He was occupied with other matters—mainly the dark beauty of Mary McNiel.

Spear, Ember and Lee Chow, took it in shifts throughout the day to question the unhappy Fray and Roach—Spear disappearing on three occasions to report directly to the Professor, and, at about four in the afternoon, leaving the warehouse to carry a message of a confidential nature into the West End.

The Wrights were kept busy with their normal work, though today they were without the assistance of Fanny Jones, for Moriarty left special instructions that Paget and his lady were not to be disturbed.

So the day passed in Limehouse.

At Scotland Yard other events were taking place. Inspector Crow chose his small staff with considerable care, being at pains to select men with whom he had worked before and knew, with reasonable certainty, were as beyond corruption as any police officers could be.

At midday Crow left the Yard, driving to Baker Street in an

official hooded gig. He spent over an hour at 221B, leaving at last with the distinct impression that Mr. Sherlock Holmes knew more than he was prepared to tell.

"As far as I am concerned, Inspector Crow," the great detective had said to him, "my feud with Professor Moriarty ended a long time ago at the Reichenbach Falls. There is no more for anyone else's ears."

Crow would have to rely on what little evidence was at hand from the events at Horsemonger Lane Jail, together with whatever else was on file about Moran, Moriarty and their known associates.

He returned to 63 King Street that evening, taking a heavy bundle of files and documents with him. The lamp in Crow's room burned long into the early hours of Sunday.

Sunday, April 8, 1894

(TAKING STOCK)

To SAY THAT Jonas Fray and Walter Roach were terrified men would have been an understatement as rank as to suggest that a nervous scholar was indifferent to the birch.

For over thirty-six hours the two men were pushed, pummeled and harried by turns. The tough Spear infused dread; Ember made oblique threats, and the small Chinese, Lee Chow, seemed to them to be the very epitome of pain as he described the tortures with which he could drag the pair through hell and back if need be. All the while the three Moriarty lieutenants were accompanied by at least two of the muscular punishers.

In the back of their minds, both Roach and Fray held the unbelievable yet indisputable fact that they had seen and come face to face with the dead Moriarty.

So they talked, loudly and long, telling of Michael Green's and Peter Butler's headquarters, the properties they owned, the people who worked for them, the rackets, burglaries and plans that were already arranged.

The three members of Moriarty's "Praetorian Guard" already knew, or a least had a rough idea of much of what the men had to tell—Parker and his lurkers having provided many details regarding the netherskens, sluiceries, and possible houses, both public and private, from which Michael the Peg was working. Yet Fray and Roach were able to put flesh on the skeleton. And when Mary McNiel had been reluctantly sent back to Sal Hodges, Moriarty sat for a full hour listening to the details as told him by Spear, Ember and Lee Chow.

Even though he was acquainted with much of the information, Moriarty was disturbed to find how deeply his own concerns had been penetrated by Green and Butler. At least two fences—John Togger and Israel Krebitz, two of the best—had most certainly been providing their services for Green's faction. When Moriarty had left England, they did business with nobody but his people. There were several other names formerly associated—though not in any major sense—with Moriarty that now appeared to have been used on many occasions by the rivals. There was also little doubt that certain night houses and hostelries, which had paid regular dues to Moriarty, were now giving weekly coinage to Green and Butler's men.

Another worry was the list of names, extracted by Spear, of the girls who were plying their trade within the one good West End house maintained by Green and Butler. Five names on that list disturbed Moriarty, for they were the names of five girls who he knew had previously been in Sal Hodges' best house.

It disturbed greatly because none of the girls would yet be much over the age of twenty-five, and even if, for one reason or another, they had become past working for Sal, Moriarty had an arrangement with the whore-mother that all the girls in her best house should be looked after once they stopped playing the national indoor game. Any woman who had worked in Sal Hodges' house was privy to information Moriarty could never afford to have passed into other hands.

After hearing all there was to tell, Moriarty sat still, except for his ever-moving head, his brow creased and his visage reflecting the concentration he brought to bear on the many problems. At last he spoke.

"Spear, get a message to Sal. I wish to see her here as soon as she can conveniently manage it. Then get Paget. I wish to talk to all of you."

Spear returned with Paget some five minutes later.

"Have you news for us, then?" Moriarty asked of Paget, who came as near to blushing as a man of his background could.

"Yes, Professor. I've asked her and she has answered yes. We are to be married."

There was a general stir, with Moriarty strangely beaming like a proud father.

"Later," he said, "we will arrange the day. But first there is the question of the slime that Green and Butler have spread."

For Paget's sake, he went over the information once more.

"I have to talk with Sal," he continued, "and then spend some time in contemplation. When we hit the Peg and the Butler, we must hit hard and right. They have to learn the lesson properly—and so has the rest of London."

The four members of the "Praetorian Guard" nodded agreement.

"Now to other matters." The smile had faded from the Professor's lips. "It appears that I was too euphoric on my return. Moran has left matters in tumult, so it is necessary that we consolidate. Today I shall require the four of you to go out and discover our true situation in the city. Take stock of our forces; be careful not to arouse suspicion." He paused, the head oscillating as though seeking out a target. It stopped, looking in the direction of the Chinese. "Lee Chow, do you know how we are placed regarding the present opium and laudanum supplies?"

"Not exacly. But I go makee good and sure."

Lee Chow had run that side of Moriarty's enterprises for many years, but the recent revelations had made even him nervous.

"Ember." The Professor fixed his eyes on the small man. "I want you to contact all our dips and whizzers, our palmers and magsmen."

Ember nodded.

"Paget, you will keep your woman inside the house until further notice. We don't want her face on the streets until the Moran business has blown over. Your special concern today will be the fences, cash carriers and collectors. Spear"—the head whipped round—"you will see to what coiners we still have working, and to the moneylenders."

Moneylending was one of Moriarty's most lucrative lines, for whether it was a sixpence to some poverty-stricken couple or several hundred pounds to those with prospects, the rate was usurious and the manner of collecting barbarous.

There were nods of understanding.

"Before we go, I think it best if you see Fray and Roach again," Spear murmured. "I would also be obliged if I could have words with you in private concerning another small matter you asked me to settle."

The Professor seemed to be lost in thought for a second, then he quickly nodded.

"Good. On your ways then. Paget, warn your woman, do not forget that; and you remain with me for a moment, Spear."

"I wish to take care of our friend, Halling, Lady Bray's butler," Spear said, once the others had left. "You've already instructed me on it and I'd like to get going today when I've completed the other work."

"If you have the time, all well. If not, then it will keep. It can be your wedding gift to Pip Paget and his lady."

Spear laughed gruffly, the serrated scar a white river plunging down the leathery terrain of his cheek. "Do the punishers remain close?"

"I do not want them loose until I have decided how best they should be deployed. In any case, we need them to look after the two turncoats." He chuckled. "There'll be plenty for them to do once we start cleaning out the Peg's midden."

Fray and Roach were still bound, but their gags had been removed. Two of the punishers shared the small room that had been allotted to them, and there was no denying the terror that lurked in the eyes of the prisoners.

Moriarty and Spear stood before them, Moriarty smiling, the twist of his lips betraying contempt.

"You have not been roughly treated, I trust?"

Fray appeared to have difficulty in swallowing.

"No," he croaked, surly.

"Good," Moriarty nodded. "And they have been given food?" he queried of Spear.

"They've both been fed."

"Then you should have no complaints. I am pleased with what you have told my people. You need not fear. You will live and be kept safe—very safe—from the influence of Mr. Green and Mr. Butler."

His laugh was unpleasant, leaving the two Green lieutenants with the distinct feeling that death might just possibly be preferable to whatever the Professor had in store for them.

Moriarty returned to his chambers to puzzle on the many things he had in hand: the rout of Green and Butler; the Harrow robbery; what he would say to Sal Hodges when she arrived; the details he still had to finalize regarding the Jacobs boys in the 'Steel; and other matters which spread beyond the Channel to the Continent.

Ember was doing the rounds, mingling with the men and women who worked the many dodges, tricks and petty thievings that brought ample returns to Moriarty and his people.

Sunday was never the best day in London, with the shops closed and some of the eating houses and other places of entertainment bereft of those who ran them. It was, however, a good day for the pickpockets, petty thieves and tricksters—those very people whom Moriarty had sent Ember to see.

The day wore on and the foxy little man traversed large areas of the city, watching those engaged in the many swindles perpetrated daily on the unwary, for Sundays were also a good time to catch those who were in London from the provinces and not wise to the ways of the magsmen, the fast talkers with their cuffs turned back doing the three-card trick, or the thimbleriggers and their three little silver cups with the dried pea, and plenty of folk sure they could tell under which cup the pea rested; or the Charley pitchers, with their weighted dice. All of them had their particular assistants, the nobblers and buttoners, the sweeteners and jolliers.

There were the dippers, who worked the pavements where good folk walked, pausing to examine goods displayed in the windows, and the fawney-droppers, looking the pictures of innocence as they inquired of passersby if the ring or watch or brooch they had just picked from the gutter could possibly be gold, and if so what a pity it was that the pawnshops were not open as they had need of a few shillings. On any Sunday, worthless rings and trinkets constantly changed hands and many a man's pocket was lighter because of his own desire to make profit.

All this time Lee Chow was moving from duly appointed house to house, mainly in the dockland areas. Moriarty had learned—far earlier than the narcotics barons who infest our cities today—that mankind is always looking for ways of escape, and the opium and dope dens of Victorian London, while not so far outside the law as they are today, brought many a rich coin to the pockets of the Professor. Lee Chow saw that the sticky sweet opium was delivered and in good supply and that other drugs, such as the costly alcoholic derivative from opium, laudanum, so favored by those who would not be seen near the opium den, was readily available.

Paget was on much more straightforward errands. The men he visited were those who had served the Professor well for many years. First the fences in their hidden rooms, secret places and storehouses behind pawnshops.

In spite of the fact that old Solly Abrahams had visited Moriarty to pay his respects only a matter of two days before, he was the first whom Paget called on—as though to assure the wily old man that the Professor looked after his own. From thence it was a case of walking long miles, of taking glasses of wine and being shown gems prised from their settings, crucibles of molten gold, rich silver ornaments, watches, seals, furs, items of jade and many assorted silks and satins, hoarded in a couple of dozen houses across London and ready to be altered, refurbished, sold to dealers, taken out of the country, or transported to towns where a certain and promised buyer or cove awaited their delivery.

Paget did not call on either John Togger or Israel Krebitz, the two fences denounced by Fray and Roach, but to the rest he brought a word of assurance from Moriarty—assurance that also contained a word of warning.

He called upon others also. The cash carriers—the ponces to whores who hawked their mutton in the streets and the bullies who carried Moriarty's cut from the houses run by Sal Hodges to the coffers in Limehouse. He visited also the collectors, men known by that name because at one time their work was solely that of collecting from those foolish enough to walk alone, and late, along secluded byways, paths and lanes. They still improved their income by this simple employment—the talents for which included only a gruff voice, menacing manner and a certain bulk—but Moriarty had extended the scope of their work. Now the collectors went day by day and week by week into coffeehouses and restaurants, to tradesmen and cabbies, who, rather than risk the wrath of Moriarty (which undoubtedly would mean at least a loss of trade, and at most severe physical damage) paid a set rate, or portion of their earnings, in return for the safety of their lives, property and business.

Spear also worked his way around the city, and he, like the others, saw men whose business provided Moriarty with the funds that kept the wheels turning within his large and variegated family. There were the moneylenders, whose loans were often repaid in blood and always with sweat and concern. Then came the coiners— the shofulmen—who worked long and dangerous hours with all their paraphernalia of molds, metals, crucibles and galvanic batteries for electroplating: whole families of them were often hidden away, jealously guarded by Moriarty's crows and a few dogs, as they produced counterfeit silver coinage. Lastly there were the forgers, men with great technical skill, producing not only bank notes but also the multitude of other documents that were the lifeblood of the whole complex system of crime—bogus references, "characters," testimonials, even pedigrees: papers to get *people* into places and to get *things* out.

Like his colleagues, Spear brought messages of goodwill from the Professor, couched in terms that could not be misinterpreted. The loyalty of these people would be rewarded as only Moriarty could reward. Treachery would be detected before it was even attempted and there was but one reward for treachery.

Spear saw the last person on his mental list at around four in the afternoon. Normally he would have returned to give Moriarty his report, but today both heart and mind were directed to settling the score with Halling. In a grim mood he took a hansom and was set down, at half-past the hour, outside The Victory, the pub where he first met the butler who had so callously allowed his friend's woman to be thrown into the street. He would not see Halling damned today, but at least the ball would begin to roll; eventually it would take the man skittling down to hell.

Sal Hodges, dressed like a duchess, arrived in the Professor's chambers at noon.

"My, Sal." The Professor rubbed his hands. "I could do a jig with you today, you look tasty as an eel pie."

Sal threw her head back in a short laugh.

"What's the matter, Professor, didn't little Mary McNiel give you enough greens? I had a noble lord in last week and he said that one night with Mary'd last any normal man a lifetime."

"What do I know of normal men, Sal? A glass?"

She nodded, sinking with some elegance into a chair and accepting the proffered glass of claret.

"I hear you've seen to friend Tappit."

"News travels."

"There's much talk."

Sal sensed, in the pause, that something was irritating the Professor.

"There'll be more within a few hours," he said, his tone giving the impression of a man spreading a winning hand at the card table.

"Is that why you want me?"

"Some of it. A matter has come to my ears, Sal. A serious matter which causes some alarm."

"You look stern, James."

Sal was one of the few people who could call Moriarty James in private.

"There is cause." He looked up at her from the desk, taking a piece of paper in the fingers of his right hand, then dropping it again. "What, my dear Sal, has become of Charlotte Ford, Liz Williams, Prudence Catchpole, Hester Dainton and Polly Mount?" He ticked the names off, right fingers on left.

Sal's glass hesitated, poised an inch or so from her lips.

"Ah," she said quietly. "I wondered when . . ."

"When I would come to that?"

"Yes." Her sharp sigh was one of annoyance with herself. "I should have talked to you of it on Friday morning. It has not been far from my mind this last six months."

"Did they leave with your knowledge?"

"I knew they had left, of course. But it was unexpected, and I had no hand in it. To be true, they simply disappeared. On a Sunday morning. Last September."

"It was not reported?"

"Of course it was reported." She was angry at the question. "Like so many other matters, it was reported to Moran; and when he did nothing, I had some of the cash carriers make inquiries."

"The five of them simply left?"

She nodded. "Exactly."

"Do you know where they are now?"

"I have not seen them. There was one report that they were in a house near Regent Street, near the Quadrant. None of the other girls has seen them and there has been no explanation."

Moriarty made a sharp sucking sound. "Sal, we have much trouble. My absence has been the cause of great laxity. Moran, whom I foolishly trusted, concerned himself with his own pastimes and not with the complexities of the family business. But you are aware of that. Now we are faced with a struggle against usurpers. Your five ladybirds have played the crooked cross, as have others, and they will all, like the children they are, go through St. Peter's needle."

Sal bit her lower lip. "I was never totally in accord with Liz or Prudence, but they were all good workers."

"And they all knew much, Sal. Too much, which has doubtless been blown about among their new masters. Now listen carefully. You'll keep your girls close for the next few days. You have enough strength in your houses?"

"I don't think we need fear."

Moriarty was silent for the space of a minute.

"I think it would be best if you send the McNiel girl here for the time being. We need another woman about. . . ."

"And I lose silver."

"A small price to pay, Sal. If you were not so dear to me, I might have felt the need to. . . ."

"To put your punishers in, Professor? I think not."

"It is a lesson of life, Sal." Moriarty's voice was sharp as a razor. "Change is an easy thing to effect. Not one of us is necessary to the whole—except, perhaps, me." His head swung from side to side as though in great agitation. "It would be a sorry matter if we had to part company now, Sal. I might even weep for you."

Sal sipped her claret, and one could scarcely note the mild tremor of her hand.

"As you say." She acquiesced, but her eyes searched the pattern of the carpet, as though seeking some way of escape.

"Then Mary comes here tonight. There will be other company for her."

"Kate Wright?"

"And more. You did not know that Paget is to wed?"

"Pip Paget? I thought he was wed enough—to you."

"There is a young woman, here in the house. They are to be hammered for life as soon as it is convenient."

Sal Hodges smiled, though not with her eyes.

"You wish Mary to teach her the tricks?"

Moriarty chuckled unpleasantly.

Half an hour after Sal Hodges left the warehouse, a young man of neat appearance, dressed in sober gray, arrived at the doors. He was no stranger to the Professor's headquarters, being clerk to the solicitor, William Sandhill—of Sandhill and Cox, Grey's Inn—who looked after Moriarty's affairs: an arrangement which in no way seemed to bother the consciences of either Mr. Sandhill or Mr. Cox, for Moriarty had bought the practice for them and was in fact their only client.

Once Sal had left, Moriarty returned to plotting, step by step, the action that would be required to smash Green's and Butler's attempted takeover. By the time he had finished with them, Moriarty mused, neither Green nor Butler would be in a fit state to work even the kinchen-lay.

The landlord of The Victory recognized Spear as the detective who had drifted in on the previous lunchtime and had a lengthy discussion with Mr. Halling. He greeted him with due deference, being a man who preferred to keep on the right side of the law. Spear accepted a glass of grog, on the house, and asked if his friend Mr. Halling had been abroad that day.

"Not yet, sir." The landlord looked up at the clock. "Another hour or so before Mr. Halling comes in of a Sunday evening. Always drops in for a glass before he has his night out. Goes for a walk around the town on a Sunday, our Mr. Halling."

There was no wink or leer, but Spear caught the meaning.

"Can you give him a message, in private, from me?"

He dropped his voice, assuming an attitude meant to convey great trust, as though the landlord were the one person in the world to be the carrier of a confidence.

The landlord nodded gravely.

"Mr. Halling is most anxious to trace a person whom he wishes to help. Can you tell him that if he is still of the same mind, he will find the young woman we discussed at number 43 Berwick Street. She will be there tonight and is in great need of help."

The address was that of one of Sal Hodges' houses—not the best, but one in which Spear had many friends, particularly the pair of cash carriers who acted as bullies for the protection of the girls. With no apparent haste, he finished his drink and went out into the late afternoon. A quiet walk down to Berwick Street, a few words with the people there, and he would have Halling on toast.

He stepped out briskly down Park Lane and into Piccadilly, eventually turning through the Quadrant, into the maze of byways that would bring him into Berwick Street.

The traffic was not too heavy, so Spear did not take much heed of the "growler" coming up slowly behind him. It went past, the cabbie pulling his horse into the curb.

As Spear came level with the vehicle, he experienced a brief second of reaction—the flash of knowledge that all was not as it should be—so that he began to shy away from the stationary "growler." Light exploded in his head, a burst of pain at the back of his skull, then darkness, through which he was vaguely aware of hands lifting him.

When consciousness returned, Spear's head was aching and his eyes would not focus properly. The world seemed to be clouded and fuzzy. He blinked twice and tried to move but his hands and feet were bound with thick rope that cut into the flesh of his wrists and ankles. Slowly his vision cleared; smoke and gin fumes burning his nostrils.

There were several people wherever he was—it appeared to be a long bare room, as he could glimpse rafters above him.

"So, Mr. Spear is awake." The voice grated, and came from somewhere near his feet. Spear raised his eyes.

"Good evening, Mr. Spear. I wonder what the Professor will say when he knows we have you snug and trussed?"

Spear knew the voice, and its owner. He was looking up at Moriarty's rival, Michael Green, otherwise Michael the Peg.

Moriarty gazed into the fire. Paget and Lee Chow had returned and given their reports. Mary McNiel was safe in the Limehouse headquarters, having arrived half an hour before in the case of one of the cash carriers from Sal Hodges' house. Once Ember and Spear were in, the Professor would have to talk in earnest about the way in which they would deal with Green and Butler.

He peered into the hot, blazing coals as though trying to see the faces of his adversaries. The pattern of his assault was already taking shape. Green and Butler, he now knew, often held court in The Nun's Head, though their main living place was a flash-house in Nelson Street near the Commercial Road—too close for Moriarty's comfort. Green also had half a dozen doss-houses near and around Liverpool Street railway station.

As for the whores, Moriarty was now aware of the names of those who controlled and carried for the street women (all soldiers' and sailors' girls), about two dozen men in all, whose known haunts boiled down to three drinking dens on the fringe of Lambeth—between the Palace and Waterloo Bridge. There were also the two brothels in Lupus Street, catering to the middle-class trade, and the one big cash earner in Jermyn Street.

The Professor also knew that John Togger and Israel Krebitz

were the only fences with whom Green and Butler had been doing
steady business; that the large Collins family, buried in their den in
the crammed streets behind High Holborn, worked exclusively on
forgeries (silver and paper) for his rivals.

There was also a mob of some twenty rips—magsmen, dips and
macers—who were totally in Green's and Butler's employ and
worked the fringes of the West End and the area around the South
Eastern District Station at Charing Cross.

Other names were filed in the Professor's able brain—those of
cracksmen, gonophs, and heavy mobsmen—some of whom had
once worked for him. Their haunts and ways were well known to
Moriarty, and none of them, he reflected with bitter pleasure, would
escape the particular justice he was about to unleash. The lesson
would be sharp and swift. More punishers were needed, but that
was a mere detail. The important matter was timing, and when
Moriarty struck, it would be with brimstone, thunder, lightning and
death.

Inspector Angus McCready Crow had spent much of the day clois-
tered in his chambers at 63 King Street examining every scrap of
paper, each note, item, report and document that contained even a
whisper concerning Professor James Moriarty.

He was surprised that so much paperwork had been gathered
together and mustered into a dossier, for, it must be remembered,
fewer than twenty years had elapsed since Mr. Howard Vincent
(former director of Criminal Investigation) had instituted such
things as photographs of wanted men, lists of stolen property, and
the system of classified descriptions and methods of known criminals (a system that has now blossomed into the MO lists).

In 1894 the paperwork of crime was only just starting its sophisticated rise, and in many ways the inspector was impressed. Like Mr.
Vincent, he was a strong admirer of the methods of the *Sûreté* in
Paris. He had a tidy mind, firmly believing that one of the answers
to successful detective work was the correlation of evidence into a
filing system.

Colleagues tended to view Crow's theories with distaste, mainly
because of their feelings regarding the inherent rights of the
Englishman. Some of the methods now being used in Europe were,
they said, repugnant to the British way of life. Crow would often try
to explain that the scientific approach to a crime index must not be
confused with the *Meldewesen*, or registration system, by which
many of the Continental countries kept track of their residents—
exercising a closer supervision over individuals than was deemed
either desirable or necessary in England.

In private, however, Crow was of the opinion that crime would only be truly contained when an efficient crime index was linked with some form of individual registration—and to hell with the privacy of the individual.

He was, naturally, a strong champion of anthropometry, as taught and practiced, by M. Alphonse Bertillon;* also of the growing science of dactyloscopy,† which, he was convinced, would eventually prove itself to be the miracle weapon of detection. But at that moment neither M. Bertillon nor the art of fingerprinting were part of his armory, and he could only wade through the tedious pile of paper.

The facts Crow had before him now seemed to add little to those of which he was already aware. Professor Moriarty, at the apogee of academic success, had resigned under a cloud, come to London, set himself up as an army tutor and then suddenly changed his way of life. Certainly his name appeared on many reports dating from the seventies.

There was, of course, the long and somewhat complicated Patterson Report of April-May 1891, in which Moriarty's name figured prominently.

Inspector Patterson had, from the summer of 1890, been alerted to and was working on the plot which undoubtedly existed both to steal the crown jewels and discredit the royal family. As the world knows, the latter part of this outrageous action all but succeeded with the so-called Tranby Croft affair concerning the Prince of Wales. The question of Moriarty and the crown jewels was, as we shall later see, a matter of some moment.

Throughout the report there were messages and cables passing between Patterson and Holmes, and it became clear that Holmes was convinced that Moriarty was the brains behind both plots. Patterson, it would seem, tended not to believe the Baker Street detective, yet appeared to humor him, as much evidence regarding the men eventually arrested came directly from Holmes.

*Anthropometry. First introduced in France by M. Bertillon in 1883, this method of classification and identification was based on those dimensions of the human body that do not alter between adolescence and extreme old age: head length and breadth, middle finger length, foot length, etc. These were further expanded into subdivisions, such as measurement of the ear, and Bertillon's famous portrait parlé. To this system he later added dactyloscopy.

†Dactyloscopy. Identification by fingerprints: first used in very early times by the Chinese; developed in Europe by Purkinje of Breslau University, but not adopted in Engand until the first decade of the twentieth century at the instigation of Sir Edward Henry.

The appendix to the case documents was of special interest, containing as it did a message, relayed to Patterson by Holmes' friend Dr. Watson, drawing attention to absolute proof of Moriarty's involvement. The proof, so the message claimed, was contained in a blue envelope inscribed "Moriarty" to be found in pigeonhole M.

Patterson noted that the pigeonhole referred to was that of the poste restante at the General Post Office, St. Martin-le-Grand, which he and Holmes often used. But no such envelope was discovered and Patterson, who was unhappily killed in a riding accident in the following year, was of the opinion that Holmes, despite all his brilliance, had made a terrible mistake—though there was still a lingering suspicion regarding the theft of the "Moriarty" letter from St. Martin-le-Grand.

During the interrogation of the six plotters, no link could be established with the Professor, and Patterson had put the final "case closed" seal on the file.

Crow read the Patterson documents twice, remembering the blank look on Holmes' face when he had talked with him earlier. Something, he concluded, had gone very wrong with that case. In 1891 Holmes had appeared almost obsessional about Moriarty's complicity. Now he refused even to discuss the man.

Inspector Lestrade himself had written a large number of the reports, mainly, it seemed, after talking with Sherlock Holmes. His private view was undoubtedly that Moriarty had for long been engaged in criminal activities of the highest order. Yet none of the reports included any firm evidence: not a shred of proof appeared to exist.

True, the late unlamented Colonel Moran was a proven rogue and cheat who had spent much time with the Professor, as did a number of other dubious characters. Though, once more, there was scant proof—nothing that could ever be taken into court.

As now, the detective force of the 1890's relied heavily on intelligence, culled from the world of thieves and villains, so the thick dossier included references to Moriarty made by dozens of informers—criminals of few principles who blew their colleagues for small sums of cash. Crow had his own blowers and, although he had little time for them, was determined to seek them out, to inquire if they could add anything to the pages of handwritten records that now littered his table. Yet on that score he was pessimistic, for the villain is a strangely gullible person. The inspector knew many who, against all logic, believed extraordinary things about the law and the police force—for instance, that the senior police officers and the judges were in league; and he shook his head sadly as he read the umpteenth notation from some detective or uniformed man.

The rogues to whom they had all talked certainly mentioned Moriarty—or the Professor, as they called him. (You could almost hear their tones hushed with awe.) According to these men and women, the petty criminals, small-time footpads, dips and failed cracksmen, Moriarty was up to his neck in villainy, running from murder to fraud, yet not one of them would volunteer to stand evidence. As soon as any officer mentioned a written statement or an appearance in court, they would shy away like nervous mares. The more he read, the more Angus McCready Crow became dubious about Moriarty, not simply because of the reluctance of the informers, but rather in spite of it. Many of them had even invested the Professor with supernatural powers, claiming that the man had ways of changing—not just his face, using the arts of disguise, but his whole body and personality.

To Crow it seemed as though a large proportion of London's criminals found the idea of Moriarty more useful than the reality: a mythical figure with magical powers. Maybe even a convenient scapegoat. In any case, thought Crow, it was absurd to think that one man could wield so much power and confusion among the shifty, treacherous criminal masses.

There was a knock at his door, and the inspector gladly pushed the papers away as the plump, sweet Mrs. Sylvia Cowles came into the room.

"I have a little cold roast beef left over, Inspector." She smiled brightly, the dark eyes inviting. "If you'd care to take a few slices with me downstairs, there's good hot mustard to go with it."

It was their private jest.

"Aye, Sylvia, I've had enough paperwork for one day; and tomorrow will be all bustle, I've to be at Horsemonger Lane by eight."

"We'll perhaps . . ." She verged on a blush. "Perhaps spend . . ."

"Make up for lost time ye mean, lassie. Aye, perhaps we'll do that." Crow waggled a provocative index finger. "It'll depend on your cold beef."

She came to him, burying her face in his shoulder.

"Oh, Angus, my dear, you do not know what a boon it is to have a man like you to lean upon. I do not have to feel . . . well . . . ashamed of my appetites. Mr. Cowles was a good man, but too good, I fear." She leaned back and kissed him on the mouth. "He would have prayed for me night and morning if I had shown desire for him. You are so different."

"Not so different. Perhaps more understanding."

Crow smiled at her, experiencing the small worry, which he had found getting larger of late. He knew well enough what it was—the unease of a bachelor who could feel himself being drawn into the web of marriage. Crow had been a successful bachelor for long, knowing of old that young widows were more able to let their hair down than most respectable women. Indeed, he had been pleasantly surprised on the first occasion of bedding Mrs. Cowles, for she had moved, panted, and even screeched her enjoyment of their coupling: something she had obviously longed to do for many years. Angus Crow was her first outlet, and they both knew that she meant business—the kind of business that led to the altar.

"How long before supper?" he asked, pulling away slightly.

"Give me fifteen minutes, Angus dear, and all will be ready."

She stressed the *all* with a voluptuousness difficult to describe in words.

Crow watched her move toward the door, roused at her kiss and the undulation of her body, the swell of her breasts and the hidden grace of those two thighs hidden under the long checked skirt. Beneath that, he knew, she would be wearing colored short silk drawers, which respectable people held to be most unladylike, worn only by women of the night; for if drawers were to be worn at all in polite circles, they should be only of a plain white color, and usually made of cotton. Those Mrs. Cowles had recently taken to wearing were the work of the devil.

Crow felt his blood rise. He nodded. Work of the devil maybe, but the removing of them was damned hot work. He sighed, not bemoaning the fact he had faced for some weeks now—that Angus McCready Crow was a lecherous man who might well have met his match in Sylvia Cowles.

Idly he picked up the next document in the pile and allowed his eyes to stray across the precise script. It was a report written by a police constable who had been called late one night to a dying man in a house near the Embankment. It appeared that the man, whose name was Druscovich, had recently been released from prison. He knew that he was dying and desperately wanted to supply the police with some new evidence connected with his crime.

But by the time the constable, who had been called off the street, got to his bedside, Druscovich was all but gone. The only words noted in the officer's report were, "Tell them Professor Moriarty was behind it all. Tell them, Moriarty."

The report had obviously been only recently refiled among the documents relating to Moriarty. Crow looked at the original date: July 1879.

Druscovich? It was a name the inspector knew, and presumably a name many other members on the force knew also, yet at the time the young constable (A 363 Jackson, D.H.) and his superiors had missed the significance. Angus Crow was missing the significance now. Yet there was something nagging away, leaving him with a feeling of great unease.

Spear's heart sank. A fury raged within him for being so foolish as to fall into such a trap. The fury was also edged with concern, for Green and Butler were now obviously alerted.

"What do you want with me?" His voice was sullen.

Behind Green, Butler lounged against a small heavy table, a tankard held loosely in his right hand. Spear also glimpsed other faces, some known to him, others belonging to men he may have seen often enough but to whom he could put no names. In all there were some ten or fifteen persons in the room.

"What do we want him for, Peg?"

Peter Butler's accent was almost affected, like a man who tried too hard to better himself and was guilty of excessive imitation of the class to which he aspired.

"What indeed, Bert Spear, what indeed? We want to know what the game is, that's what."

Spear's head was aching; it felt as though someone were swelling a pig's bladder inside it.

"What game?" he croaked from the back of his dry throat.

Michael Green took a pace forward.

"The rumors that are set about—the talk that Moriarty has returned from the grave."

"You've heard that, have you?"

Spear hoped that it was a trace of fear he detected in Green's voice, pleased in some small way that the Peg was talking about rumor: it meant they were still uncertain.

"We hear a lot of things, and it's my mind that one of you bastards is being a sight too fly."

"Oh?"

Spear shifted, pain shafting across his head like a sudden light thrown through a casement.

Peter Butler moved, pushing himself forward from the table.

"All this talk of the Professor's return," he said, smooth as treacle. "Then Moran gets the devil's whisper. It's too good to be true, Bert. Moran's been takin' his ease since the Professor got his—takin' his ease and more besides. There are only four of you who'd have the brains to see him off up the stairs—you, Pip Paget, that little yellow heathen, Chow, and the weasel, Ember.'' He paused to spit, turning his head.

"And there's only two of you would try it on your own," Butler continued. "You and Paget, or you *or* Paget. So what's the game, Bert?"

"If it's you . . ." The Peg grinned unpleasantly, showing blackened teeth. "If it's you, perhaps we can come to terms."

Spear could have shouted with relief. They did not believe the Professor was indeed back, preferring to imagine the whole thing had been arranged by Moriarty's lieutenants.

"What sort of terms?"

In spite of the throbbing and a rising nausea, Spear did his best to appear sly, even grasping.

"We'd be reasonable." The Peg's voice softened. "The Professor's organization is not altogether smashed, and you've the means to put the Butler and I in top places. We'd see you right—if it is you. We'd see you with a third share, equal to Peter and myself."

"Is it you?" asked Butler.

Spear allowed a full minute to pass, lingering for effect, keeping his eyes from meeting those of either Green or Butler. Then:

"You've more brains than I took you for. Untie me and give me a glass. Yes, it's me, with a little help from the others."

It was not possible to divine Green's true intentions, but Spear could be certain that once he and Butler thought they had control over what remained of Moriarty's lays, they would be none too choosy about what happened to him. If the circumstances had been real, Spear thought, his life would have been worth less than a duff fawney.

The Peg motioned with his hand, and two of the other men came out of the smoke and shadows to kneel and work at the knots on Spear's wrists and ankles. One of the men smelled as though he slept in a midden.

Spear climbed carefully to his feet, rubbing his wrists, fighting the sickness and the cleaving hurt that was in his head. A hand grasped one arm, and he was led, painfully, to the table and there seated in a chair. A cup of gin with hot water was placed in front of him and, looking up, he saw he was being served by a young woman.

"You can get downstairs again now, girl," the Peg said roughly.

Spear caught a glimpse of light blue eyes, holding his for a moment and felt the girl's hand brush softly against his arm. She could not have been more than twenty years of age, yet there was immense fatigue in the eyes, and lines above the nose, as though she had grown old and worn out long before her time.

"You heard him, Bridget." Butler's tone was less sharp. "Down to the others. You're paid to keep them happy, so see you do it well."

Bridget gave a quick nod and turned away, but Spear sensed that she was trying, in some desperate manner, to communicate with him. He shook his head and took a long sip of the gin, trying to clear his mind.

"You're with us then, Bert Spear?" Green was leaning across the table.

"It seems sense."

"And the others?"

"They'll listen to me."

"They'd better."

"Let me go to them and talk."

Green grinned his black smile. "Not so fast. You'll go when we've spoken more. When you've told us the full condition of Moriarty's family."

"And when you go," added Butler, "there's a pair of our family men who'll go with you."

Spear nodded slowly. He would have done the same. All he could do now was play out the time, hoping that he was in one of Green's flash-houses which Moriarty already knew. Play out the time, hoping the Professor would strike quickly.

The gaslight in the streets filtered through the eternal mixture of smoke, grime, soot and wispy fog. It hit people's faces changing their pallid color to an even more ghastly shade, making them appear as if they were the walking dead. It also cast shadows in which lurkers skulked, watching on behalf of others or out for some villainy of their own.

There were many streets and lanes in London through which it was dangerous, if not fearsome, to travel alone at night, yet the streets did not appear to hold any particular terror for the boy Slimper.

The boy could not be more than ten years old, yet he showed no fear as he ran through the eerie alleys and lanes, far from the broad and better lit thoroughfares. He turned a deaf ear to the moans and the noises that came out of the smoke and fog. His job, he had learned as an infant, was to survive the best way he could, and his survival now meant doing as he was told, which in this instance was to run as though Satan were at his heels, over the uneven cobbles, past the ghostly wraiths of beggars, and those not lucky enough to have a room or a bed to hide in at night. He scampered under arches, through the evil smells, across the more salubrious roads, with their

lighted and warm windows, swerving back into the shadow as he
saw a constable patrolling the pavement.

His trousers and coat were ragged and the shirt on his back thin,
giving little protection against rain or cold. But to run with haste and
deliver his message meant a warm place to sleep, when he was
allowed, and a glass of gin with some soup, meat and bread to fill his
belly.

So the boy ran and swerved and scampered, holding the message
in his head until he reached the warehouse; he was serving an
apprenticeship that would make him a man apart from rich or poor.

Ember, Moriarty reflected, was not a likable specimen, what with
his rodent appearance and stunted stature, and the note of a whine
which crept so easily into his voice. But there was no denying the
man was a professional.

He sat across the desk from Moriarty now, giving his report on
the day's findings—a report that barely missed a detail, whether it
was in names, places, rackets or takings.

Moriarty was pleased with Ember. "Good, as always, you've
done well. Is Spear back yet?"

"Not when I came up, Professor. He's running late."

"He had some extra work to do, but I would have expected that
concluded by now."

Moriarty leaned back in his chair and stretched to ease his
muscles. Somehow waiting always seemed to fatigue him more
than action, as though the nerves and muscles of his body became
knotted with the unease that was always with him when others were
about his business.

"I want you to pass a message out," he continued. "Get Parker
in here as quickly as is convenient. I'll need to see you all tonight."

"We're going for them this night?"

"Tomorrow, but the plans have to be laid now and, once done,
I'll want nobody off these premises until we strike. My 'Guard' I'll
trust, and the punishers downstairs, but we need others and I'll take
no risks with them once we have it arranged."

He pushed the chair back and rose, moving to the fireplace,
looking for all the world like some country squire or city gentleman,
comfortable in his own home. As one giving an order to a servant,
Moriarty said, "Get Parker then. And send Spear up the moment he
returns."

If not entirely content, Moriarty was a shade more at ease. From
the many people who had come to ask favors and pay their respects
he knew he still had a bold following; yet the intelligence regarding

the extent of Green's and Butler's advances had come as a shock. It was pleasant to know from Lee Chow, Paget and Ember, that his tentacles continued to hold and reach far in spite of the fool Moran's imprudent husbandry.

So Moriarty waited, the clock ticking off some forty minutes before there was word of Spear.

It was Paget who came with the news, knocking hard at the chamber door and disturbing the Professor, who was sitting down to lamb chops with Mary McNiel.

"There's a boy, the boy Slimper, downstairs. He's come from Parker's men."

The Professor's head turned slowly to and fro, a dark glittering light, reflected from the gas brackets, sharp and deep in his eyes, the face alert and dangerous.

"Trouble?" he asked softly.

Paget glanced toward the McNiel girl.

"You may speak in front of her." Moriarty did not raise his voice.

"You'd best see the boy, he'll not speak to anyone else. Parker has him trained well and there seems to be urgency."

The head turned twice more, then paused, eyes resting upon Mary McNiel.

"Go down to Mrs. Wright and wait."

Mary McNiel knew better than to pout or wheedle as she might have done with some of the marks in Sal Hodges' house. She rose obediently and left without a murmur.

"Get the brat up here," spat Moriarty.

Young Slimper was breathless, both with the running and the mission, yet he gave his message lucidly, wasting no words. Parker had set him as runner for the three lurkers watching Green's flash-drum in Nelson Street. During the later afternoon they had seen both the Peg and the Butler arrive together with half a dozen mobsmen and bullies. Then, less than thirty minutes before, a "growler," driven hard, had arrived at the door and three men lifted from it another man who appeared to be stunned. By chance more than their management one of the lurkers had glimpsed the unconscious man's face as the yellow light from a nearby lamp fell on it. The man was Spear, and young Slimper had been unleashed like a hound to carry the news.

"The lurkers are still in Nelson Street?" Moriarty asked sharply, knowing the answer before the boy gave it, for none of Parker's men would leave such a situation. "And the back is watched as well as the front?"

"Yes, sir." Slimper had control of his breath now. "There's Patch at the back, and Toph with Blind Sam at the front. It was Blind Sam as saw Mr. Spear's face."

"You hungry, boy?" A note of unaccustomed concern from Moriarty.

"A little, sir. More cold than hungry."

Moriarty nodded to Paget. "Take him down to Kate Wright. Let her get some fodder into him, and a hot glass of something." He turned back to the lad. "Mr. Paget'll take care of you, and Mr. Parker will be here soon; he'll have messages for you to run."

"Thank you, sir."

The boy beamed with pride, for this was only the second time in his life that he had seen the Professor, and the first he had ever spoken with him.

"Mark me, lad. You are a good boy and there'll be an extra sovereign in this for you. Never forget that I look after all my people, and if they work well for me they are cared for and rewarded."

Moriarty had all the tricks needed to inspire loyalty, and with those few simple words, together with what appeared to be an act of kindness, he knew that he had purchased another soul.

Some fifteen minutes later Parker arrived at the warehouse. Moriarty was short with words and explicit with orders. The three lurkers at the drum in Nelson Street were to stay on watch. They would be joined by another three. Slimper was to be sent back, together with another boy. If Green or Butler, or both, left Nelson Street, they were to be followed. Should Spear be removed, he would be followed.

"You'll make fast, Parker. Tighten the net. I'm to be informed of any movements, whatever the hour. You understand?"

Parker understood and hurried off to do the Professor's bidding before returning, as instructed, for the council of war, which was to be held that night.

Inspector Crow woke once in the night and in the warm, soft arms of Mrs. Cowles, smiled, burying his naked body close to her flesh.

But the smile on his face quickly disappeared, his eyes snapping open and mind alert. Around his brain the name Druscovich wove strange and uncertain patterns, and it was not until the small hours that he fell into sleep again, still puzzled by the significance of the name and its link with Moriarty.

Before waking he dreamed that he was in a large courtroom. There were three prisoners in the dock and the judge was passing sentence upon them. Yet, as the prisoners were ordered to be taken down, they turned, clapping their hands on the shoulders of the police guard, so that it was a trio of police officers who were led away by the prisoners.

On rising in the morning, Angus Crow had no memory of the dream, though it came back to him during the day.

Monday, April 9, 1894, 1:00 A.M. to 9:00 P.M.

(THE ENEMY AND THE TRUTH CONCERNING MORIARTY AT THE REICHENBACH FALLS)

THE COUNCIL OF war took place in the Professor's chambers, beginning a little before one in the morning. Those present, besides Moriarty, were Paget, Lee Chow, Ember, Parker and Terremant, the big punisher.

Kate Wright set two large pitchers of mulled claret by the fireplace, and there were several dishes of small, savory cakes, which she had baked for the purpose.

Moriarty and Paget both lit cigars, and the Professor spoke for some minutes on Spear's plight and the necessity for both speed and secrecy in all their actions from now until the strike, which would take place at nine that night.

Because there were so many areas that needed to be hit hard and simultaneously, they would need more punishers, so the three remaining members of the "Praetorian Guard," together with Terremant's men, would be out at noon collecting every bully they knew was loyal to Moriarty, bringing them in by pairs or threes, surreptitiously, until a large force was assembled. It was not until then that they would be allocated to lieutenants—members of the "Guard" and the main body of punishers, who were already at the warehouse.

"When we have them assembled," Moriarty told them, "you are to see nobody leaves here. I cannot chance one of them sneaking word to Green and Butler."

He went on to order Parker to have lurkers watching the warehouse as well as those places the punishment squads would visit.

It was an hour before the Professor finished talking and giving instructions. After that they spoke at some length regarding weapons and transportation. All had questions, and the discussion

134

went on until the early hours, until their plans for the morrow were fully prepared.

As he was leaving, Moriarty plucked Parker by the sleeve and asked if Sherlock Holmes' chambers in Baker Street were still being watched.

"I have men there night and day: two lads for runners also."

Parker was less evil-smelling today, dressed as he was in the garb of a well-to-do visitor from the country—this being his favorite disguise when he wished to pass easily and with speed between his lurkers distributed over a wide area.

"And what do they report?"

"Holmes appears to be keeping to himself. They've had but one visitor: another esclop." He pronounced the back slang in fashion, as slop.

"Lestrade?"

"No, but from the same cesspool. His name is Crow."

"A good name for a jack." Moriarty smiled at his own joke, crows being lookouts in the flash parlance.

"You know him?"

"No," Moriarty said wearily, "but doubtless I will. Did he stay long?"

Parker told him a little over an hour, which seemed to satisfy the Professor.

"I do not expect to have further trouble with Holmes," he said. "But it is as well to be alert."

As we have already noted, Crow's hour, spent with Holmes at the Baker Street chambers on the previous afternoon, had been frustrating in the extreme.

The great detective had received Crow cordially enough, though with a certain amount of reserve, even diffidence.

After introductions had been effected and Crow was seated opposite Holmes across the fireplace, the inspector set about maneuvering the conversation into the area he had already mentally prepared. He first acquainted Holmes with the news that he had taken over the Moran case from Lestrade.

"Then presumably you will have been provided with Lestrade's notes," Holmes said, somewhat stiffly.

"Indeed I have, Mr. Holmes, but I thought it advisable to go over certain facts with you."

"Admirable." Holmes nodded. "It is just as I would do it, though I doubt if I can help you more than Lestrade."

"Could you tell me why, in your opinion, Moran wished you dead?"

Sherlock Holmes remained silent for a few seconds, his whole attention concentrated on filling his pipe.

Crow suspected that he was playing for time and became slightly unnerved by this device. Too quickly he pushed ahead, taking his questioning into a further realm. "It is true, is it not, that Moran was considered to be chief of staff to Moriarty?"

Holmes raised his eyes for a brief second, fixing Crow with a suspicious gaze, then looked away again. "I have never doubted that Moran was Moriarty's chosen and closest lieutenant," he said, cupping his left hand around the bowl of his pipe and reaching forward with his right to kindle a spill.

"Then perhaps that is the sole reason for Moran wishing you dead."

"Perhaps, Inspector Crow. You have a logical mind, but maybe it is too easily sidetracked."

"There are reports that Moriarty is alive and here in London at this moment." Crow let this piece of intelligence lie flat between them—a bald statement.

"Moriarty is—nay, was—my old enemy. I know nothing of his being in London now. As far as I am concerned, Inspector Crow, my feud with Professor Moriarty ended a long time ago at the Reichenbach Falls. There is no more for anyone else's ears."

"Colonel Moran was close to the Professor. He tries to assassinate you. Now he is dead himself—poisoned in a prison cell. Do you draw any conclusions from that, sir?"

"The only conclusion is that Sebastian Moran, upon hearing that I had returned to London, knew full well that it was only a matter of time before I tracked him down as young Adair's murderer. I believe he wished to obviate that possibility. I was certainly a great threat to his life and liberty."

"And who, Mr. Holmes, would wish Moran dead?"

Homes had lit his pipe and now drew on it contentedly. "If, as I have already said, Moran was Moriarty's plenipotentiary, then I should imagine he had enemies enough—many within the walls of all the prisons in London. In my varied studies I have discovered that criminals make enemies more easily than most men; and, by the very nature of their way of life, those enemies are more potentially dangerous than in other callings."

At this point Holmes appeared to be caught up in this particular train of thought and continued at some length to propound his theories on the social habits of individuals within the criminal community.

Crow was, not unnaturally, fascinated, and by the time Holmes reached the end of this lengthy digression, the true area into which the inspector wished to research had been successfully bypassed.

In vain he attempted to bring their conversation back to Moriarty; Moran's link with the Professor; and the connection both of these men had with Holmes.

It was a fruitless task. Holmes, it appeared, was stubbornly disinclined to speak of Moriarty and, for that matter, Moran's demise. It was also apparent that he was too skilled in the art of debate to be trapped or tricked into any new statement.

So it was that Angus McCready Crow departed from Baker Street with the distinct feeling that there was much that would forever lie buried in the recesses of Holmes' complex mind.

Fanny Jones was asleep when Paget got to his chamber but she stirred and was quickly awake, even though he moved with all his accustomed stealth.

"It's late, Pip. What's going on?"

She could not fail to glimpse the serious expression on her lover's face.

"Nothing that won't keep, sweetheart."

But she was fully awake, propping herself on one arm.

"There was talk in the kitchen," she said. "I didn't hear it all but something's wrong with Bert Spear, isn't it?"

Paget sighed, sitting on the bed and removing his trousers.

"Yes, there's trouble. Since the Professor went away, a pair of right mobsmen have been poaching on our preserves. We're out to get them tomorrow, but it seems that they've got hold of Bert Spear."

Lines of worry creased Fanny's brow.

"Will they hurt him, Pip? They won't do for him, will they?"

Paget paused. It was a dangerous game in which they were involved, Fanny had no illusions about that, so there was no point in trying to pacify her with lies.

"There's a chance he'll be hurt, Fan. But then there's a chance any of us will be hurt. We'd all be scratching if it wasn't for the Professor, and I for one would rather survive well, with money in my pocket, than risk life out there alone where the pickings are good one day and poor the next."

"I hope I shall get used to it, Pip. It frightens me—all the secret things."

"What else is there?" Paget slid into bed beside her, warmed by her body.

"Out of London there's other things—like in the country." She slid her arms around the big man's neck, thrusting herself toward him.

Tired as he was, Paget felt his body respond. He kissed her gently and felt her reply to his kisses until the matter became one of urgency.

When it was over and they lay cradled together in an afterglow reminiscent of a pleasant, cloudless, summer day, Paget recalled the feelings he had experienced in Harrow: the thoughts of a new life with Fanny Jones, an existence far removed from the constant pressure and unease. He wondered if he could ever settle for that.

Moriarty prepared for bed but could not sleep. There were too many matters roaming his brain: thoughts of the morrow, plans which had to be settled before the arrival of his people from the Continent, for the Continental alliance was, perhaps, in the long term the most important thing of all. Yet his mind unwillingly returned to the last few words he had spoken with Parker. When he thought of them, they led back to Sherlock Holmes and this inevitably caused him to retrace his footsteps in time—regressing through the years into the early months of 1891.

By that year Moriarty knew without doubt that there was one man in Europe who could match him, and who might even bring about his downfall. Sherlock Holmes of 221B Baker Street. So, he was at pains to avoid Mr. Holmes, keeping only a wary eye on him.

The concluding months of 1890 had been most successful for the Professor; all his ventures had gone smoothly—robberies, assassinations contracted by governments or individuals, frauds and forgeries, not to mention the regular spoils from the daily rackets of the great European capitals. But in the August of that year he had undertaken, on behalf of a foreign power, to discredit the royal family—not a new assignment for a man like Moriarty, for had he not been the prime mover, the *éminence grise*, behind the tragic love story that had ended with the suicide of Crown Prince Rudolph of Austria at Mayerling? There was also much that he knew concerning the homosexual brothel in Cleveland Street off the Tottenham Court Road, which had brought such scandal to Lord Arthur Somerset, then Superintendent of the Prince of Wales' stables.

It had been a relatively simple matter to set in motion the events that almost brought disgrace upon the Prince of Wales at Tranby Croft, culminating in the incidents of the nights of September 8, 9, and 10, 1890, and the legal scandal in the following year.

There is no doubt that Moriarty, with his contacts and superb sense of intrigue and cunning, was able to manipulate people far removed from his personal sphere. He was a past master in this kind of human chess game, knowing exactly how to maneuver the various players in his game until they reached a point at which they could be safely left alone for the follies of human nature to do their worst.

It was during the preliminary moves in the sequence of events concerning Tranby Croft that the Professor realized it would be possible to pull off the coup of the century by stealing the crown jewels. In January of 1891 he made two visits to Rome, there concluding a deal which assured him of a safe and most lucrative market with an eccentric Italian millionaire. He then set about making the plans for the proposed robbery.

It was not until the Professor arrived in Paris, on January 20, that he discovered Sherlock Holmes had been in Rome at the same time as himself and was aware something was afoot.

During the period in Paris Moriarty busied himself in engaging the best thieves he could procure, and it was in the midst of this work that Holmes incommoded him.

The man Moriarty most wished to recruit for the robbery was a legendary French cracksman by name of Emile Lefantome. The Professor had preliminary talks with the man in his modest apartment near the Place de l'Opéra, and although the full nature of the undertaking was not revealed, Lefantome expressed interest. Moriarty was surprised, therefore, when he returned a day or so later to find the Frenchman had changed his mind.

"Monsieur le Professeur," he said. "I have thought about your offer. We have worked well together in the past, and I am tempted, but truly I am getting too old. I have been persuaded that I have enough money to keep me in reasonable comfort for the rest of my days. I do not wish to put my last years in jeopardy."

The thief was not a member of Moriarty's syndicate, having always worked as a free lance, and there was no way in which the Professor could bring pressure to bear without antagonizing the rest of his men in France—for Lefantome was held in high regard. So, with a shrug, Moriarty departed and sought the help he required from among his own ranks.

However, he did make inquiries and soon discovered that shortly after his first call on Lefantome there had been another visitor. By the description there was little doubt it was Holmes; so Moriarty knew now that the detective had brought his powers of local persuasion to bear.

By the middle of February all arrangements had been made: the plan seemed foolproof and the four cracksmen were set to arrive from France. Yet on the day of their coming only two appeared at the house near the Strand, explaining with some agitation that there had been trouble when they disembarked from the Channel packet at Dover.

The men had been traveling in pairs and the two missing thieves had been first at the bottom of the gangway. As they stepped on shore they had been surprised to find a group of police officers waiting to meet them. With the officers was a man claiming that he was a fellow passenger and accusing the two Frenchmen of attempting to rob him during the crossing. It later transpired that the accuser was Holmes, and the French thieves had been returned to Calais by the next boat.

Moriarty was furious but, hell bent on his plans, left for Paris on the following day to choose two more cracksmen from the French division of his organization—it being an essential part of the plan that the robbery should be carried out by a gang of foreign criminals.

By March the whole team was assembled in London, but once more trouble struck when it was discovered that the police, led by the tenacious Inspector Patterson, were constantly watching the four Frenchmen, who by this time had been moved to other lodgings and kept well apart from one another. Again a few questions in the right quarters, and Moriarty discovered that the police's prime informer was Sherlock Holmes.

It was at this point that the Professor put Parker and his lurkers on constant watch, following every move made by Holmes. Within a few days it became obvious that Holmes was very close to Moriarty's trail, outthinking the Professor and proving himself at least his intellectual equal.

Another essential factor in the Professor's intrigue to steal the royal regalia was that the robbery should take place in the middle of May, when the jewels were being cleaned and refurbished. Now there was another sudden change of plan. At Holmes' instigation and with the help of his brother, Mycroft, the cleaning and refurbishing was brought forward to the end of April, a move that pinned Moriarty down, giving him little room to maneuver. It was then that the Professor became determined that he must dispose of Holmes— a step he fully realized might put his own safety at risk. But he had reluctantly formed a growing respect for his adversary and so was on the proverbial horns of a dilemma: he resolved, therefore, to make one bid to solve the problem by revealing himself to the detective in a last attempt at persuasion.*

*The interview between Moriarty and Holmes is well documented by Dr. Watson in *The Final Problem*. And from the events so far related, a new perspective is now added to Moriarty's speech to Holmes, in which he says: "You crossed my path on the fourth of January. On the twenty-third you incommoded me; by the middle of February I was seriously inconvenienced

As we know, Holmes was not so persuaded and Moriarty, his back against the wall, prepared to have the great detective assassinated. Spear was put on the job with a pair of cutthroats whom the Professor often used to settle local differences. Parker was alerted, and it was made generally known that there would be a bonus if Holmes became the victim of an accident.

Three attempts were made in quick succession—the first with a two-horse van at the junction between Bentinck and Welbeck Streets; the second, following within minutes of the first, in Vere Street, when Spear himself aimed a brick from the roof of one of the houses. The brick narrowly missed Holmes, and soon the area was crawling with police.

Parker was seeing to it that the detective was followed closely—first to his brother, Mycroft, in Pall Mall, and from thence to Dr. Watson in Kensington. It was during the latter journey that one of the assassins made a frontal attack with a bludgeon, badly mistimed, Holmes once more missing death by a fraction, and his assailant ending the day in custody.

Worse was to follow: the lurkers lost Holmes, and renewed effort was put into combing the city—Moriarty conducting the operation from his armchair in the Strand house. It was not until the following morning that he suddenly realized Holmes' intentions.

Watson, who by this time was under close surveillance, left his Kensington lodgings, and within seconds it was apparent that he was moving in accordance with some cleverly prearranged plan, conceived to throw any followers off the scent. Parker's men, in fact, lost him at the Lowther Arcade in the Strand, opposite Charing Cross Station. For a fleeting moment Moriarty imagined the station to be the doctor's goal, but a moment's simple deduction told him it was Victoria, not Charing Cross, that was Watson's destination. There was less than twenty minutes before the departure of the boat train, and little doubt now in the Professor's mind that Holmes, with Watson, was heading for the Continent.

With Spear, Paget and two other men, all crowded into a pair of cabs, the Professor—in the costume and disguise of his deceased brother—made the dash through the morning traffic. They arrived as the boat train was steaming from its customary platform, and Moriarty wasted no time in engaging a special. But once more, as

by you; by the end of March I was absolutely hampered in my plans; and now, at the close of April, I find myself placed in such a position by your continual persecution that I am in positive danger of losing my liberty. The situation is becoming an impossible one.''

the world knows, Holmes had given him the slip.*

It was more than a week before Moriarty had tracked Holmes and Watson into Switzerland; but not until May 3 before he made any positive move.

By this time his quarry had arrived in Meiringen, the main village of the Halsi Valley—the "front garden of the Bernese Oberland"—through which the river Aare flows, flanked by rising and beautiful woodlands.

Moriarty was ready for the kill, having for the past four days made certain that at least one, sometimes two, of his Swiss agents were leapfrogging ahead of the detective and his companion.

On the night of May 3 Moriarty lodged also in Meiringen, not at the *Englischer Hof*, where Holmes and Watson were quartered, by the excellent Peter Steiler, but at the larger Flora Hotel. His agents were quickly deployed, and before he retired to bed that night Moriarty knew that Holmes and Watson were, on the next afternoon, planning to walk across the hills to the village of Rosenlaui, pausing to view the awesome *Reichenbachfälle* on their way. Moriarty's plans were laid accordingly.

There are, of course, two accounts of what occurred on the afternoon of May 4: one reported by Dr. Watson, and a later account rendered again by Watson, with details supplied by the great detective himself. Neither is accurate, except with regard to what took place before Watson left Holmes, after he received the message purportedly from Peter Steiler, summoning him back to Meiringen to attend the fictitious English lady, supposedly in the terminal stages of consumption.

It was, of course, Moriarty who went from the Flora to the *Englischer Hof* once word had been received that Holmes and Watson had begun their climb. He wrote the note to Watson on the stationery provided and sent his agent ahead. Watson rose to the bait, though there is little doubt that Sherlock Holmes was aware (as he subsequently claimed) that the note was a ruse.

The confrontation, however, did not take place as described. Certainly Moriarty and Holmes met one another on the narrow pathway, a sheer drop on one side and a wall of rock on the other. But Moriarty was not alone. Behind him stood one of the Swiss

---

*Watson ably recounts in *The Final Problem* how Holmes, outthinking the Professor, left the train at Canterbury, watched Moriarty's "special" steam past, and then made a cross-country journey to Newhaven, from thence to Dieppe and onward, bypassing Paris, where Moriarty doubtless lost at least two days.

agents and Paget. As Holmes saw him, he sensed a movement from behind and, turning, he was faced by Spear, a revolver in his hand.

"I think it is checkmate," said Moriarty cooly. "And I have arranged it this way, Mr. Holmes, for our mutual advantage. I have no wish to kill you, sir, though I would be a fool to imagine you would not gladly risk your life to see me dead. I can only appeal to your own sense of logic."

Holmes stood almost passively, as though expecting a death blow at any moment.

"You would not take my advice when last we met in London," Moriarty continued. "And you must be fully cognizant of what has happened. You have been successful in foiling my plans, indeed in undoing the painful work of many months. For that I respect you, and I can only hope that we now both fully understand that we are a matched pair—though on opposite sides of the fence." He took out his watch, looked at it for a moment and returned it to his waistcoat pocket. "I cannot stay over long, Mr. Holmes, but the decision on what is to follow must be yours alone. You could easily fall upon me now and we would grapple here on this ledge. My men have their orders and they will not stop us. But the result of such action can have three possible outcomes: I would go over the ledge; or you would plunge down; or the pair of us would go together. As matters stand, there are, however, only two really possible ways: that you would go down, or both of us would die; or, if I go, the good Spear, who stands behind you, has orders to shoot you like a dog."

At this point Holmes appeared to play for time, and the pair exchanged several sentences. But after a few minutes Moriarty brought the conversation back to the matter at hand.

"So the result will be death—for you or both of us. I suggest a more honorable way. That we part company here, leaving a few clues to suggest that we have both perished. After that, a truce. We would both undertake not to return to England for some three years and, when that period is up, we do not speak of this matter again—except insofar as it may suit us as individuals. After that, I will endeavor not to cross your path again, on the understanding that you will not cross mine."

We shall never know what made Holmes agree to the Professor's outrageous demands, but they were complied with. Maybe Holmes, weary of the struggle he had fought over the past months, decided it would be better for him to prolong his life and continue to serve the cause of justice in the hope that one day he would come face to face with Moriarty on more equal terms.

Moriarty recalled that as Spear escorted Holmes back onto the road to Rosenlaui, he felt no particular triumph. For once in his life he had met his match and not overcome him by true guile, but rather with superior forces backed by logic.

Now in the darkness of his bedchamber, Moriarty wondered if he would ever have to face Holmes again, and as he wondered, he experienced a nudge of real fear that perhaps in a second match Holmes would be the victor.

"And how do you make the Professor's ghost walk?"

Spear was worried by the question, which came from Green quite early in a conversation that had gone on well into the night. They had given him food—once more served by the lined and fatigued Bridget—and further drink; then the questions had come, piling one on top of the other in a manner which told Spear he would have to keep his wits about him if he were going to survive.

He had replied to the query concerning Moriarty's "ghost" in the way that came most obviously to mind—saying that they had employed an actor to simulate the Professor.

"And that has taken them in?" drawled Peter Butler.

"We have not let him be seen close, except by the four of us. Others see him only in shadow. It is an old trick."

"You have nerve, Bert," laughed Michael the Peg. "But then there's a lot at stake."

He went on to make further inquiries, which Spear either parried or gave answers that held only enough truth to make them palatable. He hoped that his captors—for that is how he had to regard them—would not trap him into making unwary statements about which they knew the whole truth.

After the first hour Green detached himself and went to talk in low tones to a trio of thickset men who sat apart, looking as though they were holding themselves in readiness for some purpose.

Two of the men left shortly after this, not returning for some three hours. Green and Butler took it in turns to talk with Spear, who by the early morning was becoming increasingly tired.

At about what he judged to be four in the morning, Spear noticed that yet another conference was taking place between Green and the men who had left and returned during the night.

"Enough for one day." Butler stretched and pointed to some bedding piled in one corner of the room. "If you want to sleep, spread yourself there."

The room was large, obviously an attic room intended for stores. There was no ceiling, only rafters, and above them, the joists and inside slates of the roof itself. The exits and entrances were made through a trap in the floor at one end. The room was lighted by three or four oil lamps; two hung from the rafters, the others on the small table. The only other light, by day, would come from the two dormer windows set into one of the longer walls. Green and Butler, Spear thought, had been careful to keep him away from the windows.

"You going to kip then, Bert?" Green had come over.

Spear, anxious to end the questioning, nodded, and the Peg moved toward the pile of bedding. A curtain hung on a short rail from one of the rafters. Reaching up, Green pulled the tattered fabric.

"Your own chamber, there, Bert. Not as good as you probably have down in Limehouse, but when we take command, you'll have all the finery you want, eh?"

Limehouse had not been mentioned before, though it should not have come as a surprise that the two villains knew exactly where Moriarty's headquarters lay. Yet Spear's concern was increased by the remark, though he could do nothing, however, but shrug, smile and take himself to bed.

He removed his trousers and coat, pulled some of the blankets around him, and stretched out on the wide mattress that lay beneath. Fatigue washed over him, and he was just beginning to drift into darkness when he sensed someone else's presence within the curtain.

"Who's there?" he whispered. He knew some of the men had gone from the attic, though at least two of the lamps were still burning, and he doubted if either Green or Butler would have left him alone.

A hand fell softly across his mouth, and a woman's voice said quietly, " 'Tis me, Bridget. He told me to come up and care for you."

There was a rustle in the darkness, and Spear could make out the figure of the girl undressing. A moment later she was beside him on the mattress.

"Are they all gone?" He did not raise his voice.

"They're downstairs, except for Brody and Lee. They're asleep out there."

Spear nodded. "And that's where you should be, Bridget."

"Out there?" Her arm moved across his chest.

"Asleep, my girl. You look done up. They always work you that hard?"

"Is there any man who doesn't? But he'll lay into me if I don't give you your greens." The hand moved down.

Spear caught her fingers, gently moving the arm away. "You rest, girl. Get the sleep you need, there's no need to peel my best end this night."

"Do you not fancy me then?"

Spear sighed, with women you could never do right.

"You looked nice enough, but you'd be better for sleep. The day will come, Bridget."

She did not argue more, but moved close to him so that they could share the warmth of each other's bodies.

Spear woke to someone shaking his shoulder. The girl had gone, and it was Green's hand on his shirt. Daylight filled the attic room and the curtain had been pulled back. One of Green's henchmen set a mug of tea and a plate of bread and dripping beside the mattress.

"You slept sound enough, Bert. Our little Bridget ride you into the land of Nod, eh?" His laugh grated. "Anyhow, me lad, it's past ten and you should be about."

Spear thanked him, on guard again, and Green rose to his feet.

"We'll have some more talking later," said the Peg and he made as though to move away, then, as if changing his mind, turned back. "Oh, we've set things going." The smile cracked over his face, dark and cunning. "That actor you've got down in Limehouse imitating the Professor. With any luck he'll be bleedin' and dead within the day."

In the Limehouse headquarters they were up betimes. One of the punishers was left to guard Roach and Fray, the rest were mustered, together with Ember and Lee Chow, and given their instructions to comb the haunts for more strength. As they prepared to go, Moriarty summoned Harkness, his driver, telling him to have the cab outside within the half hour. He then sent for Paget.

"Have you thought more about the Harrow lay?" he asked.

"If I have to go, then I will, but I'd still rather look at it from a distance."

Moriarty smiled, a brief flash of grim lightning. "We'll see, then, we'll see. In the meantime the grass must not grow. Tonight is time enough for the Peg and the Butler. This morning I want you to come over to Solly Abrahams so that we may arrange the fencing of the Harrow loot. Tomorrow we'll talk cases with Fisher, Clark and Gay."

Paget went down to the kitchen to tell Fanny he expected to be back within two hours. He was surprised to find Mary McNiel helping to roll out pastry on the big board, up to her elbows in flour—hardly an occupation for a prime whore.

While Paget was saying his brief farewells, Moriarty spent a moment with Parker.

"This Crow—can you get to our people at the Yard?"

"It may take a few hours, maybe a day."

"By tomorrow night?"

"Certainly by then."

"I wish to know about him: record; everything—particularly why he's been seeing Holmes." He paused, eyes flicking up to Parker's face as the head moved to and fro. "Is he watched?"

"Not continually."

"See to it, then. I do not care for any strange jack who circles like a vulture."

Paget returned and Parker slipped away like the wraith he was. Moriarty looked at his watch; it was nearly midday and by now the others would be pulling in his army of mercenaries. He nodded, and together they went down into the "waiting room," across the warehouse floor to the outer door.

There was room outside the warehouse for a cab or carriage, even a large four-horse van, but the exit road led only down to the docks, not a convenient route for most of the departures made from the headquarters. Normal practice was for the warehouse to be approached, or quitted, on foot. One took a short walk down a narrow lane between crushed and leaning houses, emerging through an archway into the wider, if still unsalubrious, streets.

Paget stood at the doorway and gave a long low whistle. From somewhere at the end of the lane came an answering series of short whistles—one of Parker's lurkers indicating that all was clear.

The two men set off across the court and into the lane. Through the archway they could see Harkness with the cab drawn up at the curb.

They came out through the arch into the main street, and as they emerged Paget was distracted for a fleeting second by the sound of hooves. A small single-horse van was approaching from the left. As it drew in line with Moriarty's cab sudden hell broke loose.

There were four or five shots in all, the volley coming from the back of the van, ripping the air, crashing into the cab, splintering woodwork, slamming into the bricks around the arch like a handful of pebbles projected with great force—the noise of the explosions echoing with the whine of ricochets.

Harkness cried out as Paget hurled himself in front of the Professor who seemed to do a half-turn, a small gasping grunt coming from him as he wheeled. There was the clatter of the horse, the fat rumble of wheels and two more shots from the back of the van—one of which whizzed, like an angry vicious insect, over Paget's head, the other sharding a cobble some eighteen inches to the left. Then the van was gone and footsteps echoed urgently as two of the lurkers came running up.

The Professor lay on his back, blood soaking the upper left arm of his frock coat.

"He's hit, my God, the guv'nor's hit," Harkness cried, his voice rising to a screech.

The Professor pushed himself into a sitting position.

"Stop whining, you nickey bastard, and help me up."

His face was gray, and Paget thought he could detect fear hiding in the corner of the eyes, which screwed up with pain as they got him to his feet.

Together they helped the Professor down the alley, back into the warehouse where Fanny, Mary and Mrs. Wright alerted by the noise, fluttered around getting Moriarty to his chamber and stripping off the sleeve.

It was only a flesh wound, but painful nevertheless. Moriarty kept up a steady flow of abuse as they cleaned and dressed it.

"If this is the work of Butler and Green, I'll see them with their marbles chopped."

"We'll do for the bastards," soothed Paget.

"Do for them?" the Professor snarled. "No canting flash cove uses an iron on me. By Jesus, I'll see them both do a leap: What do they take me for? A gulpy?"

They brought him brandy, and the color soon returned to his face. All thoughts of going to see Abrahams that day had gone. Moriarty could think only of the night and ruination of the Peg's organization.

Paget was in great unease, for while all indications were that Moriarty still held the whip hand, Green and Butler must have great confidence to attempt the life of the Professor so deeply within his own domain. He saw also, in Moriarty's look, the sense of concern. It was something he had only viewed once before—when Holmes had had the Professor on the run, chasing across Europe, abandoning his plans and going into exile.

Crow's sergeant, a fairhaired, beefy lad of twenty-eight, was waiting for him at Horsemonger Lane with the police surgeon; Williams, the warder who had shown the girl in to see Moran; the turnkey who had found the body; the gatehouse warder; and the governor.

Crow talked to them each in turn, making constant references to Lestrade's report. Nothing new emerged except that the pompous little doctor could now say with authority that Moran had died of poisoning by *Strychnos* nux vomica, the poison having been inserted into both the pie and the wine delivered to the colonel.

Neither were there any new features added to the description of the girl, which, Crow reflected sadly, only proved how unobservant the turnkeys and warders of Her Majesty's Prisons could be. The girl was an identical copy of hundreds of others who lived in London. Again, he thought, it was a clear case for the building up of a complete crime index. Registration cards might have solved this one; as it was, they could only issue a description and hope that among the many young women who would doubtless be brought in for questioning they might find the girl who had so insidiously taken the poisoned food into the jail.

Eventually the inspector asked to see the cell, in Men's Block A, where Moran spent his last hours. Crow was also a great believer in a thorough examination of the scene of crime. But here there were no clues, except to previous occupants. Someone had scratched on the wall

21,000 times have I walked round this cell in a week

Another, his remand obviously over and sentence passed, had chipped out

Good-bye, Lucy dear,
I'm parted from you for seven long year

BILL JONES

Below, some cynic had added

If Lucy dear is like most girls,
She'll give few sighs and moans,
But soon will find among your pals
Another William Jones

Nothing. No scratched messages by Colonel Moran, no hints or traces. Only the stale smell of humanity thinly disguised by the pervading reek of disinfectant.

Crow returned with his heavy batch of papers to Scotland Yard, where, more from irritation than conscientiousness, he instructed his sergeant to see if there were any old reports or documents relating to the name Druscovich. The sergeant did not return to the office until nearly four o'clock, this time not only with paper referring to Druscovich but also to several other names—notably those of Palmer and Meiklejohn.

Crow cursed aloud and with some profanity. He had not been able to see the wood for the trees. Druscovich—he knew the name as well as his own, and it must have been a pretty dull copper who had put in his beat report without connecting the names, and an even duller sergeant. He could only presume that no senior officer had even looked at it.

Nat Druscovich: Chief Inspector Nat Druscovich. Chief Inspector Bill Palmer, and Inspector John Meiklejohn—the three members of the detective force who were sent down in 1877. All of them had got a two-stretch for complicity in the de Goncourt scandal, which had brought shame upon the whole force.

"Tanner," he bellowed to his sergeant, "there has to be a comprehensive file under the name de Goncourt. I want it here within the half hour, then you're in charge until I've taken it home and read it."

If Nat Druscovich had mentioned on his deathbed that someone called Moriarty was behind that swindle, then chances were it was true; and if that Moriarty were one and the same man as the Professor, then there could just be a small gleam among the darkness. Meiklejohn and Palmer were, presumably, still alive; and if one or both could confirm, then maybe some of the wild stories might possibly be true. Get Moriarty on an old score and who knew what walls might tumble down.

"You're a lying bastard!"

The blow that accompanied the spat statement caught Spear in the mouth. He went down, feeling the blood running from his lip on the scarred side.

Butler, who had come in behind Green, reached forward and pulled Spear to his feet. Two of the other men—Bovey and Gibbs, Spear thought they were called—climbed through the trap and ranged themselves behind Michael Green.

Green's face was flushed with anger. He had struck with his right fist, the left crumpling a piece of paper on which there was writing.

"Bleedin' liar, Spear."

"I never claimed to be Saint Peter."

"Your plan—your plotting to control Moriarty's mob: you and Paget and Ember and the Chink, Lee Chow. An actor hired to be the Professor."

Sarcasm etched Green's words, like drawing a grater over nutmeg, all punctuated by short heavy blows to the side of Spear's head.

"Easy, Mike, we want the mandrake alive."

Nobody ever called Spear a mandrake. His right arm came back, but Bovey and Gibbs were on him with restraining arms that were none too considerate.

"It was you who didn't believe the Professor was alive."

Spear's mouth was swelling fast making it difficult to speak with conviction.

"Well, I think he's dead now." Green's smile was tight-lipped, then and greasy as workhouse soup. "You saw him go down, Bovey?"

The man on Spear's right arm nodded with the whole of his body, making Spear wonder if he was, perhaps, a little uncertain.

"Like I said, Peg. We gave him six with the irons. I hit him at least twice, and he went down like a piece of dead meat. Paget as well I think."

"I wouldn't be as sure about Paget," chimed Gibbs.

Spear could smell the powder on them, the gloom rising in his guts and head.

"They went after your actor." Green held a fist under Spear's nose. "Well, they got him with barkers in Limehouse. Only when they came back, they said he was the spitting image of the Professor—and they're men as have seen Moriarty in both his guises. That worried me, but now I've had a letter delivered—one I've been waiting for. It's from someone that's seen him and been close to him. So tell me, brother Spear, when did Professor Moriarty rise from the dead? And what was the game? The one that's blown him says there's trouble."

Spear spat the blood from his mouth.

"If you've killed him, you shoful-shit, you'd better look about you, because the demons of hell will be at your windows."

"I'll give him the demons of hell." Butler came forward, his pasty face close to Spear. "Get him in a chair and I'll tune him. He'll sing like a bagpipes before I've done."

They pulled Spear backward, dragging his heels across the boards. He tried to struggle, but there was no escape. They held him down and passed ropes about his body. Butler had his coat off and was rolling back his sleeves.

"Right, Mr. Spear. What were you up to? What the plot? What the progress?" Butler turned to Bovey. "Go down and get Bridget to heat some water—boiling water. But don't tell her what it's for—you know women when they've had their fur tickled. And bring the pincers."

Spear, confused as he was, held fast to the fact that even with the Professor gone, Paget and the rest would still carry out the plan to blot Green and Butler from London.

Monday, April 9, 1894, 9:00 P.M. onward

(THE NIGHT OF THE PUNISHERS)

MORIARTY'S ARM WAS in a sling. Apart from that his appearance and demeanor had not altered. They had all been gathered together since late afternoon, bullies and hard men alike, generating almost a holiday atmosphere, for they were to be about the work which they enjoyed most.

They were fed in shifts, with Mrs. Wright, Fanny, and Mary McNiel bringing out batches of hot pies, baked potatoes and jugs of ale into the "waiting room." There was a lot of rough laughter and coarse humor:

"What's for dinner then?"

"There's four turds for dinner."

"Aye, stir turd, hold turd, treat turd and must turd."

Then, under Paget's supervision, they got down to the serious work of arming up. Revolvers and somewhat ancient pistols were taken from the cache in the store next to Paget's chamber. Knives, life preservers and holy-water sprinklers—the short bludgeon laced with sharp nails—razors and brass dusters.

Only when all was ready did Moriarty begin to divide the men into squads, each with a leader—a process that caused the rank and file to spill out of the "waiting room" and into the warehouse itself.

The Professor, standing on a box, then addressed the evil-looking army.

"It's bloody work I'm after tonight, lads," he began. "And why not? The bastards have tried to blood me today. Michael the Peg and Peter the Butler are the first men in this city to have opened me, and if you want the likes of them as your dons, then you know what to do." There was a murmur of protest, and cries of "No!" and "You're our man, Professor."

Moriarty smiled with his whole face. "Well, if I'm your man, you're my men."

A ragged cheering, at which the Professor put up a quieting hand.

"Never underestimate your enemy though, boys. Three years ago I would not have given you a brace of new-minted farthings for Michael Green and Peter Butler, even with their ways and ambitions. But make no doubt of it, they have gained much ground and they obviously think they're a match for us. They ring our manors and yesterday they took Spear. Today they tried for me. So now, from all hell, I want them smashed come Lombard Street to a China orange, or I'll wear the devil's claws myself."

This time the cheering was unanimous.

Moriarty then began the careful work of apportioning the night's business. It took more than an hour, because there was some argument about the quickest way to descend on certain of the houses and taverns and a little bickering regarding who would use the vans and wagons that had been provided by Parker.

From six o'clock onward there had been a steady stream of lads, Parker's runners, bringing in the latest intelligence on the movements of Green's and Butler's people. The two leaders of the rival gang were still at the flash-house in Nelson Street, which was Paget's target. And, as he loaded his old five-shot revolver, the Professor's most trusted man thought briefly of Spear, wondering what they would find when they burst into the Peg's hideout.

They were due to leave, by groups, starting from half-past seven, and before he went, Paget sought out Fanny for a short and snatched moment.

She looked concerned, having covered it all night by hard work, assisting with the cooking and feeding. Now the lines of anxiety rode in a small spray of barbs between her fine eyebrows.

"There's going to be blood let tonight, Pip, isn't there? A lot of blood."

"Some." He nodded, sounding as diffident as he could.

"Oh, Pip, take care, my love." Her hands pressed hard around his arms.

Paget drew back, opening his coat to show her the butt of his revolver.

"Anyone getting in my way, I'll see his innards first."

Fanny's frown increased. "Watch for yourself."

"Shall you be all right, Fan?"

She inclined her head.

"You've kept busy enough today, girl, what with all the kitchen bustle."

"It was pleasant."

"You get on with the Professor's pusher?"

"Mary?"

"Mary McNiel, who's giving her Mary Jane to the Professor."

Fanny Jones gave a little giggle. "She's all right, a bit of a know life. But that isn't surprising, the questions she asks."

"A listener?"

"Doesn't miss much."

Paget thought for a second or two. "Watch yourself, Fan. We've got Moriarty's protection, but Sal Hodges' girls know more tricks than you've ever thought about. Don't tell her much."

She reached up and kissed him, softly, on both sides of the mouth, her arms about his neck as though to hold him close, and away from what was to come. Paget looked at her, thinking he had the finest bargain a family man could ever want. Then he kissed her full on the mouth, held her tight for a moment, and was gone.

The Collins family was large: father, mother, one grandfather, two grandmothers, six children—ranging from eighteen to eleven—eight uncles, nine aunts, three of whom were true blood relatives, and some twelve cousins.

They lived in a sprawling old house that had once been part of the great St. Giles rookery, which was still in the process of being dismantled. The Collins' house was far from unique, but it remained a warren of its own; passages, stairs and room upon room interconnected with cupboards and traps—like some burrowed lair.

This leaning and crumbling complexity was ideal for the den in which Edward Collins—the family head, a scrawny, thin scarecrow—mustered his relatives in the forger's arts. There was space, both for living and working, and, essential for safety, the place could only be approached from one direction—along an alley leading off Devonshire Street. In the alley, day and night, one of the Collins lads or a trustworthy hireling lurked as a crow to warn off strangers. Edward Collins also kept four dogs—big brutes, kept low on food—chained near the door.

Ember, leading twelve heavy mobsmen, had the Collins family as their first goal, and they took the crow—a boy of some twelve or thirteen years—in a rush before he could even spot them in the dark or raise the alarm.

One of the bullies thumped the crow unconscious while another had him quickly tied with St. Mary's knot. The dogs were another matter. Roused by the scuffling, they set up a clamor of barking, straining at their chains. But almost before the young crow was down, Ember had led the others to the door. The lock was shattered by a pistol bullet—as were the two nearest dogs—and the force was inside, rampaging through the rooms, smashing and destroying molds and presses, spilling out the molten metal and throwing the working men to the ground.

Ember had only to make an example of three—Edward, his brother William, and Howard, a cousin—for they were the three most cunning fakers in the whole pack. The foxy little man gave the orders quickly so that there was no time for pause or sentiment because of the cries of women. Edward, William and Howard Collins were held down and had their hands and fingers well broken by the two heaviest punishers in the group.

Ember then led his people away, pausing only to shout back at the wailing, cowering bunch, "The Professor sends his compliments and will find work for all loyal and true family men."

Then they were gone and the time was only half-past nine. Half an hour earlier, a gang of some fifteen ruffians, led by the burly Terremant, began their rampage through Lambeth and toward the docks where the Peg's street women had their beats. The women they treated mildly, Terremant's men thrashing those they caught with short leather straps; the cash carriers, both in the streets or drinking in their three usual dens in the area between Lambeth Palace and Waterloo Bridge, were given stronger terms. Two lay dead before it was over, the rest were cut about like carpetbags or at least knocked insensible. Terremant then carried the thrust onward, turning his band toward the West End fringes of Charing Cross to seek out the rips, dippers, magsmen, rampsmen and macers whom they knew to be in Green's and Butler's employ.

Those they found were beaten or cut—one, a leading bully whom they suspected of being in high position with Green, was shot dead outside a public house off the Strand.

By this time the police were out in force, put on alert by the swift and sudden acts of violence that seemed to be sweeping large areas of the city, and two of Terremant's men were taken down by the river.

But in the meantime Lee Chow had overseen the destruction of the two brothels in Lupus Street, and the fashionable night house in Jermyn Street.

Lee Chow treated the whores much as Terremant's men had dealt with the soldiers' and sailors' women farther east. Only here there was more scandal and many a respectable tradesman and husband, even a few men of exceptional breeding, would not go near a knocking shop for a long while to come.

The interiors of the houses were ransacked—furniture broken, windows shattered, linen and clothing ripped to shreds. Three of the five girls who had absconded from Sal Hodges' house were taken in Lupus Street, quickly bundled outside (one wrapped only in a sheet), forced at gunpoint into a waiting van, and driven away for Sal to deal with as she saw fit.

The cash carriers and protectors, both in Lupus Street and Jermyn Street, were given short shrift. Within half an hour, following a running battle, two were dead, one dying, three maimed for life and the remainder seriously beaten.

Of Lee Chow's men, one died of a knife wound in Lupus Street, another was badly injured (at the same house), and one was taken by the police in the Haymarket.

John Togger, the fence who lived across the river in Bermondsey, among the reeking smells of the tanners and leather workers, was going through a haul of silver plate when his door splintered. At first he thought it was the police (whom he had so successfully evaded for many years). But the four men who came at him were not coppers. They beat him, cut him, left him senseless, then, ignoring the evil odors of the area, calmly loaded all his hidden and valuable goods and cash into the van that had brought them.

An hour later the same four men repeated the process with Israel Krebitz in Newington.

The half-dozen doss-houses up near Liverpool Street Station were easy meat, taking only a pair of men apiece. The housekeepers offered little resistance, and the inmates were too frightened by the fists, threats and oaths of the big, iron-muscled men, to offer any convincing argument.

They carried out Moriarty's orders with a system—lacerating the bedding, taking axes to the rough tables, chairs and beds, cracking the cooking pots and dishes, and, in many cases, the doss-keepers' heads.

Also about nine o'clock, The Nun's Head—together with a number of other taverns much frequented by the Green-Butler faction—suddenly appeared to acquire much new custom: aggressive men who started to brawl and argue within minutes of ordering their drinks. The arguments became more heated, and the brawls more violent; fists were thrown, then chairs and mugs, glasses and pots.

At The Nun's Head the most damage was done to regular customers, many of whom were known to the police. The main public rooms also sustained breakages and injuries that took a long time to repair.

The strength of Parker's lurkers around the house in Nelson Street was doubled during the early evening. They were all well hidden, some in disguise, all alert. At eight o'clock the first part of Moriarty's plan for that particular target was put into action. After eight, all persons arriving or leaving the house were quietly apprehended.

Every skill and artifice was used, so at about ten past the hour two muscular bruisers arriving at the front door found their attentions distracted by a young woman of trim and pleasant appearance. The girl seemed to materialize from the shadows before either of the callers could raise the knocker on the front door. She appeared to be distressed and in agitation regarding the whereabouts of some address in the neighborhood.

The two men, drawn much by the woman's pleasant demeanor, turned from the doorway and offered assistance, but as they stood in the thin, diffused light from the one bracketed streetlamp, they were taken from behind—hands clamped over their mouths, life preservers blotting consciousness. In a matter of seconds the would-be callers were dragged into the shadows and the young woman had melted away, leaving the street quiet again.

A short time later a boy, not unlike one of the runners used by Parker, came trotting down the street, heading undeniably for Green's door; but, as he too passed the shadows, a foot reached out and tripped him thudding into the gutter, whence he was quickly lifted bodily and carried away, a hard and calloused hand stifling any sound from his small mouth.

Just after the half hour, a tall bulky man, dressed in a long, dark greatcoat with a tall, battered hat crammed straight upon his head, came from the house. He closed the door carefully behind him and stood for a moment looking furtively up and down the street. His red, craggy face, scarred and pitted like a battlefield, was clearly visible, and it seemed as though he were listening for any sound, watching for any untoward movement.

After a second or two he turned and began walking steadily in the direction of the Commercial Road. He did not get there—finishing his journey, trussed like a Christmas goose, in the back of a small van, which also contained the bound and straining bodies of the two men and the boy who had recently attempted to enter the house.

Paget and his men arrived, singly and in twos and threes, gathering in the environs of the Commercial Road a shade before nine o'clock, the omnipresent Parker creeping out of the smoky darkness to appear at Paget's elbow.

"They're all still inside, but for one fellow we've taken," he breathed.

"Green and Butler as well?"

"Been there all day. You have 'em on dripping, Pip."

"I'll make the bastards drip." Paget's blood was up, ready for the most important fray of the night. "How many you got at the back, then?"

"Four, but none of any weight."

Paget nodded and issued calm instructions, sending four of his beefiest men to the rear of the house to cut off possible escapers and trap the inhabitants in a two-pronged attack.

He already had a rough idea of the interior, Moriarty having obtained details from one of the neighboring houses that was a twin to Green's headquarters. It was a tall, narrow building, stretching back a fair length to a small walled piece of unkempt garden. Inside the front door, a passage ran to a large room at the rear, one door to the left leading to what would normally be a front parlor. The downstairs room at the back of the house led, in turn, to a small kitchen, and the stairs in the hallway took one up to the second and third stories, which contained three rooms apiece. Above these there was an attic—visible from the street by small dormer windows.

When all was ready, Paget gave the long and trembling whistle, which was the signal, and the main body of his party moved at a rush toward the front door, which they smashed in with three splintering blows of a sledgehammer.

Michael Green had undoubtedly been alerted but was not yet fully prepared. As they piled through the door, a figure flitted from the front-parlor door: a lookout who had, perhaps, dozed at his post by the window. He hurled himself toward the big rear room, from where sounds—shouts and the noise of sudden scuffling—were emanating.

About six of Paget's men were in the hall when the fleeing figure reached the doorway, turned, and fired five shots into the advancing huddle. He fired wildly, but with some success: Paget was unhurt, but three of his men fell, one of them never to rise again.

Before the echo of the first shot had died, Paget had his revolver from his belt and was returning the fire. There was a crash from the rear of the house—Paget's men at the back forcing their entry— then, like a great wave, they rushed the room at the end of the passage, a tributary of five or so men leaving the main force to pound up the stairs.

The opposing parties met in the large rear room, Green's men sandwiched between Paget's two assault groups in a ferocious hand-to-hand grapple. They fought for their lives—all of them—for it was a deadly business and they did not play it by any rules of honor or chivalry or those drawn up by the Marquess of Queensberry.

The men closed on each other, biting, punching, gouging, kicking, using the elbow and knee as well as the fist, so that the heaving and enclosed space was filled with grunts and cries, the cracking of bone and knuckles and the raw shrieks of pain.

Paget was aware of Michael Green somewhere near the kitchen door, but he did not glimpse Butler in the general melee. He heaved himself in the direction of Green, but was occupied immediately by a short, barrel of a man much experienced in the arts of hand-to-hand combat. He came at Paget, first with a wicked long-bladed knife, swinging low and dangerously, holding the weapon in front of him, jabbing forward.

Paget, reacting in the only possible way—for he still had his revolver out—pulled back with his thumb on the hammer and pressed the trigger. There was a wasted fraction of a second before he realized the weapon was jammed; then at the last moment he brought the gun down hard on his assailant's knife hand. Heavy as he was, the man sidestepped lightly so that Paget's pistol only brushed his sleeve—Paget himself twisting to the right to avoid the vicious thrust aimed at his belly.

The revolver was useless except as a projectile and Paget, recovering, hurled it full at his attacker's face, but again the man ducked, head low, his body propelled fast toward Paget's front, now offered as a large target, the knife flicking from side to side so that Paget could not tell from where the final thrust would come.

He shot out a fist, aiming a long arm at the top of the chiv-artist's chest, a little below the throat, and felt it connect hard. His aggressor let out a sudden gasp, the breath expelled from him like steam out of a railway engine, his face red, with a cluster of small warts around the left nostril, sweat filmed over the brow, below untidy hair, and running in thin rivulets down his cheek.

Paget moved, surely and with speed, while the man was still winded, before his knife arm could come up again. It took only a second to consolidate: a knee hard to the groin, and the blade of his right hand chopping, like a cleaver, across the throat.

The barreled man gave a howl of agony as Paget's knee squelched home, doubling and dropping the knife, the cry cut short as the hand sank into his throat, sending him gurgling backward to crash against the feet of other struggling men and lie still.

Paget was braced forward, lunging out to grab at his revolver, which lay inactive on the floor, the air around him heavy with sweat and the scent of blood.

As he straightened, Paget saw Green send one of the punishers spinning back into the confusion as he whirled and grabbed for the kitchen door.

Paget went after him, shouldering the struggling, fighting pairs out of the way and fending off one attacker with his boot. But by the time he reached the door Green was away. A man's body lay close to the wall, almost blocking the kitchen entrance so that Paget had to hoist him away with his heel, losing precious moments before he followed the Peg into the darkness beyond.

He had lost him again, for the back door, leading from the kitchen to the walled garden, lay back on its hinges and from the outside he could hear panting and the thud of muffled footsteps.

Paget leaned against the jamb, quickly examining his revolver, clearing the blockage before lurching toward the outer door.

Michael Green was pulling himself up the far wall at the end of the garden, outlined for a moment against the dingy sky. Paget took careful aim and fired, but as he did so, Green launched himself down the far side of the wall.

By the time Paget reached the brickwork and followed the route taken by Moriarty's usurper, the wanted bird had flown, leaving neither trace nor sound.

Unwillingly Paget retraced his steps back to the house, where the confusion had died, for his men were by now in full control—tending their own wounded and lining up those of Green's men who were still able to stand. The job was done but, it seemed, without having accomplished the main task of taking either Green or Butler.

The men who had flushed out the upper stories of the house brought down only four of Green's bullies.

"No sign of Butler?" Paget asked several of the punishers, only to receive glum negative answers.

He knew they had not much time, for it could not be long before the police would arrive; but as he stood between the rear downstairs room and the kitchen, he became conscious, among the panting and groans around him, of a quiet, though stubborn, sound of sobbing. He traced the noise to the back of the kitchen, where a girl huddled in the corner.

Roughly Paget pulled her out into the light.

"What's this, then, Green's whore?"

He could hear the gruffness in his own voice and there was a picture in his mind of the circumstances reversed: Green saying something similar to Fanny Jones.

The girl blubbered, a tired and grafile florence. Her face grimed and her brown skirt stained with grease and too much exposure to cooking; her hair was a natural light shade, but unkempt and dirty: in all a sorry sight.

"Who are you then? Come on, girl, we haven't time to waste." Again rough and jabbing, the words like blows.

"The attic . . ." the creature sniveled. "For God's sake, sir, get to the attic. . . ."

"Butler? Is Butler in the attic?"

"No, sir, he went over the wall after your men broke in. He gave me this." Paget could now see the dark swelling and broken skin on the girl's left cheek. "The attic. A man called Bert. . . ."

In the fury of the attack Paget had momentarily forgotten Bert Spear. He made for the stairs, motioning two of the punishers to follow, dragging the still tearful girl with him.

Spear was alone in the attic, lying on his back, across the dirty mattress. For a minute they thought he was dead, for Green and Butler had left him in a pitiful condition, with his face battered and caked with blood, the brands of burns on his shoulders and upper arms, and unspeakable things done to his fingernails and hands.

Only as they lifted him did Spear regain consciousness and groan.

"It's all right, Bert. It's Pip. We've got you now. We're taking you back to Limehouse."

Weakly Spear lifted his head. "You get the bastards, Pip?"

"Not all, but Green's organization's smashed for good."

Spear appeared to smile. "The girl . . . the girl, Bridget. Good girl . . . get her out."

Paget turned toward the slattern. "Is that you?"

She nodded. "I'm Bridget. He was good to me."

"You'd best come with us then."

They carried Spear out and laid him in one of the carts waiting in the side lanes. When it rumbled away, Paget took the girl by the arm.

"Come on then." He smelled the reek of Green's house still on her. "There's a cab waiting near Aldgate. Can you walk that far?"

She nodded. "Will he be all right?"

Paget drew her alongside him, stepping out since he did not want any contact with the police, who were by this time in Nelson Street.

"Who? Bert Spear?" he asked.

"Yes."

"He'll be there before us. They'll look after him."

She tried to fall into step beside him, almost running to keep up.

"Are you the Professor's men?" she asked, panting with the exertion.

"What do you know of him?"

"I heard things. Back there. Even though they kept me in the house I still heard things."

"They kept you in? For what purpose?"

"Too cook for them and serve them. . . ." She paused. "In

every way. Bastards, you should've got the Peg and that brute Butler."

"It's what we came for. But we'll catch them, girl. We'll get them yet. Their structure is shattered, and they cannot hide from the Professor forever."

They came to the cab and Paget helped her inside. It would be interesting, he considered, to find out what manner of woman lay hidden behind the dirty and bedraggled creature whom Green and Butler had undeniably so misused. There had to be something in her, some spirit or attraction, for Spear to have shown the concern he had done from his tortured condition.

Quite suddenly Pip Paget felt fatigued in mind and body. The scent of the night's business was still in his nostrils and the bruises on his aching limbs. He very much wanted to hold Fanny close and hear her whisper in his ear, and, as he felt the desire, so he experienced the same confusing sense of dissatisfaction that came when thinking of Fanny—the small sunlit picture of the pair of them, and the rose-trellised cottage with the children around the woman's skirts, and clean air in his lungs.

He pushed the thoughts away, knowing how much of his life he owed to Professor Moriarty, and how impossible it would be to live any other kind of life than the one already etched out for him by his master in crime. Paget would not have understood if someone had told him that he was a romantic at heart.

The Limehouse headquarters ran with activity: men having their wounds tended by the women, others sorting through the goods pillaged from Togger and Krebitz, taking drink and even washing the night's sweat from their bodies—not a favored pastime among their fraternity, but one encouraged by the Professor.

In his chambers Moriarty heard the news and was elated by the way in which his men had demolished his rivals, though he was profoundly disturbed and irritated to hear that both Green and Butler had so narrowly missed being taken.

"You think they had prior intelligence of our plans?" he asked Paget, who sat in front of the desk with the dust and blood of the night still on him.

"They were certain sure that you had returned. You know that by the ache in your own shoulder." Moriarty still wore a sling on his damaged arm. "But," Paget continued, "I do not think they knew any full details. Unless . . ." His voice trailed away as though carried on the wind.

"Unless?" The Professor fixed him with the deep eyes, head turning slowly twice.

Paget sighed. "Unless they wrang it from Spear, though I doubt that, for the preparation was little. It was as though they had just got wind of matters and were desperate what to do. After all, none of their other people were warned."

"Then it's simply a feeling you have? Some kind of intuition?"

"You might say that. It is a concern."

Moriarty nodded. "We must talk to Spear."

"If he can talk. He's badly hurt, Professor."

Spear had been taken to his own chambers and the women had stripped and bathed him and cleaned his wounds, putting linen rags smothered in picric ointment on the burns, and wrapping his damaged hands and fingernails in bandages spread with beeswax and sweet oil. (Mrs. Wright knew some of the simple healing arts of nursing.) They also gave him brandy in small sips, and by the time Moriarty and Paget arrived at the bedside, Spear was lying on the lip of sleep.

"You will recover, Spear," Moriarty said quietly, yet with great authority. "But you must tell us, did you break under torture? Did you blow on us, Spear? The truth will not hurt now."

Spear groaned, slowly opening his eyes. His voice was distant, but he was not delirious.

"I told nothing . . . nothing. . . . Toward the end . . . they knew something was afoot. . . . Take care, there is someone close to you, Professor . . . someone was giving them word. . . ." He was too weak to continue, but in a last effort he breathed. "Bridget . . . where's Bridget?"

"She's here and safe, Bert," Paget leaned forward, his lips near to Spear's ear. "She shall come to you directly."

He was sure that Spear did not hear Moriarty say softly. "After we've talked with her."

They went back to the Professor's chambers, pausing on the way to speed men back to their rooms or whatever places they called home and send word that the girl Bridget should be brought to the Professor.

After helping with Spear, Fanny Jones and Mary McNiel had taken Bridget in hand. They had made preparations in the kitchen to deal with the wounded, so there was a great deal of hot water, boiled upon the hobs and on top of the stove as well as in the big copper.

They now locked the kitchen door, brought out the big tin bath and set to scrubbing the unhappy girl clean, toweling her dry, then washing her hair in a mixture Mary had learned of Sal Hodges— strong liquor ammonia, spirits of rosemary, tincture of cantharides, almond oil and lavender water.

When the girl was dry, Mary McNiel rubbed at Bridget's long

hair while Fanny went off to her closet to find her one spare dress with an underskirt, long white drawers, stockings and shoes, in which they dressed the girl, combing out her hair and applying a little dry starch mixed with water and arrowroot to the livid bruise on her cheek. It was during these last stages of preparation that Paget arrived to say Bridget was required in the Professor's room.

She was, not unnaturally, frightened in the Professor's presence, but his strange and quite mesmeric effect soon calmed her.

"Tell us about yourself, Bridget," he said to her, and she responded by telling them the story of how, at the age of seventeen, she had been sent by her father from Ireland to live with an aunt and uncle in Liverpool.

Moriarty smiled and told her they would get on well, for his boyhood had been spent in Liverpool. She had been there for only a year when she met up with a young sailor called Raybet. He persuaded her to go with him to London, where she lived with him near the London docks, a situation of which she soon tired, for while he was only on short runs between London and the north coast of England, he began to spend more and more of his time with his cronies, leaving her to fend for herself. Money was always short and she admitted that for a while she had hawked herself and worse, for Bridget was a villain at heart.

Moriarty then asked her where she thought either Green or Butler might be hiding, but she seemed to have no idea: all that appeared uppermost in her mind was the fact that she was dreadfully hungry and in need of rest. Moriarty softened, telling Paget to take her down to Kate Wright and Fanny Jones and see that she was fed and given a bed.

At the door Bridget turned to thank the Professor.

"There is one matter," she said, fatigue fraying her voice. "They had a message this morning, before they got rough with Bert. It was brought by a boy I had not seen before, and after Mike Green read it he was blind angry. I heard them talking, and you were mentioned, sir. The message was from someone close to you—a woman, I think."

Paget closed the door again, ushering her back into the chair, where they carefully probed her with questions for the next half hour, discovering that Green and Butler had been expecting another message, which had failed to arrive. They also deduced that if there were a traitor, it could be only one of four people.

After Paget had taken the girl down to the kitchen he returned to Moriarty's chambers. Both men looked grave.

"See that a guard is put on her door and mention none of this to the others," the Professor ordered. "I don't want her left with any of them for long periods."

"We have the prisoners taken at Nelson Street," Paget said, meaning the two men and the boy they had caught going to the house and the man who had emerged before the assault.

The remainder of Green's and Butler's men were left at the house, and many were now in police custody.

"It would be best if we talked with them, I think. Tomorrow though, my mind is buzzing tonight."

It was the early hours of Tuesday morning before Paget lay close, though more silent than usual, beside the sweet form of Fanny Jones.

Tuesday, April 10, to
Thursday, April 12, 1894

(CROW AMONG THE PIGEONS)

THE OUTBREAK OF violence which had occurred during the night of April 9 caused Inspector Crow much concern. A number of innocent people had been injured, as well as many who were long removed from blamelessness. As always, those who were known villains offered little in the way of intelligence.

It was clear that the violence had been caused by a head-on clash between two bands of rogues, and concern ran high at Scotland Yard, for there seemed to be much organization behind the villains.

But Crow was more concerned about the matter which had come to his attention with the name Druscovich: that was the important lead for him, so he handed over the question of Monday's violence to his subordinates, instructing them to be present whenever possible at the interrogation of those concerned; to take note if the names of Moriarty or Colonel Moran drew any reaction; and to keep details, which were to be handed over to him for examination at leisure.

Having relegated this authority, Angus McCready Crow set about his own investigations concerning the three former detectives, Druscovich, Meiklejohn and Palmer, and the unhappy part they had played in the de Goncourt scandal.

The facts of the case were complex, and it took Crow much time to go through the files. In the early 1870's there had been a plague of swindles and frauds, all bearing the same hallmark, and all concerned with horse racing.

The method used is not unknown today. It operated mainly through advertisements placed in newspapers, both at home and abroad, which claimed that a company—usually with some notable names on the board of directors—was prepared to take the pain out of gambling on the sport of kings. All the punter had to do was send the money. The company would place the bets for him, offering a quick and easy return in winnings.

The human race is ever gullible as far as easy winnings are concerned—people being all too eager to send hard cash. In many cases individuals received courteous receipts, others did not. Needless to say, nobody got any winnings.

Certainly people complained, but when the company offices were investigated, all the police found was either an empty office or an accommodation address.

By 1873 it was estimated that the swindle was netting a freezing £800,000 a year, a profit too high for the detective force to stand idle; so Chief Inspector Clarke, a man with a tidy if unimaginative mind, was put in charge of the case. Quickly it became apparent that Mr. Clarke had a great deal of trouble on his hands. During the months that followed, Clarke came within an ace of catching the gang, but by the time he got to the address supplied by unwilling victims, the perpetrators of the frauds had flown, leaving little trace but for the ashes of burned papers.

At last the chief inspector was left with only one unsavory conclusion: Someone within his own force was warning the villains.

Hard though this was to stomach, suspicion pointed in the direction of a sergeant called John Meiklejohn. But there was no hard evidence and no real clues regarding the villains. Clarke and his men sifted and searched, painstakingly going about their craft.

Then the groundwork began to pay off. Two convicted criminals, a man called Walters—landlord of The Bunch of Grapes in Hilborn—and an Edwin Murray, came under strong suspicion. Eventually a petty criminal laid charges against them for assault and in the process sang a long song connecting Walters and Murray with the turf frauds, together with a so-called mastermind named Kurr.

Walters and Murray were arrested, but Kurr escaped by his teeth's skin, having been warned in advance. Walters and Murray were tried on the assault charge, found not guilty and discharged, only to be rearrested on charges of conspiracy to defraud.

The evidence against Meiklejohn being the gang's man at the Yard was inconclusive, as indeed was the case against Walters and Murray. They were both given bail, which they broke, disappearing, it was rumored, to America.

In the meantime the chief inspector received information from a Mr. Jonge, resident in the Isle of Wight. Jonge, as it turned out, told little, except that he had been asked by Walters to translate some newspaper advertisements for insertion into foreign papers. Needless to say, these advertisements concerned the turf frauds.

No action could be taken against Meiklejohn, but as a precaution he was lent to the Midland Railway and given the rank of inspector with the company's police.

The whole fraudulent carbuncle revealed its second head in the winter of 1877, when a firm of lawyers, based in Paris, called on Superintendent Williamson, head of the detective force. Their client was the Comtesse de Goncourt, who, they suspected, had been swindled out of £10,000 by the English racing investors. The initial approach had been made by a Mr. Montgomery, who foolishly supplied the Comtesse with details of his address in London.

Chief Inspector Clarke, who spoke no other language save his native tongue, handed the case over to Chief Inspector Nat Druscovich, the Criminal Investigation Department's language expert.

Druscovich set off to arrest Montgomery, but returned alone and unhappy. Clarke had told no one else that the arrest had been imminent; yet once more there had been prior warning—and this time without the help of Meiklejohn, who was busy dealing with the criminal tribulations of the Midland Railway.

The finger could point to only one man—Druscovich, who was left in charge of the case. In a matter of days Druscovich appeared to have won back trust, for he traced some of the notes paid out on the Comtesse's check. The trail led to Edinburgh where the notes had been cashed by a man answering the description of none other than the helpful Mr. Jonge, who had been so forthcoming at the time of Walters' and Murray's arrests.

Jonge was shadowed and traced, with a man named Gifford, to the Queen's Hotel, Bridge of Allan, where they had met up with another suspect—Inspector Meiklejohn. Druscovich was dispatched to make the arrest, again missing the criminals by a short head.

Clarke and the superintendent immediately ordered both Druscovich and Meiklejohn to explain themselves in writing. Druscovich said that these criminals were known to be elusive and he was only fallible; Meiklejohn claimed that he had every right to be at the Queen's Hotel, Bridge of Allan, as he was on company business, looking for a missing trunk. He had no idea he was talking with wanted men when he had shared a meal with Jonge and Gifford.

Druscovich then took the action that led to his downfall, presumably in an attempt to show innocence. He forwarded three pieces of evidence to the Yard. First, some blotting paper taken from the hotel smoking room, upon which were the smudged, blotted words, "Keep the lame man out of the way." Jonge was lame.

Second, a telegram addressed to Mr. Gifford at the Queen's Hotel, reading:

IF SHANKS IS NEAR THE ISLE OF WIGHT LET HIM LEAVE AT ONCE AND SEE YOU. LETTER FOLLOWS. W. BROWN. LONDON.

Jonge's home was in Shanklin.

Last there was a letter:

Mr. William Gifford—
Dear Sir.
There is very strong particulars from Edinburgh, which I suppose you know of. They have the address at the shop here. It is also known that you were in London a day or two ago. Perhaps you had better see me, for things begin to look fishy. News may be given to the Isle of Wight—where Shanklin is. You know best. D goes to Wight tomorrow. Send this back. W. Brown, who was with you at the "Daniel Lambert."

The handwriting was that of the most senior and trusted officer in the CID—Chief Inspector William Palmer.

A few days later Jonge, Kurr, Murray, and three others were arrested by the Dutch police in Rotterdam and brought back to London for trial. Jonge was sentenced to fifteen years' penal servitude; Kurr and three others got ten years apiece; and Murray eighteen months as an accessory.

Within a few weeks Druscovich, Meiklejohn and Palmer drew two years apiece, and even Chief Inspector Clarke was implicated by Kurr—a particularly vicious and slanderous attempt, which failed.

Inspector Crow mulled over the files, reading the details three times. There was this one shred of evidence, now linking Moriarty with the event, coming from Nat Druscovich's deathbed. It was a matter for serious thought and detailed investigation. More than ever Inspector Crow yearned for the kind of crime indexes and registration systems the Continental police had at their fingertips. He was also starting to wonder about Moriarty, possibly for the first time in any serious context.

It was essential that he should talk quickly to at least one of the main cast of characters who had been involved in the de Goncourt scandal. Even if they could be found he had no desire to talk with Jonge or Kurr or any of that ilk. He would have to make his first appeals to the sensibilities of either Meiklejohn or Palmer.

Within half an hour he was in possession of the fact that the last report on Palmer was that he managed a public house in Horton. Crow believed in striking with a hot iron and immediately made the tedious journey—to no avail. On arrival, late in the afternoon, he discovered that Palmer had only recently given up the public house in order to emigrate to Australia and a new life. It puzzled Crow, for Palmer must by now be almost sixty years of age—an odd time of life to start growing new roots.

It was late when the inspector got back into London. He collected the day's reports—concerning the violence of Monday night—and wearily retraced his steps toward the tender charms of Mrs. Sylvia Cowles in King Street. On the following day he would start looking for Meiklejohn.

At a little before ten o'clock on Tuesday morning Moriarty called a short conference with Ember, Lee Chow, Paget and Parker. Spear had spent an uneasy night, was still in much pain, but the fever that had initially swept over him appeared to have abated.

Lee Chow was entrusted with getting the loot taken from Togger and Krebitz over to Solly Abrahams, together with a message that Moriarty himself would be seeing the old fence within twenty-four hours.

Parker, who was still making inquiries about Inspector Crow, received orders to send his men out and about to judge opinion in the underworld, to reinforce Moriarty's case, and to continue the search for Green and Butler. Ember's job lay in contacting the trio of thieves, Fisher, Clark and Gay, ordering them to the Limehouse headquarters for conference with their leader.

"I have to talk with them about the Harrow business," the Professor said. "There's swag enough in that for all." Then, turning to Paget, "I shall need you with me, as you have the lie of the land."

Paget looked glum, hoping Moriarty was not going to insist on his going on the actual crack.

"No need to look so hang-dog, Pip." The Professor rarely addressed any of the "Praetorian Guard" by their Christian names, particularly in front of the others. "You are to be married. Has Fanny set the date yet?"

Paget shook his head, flashing Moriarty what could have been interpreted as a dangerous look.

"Well, then, I'll set it for her." Moriarty smiled. "How about a week today? We should have need for jollification by then."

There was murmured assent and Moriarty instructed them that word should be passed.

"It will be a day of celebration. A proper hammering, Pip, that's what you'll get. A wedding fit for a king and queen."

The big, tough Paget came near to blushing.

"We must consolidate." The Professor switched easily to another subject, shifting his weight in the chair, and fingering the sling in which his damaged arm still rested. "I will not have any other fumbling villains trying to oust me from my rightful seat or split my family. On Friday my people arrive from Paris, Rome, Madrid and Berlin. They must see we are on top of matters here. Before then I'll need the Jacobs boys back in the Chapel. Ember"—turning sharply to the little man—"after you have relayed my message to Fisher and the others you are to get Alton at the 'Steel. I'll talk with him tonight."

The meeting was over and Moriarty was left alone with Paget, whom he had instructed to remain behind.

"Have you had more thoughts on what we discussed last night?" asked the Professor once the others had removed themselves well out of earshot.

"It can only possibly be one of the four." Paget's face registered extreme unease. "Yet that's almost unthinkable. We should question those that were taken outside Nelson Street last night." He bit his lip. "Are you serious about the wedding?"

Moriarty was silent for a full minute before he nodded in acquiescence. "Deadly serious." His good arm flapped imperiously as though signaling that part of the conversation was over. "Is Terremant still in the building?"

"Terremant and four of the others. One watching Roach and Fray."

"Good, we shall need them."

"The others are keeping an eye on the Nelson Street crew."

"And the boy has been kept separate?"

"The three men are together. The boy has the secure chamber next to mine."

"Good, then we will see the boy first."

The architect and the builder who had made the secret conversion of the warehouse were both cunning men. Moriarty's chambers were constructed on the second story of the building, occupying the rear, and placed above the area which formed the "waiting room" and kitchen. When one walked into the main, ground-level floor of the warehouse, it appeared barren, deserted and broken down to a state of near decay. Few would have guessed that the long walls running to left and right, were false, concealing connecting passages linked with the kitchen area.

From these passages, spiral iron staircases ran up to the remainder of the second floor, the whole being a hive of living and sleeping rooms, storerooms and small, bare brick cells perfect for housing weapons, loot or, at times like this, prisoners.

Paget's room was large, with windows, reminiscent of those one saw in artists' studios, angled toward the dirty sky yet providing good light. It contained the cozy necessities of life—a bed, writing table, another table, from which he and Fanny took their meals, stand chairs, armchairs, and in one corner a wardrobe of modern design, which was complemented at the other side of the room by a matching chest of drawers.

Several pictures decorated the walls, mostly cheap prints, the remnants of small robberies or petty filchings, and on the chest of drawers a pair of silver-backed brushes lay neatly next to a lady's silver hand mirror.

The room was flanked by two of the many brick cells: one used as a storeroom for weapons, the other at present occupied by the boy whom Parker's men had waylaid outside Green's house in Nelson Street. It was to this cell that Paget and Moriarty made their way—Paget having collected the key from the kitchen where Bartholomew Wright had charge of the locks and their attendant pieces of machinery.

The boy was lying on the floor, his knees pulled up to his stomach, the small undernourished face thrown back and contorted with pain. He was very still, and Paget's first thought was that this must have been how Moran looked when they found him in Horsemonger Lane Jail. There was a little vomit and the remains of a meal—some bacon, sausages and a mug of beer—scattered across the table. The memory Paget always retained thereafter was, oddly, the child's hair, matted, curly, stiff and springy with grime.

Moriarty cursed softly and Paget's heart dropped, as though to his bowels.

"Poison." Moriarty spoke in a whisper. "Poison, the same as the colonel."

Paget's face was set like a granite figure on some churchyard memorial.

"His breakfast." The voice was dead as the lad on the floor. "Fanny fetched him his breakfast this morning. I heard it while I was in the kitchens. She took breakfast to Roach and Fray first, then the other three, and the boy last."

Moriarty's tone was bitter cold. "I am on the brink of controling the crime of Europe, yet I cannot wholly control my own people here in the Great Smoke." He took a long, tremulous breath, and Paget could feel the fury building, so tangibly that he might almost have touched it. "Say nothing yet. See if Parker is still in the house. If so, bring him here. Did Fanny take the breakfasts on her own?"

Paget shook his head slowly. "She had one of Terremant's lads with her, I think."

"I'll have him up also. Leave him at the end of the passage until we're ready for him."

Paget set off quickly in search of the chief lurker and the punisher who had been Fanny's escort, his mind confused and grim, for he did not doubt the boy's death was the work of whoever had infiltrated Moriarty's domain.

Parker had not yet left, and within minutes Paget returned to the cell with him, leaving the punisher, as instructed, at the end of the passage.

Parker frowned as he entered the cell, bending quickly over the young corpse. He straightened and stepped back with a long whistle of surprise.

"I did not see him in the light last night." He looked up at the Professor. "This is young Slimper's brother. I was about to start using him—been pestering me for some weeks."

"Then get young Slimper to me," snapped the Professor. "Call Terremant's man."

The burly punisher came up at Paget's shout.

"You went with Fanny Jones this morning when she took breakfast to the prisoners?" Moriarty asked.

"I did, sir."

They kept the man a little to one side of the door so that he could not see into the room.

"Tell me the order of things."

"We went first to Roach and Fray. Then back to the kitchen for the food for the other three—we had to make two journeys, young Fanny made a joke, saying it was worse than being in service again."

"Did she now?" Moriarty showed no humor.

"Then we went back down again and she got the lad's breakfast. I was going to come up with her, but she said there was no need seeing how he was only a lad."

"And who was preparing the food?"

"Mrs. Wright, sir, as always. I think Mary McNiel was helping this morning."

"Helping her? How, with the frying?"

"No, with the dishing out. She dished out the lad's sausage and bacon, I know that because Mrs. Wright poured the beer for him."

Moriarty frowned. "And the new girl, Bridget?"

Paget answered for him. "They've let her sleep late today."

The Professor made a grunting noise, gruff from the back of his throat.

"Tell nobody we've talked to you." He looked hard into the punisher's eyes, dismissing him with a curt nod.

Together, Paget and Moriarty carefully locked the cell door, Moriarty returning to his chambers while Paget, under orders to retain the cell key, went to fetch the first of the other prisoners.

Ten minutes later the man whom they had grabbed coming from Nelson Street stood between two of the punishers, in front of Moriarty's desk. Paget sat to one side, conscious that he was now wholly working as the Professor's chief of staff.

The prisoner's name was unromantic enough, Zebedee Smith, a man of around forty years of age, big though flabby from drunkenness and fleshly lusts. Paget knew him both by sight and reputation. Some ten years previously he had been in clover, a leading man in the Swell Mob, an expert pickpocket, caught only once, for stealing a gold watch near St. Paul's—for which act he had served two years in the 'Steel. It said much for the harshness of that prison that Smith had been a lost cause once released, reduced within a few months to working the kinchen-lay. But old lags die hard, and from stealing from children he gravitated to running a small school of young lads who did the thieving for him.

It was only now that Paget remembered the couple of whispers that had come to him in the past year about Smith: that he was becoming a man of resources once more, being expert with his lads, who appeared to like him and were prepared to work long hours on his behalf.

Moriarty's voice cut like a butcher's blade when he spoke to the prisoner, his eyes small and gleaming, the head performing its iguanalike oscillation.

"We know about you," he began. "So there's no need to lie or pull the faker with me, Smith. If my lads had their way, you would have been meat last night, but I'm a just man."

If there was fear in Smith he did not show it as he stood silent and stock still.

"You are good with the kinchen. You worked for Green, so bear with me, Zebedee Smith. Green is smashed, so it follows that you are smashed also. But there is a chance that you may work again if you answer honestly and can be proved, in time, to be loyal."

"You shouldn't trust one like that, Professor." Paget, acting the part, spat, turning his head away. "That one holds a candle to the devil."

"I know my business, Paget. There's work in this horse yet." He turned back to Smith. ''You know a boy called Slimper?''

''I know a lot of boys.''

''He's on the dodge. Do a ripper on him and let's have it finished.'' Paget feigning disgust at the seeming kindness of his leader.

''A boy named Slimper, Zebedee?''

Moriarty took no notice of the inherent violence in Paget's tones, it was a piece of dialogue well rehearsed.

Slowly, ''I know a Slimper, yes.''

Moriarty nodded to Paget, who went to the door, returning with young Slimper who worked for Parker.

''Is this the lad?''

Smith shook his head. ''Like him, but this one is bigger built.''

''You know this gentleman, Slimper?'' Kindness oozing from Moriarty to the frightened boy.

''No, sir. I never seen 'im before.''

Moriarty dismissed the boy.

''The other Slimper, now. He worked for you, yes?''

Silence for a brief second before Smith answered. ''Yes, I had a Slimper working.''

''What kind of work?''

''Dipping and the like.''

''Nothing else?''

''Not for me.''

''Then for Green. Did he do anything for Green? Remember that Green is a dead man and cannot help you now.''

''All right. Yes, he did running errands for Green.''

''What errands?''

''I don't know. Messages and the like.''

''And he ran messages for Green yesterday.''

''Aye.''

''Between Green and whom?''

''I don't know, I swear I don't know.''

''But he brought a message to Nelson Street yesterday morning.''

''Yes.''

''And you were expecting him again last night?''

''The Peg was expecting him.''

''With a message?''

''Yes.''

''And he did not turn up?''

Smith was on edge now with all the fast questions. Paget tipped him further.

''Have done, Professor. He'll not help you. I'll slit him myself.''

"I don't know who it was from." The rest chased out in a rush from Smith's lips. "I know it was about you, Professor, and it was from some woman. They had a message brought by the lad in the morning. Then there was trouble with Bert Spear. Green and Butler were like cats on hot coals, waiting for the lad to return. When he didn't come, they sent me to find him. That's when your people collared me, and that's the truth, Professor, the stone truth."

"I believe you, Smith."

Paget made a noise meant to convey doubt.

"Paget!" Moriarty made the order sound harsh. "Put Smith in a secure chamber by himself. It would be best to keep him apart from the other two."

The pair they had caught on their way into Nelson Street were nothing: a couple of bullies sent for by Green, obviously knew little, were frightened particularly by Paget's bellicose attitude, and the fact that they were facing the great Professor Moriarty for the first time, uneasy with the knowledge that they had been allied to the losing side. They could add no intelligence, so were sent back to their cell in great disquiet.

"You understand the personal risk you take now?" Paget asked.

Moriarty smiled, as one would condescendingly look upon a bright child.

"Indeed, Paget, I know all too well what risk I run, and we must be careful to lull suspicion and yet be certain not to overlook anything."

"I hope you are not looking toward me as a food taster, like the Eastern potentates have in their service."

"It would be a good position for friend Smith." Moriarty was still smiling, his lips and eyes changing slightly so that more than a hint of evil now lurked in the face. "No, my friend, I think more drastic measures are called for."

They spoke for some ten minutes, after which Paget went up to the boy's cell, tidied the body, wrapping it in a blanket and circling it with stout cords. That night they would add chains and weights; then the body could be consigned to the river and a safe eternal rest.

When he got down to the kitchen, Paget saw that Mary McNiel was gone. She would be with the Professor now as they had arranged. His instructions were to talk with Fanny, and it would not be easy, for having the girl he loved suspected of such a murder was no simple matter—especially as he was duty bound not to arouse her own suspicions. He called to her from the doorway, making apologies to the Wrights for borrowing her for a few moments. He was pleased to see that Terremant and one of his other men were out in the "waiting room," their eyes watchful: Moriarty had undoubtedly already made arrangements with them for what was to follow.

"What is it, Pip, you look so serious?" she asked when they reached his chambers.

Paget kissed her lightly on the mouth and smiled.

"Some of it is grave, some happy. Which would you like to hear first?"

She threw back her head, laughing.

"I think I know your happy news. They were teasing me in the kitchen. Is it true? The Professor says we're to be married next week?"

"A week today, girl. Spliced and banqueted like kings and queens, the Professor said."

"Oh, Pip."

"How will you like being Mrs. Pip Paget, then?"

She gave a series of little squeals as Paget lifted her in his big hands and whirled her around, his face becoming serious as he gently let her down to the floor again.

"Now there's some unpleasantness, Fan."

She looked at him with large, innocent eyes, full of questions.

"There's been a horrible accident, Fanny, and this may upset you."

"Accident? Bert Spear's all right, isn't he? He hasn't. . .?"

"Bert's fine. It's the boy we took last night. The one in the secure room next to us here."

"That little fellow. Oh, Pip, he's such a frightened rabbit."

"He was."

"What?"

"He *was* a frightened rabbit, Fanny."

He held her in his eyes, watching for any flicker, any sign that might give her away. She merely looked at him, her eyes widening.

"He *was* . . .?"

"He's dead, Fan."

"But I saw him this morning. I took his breakfast in to him."

"That's just it, Fan. His breakfast."

It took a few seconds for the light to break into her muddled brain and her mouth to open in a gaping tremble.

"Not like the colonel? Oh no, Pip. Oh God, the Professor wouldn't do a thing like that to a—No."

Paget caught her hard by the shoulders.

"No, Fanny, not the Professor. It can only have been an accident. He'll be talking to Kate and Bart Wright soon enough: Some

of the stuff they used on Moran must have found its way into the
beer or the mug or even onto the plate you used for his sausage. It
can only have been an accident.''

She was crying, shoulders heaving, nose reddening and the tears
welling out, chapping her pink cheeks in raw streaks. If she was a
bad one, thought Paget, she was a good actress and ought to be on
the stage where she rightly belonged.

He left Fanny, eventually, still upset, blaming herself.

''That's twice, Pip. Twice I've taken the means of death to
people. I'll burn in hell for it, burn in hell.''

He quietened her, told her not to fret, and to stay in their room
until she felt better.

''There will be a lot going on around the place for the next hour or
so, Fanny love, you're best out of it.''

Mary McNiel had left the Professor by the time Paget got to his
chambers.

''I do not know.'' Moriarty was gazing from his window. ''I
really have no idea, Paget. And you?''

''The same. Shall I get Bart and Kate?''

''Let's have it over with. I'll not eat or drink happy until we've
done with them all.''

Paget returned a few minutes later, shepherding the Wrights into
the room, closing the door behind him and standing, arms folded, in
front of it.

Moriarty motioned the Wrights into chairs and began, telling
them that there had been a fearful accident and that somehow the
boy's meal had become tainted with the strychnine they had used on
Moran.

''But I keep it locked, in my private cupboard.'' Kate Wright was
suddenly white with fear.

''If it could have got into the boy's food or drink, then other
things might be poisoned also.'' Bartholomew Wright's voice
moved, falsetto, up the scale.

''Quite so.'' The Professor leaned back. ''That is why Terremant
and one of the other punishers are at this moment destroying all the
food in the house and emptying all the ale and wine that is not safely
unopened.''

''But—'' Kate Wright began, changing her mind because of the
look in the Professor's eyes.

''I want you, Kate, to go down with Paget here, and give him the
poison. He will get rid of it. After that we are making arrangements
for you to have one of the carts. Terremant and the other will go with
you to buy fresh food and replenish the drink. I cannot take chances,
Kate. We will have all the plates, mugs, knives and the like

thoroughly washed in boiling water also. The girls can do it while you are getting the provisions. That way we'll avoid any similar unpleasantness.''

Paget went down with Mrs. Wright, returning with the small blue bottle marked with the distinctive skull and cross bones. When the Wrights finally left, Moriarty went again to stand by his window.

"They will all be watched like hawks from now on. I have sent for Parker to bring in another pair of his best people. The moment he or she makes a mistake, we will know.''

Paget was to remain greatly troubled for some days.

In the early afternoon Moriarty went with Paget to visit Spear, who by now had been propped up and was sipping beef tea, specially brought in for him, the feeding cup held by Bridget. Now that she was rested and her hair well dried out, they saw that she was indeed a pretty girl, and although she would retain the thin, under-nourished look for a while yet, a pert cheekiness could be discerned in her face and eyes; the whole was framed by a mass of golden hair which hung full-bodied to her shoulders.

Spear smiled weakly when they inquired how he fared, saying that in a few days he would be up and about again, softly cursing his lost opportunity with the Bray's butler, Halling, and even managing to ask after the Professor's wound.

"It will take time before you can use your hands again.'' The Professor bent over the bed like a surgeon.

"When I can, there'll be many who'll need to watch themselves.'' Spear's cut and bandaged face was a disconcerting and bizarre mask. "I pray you'll not get Green or Butler before I can have a piece of them.''

"You just quiet yourself,'' soothed Bridget, then turning to Paget and Moriarty, "I think he should be allowed to rest again now.''

Moriarty raised his eyebrows, the lips softening into a thin, humorless smile.

"Miss Nightingale,'' murmured Paget.

"A spirited girl, young Bridget,'' mused Moriarty once they were outside. "It is hoped that she can be trusted.''

"I'll see to it that she is watched.'' Paget was sullen, his humor reflecting the dark thoughts he secretly nursed, for he did not know whom to trust anymore.

A little after six, the trio of thieves, Fisher, Clark and Gay, arrived at the warehouse, and for the following two hours they discussed plans for the proposed robbery at Harrow: Paget voiced his opinions, based on the reconnaissance he had made, and the other men—all well experienced in matters of this kind—took the Professor step by step through their designs. Moriarty listened for a

while before he pronounced his ultimate blessing on the scheme
with, naturally, a few modifications. He also authorized the use of a
two-horse van for removal of the loot, and directed Paget to travel
down to Harrow on the day of the robbery.

"Just to make sure the matter is still possible. If our fine customers have changed their plans and perhaps come home unexpectedly,
it is better that we should be warned." He caught Paget's worried
frown. "You can return long before the crib's cracked open, Paget;
I have my eye on two very likely fellows of ours to join this trio."

At ten o'clock a cab brought Alton, muffled against both the chill
night air and the possibility of recognition. He was ushered into the
Professor's chambers where Lee Chow, Ember and Paget were also
gathered. A table was set up in front of Moriarty's desk, and upon it Alton spread out a large ground plan of Coldbath Fields
Prison.

For the better part of an hour he talkd quietly and with great
concentration, interrupted only occasionally by remarks from Moriarty and small queries from the three members of the "Praetorian
Guard."

By the time he left the warehouse Alton was satisfied: half his fee
jingled in his pocket. The remainder would be his late on Thursday
evening when William and Bertram Jacobs became free men.

Moriarty dismissed his three lieutenants after a brief word to
Paget regarding the watch being kept on the women and the kitchens, also on the work for the morrow. He needed to talk with their
first prisoners—Roach and Fray—and make the journey, at last, to
Abrahams to arrange details of fencing the loot from the Harrow
affair.

But the day was not yet concluded for the Professor. Mary
McNiel hovered at the foot of the stairs leading to his chambers,
wishing to get to bed and knowing that when she did there would be
no sleep for a while, Moriarty's carnal appetites being what they
were. Indeed, he had told her earlier, "Tonight, Mary, you can
prepare for a long ride to Mount Pleasant and Shooter's Hill."

Before bed, though, Parker was waiting to see the Professor.

"I have talked to our man at Scotland Yard," said the chief lurker
once he was settled in the armchair in front of Moriarty's desk.
"This Crow is a hard man, one who as often as not walks alone, and
there is little to make us doubt that it is yourself he seeks. There are
certain files and papers that have been made available to him, and
his staff have been asking questions."

"And not getting answers, I trust."

"I think not, but he is a worthy opponent."

Parker went on to outline Crow's career, his theories regarding the work of police detection, which made him, to some extent, an unpopular figure at the Yard.

The lurker continued giving many small details of Crow's life, including a description of his rooms in King Street and the association with Mrs. Sylvia Cowles.

"She might be the fulcrum of his downfall, then," mused the Professor.

Parker grunted. "Do not take him too much for granted. He is an avid reader and his shelves contain some strange selections for a man in his profession."

"Such as?"

Parker pushed a sheet of paper across the desk. He knew Moriarty's theories well, for the Professor always held to the maxim, "Acquaint yourself with your man's bookshelves and you will know him." The list was a detail of every book in Crow's rooms.

There were the usual titles of literary merit, though one or two showed a certain paradoxical romanticism in the detective. Among the more specialized volumes, he expected to see such things as Havelock Ellis' *The Criminal*; Guyot's *La Police;* a translation of Purkinje's 1823 lecture on fingerprint impressions; Bertillon's *Signaletic Instructions, Including the Theory and Practice of Anthropometric Identification*, and a number of specialized journals, including a copy of the *Revue politique et littéraire* for April 28, 1883.

What he did not expect to find were such items as John Locke's *Essays Concerning Human Understanding*, the works of Aristotle, and Bacon's *The Advancement of Learning*.

Moriarty pondered. This man Crow might well prove to be of similar mettle to Holmes. A trial of strength with Crow would mean a testing of the deductive method of logic, combined with scientific skills not yet fully practiced in England.

"Has he been around and about, or does he just sit and brood?" the Professor asked.

"He has been out today. To Horton."

Almost indiscernibly Moriarty's face twitched. He was too tired to think the business out fully tonight; also he had need of the charms and seductive thighs of Mary McNiel—even though she was suspected of treachery. He would sleep on thoughts of Crow, and tomorrow look at the tactics and strategy that would best be employed to meet this new adversary.

It was some time before Angus McCready Crow slipped into the sweet arms of Morpheus. He was first embraced by the sweet arms and honeyed fingers of the eager and voluptuous Mrs. Sylvia

Cowles, under whose ministrations his fatigue soon departed to be replaced by that virility which is the motive force of all mankind.

Mrs. Cowles was asleep first, leaving Angus Crow to bask in the gentle glow and aftermath of their congress. His thoughts slowly began to revolve around Moriarty, who was stealthily becoming his unseen, unmet and unknown adversary. All the tiny pieces of intelligence, gleaned from the files, started to take on a new shape and significance. Holmes' own obsession with the man as leader of organized crime, the oblique references to him as a sinister mastermind appeared, in the dark watches of the night, to assume greater proportions and a new three-dimensional quality.

He slept fitfully through the night, waking fully at around seven in the morning, urged into complete consciousness by the ever-ready Mrs. Cowles whispering,

"Angus, my love. Again, Angus dearest, oh, please, again."

With a responding grunt the craggy Scot plowed another long sweating-sweet furrow, much to their mutual satisfaction, but with the result that on this morning of Wednesday, April 11, the inspector was a good fifteen minutes late in getting to his office.

It was not until after ten o'clock that Crow's sergeant, Tanner, winkled out the whereabouts of former Inspector John Meiklejohn. By that time Crow had taken more than a cursory look at the interrogation reports that had followed Monday's black night of violence. Moriarty's name appeared more than once, as did the names of Michael Green and Peter Butler. As was suspected, another pattern was emerging, that of two rival criminal factions clashing over disputed territory and powers. Though there was little concrete evidence, Crow knew that if Green or Butler could be found—and the Yard knew that pair well enough—the chances were that they might eventually lead to the dark and brooding specter of Professor James Moriarty.

By half-past ten Crow and Tanner were both seated in the back of a fast-horsed cab, starting the journey to meet the erstwhile Inspector Meiklejohn in the City Road.

Moriarty and Paget were up and out by eleven, riding over to see Solly Abrahams. It was a bright morning but Paget found his master far removed, uncommunicative, deep in thought. The Professor had wrapped himself in numerous matters, in particular the address he would give to the emissaries from the European capitals—a speech of some import, for on the results of Friday's meeting rested the whole future of Moriarty's dream to be overlord of the criminal denizens of the Continent.

Beneath these thoughts lay the obscure fears, those weird fantasies of mind, which came, Moriarty knew well enough, from the still-present threat of Green and Butler and the undeniable fact that there was a chosen agent of death well entrenched within the Limehouse lair.

Crow was also hiding away in Moriarty's secret consciousness—a figure of law and justice who appeared to be girding his loins for an assault against all the Professor stood for and had worked for.

The business with old Abrahams did not take more than an hour and a couple of glasses of port wine. (The Jew kept a fine cellar, and it was rumored that he had once personally employed a team of cracksmen whose sole duty was to rape the cellars of the nobility.) The Harrow matter settled, they drove back to Limehouse and Moriarty instructed Paget to present himself at his chambers after they had eaten. This afternoon he would talk with Roach and Fray to inform them of their choice for the future—death or life with a term of very legal imprisonment.

There was another matter that had been troubling Moriarty, and at last his mind was rightly made up. Before his food was served by Mrs. Wright—now accompanied by an omnipresent punisher—he sent for Lee Chow and gave him quick and ruthless orders.

"The man, Zebedee Smith," he said with no trace of emotion.

"You wishee I. . .?"

"Yes. We have no further use for him; he has lived out his purpose. He also knows too much. Tonight, Lee Chow, see that his throat is slit and the body well stowed."

The Chinese bowed a solemn bob and retreated, smiling. This was no time for any sentiment, and probably the other two taken entering Nelson Street would go the same way on the morrow.

John Meiklejohn was now a man in his middle sixties, but of necessity he still worked for his living. His office was small and furnished in a simple manner, being on the second floor of a building near to where the City Road joined with Old Street. A brass plate on the door signified that this was the office of JOHN MEIKLEJOHN. DETECTIVE & LEGAL INVESTIGATOR.

Crow tapped on the door and pushed it open. Old Meiklejohn sat behind a large desk strewn with papers. In the corner, near the one grimy window, a young man sat laboriously writing in a large ledger.

Crow introduced himself and watched the smile of welcome fade from Meiklejohn's tired and lined face.

"Is this a business matter or something personal?" the private detective asked, worry plain in his rheumy eyes.

"It is somewhat of a personal business, I'm afraid." Crow's rich burr had a kindly touch to it.

"Ah, personal. Some trouble you wish me to settle for you, perhaps?"

"No." Crow was firm. "Some past trouble of your own, which you can perhaps help us with."

Old Meiklejohn nodded sadly and called to his young assistant.

"Bernard, the gentlemen have a little private business with me. I'd be grateful if you would step out for a few minutes." He gave a short and not unpleasant laugh. "You can go across the road and ogle that young woman in the draper's, eh?"

When the lithe and blushing Bernard had departed, Meiklejohn waved his visitors into chairs.

"I suppose it's something from the de Goncourt affair. It usually is."

"Usually?" Crow on the alert. "What do you mean, man, usually? You have many inquiries about that? I thought it was well forgotten by most people."

"Oh, I suppose I exaggerate, but once in a while someone recalls it, usually when there's a similar swindle. It is then that I get a visit. Another lot of magsmen on the con?"

Crow smiled gently. "Mr. Meiklejohn, I have no wish to remind you of the past. It is dead and well buried as far as I am concerned. You were a fool, but like the other two, you paid your debt." He glanced around the bare office. "And go on paying, too, I imagine."

Meiklejohn sighed. "It hasn't been easy, but I've managed; good times and bad. There is quite a call for private investigation, you know, though I should have taken myself off to America, I hear that is where there are real pickings. A countryman of yours has done well with his agency there."

"Aye, Allan Pinkerton."

"Yes, that's where I should have gone. A fool should not stay near the spot where he has befouled himself."

Crow gave a long, sage nod. "I suppose you're right, but you can leave it too long, you know. Had you heard that Palmer's gone to Australia?"

"No." It was almost a shocked sound. "No, has he really, now. Well, he's left it late, and poor old Nat gone also—a different kind of emigration."

"It was concerning Nat Druscovich that we called."

Meiklejohn gave a bitter laugh. "Don't say that after all this time you've found he left a will and two thousand pound to me. That would be irony indeed.''

"He died a broken man; but you know that. There is something, though, that we did not know until recently. Or I should say that it was known but nobody heeded it. You can be of great help.''

"I'll do what I can, of course.''

"Then you'll add another name to those of Jonge, Kurr and Murray.''

Meiklejohn looked started, puzzled and a shade gray.

"Another name? You have all the names. Everyone was caught.''

"Walters was not caught.''

"Well, he skipped it, didn't he? America, they said.''

"They said the same about Murray, but he turned up.''

"Well, I don't know what happened to Walters.''

Crow took a deep breath. "What about Moriarty?''

Meiklejohn blanched. "Who?'' he asked, a tremble in his voice, eyes darting about the room as though looking for a way of escape.

"Moriarty?'' said Crow pushing.

Meiklejohn shook his head. "I never heard that name. Not in connection with the turf racket, anyway.''

"About any other rackets?''

"Well . . .'' He was hesitant. "Well, one does hear the odd whisper from time to time. In this business you can't—''

"Moriarty was behind the swindle in which you were involved, man. We know it and so do you. All we need is a sworn statement.'' His Scottish burr was more marked.

"You'd never get him, Inspector. Nobody'll ever get Moriarty and you know that.''

"I don't know it, and I want your statement saying that he was heavily involved with Kurr and Jonge. The truth.''

The minutes ticked by, Meiklejohn shaking his head again.

"Who says he was involved anyhow?''

"Nat Druscovich for one.''

"I don't believe that. If Nat had talked, you'd have been racing about like whippets.''

"On his deathbed. He said it all right, but it got overlooked.''

"You've a signed statement?''

"We've got enough.''

"I doubt it.''

"Enough to collar you and make life unpleasant, and it could be very unpleasant for a man of your age. Good God, man, you must know that.''

Once more a protracted silence. Then—

"If I do some chanting, what then?"

"We'll leave you alone, Mr. Meiklejohn."

"You might, but . . ." The sentence trailed off into an unspoken query.

"Is it your safety that concerns you?"

"What do you think, Mr. Crow? What do you really think?"

"I have no idea, Mr. Meiklejohn. All I know is that we have strong evidence that the name of one man was withheld in a case which is dormant. I have reason to believe that you know that name. It is your public duty to make a statement to me now, because it is important for me to have evidence that will stick."

Meiklejohn let out a long sigh. "You are saying that you'll hound me to the grave if I don't tell you."

"I would not use such strong terms."

"Does it have to be a formal statement?"

"I'm afraid so."

"Well, I'll tell you all that I know, which is not great. Kurr and Jonge were, as far as I was concerned, the two ringleaders of that particular series of frauds. As you know, they paid me to tip them when the police were getting close. The details are all set down in the text of the trial. It was not until almost the end that I became aware they were not acting alone, that they were marionettes for another man. I heard his name on several occasions and saw him once—in Jonge's house at Shanklin. His name was Moriarty. James Moriarty."

"Would you be able to identify him?"

"It's a long time ago—but, yes, I think I would."

"Can you give us dates?"

"I kept no records—no diaries, and my memory is not what it was."

"Which means that if we took you into court, your memory would fail you regarding the identification?"

A small and watery smile crossed Meiklejohn's face.

"Possibly."

Crow concealed his frustration as Tanner penned the statement, handing it over to Meiklejohn to sign—an act he performed with some reluctance.

Crow noted, as they left, that Meiklejohn appeared to have aged in the half hour or so that they had spent with him. Crow would have preferred to ask more, to have probed and questioned at length, but that could come later. At least this document, small as it was, might be the battering ram to send the Professor on a downward slide. The rest of his day would now be spent examining the Monday night's reports and, possibly, talking to some of those involved.

Back at the Yard he instructed Tanner to get about the second line of his investigations: to make a detailed examination of the life, times, friends and relatives of the departed Colonel Moran.

Roach and Fray had been dreading the moment when the Professor would give final judgment upon them. They were both aware by now that some major battle had been fought and won against their former leaders, Green and Butler. It remained only for some kind of sentence to be passed, and Moriarty's cold ruthlessness was legendary among the brotherhood of crime.

Paget came with one of the punishers, leading them from their cramped quarters, down the spiral staircase, along one of the passageways, through the "waiting room"—in which a number of men and women sat intent on seeing the Professor—and up to the leader's chambers, where they were placed in front of the desk, much after the manner of prisoners in the dock awaiting the verdict of the court.

Moriarty, his arm still in the white sling, had the air and manner of a hanging judge. When he spoke, the words dripped from his lips with the same self-satisfied plumminess both men had heard in the court of law.

"In other circumstances I would have had you done away with, like anyone else who had abused my patronage," he began. "But I have promised that you will hold your destiny in your own hands." He paused, as though for dramatic effect. "The choice is simple: You can either die—tonight, quickly and with no fuss"—his good arm moved in a graphic mime across his throat—"or you can remain silent, do exactly as you are told, and serve a term of some three years—in the 'Steel."

It was hard for the two men to digest. In those few words Moriarty appeared to conjure all the legends that surrounded him. Here he was, the all-powerful leader of the criminal world, proposing to send the prisoners to jail: to use the legal powers of the land for his own advantage, by having them incarcerated in the most dreaded of London's penitentiaries.

Hard as it may be, the men were not foolish. Three years' misery was little to pay in bargain for their lives. It took them only a few moments to murmur out their acceptance of the sentence.

Moriarty nodded, as though to signify that they had made a wise choice.

"You must understand," he said, the voice dropping to a whisper, "that any breach in our arrangement can only bring you certain death. You know me well enough to be sure that my arm has power to reach you wherever you may be. Retribution can be swift.''

They were told to stay quiet in their cell. Tomorrow the full instructions would be given to them.

Once Fray and Roach were removed, Moriarty sent for Lee Chow and issued orders regarding the people waiting to see him. The remainder of the day would be spent giving audience, dispensing favors, dealing with complaints; for this was part of the pattern of life which surrounded a man in Moriarty's position.

Thursday, April 12, 1894

(THE MANNER IN WHICH MORIARTY PROCURED FREEDOM FOR THE JACOBS BROTHERS)

EVEN THE CHARMS of Mrs. Cowles were lost on Crow during Wednesday night. The bit was between his teeth, and he had lost little time making some discernible method of the muddle of paper and dossiers littering his office.

"Planning," he said to Tanner. "Planning and organized method. It is the only way we can possibly expect to catch this villain. If he is a villain—for never be foolish enough to forget that any man is not guilty until he is so proved."

With the tiny chink of light glimpsed during the short interview with Meiklejohn, Crow now set out to take a bold look at the major crimes of the past twenty-five years, giving special attention to those in the five years preceding 1891—the year in which Moriarty was said to have disappeared.

He also had men looking at the crime reports of the last week, and by Wednesday night there was at least one small act among many which seemed to interest him—the unconfirmed report of a shooting incident in Limehouse, near the docks.

He sat until the early hours of Thursday morning going through the painful process of thinking himself into the shadowy Moriarty's skin—an exercise which had proved most useful on other occasions when dealing with much smaller fry.

It was only when he arrived at the Yard on the Thursday morning that Inspector Crow realized he had not followed one glaring line of reasoning. Meiklejohn was a frightened man; even the name of Moriarty had unnerved him. True, he had admitted to a man of that name being behind the old turf swindles, but in the end even that admission was overshadowed by the obvious fear radiating from the man like the new miracle, electricity.

If Moriarty was to be feared that much by a man who was once deemed to have the intelligence to be a detective, then there had to be a reason for it. He immediately dispatched Tanner and another officer to bring Meiklejohn into the Yard. But as he feared, they were out of luck: Meiklejohn's office was closed, and other people in the building said that he had mentioned retirement. Further inquiries elicited that John Meiklejohn had paid off his assistant, packed his few belongings and taken the morning boat train to Dover. He was never seen again.

"Terror," observed Angus Crow, "is a great force. If we could harness terror to machines, we could move whole cities—no need for horses or these wretched carriages built to be driven without a four-legged beast. Terror could drive most things."

Indeed, terror could drive men across oceans or in other cases to silence. Crow remained unaware of Moriarty's next move simply because a number of men—some in Her Majesty's service—were prepared to remain blind, deaf and dumb; some because of money, but most from terror.

The area surrounding the Middlesex House of Correction, Coldbath Fields, was drab, gray and unpalatable. Houses, once desirable red-brick dwellings, had over the years become seedy and neglected, for few people sought to live within sight of the grim, spiked walls of that vast prison.

The 'Steel—an ironic nickname culled from the French Bastille—lay to the east of Grey's Inn Road, flanked by Farringdon Road and Phoenix Place, fronting on Dorrington Street. All nine acres were enclosed by massive, buttressed brick walls, which obscured all signs of life except for the darting beam of the treadmill fan, which could be observed by daylight turning its monotonous and weary circle.

In front of the prison was a small grass area, kept trim by sheep, the tall bow window of the governor's house jutting onto it. To the right of the window was the familiar prison doorway topped by a black-lettered inscription dated *1794;* below this were the stern, green folding gates, huge knockers, the decoration of vast iron fetters and the gridironlike wicket. Mounted on the stonework, on either side of the doorway, were black notice boards providing *Information Respecting the Terms of Imprisonment and Fines to be Paid* and announcing *No provisions, clothing, or other articles for the use of the prisoners.*

The evening roster of warders and turnkeys came on duty at half-past five in the afternoon, while the prisoners were at supper, the changeover taking place in time for the duty warders to supervise the locking up, which began at six o'clock.

On this evening Frederick Steadman Alton, one of the senior turnkeys at the 'Steel, came on duty with the night roster, having had two days' leave following six months of day-roster work.

With the other officers he waited outside the gates until the wicket was opened, a little before the half hour, and stepped into the narrow yard that housed the gate warden's lodge on one side and, on the other, a gravelled court enclosed by the walls of the governor's house and leading to the stables and offices.

A glass awning covered the way to a double iron gate, which was opened to allow the prison officers passage into the brick and spike-hemmed yard. Alton took his place in the three ranks of warders and turnkeys as they formed up for a cursory inspection by the dapper little deputy governor. In Coldbath Fields the prisoners' heads were counted night and morning, but few would have thought of doing the same to the warders. Certainly on that evening nobody noticed that there were three extra men wearing the blue uniforms of the Prison Service, or that one of them was carrying a small pocket pistol under his jacket.

Coldbath Fields was in reality three prisons in one: a large and forbidding central building, the Felons' Prison, and two others, one at each corner of the main block. These other jails were, respectively, the Vagrants' and the Misdemeanants' Prisons, both having been built to similar specifications—four long blocks spaced equally in a half-circle like the spokes of a wheel.

In 1894 the 'Steel was nearing the end of its long and unhappy life, but it still bulged with inmates; so much so that many who should rightly have been quartered in the Felons' Prison were fitted into cold and tiny cells within the Misdemeanants' Prison. Two such unfortunates were William and Bertram Jacobs, housed in cells on the second floor of B Block. Alton was the senior warder of B Block, and it was to this area that he walked as soon as the deputy governor dismissed the incoming roster.

A few paces behind Alton came the three extra warders, two walking ahead, the third a little behind them, his right hand in his uniform jacket pocket.

The changeover of warders usually took around twenty minutes, some going straight off duty as soon as their replacements arrived, others forced to linger and assist in the counting of prisoners as they returned from work and were locked up for the night.

The warders coming on duty slowly converged on their variously appointed buildings and blocks. Alton was the first to arrive at B

Block in the Misdemeanants' Prison. He greeted his daytime counterpart, signed the docket, and told him that he could move his warders out—the takeover always being an easy matter as far as he was concerned.

The three warders coming up behind Alton lingered for a moment near the doorway, allowing others to pass them and listening to the greetings and chitchat that passed between the officers.

The cell floors each had an allotment of three warders and, standing by the door, Alton quietly held back the three men from his roster assigned to the second floor. There was an unhurried conversation, during which Alton told them to go back to the administrative office and take their tea now instead of waiting until after their charges had been locked away: a perfectly normal practice by which senior warders—with their gilt metal collar plates—showed favoritism to their juniors.

As the three warders left, so the trio of extra men entered B Block and made their way up to the second floor, the largest of them taking the bunch of keys offered to him by Alton.

At six o'clock the prison came alive, and for about twenty minutes the dull tramp of boots echoed through the yards and courts, up the stairs and along passageways as the drab-uniformed prisoners moved in regulated lines, from work and their meager supper to their allotted cells and dormitories.

The prisoners looked exceedingly fatigued, as indeed they might, having worked a day which started at twenty-five past six to the sound of the cannon, with work beginning at seven and going on until half-past five; but for a break of one and a half hours for meals, the day was spent on the body-breaking treadmill or in moving piles of heavy cannon balls from one place to another in the shot drill field. Some, of course, picked oakum, and a few worked in the mat room or at a trade, such as plumbing or glazing, yet these fortunates were but a small number among the twelve-hundred-odd convicts forced to conform to the soul-destroying routine. Even then, some remembered that they could regard themselves as lucky—for a few years earlier the life at Coldbath Fields meant day after day of silence with no contact or converse between their fellow sufferers under the experimental silent system.

Alton and a junior warder, identifiable by his silver metal badge, counted the heads of their charges in B Block, Alton hardly raising his head as the Jacobs brothers, clad in their rough, shapeless prison jackets, trousers and caps came through the entrance to B Block.

With the other prisoners they marched up to the second floor where by now there seemed to be only one warder on duty—a very tall, broad-shouldered, muscular man with his uniform cap pulled down over his eyes. This warder had stationed himself midway between the cells normally occupied by the Jacobs brothers, which were halfway down the passage. From this vantage point he could see Roach and Fray inside the cells, stripped to the buff, their warders' uniforms discarded and lying on the floor. They both looked miserable, yet resigned to the inevitable.

As William and Bertram Jacobs entered their cells, so Terremant —for he was the third "warder"—turned away, walked up the passage and began to lock the cells.

By the time "Warder" Terremant reached the cells formerly occupied by the Jacobs brothers, the two men were outside, dressed in the uniforms formerly worn by Roach and Fray.

The trio moved slowly down the passage, pausing to lock each door and call good-night to the occupants. When this was complete, they made their way, unhurriedly, down the stairs, hardly changing their pace as Terremant passed the bunch of keys back to Alton.

Without any undue haste the three men headed toward the main gate. The day-roster warders were still filtering through, tired and glad to be away to their own homes and hearths, and it was a simple matter for the unauthorized trio to mingle with the departing officers, lingering for a few seconds within the yard outside the gatehouse without actually entering to sign off. Nobody challenged or questioned them as they stepped back to allow a pair of senior officers to go through the wicket before them. A few seconds later they too were outside and free.

A pair of hansoms waited in Gray's Inn Road, Harkness and Ember in the driving seats whipping up the horses as soon as their passengers were aboard and setting off at a steady trot toward Limehouse.

By quarter to eight Bill and Bert Jacobs were climbing the stairs to the Professor's chambers, each clutching a tidy glass of gin.

The stay in the 'Steel did not seem to have done either of the lads any harm; if anything—apart from the fatigue that showed under the eyes—their young frames appeared harder and their faces tougher than ever. The Jacob boys were both in their late twenties, sturdily built, though in no way running to fat, their faces strong with good jaw lines and noses belying their natural parentage—chiseled and without the twists or breaks so prevalent among their class. Both had clear blue eyes, reflecting a capacity for deep tenderness and, conversely, fearsome cruelty. In plain language they were very hard men who could, given the correct mode of dress, pass as gentlemen.

Moriarty greeted them as he would have greeted long lost

sons, embracing each in turn in the Continental manner, while the lads themselves poured out their gratitude, though in no fawning way.

When they were all seated, Paget appeared in the doorway, leading Mrs. Hetty Jacobs by the arm. For the next minutes the room became a place of profuse and fulsome thanks, coupled with the natural tears of a mother reunited with her sons.

Presently the Professor quietened Hetty Jacobs.

"I think it unwise, for the moment, for your boys to return home," he said kindly. "They must stay here awhile, but you may see them as often as possible."

Still with tears lacing her plump cheeks, Mrs. Jacobs kissed Moriarty's hand for the umpteenth time.

"How shall I ever thank you?" she muttered. "How shall I ever repay?"

"You are of my family, Hetty. You know that. There is no need for repayment. Not yet. But I can tell you that both Bill and Bertram can offer much in return for their freedom. I need well-set-up boys like this, so getting them from the 'Steel is a doubled-edged favor; it gladdens both our hearts."

When Hetty Jacobs was finally sent on her way, the Professor got down to business, as the boys drank their gin and ate the meal Kate Wright and Fanny Jones, still watched over with great care by the other men, had prepared and brought to them.

"It's a pleasure to have you back." Moriarty's thin smile lit his lips but not his eyes.

"You can see it's their pleasure also," Paget nodded. "Look at them, grinning like baskets of chips."

"There is work, lads. Much work. I need you about the house, both for protection and special labors that are being arranged."

He went on to speak of the difficulties they had experienced with Green and Butler, letting them into the secret of the traitor in their midst, and the facts concerning the important meeting with his Continental agents, set for the following day.

"I need you close, with your eyes skinned and fists ready. Then, of course, next week we have a celebration. Friend Paget here is to be married on Tuesday. After that there is a caper that should bring us a mild fortune—silver, gems, some paintings of note, and cash." He continued to talk of the arrangements already made. "The three lads who brought it to me are of good reputation, but it is necessary that I have a least one I can trust to go with them. Two heads are better than one and your muscle could be a help. I'd feel happier with you two there."

"You can count on us for anything, Professor," said William Jacobs.

His brother nodded. "Your life itself would be safe with us."

"Good." Moriarty came near to beaming. "I need stout and true boys around me at this time. I want both of you close to me at tomorrow's meeting. Paget and Lee Chow will be there also, so stick by them. And remember that in my absence they are to be obeyed as if it were myself."

When he had seen the Jacobs brothers settled for the night, Moriarty went over to Spear's chambers. The invalid was sitting up, propped by pillows, the faithful Bridget still by his side. Moriarty noticed with interest that she was reading to her patient from an old copy of *Harper's Magazine*. The thought of Spear listening to the middle-class jottings of that periodical made Moriarty smile inwardly as much as the fact that Bridget could read made him wonder.

"Well, has your little nurse not left your bedside?" he asked brightly.

"Hardly for a moment."

Spear's voice was still weak, though the look of adoration which passed between him and the golden-haired Bridget spoke of one thing only.

"You're being a good girl to him, Bridget?"

"And why not?" she answered, forthright as ever. "He is one of the few men in my life that's shown kindness to me."

There was little arguing with her and, after a few minutes inquiring after Spear's wounds, the Professor departed, to await news from Parker, who had been down to Victoria Station with some of his men to watch for those arriving on the boat train from the Continent.

Parker and his lurkers saw all four of them come off the train. First, the short, thin Jean Grisombre from Paris, a rare jewel thief who had long worked the capital city of France with his own band of burglars and cutthroats until, some years before, Moriarty had suggested a form of alliance. The pair had worked in loose harmony ever since, and it was during his three years' sojourn in Europe that Moriarty had spent much time with Grisombre—as he had with the other Continental arrivals—in an attempt to found a grand alliance.

Jean Grisombre had with him a pair of young men whose manner and bearing was distinctly that of the apache: lithe, slim and deadly. One of Parker's men strolled after them, following their hansom and making certain that the party booked into the Royal Exeter in West Strand.

The visiting representative from Berlin was the tall, correct-looking Wilhelm Schleifstein, who had more of the appearance of a banker than an organizer of crime, his full beard making him look older than his thirty-nine years. In face he had been in the world of commerce as a young man, though forced to leave the banking house which employed him after it was discovered that several thousand marks were missing and his books did not balance.

Schleifstein had progressed from those relatively small beginnings to become somewhat of an expert in defrauding banks and gathering of intelligence concerning the most rewarding areas for jewel robberies. He also gathered together a growing band of dippers, whom he sent out after particular quarry, earmarked as carrying large quantities of currency.

During his many visits to Berlin since 1891 Moriarty had discovered that the German's large hand was in the flesh trade—running numerous brothels and taking a share from vast numbers of street women. The Professor was also acquainted with the huge fellow who walked with his Berlin visitor—Franz, a seven-foot giant who acted as Schleifstein's personal servant and bodyguard.

This pair was followed by one of the lurkers who later reported they were staying at the expensive Long's Hotel in New Bond Street, where it could cost you as much as a pound a day including meals.

The fat, suave Italian who came off the boat train was Luigi Sanzionare, the son of a baker now risen in the hierarchy of Italian criminals, becoming, at the age of thirty-three, one of the four most sought-after men in Rome—looked for by the *questori* and villains alike.

Sanzionare brought with him a pair of smooth-faced, swarthy young men, dressed somewhat floridly. He was also the only visitor to be accompanied by a woman—dark, oliveskinned, and emanating a beauty that smoldered behind her eyes and stirred men's loins when she walked. If the Italian had wished to draw attention to himself, he could not have done better, for the eyes of all men on the platform were drawn to the lady, as though by a feat of mesmerism, as she promenaded haughtily from the train.

Sanzionare's party was lodged at the Westminster Palace in nearby Victoria Street, and Parker's man was not slow in learning that the lady, a Signorina Adela Asconta, had a room adjoining that of Signore Sanzionare.

By comparison with the other visitors Esteban Bernado Segorbe was positively dowdy. Short, neat and quietly dressed, he carried his own portmanteau from the train, was diffident in engaging a porter, and almost slipped through Parker's net. But not quite, for it was later reported that Segorbe had put up at the modest Somerset House in the Strand.

Esteban Segorbe was the least known to Moriarty. When sounding out representatives in Spain, the Professor had been advised to contact this quiet resident of Madrid, who had welcomed him into his pleasant, though not luxurious, home, listened carefully to all Moriarty had to say, agreed in principle to some form of alliance, and thereafter conducted any business between them with minimum fuss and scrupulous fair dealing.

Moriarty was aware that the man controlled large areas in prostitution and had a hand in numerous unlawful interests. There was little doubt, for instance, that he was engaged in the pernicious white-slave trade. Yet Esteban Bernado Segorbe was something of an enigma.

''What's up, Pip, you've been so strange, as close as wax?''

Fanny sat at their makeshift dressing table, clad only in her chemise and drawers. Paget reflected that she was very different from other women he had known. For one thing, in his limited experience only high-class whores wore drawers, though they seemed to be correct for the snotty middle-class ladies if the drawings in the magazines were anything to go by. He remembered looking through a copy of *The Gentlewoman*, which Ember had picked up somewhere, and laughing at the advertisements for stays and other undergarments. There were also the postcards Spear had got hold of—from Paris he said—showing young women in colored drawers trimmed with yards of lace. They had made him exceedingly hornified, just as the sight of Fanny sitting there was doing now.

Yet Paget could not get the terrible suspicion from his head. It haunted him practically all the time now. Fanny Jones had come from nowhere and yet everywhere, a woman of so different a background and experience that it almost made Pip Paget afraid on some nights even to touch her. He supposed that what he felt was the strange thing they called love, though Christ knew what that meant.

He could not have truly put the fears into words, yet they were strong enough. If Fanny turned out to be Green's agent, or—and the thought had crossed his mind—some interloper inserted like a chimney boy by the police, he did not know what he would do. The Professor would have only one answer, and that frightened Paget to the limit.

''Pip?'' Fanny called again. ''Is something troubling you? Is it our wedding?'' She rose from the chair and came to him, putting her arms around his neck so that his nose was nuzzled in her hair. ''Is it that? Do you not want to wed me?''

Paget, basically a rough man with women, held her close. How could he tell her that more than anything else in the world he wanted them married? How could he admit, even to himself, that in truth he would do anything for her, even if she had cross-bitten Moriarty.

''I love you, Fan,'' was all he said. ''I love you and we'll be married on Tuesday. There's little else I think about.''

Friday, April 13, 1894

(THE CONTINENTAL ALLIANCE)

ANGUS CROW FELT that he was making a little headway. He did not quite know in what direction, but there were now some distinct leads. He also found it heartening to know that if he came close to Professor James Moriarty, there was a legal reason for arrest.

Some names had cropped up both from the original files and the questioning of those arrested on Monday night. Holmes himself had mentioned a man called Parker who, it seemed, acted as a spy, or watcher. Among Moran's more shady acquaintances the name Spear constantly recurred, and from the Monday's gleanings there were references to a Chinese called Lee Chow and a man called Paget—this last had certainly been present at the affray in Nelson Street.

But there was still no sign of either Michael Green or Peter Butler, though a good number of their associates were in custody. Crow ordered these men to be questioned regularly and with considerable tenacity. Meanwhile the watch for Green and Butler continued.

It was almost eleven o'clock when the telegraph arrived from the *questore*'s office in Rome. It was addressed to the commissioner and read:

SUBJECT LUIGI SANZIONARE REPORTED TO HAVE ENTERED ENGLAND STOP SUGGEST HE BE WATCHED IF CONTACTED STOP WANTED HERE SUSPECT MURDER THEFT AND OTHER CHARGES STOP SANZIONARE ACCOMPANIED BY TWO YOUNG MEN AND WOMAN KNOWN AS ADELA ASCONTA STOP

There followed a description of Sanzionare based on the anthropometric system. The message was circulated, and Crow, paying little heed to it, reflected on the efficiency of the Italian police. One day, he dreamed, there will be a united organization of both British and Continental forces to ensure any criminal moving from one country to another can be traced and hunted down.

But that was thought for the future, of little value in Crow's present investigation. He set his mind, therefore, to the task. If Moriarty was the general of some criminal army, then some of the stories that appeared and reappeared in the files must have at least a germ of truth.

Crow began to examine the most incredible of the recurring themes—that Moriarty was the same Professor Moriarty who had achieved fame in the academic world, yet somehow possessed the power to change both face and body at will. By sifting the evidence, he was able to separate at least one fact—Moriarty appeared to manifest himself in only two ways: first, as the tall, very thin man with the unmistakable physiognomy known to countless academics; second, as a shorter, younger, and more stocky man, who, instead of the domed bald pate, possessed a good head of hair.

The logical conclusions were simple: Professor Moriarty, the criminal commander, must either be two men masquerading as one; or one man masquerading as two. If the latter conclusion was correct, then the man concerned could *not* be the academic Professor Moriarty. He had to be the younger man. *Quod erat demonstrandum.*

Crow smiled and began to hum to himself, eventually breaking into song.

> Oh! Mr. Porter, what shall I do?
> I wanted to go to Birmingham,
> But they've taken me on to Crewe. . .

Mrs. Cowles had gone with him to see Miss Marie Lloyd at the Empire Theatre in Leicester Square only a few weeks before, and they had both nudged one another at the salacious innuendoes Miss Lloyd was able to convey.

> Take me back to London,
> As quickly as you can,
> Oh! Mr. Porter, what a silly girl. . .

He stopped short at the discreet cough from the doorway.

"Did you call, sir?" asked Sergeant Tanner.

"No, no, I didn't call," Crow huffed, his accent more pronounced with his embarrassment. "But now y'here there's a job for ye."

Tanner was deployed with one of Crow's other detectives to begin a long and detailed search into Moriarty's life—his relatives, the affair at the university, anything and anyone who was connected with him before his arrival in London as a military tutor.

In the outer office the harassed Sergeant Tanner rearranged his schedule, had another detective carry on his work regarding the late Colonel Moran, and started out on his new duty, leaving Crow to let his mind and logic dwell on other aspects of the situation.

"What do you think all the fuss is about then, Jim?"

It was the punisher with the bent and mutilated nose who addressed Jim Terremant.

"Don't know and I don't know that I want to know," replied Terremant. "There's been some trouble with the women, no doubt about that, what with the lad an' all. The Professor's a careful man. My advice to you is to do as you're told, keep your eyes peeled and trust nobody, except the Professor, Mr. Paget, Ember and Lee Chow."

"That yellow 'eathen, he gives me the creeps."

"Then if its 'eathens that give you the creeps, you'd better mind yourself today, that's all." Terremant spat with some feeling. "We'll have the place full of 'eathens before long. Foreigners, Eye-talians, Germans, Froggies and Spaniards. They're all coming in 'ere for this meeting the Professor's got together."

"Then we really will have to watch the women. I 'ere as how you couldn't trust them Eye-talians with yer grandmother."

"Well, you watch away: the women, the grub—and the bloody silver."

Promptly at quarter-past eleven the cabs arrived at the various hotels. One of the young Italian men accompanied Luigi Sanzionare from the Westminster Palace; from Somerset House Esteban Segorbe traveled by himself; Fritz, the huge German, left Long's with Herr Schleifstein, and both the French bodyguards were with Jean Grisombre when he walked from the Royal Exeter.

Moriarty's desk had been moved into the bedroom, a large dining table taking its place. Around the table were six chairs. Of Moriarty's men, only Paget, Lee Chow and the two Jacobs brothers were going to be present in the room, though Terremant and his men would be within easy reach as they watched over the preparation of food and drink and its conveyance from the kitchens to Moriarty's private rooms.

Parker and a detachment of his lurkers, some of them armed with pistols and revolvers, were guarding the warehouse from all possible angles.

Moriarty, not in his brother's disguise, was dressed in black: a long frock coat, trousers and waistcoat, and a somewhat old-fashioned Mornington collar, looking for all the world like a doctor or banker. He waited, with Paget standing to his right and slightly behind him, to greet the arrivals at the top of the stairs. There were handshakes, smiles, bows and elaborate greetings. Sanzionare had not met Schleifstein, and Schleifstein had never met Grisombre. None of the visitors had ever seen Segorbe before today.

Already there had been agreement about the language problem, and the conference was to take place in English. Some of the accompanying personnel, however, did not speak English, so there was a great deal of sign-language passing between the rank and file.

Before matters could proceed toward luncheon, Moriarty called for silence.

"Gentlemen," he said, "before I welcome you here officially, I have taken something of a liberty. We have another guest."

There was an exchange of brief, yet nervous, looks.

"You need have no fears," Moriarty smiled. "He is one of us. Indeed he hails from Europe, though he has taken on a new nationality." He paused, his eyes searching the faces of his colleagues. "We are told that the United States of America is the great progressive country of our time—as indeed it is, for our friends there are already well organized. It is with our own interests at heart, then, that I have invited an emissary from that great country to—how can I put it?—to observe our deliberations."

He nodded toward Paget, who opened the door, admitting a tall, burly man, about thirty years of age, dressed soberly in dark suiting, a pearl-gray cravat at his throat.

"May I present"—the Professor spread his arms wide in an extravagant gesture—"Mr. Paul Golden of New York City."

Though he was heavily built, Golden gave the impression of remarkable alertness, with bright eyes that never ceased to move in an inquiring manner. When he spoke, there was a heavy nasality underlying the strong, almost Germanic, guttural accent.

"It is good to be here," he said, a wispy smile crossing the thick lips. "My friends in The City—as we call New York—have asked me to carry their good wishes to you all. And I must thank you for the invitation which has allowed me to make the journey over the ocean. As the good Professor says, we are doing our best to work in an organized fashion. I shall enjoy and listen with interest.''

With some diffidence the other guests approached the American visitor; they shook hands with him and exchanged a few words.

Paget noted that Golden—whom the Professor had told him of only a short time before the meeting was about to commence—seemed reluctant to engage in any lengthy conversation.

After two or three glasses of sherry the party sat down to luncheon, served by Bill and Bert Jacobs, overlooked by Paget and Lee Chow, correct as butlers of long experience; the dishes were brought up from the kitchens by Fanny Jones and Mary McNiel, each with one of the watching punishers in tow.

Mrs. Kate Wright had excelled herself. Red pottage (made of haricot beans, tomatoes, beetroot, onions and celery) was followed by lobster cutlets. The meat course consisted of traditional roast beef with Yorkshire pudding, buttered carrots and turnips mashed together, baked potatoes and spring cabbage. Sanzionare made a joke by saying that Segorbe, Grisombre and himself should really have a papal dispensation, it being a Friday and them coming from families of the Roman Catholic persuasion. Schleifstein looked down his nose, thinking the remark neither funny nor in good taste. Golden smiled, as if he possessed knowledge of some secret jest.

Kate Wright's favorite London pudding was served next—a concoction of apricot jam, sponge finger biscuits, butter, milk, lemon and eggs. The meal was completed with Angels on Horseback, that particular savory being one of Moriarty's favorites; the Professor had always been partial to bacon and oysters.

While the five leaders ate lunch, their lieutenants ate from a cold buffet, laid out on a trestle table set under the window, though none of them let their eyes stray long from their particular chief.

When the meal was finished and all were replete, Moriarty called the table to order. Paget went out to make certain that Terremant had posted one of the punishers outside the door; the bodyguards and others took up their places, ranging themselves behind their respective leaders, and they all fell silent.

First they toasted one another by turns—Moriarty coldly businesslike; Sanzionare and Grisombre effusive; Schleifstein correct and distant, without warmth; Segorbe quiet and with a mocking quality; Golden respectful, maintaining his position as observer.

Moriarty then rose and began his long speech.*

*The text of Moriarty's speech is taken directly from the journals, the indications being that the Professor set down what he said from memory within twenty-four hours of its delivery.

"Gentlemen, I wish to welcome you here and thank you all for making the long and irksome journeys you have each undertaken from your homes and natural environments.

"In the last few years we have talked individually about the plans I have long conceived. All of us have had experience, which has taught us that where so-called unlawful activities are concerned, there is more to be said for concerted action than the individual and lonely forays made daily by men and women acting on their own initiative.

"The sneak thief, cracksman, dipper and mobsman, the macer and magsman, even the assassin and whore, can go about their business and net certain small benefits. They can be successful, fence their loot, plan their capers, but all in a vacuum. We have, I believe, all proved that the man acting in concert with those of his kind has more opportunities, more certainty of profit, more chance of evading the law.

"It may well be that I am an arrogant man, but I have reason to believe that of all of us here, I have the greatest experience—my organization being the largest, and controlling, as I do, the major elements not only in London, but also the bulk of England, Scotland and Wales.

"The loose and reciprocal arrangements we have had in the past few years also appear to have proved beyond doubt that an organization based on mutual trust, understanding and sharing is not only possible but decidedly in our interests. I make no bones about it, gentlemen, my object in calling this meeting today is to discuss the foundation of a superior network that will stretch throughout the length and breadth of the Continent of Europe—for the Continent is a vast storehouse of treasure and power: there for us to use, to take, to plunder, if you like.

"We are all aware that the men and women who work for us and under us are in the main creatures of limited education, with narrow intellects. So it strikes me that it is our duty, our responsibility, to care for these men and women, to guide, comfort and direct them and to see that their very able talents are deployed to the best advantage. If that can be done here in Great Britain, it can certainly be done on a Continental scale. That is my object.

"Now, none of us are fools—otherwise we would not be sitting here together, today. There is a need for lengthy discussion about many aspects of control, of the methods which we would need to maintain such an alliance—for that is how I see it: a grand alliance based on modern methods.

"This brings me to what may be the most important point I have to make. Progress, gentlemen, progress. For too long our brothers in crime have clung to old and hardened ways, neglecting even to notice that around us we are seeing the world alter as never before. Many of the advances in science are, I fear, regarded as mere fads and follies; not just by the world in general but by our own world in particular. The signs and portents of change are all about us, yet we do not see our lives being drastically altered Think for a moment what difference has been made by the railway: the huge distances that can now be covered in a relatively short space of time. It is a shrinking world and I foresee it shrunken even more drastically. We must be alive to these matters, alive to them and harness them to our own advantage.

"For instance, the telephone and telegraph are already making strides so far undreamed of. In a matter of minutes it is possible to talk to somebody who is miles away, at the other end of our cities. In a matter of hours we can be in touch, by telegraph, with the far corners of Europe. We have already used these modern methods, but do you imagine that this is going to stop here? It should be obvious to any thinking man that our present telephone, telegraph and cablegram services are not going to remain as they are. They will progress; there is little to stop them. Within years we will be able to speak to each other over great distances. Imagine how that will affect our aims.

"Not only *our* aims, though, for it will also have bearing on the police forces of the world, governments, banks and industries. It is with these things in mind that we must plan. If we accept, then, that we are going to be able to communicate with more ease with each other over great distances we must also look at some of the other factors.

"I have spoken of the railways. There is also a new evolution taking place which concerns other forms of traveling. We are told that on the sea ships will be built that will not only be bigger and better but also faster. On land we all smile a little at the strange phenomenon of the horseless carriage. I would say to you, do not smile. What we are seeing in these noisy, shuddering and bumping vehicles is the dawn of a new kind of transportation, which will eventually totally outstrip anything we could dream of. Make no mistake about it.

"You will also be inclined to laugh at my next suggestion. We know the way the balloon, and ballooning, is becoming an increasingly popular novelty; and who amongst us has not smiled dubiously at the strange drawings and ideas held by many that man will one day be able to soar and fly like the birds?

"Yet, when you consider the achievements made in other fields, who can really doubt that the theories of seeming fools and dreamers will, in a short space of time, become a reality with which to be reckoned? Who has heard of the experiments taking place at this moment under the guidance of men like Otto Lilienthal? The time will come, as certainly as tomorrow, when men will travel through the skies just as they will travel with ease and comfort at ever increasing speeds on land and sea.

"My friends, I have spoken about the natural line of progress, fast overtaking us, that will inevitably have a bearing on our lives and on the manner in which we work. We now have to consider what the climate will be; who will control these changes. The answer is simple—politicians, industrialists, generals and the rich. They hold the key to all power and if we are to have any share in the fortune that awaits, we must also have a share in that power. How is this to be achieved?

"Our manner of business is classed by many as the business of evil. So be it. But in what conditions can this so-called evil best flower? I would suggest the word *chaos*; I would suggest the word *instability*; I would suggest the word *uncertainty:* three words that should be the cornerstones of our thinking.

"In the world today there are great revolutionary political movements smoldering under the surface of life, ready to erupt with the fire and violence of a volcano. From all parts of the Continent we hear of anarchy—assassinations, the detonation of bombs, the disruption of normal everyday existence, all performed in the name of political ideals and fervor.

"I would suggest to you that these methods of anarchy and unrest can be used by us to furnish our own interests. If we can assist and foster conditions of unrest, even perform anarchistic acts of our own volition, we can create a situation where the ripe pickings will fall to us like apples from the tree.

"It remains now for us to plan, to decide, to make ready for the harvest we can reap."

There was silence as the Professor sat down. Then Grisombre began to applaud. With slight hesitation the others joined him, Schleifstein slapping the table soundly with the palm of his hand.

When the small but sincere ovation subsided, Grisombre rose, speaking in a strongly accented English, choosing his words with care.

"I find it interesting to hear the good Professor expound this theory. From my own experience I can attest to the fact that it is all valid thinking. It is true that I was a very young man in 1871, but I recall vividly the conditions which reigned in Paris at the time of the siege."

His eyes darted toward Schleifstein, as though seeking some confirmation from a member of the race that had bested the French at the culmination of the Franco-Prussian war.

"The conditions were terrible, with food so scarce that some were reduced to eating rats. I remember the day they shot the elephants in the zoological gardens for food. But my overall recollection is that of a city open to plunder. I know of many men who made fortunes. The disruption of society can only lead us to greater strength and I, for one, welcome Professor Moriarty as our inspirational leader."

One by one the others threw in their hand with the Professor. It remained for the complicated governing details of their intercontinental organization to be thrashed out. But before the conversation could turn in that direction, Sanzionare rose to his feet.

"As the Professor's guest, I would like to pay my respects in a tangible manner," he announced, flicking his fingers in the direction of the young man he had brought with him.

The dark young Italian was at his master's side, moving with a quick skill that Moriarty considered could, under different conditions, be deadly. A small, oblong package appeared as if from nowhere. Sanzionare took it, walked the length of the table and placed it in Moriarty's hands giving a short but reverential bow.

Moriarty unwrapped the package with care. Inside was a box, carefully tied with ribbon. The box contained a book, bound in calf and beautifully decorated with gold leaf—an Italian translation of *The Dynamics of an Asteroid* by James Moriarty. Its feel was beautiful to the hands, and to the gaze of anybody with artistic sensibility it was in itself an *objet d'art*.

"I had it done especially by our most skillful craftsman in Firenze," said Sanzionare, and Moriarty wondered at that moment if the Italian's eyes were tinged with mockery. He felt a well of unexpected anger rise in him and the color flood high on his cheeks. But in a second Moriarty recovered his composure, making a short and gracious speech of thanks.

The Frenchman, Grisombre, not to be outdone, made a sign in the direction of his two slim, olive-skinned escorts, who, reacting somewhat dramatically, produced a flat square package that had been stowed under the table. This was revealed to be a book also—a slimmer volume than that offered by the Italian, but larger in size and bound in hand-tooled Morocco leather.

"Monsieur le Professeur," Grisombre licked his lips. "I know that you, like myself, have an eye for the ladies. You are a connoiseur in the arts of love. The photographs in this volume are made by some of the best at my disposal."

The album contained over two hundred photographs that would today bring a fortune from any wealthy collector of erotica. Moriarty allowed a smile to trace briefly over his lips as he let the pages waterfall quickly from his thumb, getting a small first glimpse of the exquisite ladies from Paris in various stages of undress, in poses of a most seductive nature—alone, together and with various young men of well-endowed physique.

Schleifstein was now at the Professor's elbow, an unwrapped, heavy, polished mahogany box in his big hands. He clicked his heels, after the Prussian military manner, and placed the box in front of Moriarty.

"I have a gift which I think will be of more practical value."

The lid swung back on hinges to reveal, nestling in a dark blue bed of velvet, an unusual pistol. Moriarty had seen nothing like it before and, in truth, it was the most interesting of the three gifts so far offered. To begin with, there was no chamber and no visible hammer.

He picked it out of the box and weighed it in his hand. It had a masculine, workmanlike, feel. He looked questioningly at the German.

"It is an automatic pistol," said Schleifstein. "Another mark of progress, you see." He took the weapon from Moriarty. "The cartridges fit into a magazine, which slides into the butt and the weapon automatically recocks itself when you fire. It is copied from an idea incorporated in the Maxim gun, and is the invention of a Hugo Borchardt, manufactured by Ludwig Loewe of Berlin. I have brought cartridges also, and I venture to suggest that in all the many signs of progress you have spoken about, this will also bring a drastic change to our business."*

Moriarty nodded. Firearms fascinated him, and this one sent strange tingles up his arm as he held it. He looked around, catching the eye of the Spaniard, Segorbe, who held him steadily in his gaze.

"These gifts make mine look somewhat puny," smiled Segorbe, rising and passing over a long, slim parcel.

It contained a Toledo dagger, the hilt pocked with rubies, the blade honed razor sharp.

"It has the advantage of silence when compared with the pistol,"

---

*The Borchardt automatic was, in fact, the precursor of the Luger. Hugo Borchardt had successfully invented the design as early as 1890 while living in America, but no manufacturer in the United States showed any interest. Finally Borchardt took the design to Germany, where Loewe put it into production in 1893. It was one of the first automatic pistols to be sold commercially in any large numbers.

Segorbe said smoothly.

Moriarty looked down at the collection in front of him, lips curving slightly.

"Your gifts," he said almost in a whisper, "represent all the classic facets of the great intriguer. I now only need a vial of poison and some kind of explosive and I can be regarded"—he swept his hands across the pile of presents—"as scholar, libertine and assassin."

There were quiet chuckles from the men around the table.

"But there is no need for gifts," he continued. "To have gathered you all here; to share experiences and thoughts; to build a structure and plan ahead is all we need. The ultimate outcome of this meeting will be reward enough for all of us."

Paul Golden said nothing, yet took in everything.

"That automatic barking iron looks real wicked," said Paget later. "It'll be some moment when we get to see it fired."

He was talking to Spear, who was obviously mending, even though his face still looked bruised and battered and the dressings on his hands contiued to need changing twice a day.

"What about the book the Frenchie gave him?" Spear winked broadly and Paget grinned.

"Where did you hear about that, then?"

Spear nodded in the direction of Bridget, who sat in her usual place by the bed. "She told me." His look was of one jesting at the embarrassment of another.

Bridget blushed scarlet, biting her lip.

"She got it from her." Spear nodded again, this time toward Fanny.

Paget looked at his betrothed, a query in his lifted eyebrows, amusement around his mouth.

"Well . . ." Fanny hesitated.

"And you, Fanny Jones, saying you thought it was disgusting." Paget smiled, remembering the girl's forthright statements when he had described the photographs to her.

"Well . . ." said Fanny again, with no other words of explanation.

"You girls have got dirty minds." Spear looked at the two of them, not caring about the fact that grinning was still a painful exercise.

"We're inquisitive, that's all." Bridget still showed spirit.

"You'll know all about it when I'm back on my feet and well," said Spear.

"Maybe—" Fanny was cool, her hands folded in her lap. "Maybe we should plan a double wedding on Tuesday."

Both Spear and Bridget appeared to be wrapped in thought.

It was early afternoon when the news came into Scotland Yard that Sanzionare was staying at the Westminster Palace and that he had gone out with one of the young men, leaving the other in the hotel with the girl, Adela Asconta.

Though Sanzionare had nothing to do with him officially, the fact was passed on to Crow, who made a note of it, and continued to work away at the logical possibilities concerning Moriarty. In a day or so he hoped to have all the facts on the strange Professor of Mathematics, his background, resignation from the university and the move to London.

In the meantime something else had materialized. Word had come from an informant down near the docks that the man Paget, whose name had been revealed during their examination into Moran's associates, was to be married on Tuesday at St. Andrew's, Limehouse.

If Paget were an associate of Moran, Crow reasoned, and if Moran had been an associate of Moriarty, then Paget could be in some way connected with both of them. It would be interesting at least to see this person and his bride.

The thought of a bride brought Angus Crow down from his logic, to the earthiness of Mrs. Sylvia Cowles. There was no logic there, simply passion, and after a few moments with his mind drifting about the bedroom delights afforded by Mrs. Cowles, Crow was obliged to loosen his collar.

It was a waiting game, he thought: waiting for Moriarty; waiting for some further hints or clues; waiting until his own powers of deduction could be set against hard facts and proved to be either right or wrong. In some ways he was also waiting for himself, and that was the most illogical matter of all—waiting to make his mind up about Mrs. Cowles. Angus McCready Crow decided that his emotions, as far as Mrs. Cowles was concerned, were in some chaos.

On Friday evening Luigi Sanzionare returned to his hotel suite and spent the night hours with Adela Asconta; Wilhelm Schleifstein went to eat at the Café Royale, eventually going back to his hotel to a glutted sleep; Jean Grisombre and his two companions went, on Moriarty's advice, and with special facilities, to Sal Hodges' house; while Esteban Bernado Segorbe sat down in the writing room of Somerset House to pen a long letter of instructions to his chief lieutenant in Madrid: Señor Segorbe's business interests needed much of his time and attention.

In Limehouse the punishers still kept the kitchens and the womenfolk under close watch; Professor James Moriarty sent Mary McNiel to bed without him and spent the time until the small hours working on notes for the continuation of their meeting on the morrow; Spear dozed, and Bridget kept her vigil; Paget and Fanny slept entwined, though Paget dreamed vividly of prison cells and policemen in full cry after him, shrunken to the size of a rat and facing death by being squashed by a huge boot. Ember and Lee Chow were out and about, as indeed were many more of Moriarty's people, for there was a wedding party to attend on Tuesday and gifts had to be procured. No self-respecting member of the great family of villains could be expected to buy wedding gifts with money.

Saturday, April 14, 1894

(AN ASSASSINATION IS ARRANGED)

THE STRUCTURE OF the organization had been thrashed out during the period that followed the luncheon party on the previous day. The more serious problem of implementing the plans for chaos throughout Europe was left until Saturday afternoon when each of the protagonists put forward their own possible actions.

All were agreed in a campaign aimed at the disruption of peace, harmony and the serene way of life in the major cities across the Continent—actions that would undoubtedly be attributed to the extreme political factions that already bedeviled Europe. But it was Grisombre who made the first concrete suggestion of political assassination.

"There is nothing that will bring alarm more speedily," said the Frenchman. "And I intend that in my area there will be a quick outrage, which should spark immediate turmoil. Within the next few weeks I shall see to it that the President of France is murdered."

Grisombre, as we now know, was as good as his word. The meeting, headed by Moriarty, was undoubtedly the signal which heralded a sudden upsurge of anarchist activities throughout the Continent. In June the French President, Sadi Carnot, was assassinated in Lyons. It is interesting to note that the assassin was an Italian, so the possibility remains that the Continental branches of Moriarty's empire were, even then, working in harmony.

Neither can we now doubt that other events in the history of the late nineties and early 1900's are directly attributable to the London meeting of April, 1894. There appears to be evidence that even the death of President McKinley of the United States in 1901 was part of the later plan. Certainly the tragic event of the death of Archduke Franz Ferdinand at Sarajevo—which culminated in the

First World War—was a direct result of Moriarty's actions. The immediate effects in England itself—which we can now examine—have long been a closely guarded secret.

The resolve apparent in Grisombre's promise startled Moriarty. It was as though the Frenchman were attempting to outbid him in some deadly game, and the Professor felt the eyes of his colleagues looking at him for a lead.

He remained silent for a full minute, then his head nodded almost imperceptibly.

"Good," he said. "Good. This is the kind of foresight we require."

Moriarty looked in turn at each of his allies. "I too have plans," he said quietly. "In this country there is little point in killing off a Prime Minister nor yet any parliamentarian. Also our Queen—our figurehead—is an old lady who will soon die anyway."

He paused for effect. "My plans concern the next in line: the one who will reign once Queen Victoria has, as Shakespeare put it, shuffled off this mortal coil. The Prince of Wales, the illustrious if somewhat debauched Albert Edward, will be my personal victim. And to that end, gentlemen, I would like you to be my guests at a rather special performance tonight. You may rest assured that in a matter of weeks the Prince will be a dead man."

The brooding silence which fell upon those gathered about the table spoke eloquently of the respect that was generated.

It was Paul Golden who finally broke the silence.

"Professor. Gentlemen." His mouth was set, without the hint of a smile. "I have found all this both instructive and interesting. I am afraid that I will not be able to join you in whatever else the Professor has arranged tonight for it is time for me to begin my somewhat arduous journey back to New York. I will, however, take with me a glowing report to my colleagues. Providing your plans go smoothly, I see no reason why we in the New World cannot at some future date do business with your organization here in Europe. You may certainly call upon us at any time for help or advice. I look forward to developing a beneficial relationship."

Paget, sturdy by the door, did not really understand what it was that now disturbed him. He had spent much of his life in squalor, clawing his way from the gutter. Since Moriarty had become his father in crime, life had fallen into a pattern and he was certainly not averse to performing most of the acts deemed unlawful by society. But like many of his persuasion, Paget held the royal family in awe and reverence. Now, in a few words, his leader had embarked them on a journey which to him appeared one of abject futility, waste and folly.

The performance Moriarty wished his Continental visitors to attend took place at one of London's best, and most famous, music halls—the Alhambra Palace of Varieties in Leicester Square, where there was a particularly good bill playing.

Strangely Moriarty was a man who delighted in the roistering, sometimes vulgar, always colorful spectacle afforded by the music hall, and he had gone to great pains to procure the best box in the house, not only for his four principal guests, but also for the bulk of their combined retinues. As for himself, Moriarty allowed only Paget to accompany him, insisting that his lieutenant should come armed.

Paget naturally felt honored, but he could not throw off the feeling that the new Continental alliance had tipped the Professor into realms that were unbelievably dangerous. He had vaguely known that in the past Moriarty often engaged himself in commissions for other powers, calling for nefarious dealings with politicians and royalty. But for all Paget knew, the royalty was foreign and so did not count. This was different.

The final gathering of the Continental emissaries ended in Limehouse a little before five in the afternoon, and arrangements were made for everyone to meet in the plushly appointed foyer of the Alhambra, some fifteen minutes before the second evening performance.

The entertainment on that particular night was of exceptional value. As well as the two ballets (the Alhambra spared no expense to provide magnificent spectacle centered on its *première danseuse*, Mlle. Catherine Geltzer), the program included Mr. G. H. Chrigwin, the White-Eyed Kaffir; Miss Cissie Loftus; Mr. George Robey—still making the audience reel with his humorous song, *The Simple Pimple*; Lieutenant Frank Travis, the Society Ventriloquist; Miss Vesta Tilley; and Mr. Charles Coburn, the Man Who Broke the Bank at Monte Carlo.

The one artist, however, whom Moriarty wished his colleagues to see, and who indeed held the Professor himself in fascinated concentration, was billed as Dr. Night, Illusionist and Prestidigitator Extraordinary.

Apart from other considerations, Moriarty could not resist the feats this kind of entertainer was able to perform; for in some ways the magician and the Professor were in the same line of business: illusions, disappearances, manipulation and the casting of spells. This very night, for instance, he was sitting in public with his four Continental henchmen, appearing in the visual shape of that Professor Moriarty who had once been fêted as a new mathematical genius.

The pit orchestra produced a shimmer of strings and brass, with perhaps a shade of heavy-handedness from drums and cymbals; then the tabs rose to display the stage hung with black drapes and set about with small ornate tables and pieces of intricate and undeniably magic apparatus.

The drums rose to a crescendo, and Dr. Night appeared, a man of medium build, immaculate in full evening clothes, his hair and small beard black, and the aura surrounding him undeniably Satanic. His eyes swept the audience with a look which almost conveyed contempt.

"Ladies and gentlemen. The wizardry of the East and West," he announced, reaching into the air and plucking forth a deep blue silken handkerchief. "One and one make two." Another color silk came from the air into his other hand. "And three . . . and four."

The hands, delicate with long fingers, reached alternately into the air until he had collected some ten or eleven multicolored pieces of silk, which he rolled together to produce a pear-shaped ball some eight or nine inches long. Then with a quick upward movement Dr. Night threw the ball into the air where it appeared to be poised for a second before expanding and opening into a huge butterfly suspended before him.

There followed an array of flamboyant mysteries that held even the noisy gallery silent and in suspense: an Egyptian sarcophagus, complete with mummy, was shown from all sides. The mummy was removed and proved to be in a fragile condition (in fact at one point the head was separated from the body). The mummy was replaced, the sarcophagus whirled round, suddenly beginning to shake violently with a knocking from within.

With a flourish Dr. Night opened the quivering sarcophagus, and, to weird Eastern music, a magnificently attired Egyptian Princess stepped from the casket to perform a sinuous dance.

Great glass bowls of water were produced from the air under a large silken square, each bowl bursting into flame seconds after the silk was removed. Then Dr. Night passed into the audience to have eight playing cards selected, and to borrow three rings from somewhat nervous ladies. The eight chosen cards appeared suddenly and in full view on the points of a large ornate silver star. The mystic doctor then took an omelette pan into which he broke eggs, added the three rings and topped it with brandy, setting the mixture alight and dowsing the flame with the lid; immediately removing it to display three snow-white doves, each with one of the borrowed rings on a ribbon around its neck.

The Egyptian Princess was brought on again, this time to be mesmerized by the doctor, who then caused her to levitate, floating in midair before the eyes of the assembled audience.

It was the culmination of a splendid performance, Dr. Night leaving the stage to rising applause. Moiarty sat, like a small boy, entranced, even a hint of jealousy in his mind. It was as though the spectacular Dr. Night had touched Moriarty's Achilles' heel, for most of the illusions and their performance baffled him, and he was determined to discover the secrets of these impressive arts. He did not know, however, that other fates were conspiring against him.

Earlier, as Moriarty's party gathered inside the foyer of the Alhambra, Sergeant Cuthbert Frome, an officer of Scotland Yard's Criminal Investigation Department, was taking a walk around the West End; more to familiarize himself with certain locations than anything else. Frome was twenty-eight years old, recently transferred from the city of Manchester to the metropolitan police; he was a keen man, eager to make his way and full of the enthusiasms of his age. After only six weeks at the Yard he had confidently brought himself up to date with all the wanted lists and descriptions of persons to be watched, reported on, or apprehended.

He was passing the facade of the Alhambra when his attention became drawn to a carriage discharging its occupants: a very beautiful young woman accompanied by two young men with Italianate good looks and a slightly older, more swarthy man.

Frome had seen the man's description on a circular passed around the office and his brain searched for facts. The woman and two younger men had also been mentioned. An Italian name, Santo-something? Sanzionare. He had it; but by then the party had passed on into the theater. Frome followed, pausing briefly to show his credentials to the front-of-house man.

His quarry was not in the foyer, so the sergeant went through to the long refreshment bar, which was already crowded with men and women, most of them in full evening clothes. Among these theater-goers, Frome recognized not a few ladies of the town, for this was a favorite place in which they plied their nubile wares—in spite of Mrs. Ormiston Chant's efforts to close the variety palaces because of the temptations afforded therein by the frail sisterhood.

At the far end of the bar Frome spotted Sanzionare's party with another group of men. One of this company stood out from the rest like a signal beacon, for he was tall and very thin with a great domed forehead and eyes that appeared sunken into his face and surrounded by dark circles. Frome knew this one also by his description.

The temptation was to leave and make his way with haste back to Scotland Yard, for the sergeant was well aware that many questions were at this moment being asked about the tall and gaunt man. But he held his ground, watching until the party made their way up to the circle boxes.

A few minutes later the young detective was admitted to the house manager's office, rapidly regaling the manager with a story that gave little of the truth but allowed Frome access to a spot in the circle from where he could view the box now occupied by Sanzionare and the others. From his vantage point Frome was able to make rough sketches of the men and women present—an action that turned out to be of great importance.

Nobody had, of course, informed Frome that Sanzionare's hotel was being watched and the Italian followed. But the detective detailed for this chore had simply obeyed his instructions to the letter; so while Frome was inside the Alhambra, carefully making a visual picture of each member of the suspect group, the detective charged with the surveillance of Sanzionare, sat in a nearby public house, his eye on the clock, waiting to pick up his subjects once the performance ended—an act which was to earn him a severe reprimand Monday morning after Frome's detailed report reached Inspector Angus Crow's desk.

Sunday, April 15, to Wednesday, April 18, 1894

(THE WEDDING)

FROME'S REPORT WAS not seen by Angus McCready Crow until Monday morning because in spite of the building pressures of detection Crow was determined to observe Sunday as a day of rest and recreation. He also knew that he could not hold off the growing problem of his emotional involvement with Mrs. Cowles for much longer.

Mrs. Cowles had been sweet, loving, tender and understanding; yet of late her passions appeared to become more demanding and the whispered endearments that took place on their regular coming together were sprinkled with hints and importunings which meant but one thing. Though she did not come right out with it, Mrs. Sylvia Cowles was suggesting to Crow that she either had to lose a lodger or gain a husband. Crow, the onetime confirmed bachelor, was as reluctant to move out of the comfortable diggings as he was to take unto himself a wife who might well come between him and his dedicated task—bringing villains to justice and justice to villains.

Yet Crow was a prudent man, well aware that any further prevarication on his part might lead to unpleasantness. However, though much of his reasoning told him he should be out and about—searching for the truth concerning the power wielded by the shadowy conundrum, Moriarty—the question of Sylvia Cowles could not be shelved forever.

It was with these thoughts in mind that Crow suggested to his landlady that they spend a quiet day together. They ate luncheon at 63 King Street and then went for a stroll, taking a cab as far as Marble Arch, before walking gently in the now warm spring sunshine across Hyde Park to the banks of the Serpentine.

It was late afternoon when they returned to King Street, and Crow, having talked about everything imaginable—except for that which was most on his mind—swallowed all pride, doubts, and a few of his fears.

"Sylvia," he started gruffly, "there is something I have to ask you." It sounded like words from a cheap romance. "Tell me, have you been happy since I came to lodge here?"

"Angus, you know I have been happy, but you must also know that, like other people, I have a conscience." She smiled sweetly.

"That is what I wish to talk to you about. This happiness, my dear, cannot last if we go on as we have been doing."

There was a long pause as Sylvia Cowles looked hard at him, her eyes narrowing a little.

"Yes?" she said coldly, as though expecting the worst.

"What I am trying to ask, my dear . . ." *Oh God*, he thought, *is it me saying this?* "What I am trying . . . Sylvia, would you do me the honor of marrying me?"

There. It was out. And at the back of his mind Crow wondered if he would ever be able to take back the words.

"Angus." Mrs. Cowles' eyes seemed to brim with tears. "Angus, my dear. As they say in romantic novels, I thought you'd never ask. Of course I will marry you, nothing is nearer to my heart's wish."

She then descended on the detective, showing him exactly how near to her heart's wish it truly was.

Later Inspector Angus McCready Crow began to think perhaps it was for the best that his bachelor days should be considered over at last.

Sal Hodges came down to the warehouse late on the Sunday afternoon and spent an hour, taking sherry and talking business with Moriarty. She then went to see Spear.

"Bridget," Spear said softly once the introductions were over, "will you be a pet and leave me alone with Sal. I have things to discuss with her."

"And you can't say them in front of me?" Bridget colored.

"No. No, I can't. There are some things that are private, from times before you, Bridget."

"I'll go," she spat, "but don't forget that I'm no lady's maid like Fanny. I've scavenged, clawed, stolen and fought with the best of them. I'm a family girl, and when my heart's set on something, I'd like as not kill for it." She left with a flounce, face scarlet with suppressed anger.

"Yours?" asked Sal, sitting beside the bed, her eyes twinkling and head cocked cheekily on one side. In the free and easy world of Moriarty's family, Spear was the last person she would ever have wagered on to be caught by a pretty face.

"It'd seem so."

"Indeed it would, but if you ever want to get rid of her, I've always got a place for a girl with spunk."

"I doubt there's any chance of getting rid of her. She's a sticker, Sal, and I could be worse off. But that's not what I want to talk about."

"Are you better?"

Spear looked his bandaged hands. "Not ready yet to use these as I'd like, but better than I was. How often do you go into your shop in Berwick Street?" The muscle on his right cheek contracted, making the uneven scar show livid against the healthy skin.

"A couple of times a week. Why?"

"I sent someone there last Sunday. Look, Sal, I was trying to do Pip Paget and young Fanny a favor. Fanny Jones lost her post because of a lecherous butler called Halling. I had him marked up last Sunday evening: left a message for him saying as how Fanny was at the Berwick Street place. I reckoned I'd get there before him, and I was going to put the carriers right. As it was, bloody Green and Butler nabbed me."

"He went there." Sal chuckled. "I was in on Monday and young Delphine said they had done business. Apparently he was annoyed at them knowing nothing of the Jones girl, but Delphine made it up to him. Pompous bugger, it seems. Delphine said he was a puffer."

"If he goes back, could you get him fixed?"

"The carriers there will need to be paid, and I don't want no trouble on the premises."

"Twenty guineas?" Amidst the bruising on his face Spear's eyebrows were raised.

"It should be enough."

Spear flapped a bandaged hand toward the old chest of drawers that stood near his window.

"In there. The top drawer. There's a cash box."

Bridget returned as Sal was about to leave and the elegant, sophisticated madam could not resist a parting shot.

"I'll give your love to the girls then, Bert."

"Sod the girls."

"They all miss you."

"Just get that one thing done for me."

"And what might that one thing be?" asked Bridget, tapping a foot, once Sal Hodges was out of the room.

"You're jealous already and I haven't even shown you how to dance the old buttock jig yet."

"You'll show me soon enough, Bert Spear, and I'll learn you as well. Just what's that whore-mother doing for you?"

"If you must know, she's getting a wedding present for Pip Paget and Fanny Jones."

"I could have done that."

"You're not allowed a step outside this building and you know it. Not yet. Anyway, it's a special present that only Sal can arrange."

Bridget treated him to a sunny grin. "Something Paget can practice on?"

"Enough of that, girl." His tone softened. "Will you not go on reading that tale to me?"

"I'll give you tale." She moved archly, thrusting forward.

"Tale or tail? You move as though you crack nuts with yours."

"I shall. Your nuts, Bert Spear. I can be a rare nutcracker when I've the mind."

Moriarty used the letterhead of his former house off the Strand when writing to Dr. Night, the illusionist. The note was short, praising the performance and asking for an appointment with the doctor to discuss matters of mutual advantage. The advantage of which Moriarty wrote was undefined but concerned the payment of a large sum of money to Dr. Night in exchange for professional secrets. The Professor was obsessed with the whole idea, as though the tricks and stratagems of the illusionist would provide him with more personal power. As, indeed, he considered they could. However, he still had to proceed with the everyday workings of his business.

While he waited for Ember to return—for it was Ember who had been entrusted with delivering the letter and bringing the illusionist's reply—Moriarty ticked off the multitude of items he seemed to be juggling. Foremost in his mind was Paget's imminent marriage, but that was in many ways clouded by the knowledge that they had yet to unmask the traitor in the warehouse.

Since the moment Moriarty had concluded that there was an apostate in their midst, the watch had been kept on all four suspects. Moriarty's not inconsiderable knowledge of human nature told him now that in all possibility the culprit would be revealed by precipitate action within a few days—maybe even before the wedding celebrations on Tuesday.

There was the question of the robbery at Harrow, which would follow hard on the wedding. The cracksman Fisher had, that very morning, supplied the Professor with a complete list of items they

hoped to bring away from the Pinner estate. These included some
rare silver and gold plate: at least £20,000 of jewelry, kept in a
"Country Gentleman's Deed Safe"—by George Price Ltd of Wol-
verhampton—in the study on the first floor; and several valuable
objets d'art, two of which were Canaletto paintings.

Moriarty had already known about the Canalettos, and they were
earmarked for special shipment back to Italy within a few hours of
the robbery, their disposal having been planned in conjunction with
Luigi Sanzionare.

Overriding all these things was the Professor's move respecting
the Prince of Wales. Already copies of the court circular were on his
desk. Place, time, date and method were all things that had to be
clear and plotted.

Shortly after nine Ember returned with an envelope addressed to
the Professor in a florid script much occupied with whirls and fancy
scrolls.

> Most honored Professor,
>   You do me great service in showing interest in the noble art
> which I practice. I should be more than happy to meet a
> gentleman of your learning and position to discuss, as you
> write, the proposition "to our mutual advantage." If you
> would do me the honor of calling on me in my dressing room at
> the Alhambra Theatre after the last performance on Wednes-
> day night, that is to say at eleven o'clock, I would be most
> happy to see you. If this is not convenient, perhaps you could
> suggest another time and date with which I will endeavor to
> comply.
>   I remain, sir,
>   Your obedient servant,
>   *William S. Wotherspoon.*
>
>   *(Dr. Night)*

Moriarty's lips lifted in a sour smile. A magsman, he thought.
William S. Wotherspoon. Dr. Night. A cheap magsman.

What a pompous bastard he is, thought Delphine Merchant. Her
client, Mr. Halling, was carefully brushing his hair, as though each
thinning strand had its own particular place on the scalp. In bed he
went at it with lecherous vigor, yet without the style of most men,
but once out and in his trousers again, he eyed her as though he was

some lord or duke. By God, she had known lords and dukes and they were better men than this skinny-ribbed beanpole—and better at flopping.

"You can stay all night with me, you know, my duck," she said, letting her small voice sweep up and down the scale.

Sal Hodges had once told her that using her vocal charms in this way could well set a man on.

Halling turned and looked at her as though she was a piece of gutter turd.

"My child, I have to be back." He consulted his watch, replacing it in its pocket with much exaggerated care. "It just wouldn't do. I have a duty to the servants. Some of them are only young girls. No, I have my responsibilities. Private pleasure must never conflict with public duty."

Public duty my arse, thought Delphine, *and servants as well. You have the look and the smell of butler written all over you, my friend, for all your coming so heavy.* She pitied the young girl servants in that household. Delphine knew the hell that lecherous, demanding, double-faced butlers could create among little parlormaids. Respectability was a word that covered sins and hypocrisy like thick glue.

It was near enough ten o'clock when Halling left Berwick Street to make his way back to the secure portals of the Brays' mansion in Park Lane. He turned left, crossing into Broad Street, then down toward Brewer Street and the Quadrant. Though there was no fog, the smoke hung heavy above the houses, blowing wispy along the gullies of the narrow lanes.

They took him from an alley off Brewer Street, two of them, big rough men who seemed to the butler to be the size of gorillas. Later the police decided that it was a simple case of robbery, but Halling, ruined for life, always wondered, for they knocked him down quickly with blows to his head; nor did he try to resist as they went for his purse and snatched the watch from its chain. It was only when he was down and the things taken from him that they cobbled him, first in the ribs and then lower, damaging him in a way that, though it still left him alive, removed what manhood he had.

Spear's reaction, on hearing the details, was one of outright pleasure. It was justice, as far as he was concerned: a justice made sweeter by the fact that he did not tell either Fanny Jones or Paget. Never again would the unctuous Mr. Halling bother or blackmail helpless girls in service.

The hams and the veal, chickens, turkeys and rabbits were brought into the warehouse on Monday morning. Out of respect for her position as the bride, Fanny was excused all duties in the kitchen, her place taken by Bridget—though she was loath to leave Spear's side, particularly on the day when he was being allowed to get up and sit in a chair in readiness for the wedding: Albert Spear was not going to be left out of the celebrations even if they had to bring him downstairs on a shutter.

The activity in the kitchens began gently, gaining momentum through the day, until by late afternoon it reached a frenzied peak— all watched by successive teams of men whose instructions were precise and whose eyes followed every move made by those engaged in preparing the delicacies.

At midday they began to unload the wines: crates of Vauban Frères champagne, which had been diverted from their original destinations by numerous ruses, including bribery and the more barefaced forms of violent robbery.

The main outer floor of the warehouse was swept and cleaned by a team of Chinese whom Lee Chow had mustered for the purpose. Extra lamps were trimmed, filled, and hung in place, and long trestle tables were set to run down the length of the floor, to left and right, while others were erected in front of the entrance to the "waiting room."

When all this was completed, the women—wives and girls drawn from many areas of Moriarty's organization—came in with armfuls of spring flowers and garlands, to decorate what was normally a bleak and dreary interior. It was plain to see that the Professor was determined to do it right by Paget and his betrothed.

Yet business continued as usual. Moriarty held his daily meeting with the three remaining members of the "Praetorian Guard," together with Parker and the Jacobs brothers, who were quickly assuming a new importance within the structure of power. He also dealt with a steady stream of callers. And Paget himself was kept busy receiving various moneys, from cash carriers, bullies and collectors who had been out as usual over the weekend, wringing Moriarty's tribute from those who regularly paid tariff to the Professor's coffers.

During the midafternoon, Paget took the opportunity of catching the Professor alone.

"I'd like to thank you for all you're doing for Fan and myself." There was genuine appreciation in his manner.

Moriarty looked up, eyes dull and watchful. "It is right that I should do this for you, Paget. After all, you have been with me a long time and you are now my most trusted man. I only hope, for your sake, that the woman will not prove to be like most of them; that she will not let you down."

A flash of pain crossed Paget's face, the suspicion still ever-present, a constant worry.

"I cannot believe it is Fanny." The words were brave enough, but doubt still lay buried behind his eyes. "As for being your most trusted man, indeed I try to be worthy of that, but I have concern over one matter, and I have to speak to you of it."

Moriarty's head came up, face dark, glowering with the first hint of reaction, which would come like a storm if Paget proved to be in disagreement with any of the Professor's well-laid projects.

"Go on." The voice chilling as ice in the face.

Paget straightened, firming his resolve. It would be wrong to remain silent over this.

"I will do—and have done—most things, Professor. You know that. Thieving, punishing, collecting, murder even. But I cannot be asked to perform the thing you have promised to the Continental gentlemen."

"And why not?"

"I cannot, that's all there is to it. I could never take violent action against the Prince of Wales."

"Sentiment," spat Moriarty. "You're like all the rest. Pilferers, thieves, murderers, yet the royal family is sacrosanct. Sentiment and superstition." He gave a half laugh. "But you have no cause to worry, Paget, you will not be asked to assist in the demise of Bertie Wales. I shall see to that one myself and make it a personal matter. Now go and concentrate on your nuptials."

Inspector Angus McCready Crow did not make his engagement public knowledge at Scotland Yard when he went in to work on the Monday morning. The word would be out soon enough, for the ecstatic Mrs. Cowles was pressing for an announcement in the columns of *The Times*.

All thoughts of his future matrimonial predicament went straight from his mind when he saw young Frome's report on his desk. Under normal circumstances it would never have been passed on to Crow, but the assistant commissioner who had viewed the document and the drawing, saw at once that if the young policeman was accurate with his pencil, one of the group could be nobody else but Professor James Moriarty.

Crow had no doubt that it was Moriarty; the likeness was exact, just as he was described by Holmes. It concerned him deeply that here was an indication of the possible scope of Moriarty's control. Luigi Sanzionare was certainly sitting with him in the box at the Alhambra, and the girl Adela Asconta, her head cocked to one side, the face puzzled. To his eye, Crow reasoned, most of the others present were foreigners also.

He first referred the matter to the assistant commissioner, then, on his authority, ordered the drawing to be copied and circulated to police forces on the Continent, with a view of identifying some of the other faces present. It was shortly after this had been done that Crow interviewed the detective who had been on duty, shadowing Sanzionare. But the horse had bolted; the Italian and his party had left the Westminster Palace that morning, taking the boat train, presumably en route for Rome via Paris.

It was disturbing to know that Moriarty was openly consorting with foreign criminals in the capital, and it did not take such an agile mind as Crow's much time to deduce what they were about: At least it would be some very large robbery, at worst a union of the criminal elements of all Europe.

The temptation to mount a full-scale search for Moriarty, collar him and use the old de Goncourt business as a holding charge, was great. But Crow was only too conscious that a clever legal man would break the de Goncourt charge with little trouble. The most they could accomplish that way would be a chance to talk to Moriarty for a day or so—if that. His real chance was to continue the waiting game.

By early afternoon Tanner had returned with what intelligence he had been able to glean. It disclosed little except that Professor Moriarty had been forced to resign from the university because of a scandal concerning two of his pupils—and it was thought that he had finally left the academic cloisters in the company of his youngest brother, who appeared to have visited him at the university on a number of occasions.

Crow also learned a little about Moriarty's family: his upbringing in Liverpool and the two younger brothers, both named James, one of whom was an officer in the 7th Lancers. As for the youngest brother, there seemed to be no information except that he had left home to work with the Great Western Railway Company, which, strangely, could not trace an employee of that name.

Crow wondered if it were possible. The youngest brother was not traceable. So? He came back to his original line of reasoning. If the Professor was able to appear in two guises, one younger than the other, it might be that the Moriarty they sought was in reality the famous professor's youngest brother. He instructed Tanner to continue the search for any further facts concerning James Moriarty minimus.

Crow then turned his attention to the morrow and the man Paget who was to be married at eleven o'clock, by the curate of St. Andrew's, Limehouse. He had this on the word of a sergeant in his late thirties, with much experience in the clam-closed dockland world. So Crow sent for the man.

It was natural that Crow should be anxious about the source of the intelligence concerning Paget's wedding, and his interview with the sergeant lasted for the better part of an hour. But like all good detectives, the sergeant was reluctant to reveal the name of his informant.

"It's not easy down there, sir," he told Crow. "You can be working in the thick of villains and transgressors of the worst kind, yet not know a damned thing. You plod on and trust to luck. All I can tell you is that this Paget's a big bloke with a lot of connections, and he's to be hammered proper tomorrow. As for my informant, I've never had anything from her before, but it does seem to be a straight tip. I did get the impression she was nervous in talking to me, that she was being watched and held some kind of grudge—but that's only intuition."

"Nothing wrong with intuition, Sergeant, not so long as it can be backed up with common reason and logic."

The sergeant laughed. "I've yet to associate common reason or logic with a woman."

Crow was immediately depressed for the thought of the imminent departure of his freedom rushed back into his mind. Weddings appeared to be the vogue, so tomorrow he would take a trip down to Limehouse and see this Paget and his bride turned off. If nothing else it should prove an interesting venture.

That Moriarty could pull strings at all levels was a plain fact of life, so nobody questioned what methods he had used to arrange the wedding without the formality of banns. It was enough to say that the Professor decreed the marriage would take place at St. Andrew's at eleven o'clock, and only a very limited number of people would be allowed into the ceremony. The celebrations afterward in the main floor of the warehouse would be another matter.

As always, the Professor's orders were obeyed to the letter, and at five minutes before eleven o'clock only a handful of people were waiting at the church. Paget was sitting in the front pew with Parker—spruce and smartly dressed, shaved and looking almost respectable—beside him as best man. Spear was not allowed to come over to the church, but Bridget, Kate Wright and her husband were there, as were Ember, Lee Chow and a couple of the punishers

with Terremant. There was no fuss, no choir or organ, for Moriarty
did not wish to call any undue attention to the church wedding. The
music, dancing and loud roister could safely be conducted behind
the locked and bolted doors of the warehouse later.

Parker had set his watchdogs around and about, but nobody paid
any special heed to the few old ladies, and a couple of men roughly
dressed in corduroy, with red chokers at their necks, who sat at the
back of the church. Weddings, christenings and funerals always
drew a few strays who liked to wallow and weep for people they did
not know.

Angus Crow felt conspicuous in the unaccustomed garb, but the
detective with him was quite used to posing in disguise and he
assured his inspector that he looked nothing like a policeman.

Promptly at eleven o'clock there was a stir at the back of the
church. The curate appeared before the altar and walked down to the
nave as Paget, nudged by Parker, took up his place.

They came slowly down the aisle: Fanny, composed and radiant
behind her white lace veil, clad in a dress she had labored over for
many hours—white silk, tight-waisted with a short train and high-
necked lace cape. She looked undeniably small on the arm of the
tall, dignified and stooping Moriarty, who had removed the sling
from his damaged arm for the first time since the attempt on his life.
Behind them walked Mary McNiel, the maid of honor, nervous and
ill at ease.

Crow was fascinated, particularly by the man on whose arm the
bride leaned. This was his first glimpse of the Professor, and the
whole scene had about it an air of unreality for him, as though the
characters in a novel were suddenly coming alive before his eyes.

The bridal procession came to a halt, the couple giving each other
a quick and hesitant glance before the curate began to intone:

"Dearly beloved, we are gathered together here in the sight of
God and in the face of this Congregation, to join together this man
and this woman in holy matrimony. . . ."

Crow hardly heard any of the service, so intent was he in gazing
at Professor Moriarty. It was a strange, depressing and brooding
feeling to see the man standing there in the church. In some ways the
very fact of Moriarty being in such a holy place made it worse; as
though a great sea of invisible evil surrounded the man, emanating
from him. Crow experienced odd and vivid sensations, associated
with clear pictures in his mind, of huge and unquenchable waves
breaking remorselessly upon rocks. The rock of the church, he
thought, under assault from the heavy swell of Moriarty's powers.

When the time came for the bridal party to follow the curate into the vestry, Crow could have sworn that Moriarty turned and looked down the church, the deeply circled and sunken eyes seeming to gaze straight into his own, penetrating through his skull. It was an unnerving moment that sent an unaccustomed icy shiver running from the back of Crow's neck to the base of his spine.

When the happy couple emerged to return down the aisle, two things took the inspector by surprise: First, the man Paget was most certainly one of the people shown on Frome's adept sketch of the party at the Alhambra; secondly, the bride, looking happy and most fetching with her veil now thrown back, answered the description of the young woman who had taken the basket of victuals into Horsemonger Lane Jail on the day Colonel Moran died.

Though Crow was outside the church as quickly as possible, he was amazed to find that the whole wedding party appeared to have melted into the side streets, lanes, and alleys like the thin wraiths of smoke that drifted through all the byways of this area. The whole episode had about it an eerie quality, akin to what he had felt on first sighting the Professor.

The evidence and his reasoning did seem to be adding together, and although he had not been able to detect anything strange in the Professor's appearance—such as the use of disguise—he was sure and certain that the connection between Moriarty, the professor of mathematics, and Moriarty, his youngest brother, was the answer to one of the problems. The man, Paget, was now fully proven to be an associate, not simply of Moran, but also of Moriarty; it would also be of importance to speak with the woman who had become Mrs. Paget; Crow was positive that the servant girl at Horsemonger Lane and Paget's bride were one and the same.

But how best to act? That was difficult. To begin with these people had to be found in the warren of byways that ran through the maze of the city's East End; then, once found, could they be held? If Moriarty's power were really as great as Sherlock Holmes had originally indicated, then he would be protected by almost an army and his ways of escape would be manifold. Should they wait for him to show himself again? Issue a directive for his apprehension? The latter course seemed unreliable, for a directive of this sort meant dozens of people being alerted, and undoubtedly the word would get back to Moriarty within the hour. The last thing Crow wanted was for his man to go to earth.

In the meantime, Crow decided as they rattled back to Scotland Yard, he would still have to wait. Inevitably the Professor or one of his confidants would make a move. The feeling of gloom and frustration began to lift. The answers were there, near to the surface, and it could only be a matter of time now before this archvillain would stretch his head too far from his world into Crow's.

Nobody had ever seen the warehouse looking like this before. The place smelled of flowers, the lamps were lit and the atmosphere bright with gaiety. It was also full to capacity: a very wide cross-section of Moriarty's family of villains present to pay respects and celebrate Paget's wedding.

The newlywed pair sat at the table set before the "waiting room" door, together with Moriarty himself, Ember, Lee Chow, Parker, the Jacobs brothers, Terremant, and Spear propped up in a chair. On their right a small dais had been set up for a band—a brace of violins, a cornet, two banjos, a zither and an accordion—ready to launch into *The Happy Peasant, Il Corricolo, Mona,* and later, when the party was in full swing, *'Appy 'Ampstead, Knocked 'Em in the Old Kent Road* and *My Old Dutch.*

At twelve noon the wicket gate, set in the big double doors, was locked and bolted, the warehouse full and the party ready to commence. Moriarty's orders were no admissions after noon.

The long series of trestle tables running down the left side were crowded with pies and molds, cold chickens and turkeys, hams and pickles, in the center of which stood a three-tiered wedding cake. There was champagne and ale to drink and a myriad pastries, jellies and trifles to choose from. In many ways it was a strange sight, as though this odd mixture of people were trying to ape the manners, style and etiquette of the middle classes.

This was most apparent on the table running down the other side of the floor, crammed as it was with gifts for the pair. The finders had been out and about to provide their tokens and tributes, though, apart from one or two objects, a certain sameness was visible. There were gold Albert chains and Langtry Alberts, bracelets and bangles decorated with Oriental pearls and diamonds; "Love Laughs at Locksmith" brooches; rings in abundance; gold keepers and knot rings, signet rings and heart charms and gold scarf pins. There were at least a dozen silver pencils, and four of gold; watches, both ladies' and gents', with Swiss horizontal and lever movements, and barrel movements; two sets of antique patterned fruit spoons; a solid silver-back brush set in a case, for Fanny; a silver combined match box and sovereign purse; a pair of field glasses; bottles of the Royal Perfumery's Chypre and New-Mown Hay.

In effect all the gifts were things that could be easily pocketed or taken quickly from their rightful owners. The only larger items being those given by the Professor himself: a haberdashery cabinet for Fanny, containing cottons, silks, tabs, buttons, needles, pins and all the paraphernalia women used; and, for Paget, a dressing-and-shaving case in dark French Morocco, with razors and the usual cutlery.

The guests who crowded the warehouse were of an unlikely variety: men and women dressed fashionably, some with taste, others looking flashy, gaudy even, in contrast with the more sober-suited men, who could easily have been professional people, doctors and bankers, maybe politicians; and it was notable that both these groups were at variance with the rougher, down-at-heel folk —people one could see daily on the streets of East and West Ends alike.

To an outsider the strangest thing of all was the fact that all these class divisions appeared to intermingle easily, laughing and jesting with each other, so that a bruising bully was seen talking merrily with an elegant city gent; a recognizably flash woman could be observed twinkling her eyes and undulating her charms at an elderly man who might have just walked in from the Stock Exchange; a delicate lady of high fashion clinked her champagne glass with a man who, even to the least experienced eye, could be little else but a person of dubious habits.

Paget and Fanny remained almost oblivious to the throng, except when one or another of Moriarty's employees—for everyone there served the Professor in one way or another—came over to the table to offer congratulations, after first paying their respects to Moriarty himself.

Yet in the far corner of Paget's mind there were the two-pronged, irksome nags of concern and despair. He could not deny that he had never before felt the warmth and tenderness that flowed between him and Fanny; nor could he deny the paradoxical sense of suspicion that his bride could just possibly be the one within the Professor's private domain who had already betrayed Moriarty and was willing to do it again. There was also the overriding unease, which had first come to him at Harrow, manifesting itself in the consistent knowledge that his present life was no way to achieve that happiness he so earnestly desired for the two of them.

Moriarty sat near, receiving the guests as they came to the table, rather like some princely father: shaking their hands or accepting their embraces, listening to their sweet, dripping words or requests with the same firm and unshakable concentration he always displayed. Yet deep within him there was a disquieting anxiety. He doubted if anyone else had noticed the two men sitting at the back of the church during the wedding ceremony. He had. He had also smelled the danger, that same scent that had reached his seventh sense when Holmes had come too near. The two men were he was certain, police; and one of them probably bore the name Crow.

Moriarty glanced along the line of favored men who sat with him and the bridal pair. Spear appeared to be enjoying himself, but the bruises were far from healed and his hands would need time yet before he could use them properly. The Professor sighed inwardly. Paget was his best lad, no doubt of that, but the bright Fanny Jones had him by the balls and there was no accounting for men who became enslaved by women. If only Spear had been better recovered.

The afternoon wore on, food, drink and music flowing through the heads and bellies of the guests, generating a false sense of security. Even the punishers were relaxing, and outside the few lurkers whom Parker had placed on watch began to grow restive, bored and not a little discontented that they were banned from the festivities.

Inside people began to sing to the band and groups started to dance, until the whole ground floor of the building reverberated to the music and stamp of feet.

The woman passed through the crowded floor, pausing for a word here and there, stopping to be kissed by some old comrade, quipping a jest with others. Nobody took heed when she reached the wicket gate in the warehouse doors; nor were they concerned— even if they saw—as she slipped back the bolts and snapped the lock free.

By late afternoon the mists came in to join with the smoke in the streets, making it difficult for a man to see much more than a couple of yards ahead, distorting the sound of footsteps on the roads and cobbles, damping the echo and confusing the sense of direction.

The neat little coach drawn by a pair of grays set the two men down some three hundred yards from the archway and alley leading to the front of the warehouse. They moved without sound, shadows clinging to shadows, pressing against walls and doorways, flitting between the darker patches of mist and smoke like specters on the haunt.

Finally they reached the archway and the last yards through the lane, which brought them in front of the warehouse.

"You think she'll have got the latch off the wicket by now?" one whispered, peering hard through the murk at his companion's muffled face.

"If not, then we have to wait," replied the other.

Gently they glided into the open space, nearing the door, the first man pressing himself against the flaking woodwork, his hand gripping the iron hoop of the wicket latch, testing it. From inside the sounds of revelry penetrated doors, windows and walls alike.

The latch responded and the door moved a fraction.

"We go like lightning once we're inside," breathed the one at the latch. "You ready?"

His partner nodded, and together they slipped out of their top-coats, revealing themselves to be dressed soberly in gray, with long fashionable jackets falling just below the knee. Both were bearded, almost distinguished looking, with gray streaking their hair.

The man at the door looked back, nodded again, appeared to take a deep breath, and then quickly pushed the door open. Within seconds they were inside, few even noticing them as new arrivals, so fast did they mingle with the guests.

Both men ate a little chicken and drank two or three glasses, before surreptitiously weaving their way through the chattering and happy groups, until they reached a vantage point to the right of the top table. Again they chose their moment; when Moriarty was engaged in earnest discussion with two men—whom they recognized as cracksmen named Fisher and Gay—and there was much toing and froing through the door to the "waiting room," kitchens and the Professor's private quarters. Using stealth, as before, the pair of interlopers casually slipped through the door and moments later were padding silently up the wooden stairs to the Professor's darkened chambers.

The party showed no signs of ending: Moriarty knew well enough that if left to the guests, it would go on throughout the night. But being a man with a constant eye to the needs of his organization, he intended that all would be well finished by eight. It was seven o'clock, therefore, when he leaned over and whispered to Paget, telling him that the time had come for him to remove his bride to the privacy of the bridal chamber.

Paget had been reasonably abstemious, but still could not resist a crude gibe, pointing out to the Professor that all that was required from bride and groom had long since been accomplished. The remark was met with withering disapproval and a cold reply that left Paget and Fanny in no doubt that however they felt, this was their legal bridal night and out of respect for their marriage it was necessary for them to go through at least the motions of "the leg business," as Moriarty put it.

"If I don't get these fuddlers out of here, the lot will be hoodman blind and there'll be no work done tomorrow. So get at it, the pair of you.''

There was much raucous laughter, jeering and cheers, as the newlyweds attempted to take their farewells, and it was almost a full half hour before they were able to complete their departure through the ''waiting room'' and back along the passage to the spiral stairs leading to the second floor and Paget's room.

Moriarty immediately signaled to Terremant, and those punishers who were not already too tipsy to comply began the task of speeding the parting guests on their way.

It was plain that a good number of those residing within the warehouse had made arrangements with ladies they had met during the celebration. There would be more people than usual sleeping within these walls tonight.

The atmosphere, combined with the drink, had taken its toll, and even Sal Hodges was flushed as she approached the Professor's table, bending low and whispering in his ear:

''You said you'd like to dance a jig with me, then why not tonight? Get rid of little fairy-Mary, and I'll give you a prick in the garter you won't forget for a long year.''

Moriarty smiled with undisguised lechery. ''Sal—'' he leered— ''it has been too long since we played the two-handed put.''

He glanced around to catch Kate Wright's eyes, signaling for her to join them.

''Get young Mary out of the way.'' He spoke low. ''Let Terremant or one of the others have her tonight; then make up the fire and light the lamps in my chambers.''

The housekeeper registered mild surprise, then grinned, nodded, and turned away, pushing past Spear, who was being helped up by the tenacious Bridget.

As the slow procession of wedding guests made its way from the warehouse, Pip Paget clutched his new bride to him in their bed.

''I reckon I love you, Fan,'' he whispered. ''How does it feel to have it legal?''

She lifted her head, kissing him gently on the cheek.

''I didn't really notice that time, dearest. Try again and I'll pay more attention.''

They both giggled.

Later he said, ''Truly, Fan, how will you like it, being here permanent with a husband?''

She was silent for a long minute. ''I'll like it fine, having you and looking after you, Pip. But it worries me, all the things you have to do. Is it truly to be permanent? I'm sometimes at sixes and sevens in case you get taken like Spear. Or worse, by the coppers. I got the horrors after going to Horsemonger Lane, and I couldn't bear it if they put you in one of them places.''

Paget had no answer, and did not dare reveal what was in his heart.

It was only a few minutes later that the loud knocking came at their door, and shouts along the passage. The warehouse was almost cleared by the time Mrs. Wright came down to tell the Professor that his chambers were warm and ready.

"I put out a pretty cambric nightgown for you."

She looked archly at Sal Hodges, who could not but smile in return.

The Professor rose, gave Sal his arm, and escorted her through the "waiting room" and up the stairs.

He knew something was wrong the moment they stepped inside the door: the smell, a sense made sharp through years of guarded actions. This second of knowledge gave the Professor a tiny advantage, allowing him to leap forward from the threshold, so that the two men—poised on either side of the door, knives held high and ready to strike the blows as he entered—were momentarily set off balance.

By the time they recovered themselves, Moriarty had made an agile spring over his desk, his hand moving fast toward the drawer in which lay the Toledo steel dagger presented to him by the Spaniard, Segorbe. He would rather have gone for the Borchardt automatic pistol, but that was prudently locked away.

Moriarty faced them, the dagger held low and straight in his right hand, legs apart and slightly bent at the knees—the classic position of the knife fighter.

"You're flushed at last then," he hissed, with traces of excitement from the back of his throat.

Behind the beards he could clearly recognize the countenances of Michael Green and Peter Butler, who were now moving, firm-footed, crabbing away from each other, in a pincerlike action that would bring them to either side of the desk.

Moriarty backed away, to give himself more space and room for maneuver, conscious that the fireplace was behind him. He countered by moving to the left, in an effort to bring the door of his bedchamber in line with his left hand.

They came on, clearing the desk: Butler in a crouch, Green smiling, tossing the knife from hand to hand, a ploy calculated to confuse the victim. Moriarty's eyes moved from one to the other as he kept backing.

Then there came a crash from the stairs.

The moment's hesitation and Moriarty's bound forward as they entered the room had given Sal Hodges time to act. Her brain, slightly slowed by the champagne, did not react as quickly as it would have done in other circumstances, so a small edge of time was lost. It took a second or two for her to grasp the situation, turn on her heel and descend the stairs.

She had almost reached the bottom when she saw Kate Wright standing in the middle of the "waiting room" floor, like a statue, still and listening.

Sal shouted, "Kate. Kate. Quickly. The Professor. They'll murder him."

But Mrs. Wright, instead of taking quick action, advanced softly toward the stairs, lifting her right hand, which held an empty candlestick.

Sal was two steps from the bottom of the wooden stairs when the game became clear, but by this time Kate was gathering speed, her arm fully back to strike with the candlestick.

"Shut your mouth, you whore, he's only getting his due. Let them stick him proper," mouthed Mrs. Wright.

"Bitch snake," screamed Sal, hoisting her skirts high and lashing forward with a silk-enveloped leg, the delicate toe of her boot meeting hard on the forward-moving Kate's stomach.

Kate let out a grunt as the kick went home, falling backward as Sal, now off balance, toppled, to come crashing and sprawling across her.

Upstairs Moriarty's hand found the doorknob, and with a quick twist he stepped backward. At that moment both Green and Butler sprang, but the Professor was too quick; he turned sideways and sprang away, leaving the two men almost jammed in the doorway.

With a quick glance behind him, Moriarty took two backward strides into the room, bringing him close to the bed, which was turned down, the cambric nightdress—all frills and lace trimmings, just as Kate Wright had described—laid across one pillow. With a sweep of his left arm Moriarty had the nightdress in his grasp, turning as Peter Butler lunged forward, his knife connecting, not with Moriarty's ribs, but with the soft material that had been destined to cover Sal Hodges' nubile body.

The knife was well entangled, and with a quick and hard pull, Moriarty had Butler off balance. The Toledo blade jabbed forward, a straight movement from the shoulder, the razored steel slicing into Butler's stomach like a kingfisher through water.

Butler had time for one scream, shrill and short, descending to a gurgle as he pitched back, Moriarty following through and throwing him from the blade.

On the "waiting room" floor, Sal Hodges grappled with Kate, both women with their skirts in disarray, showing legs, garters, even Sal's lace trimmings around the legs of her white drawers, as they grunted and puffed, rooling, pummeling and struggling for the one handy weapon, which was still grasped tightly in Kate Wright's hand.

In the bedroom Moriarty and Michael the Peg circled each other, Butler now silent on the floor.

"Come alone then, Peg, my bold lad," Moriarty was smiling, flushed with the success over Butler.

Green remained placid, crouching low, with knees bent ready to spring, trying to position himself so his back was not to the door, for the sounds from downstairs were becoming louder.

Sal clung to Kate Wright's hand below the wrist, to stop the woman from wresting clear and using the heavy candlestick as she intended. Sal's other hand fought for her adversary's throat, but Wright was having none of it, scrabbling and scratching at Sal's hand with her own free paw. Then with a mighty effort Kate drew herself clear, throwing Sal Hodges back and rolling away. Sal knew she was all but done, as she twisted on the floor in a last attempt to meet Kate, who was up and bearing toward her, the candlestick once more raised. In a final gathering of agility, Sal grabbed for the woman's boot. Her hands felt the leather around the ankle, and she heaved backward.

Kate Wright let out a harsh cry, the candlestick fell, hitting the stone an inch or so from Sal's head, as her attacker, legs pulled from under, went down with a heavy crash.

Sal was on top of her in an instant, this time pressing home the advantage, her small bunched fists smashing into the housekeeper's face.

Green was thrown by the crash and cry from below; for a fraction of a second his concentration wavered and Moriarty, poised on the balls of his feet, leaped forward for the kill.

But Green was still too quick for him, turning and thrusting back with his own knife so that Moriarty's blade ripped harmlessly at his sleeve.

The two men recovered their balance, facing one another again, panting heavily, their eyes shining like two animals at variance over a mate.

Sal did not know if Mrs. Wright were conscious or not. She lay still though, for long enough to allow Moriarty's madam time to take to her heels. She ran as if all hell were after her, through the connecting passageway, tripping and stumbling up the iron twisting stairway toward the door she thought belonged to Paget, shouting all the time, a strident cry for help.

Paget was out of bed, away from his warm bride in a second. The commotion had about it too much urgency to linger, and it was in a confused state of nakedness that he opened the door to Sal Hodges, who breathlessly poured out a string of disjointed words. It took but a moment for Paget to reach for his trousers—and the old five-shot revolver.

Green made another lunge, Moriarty countering, throwing himself backward across the bed so that Green's blade switched wide of its mark.

Rolling over the back-turned counterpane, the Professor recovered, his feet firmly on the floor at the far side, the bed between them. He was uncomfortable, the harness he used in his disguise now hampering him, and the pistol wound from Green's previous attempt, throbbed, pulled open by the exertion.

Green's eyes moved ceaselessly as he tried to decide which way to go. Moriarty stood his ground, and there was only an instant's hesitation before Green made up his mind and came at a rush around the bed, forcing Moriarty to turn and face him. Both men's hands moved as one, and in a second they were locked wrist to wrist. It was now not so much a question of skill, but of strength and who could first break the other's wrist grip.

They strained for what seemed to Moriarty an age of time, his wind and strength ebbing with each new exertion. Twice he lashed out with his right foot in a vain attempt to hook around Green's ankle, but the Peg was slowly forcing the issue, his grip unwavering around Moriarty's wrist, while the Professor's own grasp slowly slipped. He could feel his thumb being pushed back, and then with a hard downward pull of his arm Green's knife hand was free, back, and descending in a final wicked arc of steel.

The shot was like a cannon exploding in the room. Green's face was transformed, the mouth sagging open, his arm falling limp, as though the muscles had been severed.

The bullet took him high in the chest, an ugly fountain of blood bubbling out before his body hit the floor. There was the smell of powder, and Paget stood in the doorway, chest bare and his hair in disarray, his revolver still trickling smoke.

Green lived for twenty minutes, no more; and he was lucky at that. The wound had him breathing out pain and raving, crying for help; but Moriarty, having cleared the room, ordered nobody to touch him but sat on the bed and watched until the wretched man expired.

Paget brought up four of the punishers—fuddled and bleary from the party—to remove the bodies. Kate Wright was bound, and with Terremant as guard, locked in one of the secure rooms.

Fanny, Ember and Lee Chow were up; Fanny tending the cuts and bruises sustained by Sal Hodges, who took the opportunity to consume a couple of glasses of the Professor's best Hennessy's brandy—the 1840. Once the bodies were taken away, Lee Chow and Ember set about the menial task of cleaning the bedroom, washing out the bloodstains, and remaking the bed.

Moriarty, his disguise now removed, and his body clothed in a long silk robe, sat by the fire also sipping brandy. Paget, fully dressed, stood beside the desk.

"I cannot credit Kate Wright," said Moriarty's most trusted man.

The Professor stared broodingly into the coals.

"What of her husband?"

"We have him downstairs. He's to pieces—cannot explain anything."

"And swearing eternal loyalty, I've no doubt."

Paget nodded.

"We'd best have him up, and Paget—"

"Professor?"

"I have no way of thanking you. I was finished but for your pistol."

"That's my duty. Any of the others would have done the same."

They brought Bartholomew Wright up, his face drained, undeniable fear showing in his eyes and at the corners of his mouth. He spoke like a man stricken by some unexpected family loss, as though he could not fully grasp the nature of what had occurred.

Moriarty spent only a few minutes on him before irritably ordering them to take him away. When he had gone, the Professor called to Lee Chow, instructing him to take a bottle of the cheaper brandy and sit with Bart Wright, making sure that the man got the spirits inside him. Lee Chow did not waste either words or time.

Then Terremant and Paget brought Mrs. Wright up the stairs, into the chamber. With the woman it was a different story, even though she was still shaken from her fight with Sal Hodges, the deep and livid bruises beginning to color about her face.

"So, Kate." The Professor looked at her with undisguised contempt.

"So."

Paget could have sworn that she had almost laughed the word.

"You sold me to Green and Butler then?"

"And would do again."

"Young Slimper?"

"Yes, young Slimper also. He would have told you quick enough that he carried messages for me between here and Nelson Street."

"Mmm!" Moriarty looked away, into the fire. "Why, Kate? Have I not always looked after you? Why?"

She was silent, erect and head tilted. "For women's reasons."

The Professor's eyebrows arched. "Emotions? I thought you were beyond that, Kate."

"Aye, so does my husband, but I've had the horns on him for three years."

Moriarty's brow wrinkled deeply, then as suddenly cleared as he saw the only possible truth. His face broke into a smile flecked with evil, lips opening to emit a laugh.

"Moran," he chuckled. "So Moran had you, did he?"

"Yes, Sebastian treated me like his queen. . . ."

"When he wasn't off with his whores."

"He had his whores." She was quiet, in complete control of herself. "But the colonel always came back to me. I think the three years you were away were the three happiest of my life."

"But Kate, you prepared the basket for Moran in Horsemonger Lane. You didn't try to alter that."

She shrugged. "What would have been the point? Bart did it anyway, not me. It was quicker for Sebastian Moran that way; better than the wait for Ketch's tree. After he went, it was up to me, and we damn near had you." She wrenched free of Terremant, leaning forward to spit full in Moriarty's face.

"Get her out." Moriarty did not watch as the big punisher dragged her, shouting abuse, from the room.

Paget hovered, knowing what was to come.

"I don't care which one of you does it," the Professor said with no sign of feeling. "Nor the method. I want her dead and disposed of tonight. Then send young Fanny to me; and I want to see Lee Chow as soon as Bart Wright's full of brandy. We cannot take risks."

"You're not—" Paget stopped himself.

"I'm not what, Pip? Not going to let Bart Wright go the same way? How can I do otherwise? What respect or loyalty could I expect from him now? You get on with the woman. Leave the man to Lee Chow."

Much troubled, Paget left the room. He had seen enough of death that night and certainly had no stomach for killing women, but he was the Professor's most trusted, and it would be difficult to delegate the duty to any other. All he could do was see it was a quick end for Kate Wright.

Fanny faced Moriarty with unease blatant on her pretty face, for she was no fool and could guess at what was now going on.

Moriarty's face bore signs of strain, which Fanny, naturally, put down to the ordeal he had endured with Michael Green and Peter Butler. She was not to know the pressure was building up inside the Professor like a head of steam in a railway engine.

The fight with Green and Butler, the unmasking of Wright, and the subsequent dispensing of rough and quick justice had all played a part; but within the Professor's mind there still lurked the unease he had felt on seeing the two strangers in the church.

Crow was a man of tenacity; he was also a man with a good mind and a sense of logic. Moriarty did not need crystal balls or any other artifice of fortune tellers to reveal truth to him. He knew, with that supreme sense of mental illumination which ran in his family, that Crow was on the hunt. His brain ran wild with ideas and feelings and shadowy pictures of Crow's men watching, waiting, following— Crow at the center (rather like Moriarty at the center of his own world) organizing, outthinking, using his brain and intuition.

"Mrs. Paget." Moriarty addressed her wearily, and Fanny experienced a slight shock at hearing her new name for the first time.

"Mrs. Paget, we have had some bother of which you are, no doubt, aware."

"Yes." Her voice was small.

"Our good friends and servants, Kate and Bart Wright, have had to leave us, quite suddenly it seems. I am, so to speak, incommoded—without a housekeeper." His head swung from side to side in the familiar oscillating motion. "Without a housekeeper," he repeated. "So the position is vacant; it is a demanding one, but can be rewarding. I've no need to tell you that." He breathed a deep sigh. "What I am trying to say is, would you now consider taking over the situation?" He passed one hand across his brow.

Fanny was confused; she had not even considered this aspect. She opened her mouth to speak, but before words came, Moriarty said:

"I realize you will have to speak with Paget about this matter. You cannot be expected to make a decision on your own. The position is one of responsibility, and if you take it, I will see that you are well recompensed. In any event I would be grateful if you would continue with Mrs. Wright's duties at least for the time being.'' He lapsed into a moment's silence, appearing to be preoccupied, before he continued. "It may well be that we will have to change our style of living, by which I mean that we may soon be involved in moving house. If you take the post, I would have to rely heavily upon you during the change. Talk to Paget.''

"Yes. Yes, Professor. I'll talk to him; and I will carry on Kate's—Mrs. Wright's—duties for the time being."

Moriarty fluttered a limp hand in her direction: a dismissive signal.

Fanny left, bewildered and uncertain. There were wheels within wheels and while the horror of the night could not be wholly blotted from her mind, she was strangely disturbed by the Professor's talk of changing their abode.

Moriarty was also disturbed. The warehouse had been an excellent headquarters. It was in the heart of his territory and had all the appurtenances necessary to his livelihood and that of his organization. He also liked his private quarters, particularly the refurbishing that had been carried out during the enforced exile. But the appearance of the two coppers during Paget's wedding had caused the Professor to start thinking seriously of alternatives. He had long ago made provision for a time such as this—an estate in Berkshire, kept in excellent repair and condition, though the largest part of the place was shut off and the rest occupied only by a couple hired for that specific purpose. A number of men and women in Moriarty's service had seen the place, for it was often used as a hideaway for those wanted by the police, or for special cases that needed holing up until they could be transported from the country. Perhaps, Moriarty reflected, the time was coming when he would need to move his entire entourage, a step that could prove disruptive, if only because a base in London had always been deemed necessary.

Moriarty waited a further hour, until Paget returned, looking weak and ashen, with the news that all had been done. Lee Chow had also been given his instructions and would report in the morning. Moriarty had no cause to be concerned about that: The Chinese was without qualms regarding life, death, and loyalty. If Moriarty told him to slit his mother's throat, it was certain he would do it without question or conscience.

Sal Hodges joined Moriarty, as arranged, for what was left of the night; but the sharing of a bed proved to be more in the nature of mutual comfort than participation in the lusts of the flesh. For most of those close to the Professor the night was a period of uneasy sleep, decorated with nightmare fantasies and dreams of an unpleasant nature.

Cuttings from The Times for Wednesday, April 18, 1894

ENGAGEMENTS

Crow-Cowles. The engagement is announced between Inspector Angus McCready Crow, Metropolitan Police, son of the late Dr. & Mrs. James McCready Crow, Cairndow, Argyllshire; and Sylvia Mary Victoria Cowles, daughter of the late Mr. & Mrs. Robert Ferridole, Chester Mansions, W.1.

COURT CIRCULAR

Their Royal Highnesses, the Prince and Princess of Wales, will be holding a small house party at Sandringham, from Thursday to Monday, April 26-30. There will be a dinner party on Friday, April 27, when the entertainment will be provided by the celebrated illusionist, Dr. Night.

Inspector Crow put up with a good deal of chaffing at his expense on the Wednesday morning. Most of the senior officers read *The Times* with their breakfast, so the news was well out by the time he reached his office.

At 63 King Street, Mrs. Cowles had primped and preened from the moment the newspaper arrived, and when Crow left, she was preparing to go out herself in order to purchase a number of copies, so that the clipping could be sent to her numerous relatives.

When the commissioner sent for him, Crow naturally assumed that he also wished to add his hearty congratulations. Indeed the commissioner did extend his good wishes, as did the assistant commissioner, who was also present. But that part of the proceedings was brief. The commissioner was anxious to talk about Crow's progress on the Moriarty business. Reports were, to put it mildly, unnerving: particularly the news (which had come from a number of sources) that not one, but several Continental criminals had been in London over the past few days—doubtless for some kind of meeting.

Crow added little to what he had already told the assistant commissioner. He was at some pains to point out the reasoned way in which he had gone about his investigations, making no bones about the fact that he had been skeptical when first given the assignment: a viewpoint that had been dramtically altered during the course of his sleuthing.

The commissioner saw the wisdom of not putting out an alert for Moriarty's immediate apprehension, but was not altogether happy about the waiting game his inspector had chosen as a course of action. He remarked, "It is more a course of inaction."

After an hour or so it was agreed that Moriarty was almost certainly using some den in the heart of the East End, probably Limehouse, as a center of operations. So the commissioner assented to have another ten men transferred to Crow's staff to be used for the express purpose of moving in disguise around the suspect area in a concerted attempt to discover the exact location of the Professor and whatever forces were at his disposal.

"I do not like the idea of my officers mixing and hobnobbing with the criminal element," said the commissioner, "but it would seem there is no other way."

Crow mentally raised his eyes toward heaven. How else, he silently questioned, does one gain knowledge of villains, if you do not mix with them? Progress in methods of detection, thought Crow, moved at a snail's pace here in London. Later he reflected that his own deductive methods, combined with the work Tanner and others were doing on the ground, had not seemed to accelerate matters.

By midafternoon the extra men were out and about, eyes skinned and ears cocked, their one aim being the arrest of Professor Moriarty on some major charge and the ultimate breaking of whatever criminal union he controlled.

Moriarty spent most of the day wrestling with the problems at hand, notably the decision whether to move his headquarters from the heart of things to the more lush landscape of Berkshire. The matter concerning a new housekeeper was solved at lunchtime, when Fanny came to tell him that she was prepared to take on the position. He spoke with her for some time, carefully explaining his own preferences in food and drink, instructing her in the main duties that would be expected of her and transferring custody of the house keys.

Kate Wright had run the place with the help of her husband, and Moriarty told Fanny that he would provide her with an extra pair of hands as soon as it was convenient. In the meantime Bridget would assist her, with occasional help from Mary McNiel, who had so far spent the day in the sulks.

The item in the court circular had not escaped the Professor's eager eyes, and his brain was already working days ahead, toward fulfillment of the promise he had made to his Continental colleagues.

He was anxious for the evening to come, for he could not deny an almost childlike excitement about meeting the magical Dr. Night.

He dined alone on a meal Fanny had taken great pains in preparing and at about half-past ten left the warehouse, without his disguise, for the Alhambra.

The stage-door keeper had been advised of Moriarty's arrival, and a call boy led the Professor through the passages to Dr. Night's rather cramped dressing room. As he followed the lad, the Professor felt that behind the scenes, a music hall after the last performance had little magic about it.

William S. Wotherspoon (Dr. Night) had no large sense of mystery about him either. Close up he was a small man, unctuous in manner and completely lacking in the presence that radiated from him on stage. The dressing room was over-hot, smelling of a mixture of fish and chips, greasepaint and pale ale, which, if the number of empty bottles were anything to go by, the magician consumed in large quantities.

"An honor, Professor. I cannot tell you what an honor it is to receive you." Dr. Night went through the motions of hand washing. He wore a rather loud check suit, which also seemed out of character.

"You are surprised at my getup?" He grinned. "I do it on purpose, my dear Professor. If I did not, I would have to be on show twenty-four hours a day. Some of my colleagues prefer it like that, but I find it enough strain being an illusionist on stage without having to do it off. So this is my own little illusion—a disguise, if you like. Do take a seat." He swept some papers from the easy chair, which was badly in need of repair.

Moriarty had been unprepared for this kind of man and was forced to remind himself of how brilliant Dr. Night's act had really been.

"It is my pleasure, Dr. Night," he said with courtesy.

"Bill. Please call me Bill. Dr. Night's for them out there." He cocked his head in the direction of the door.

"Bill, then. I was most impressed by your performance. Most impressed."

"That's nice of you, and gratifying. Others have been impressed also, it seems." He lowered his voice. "Did you happen to catch the piece in today's court circular?"

"Indeed I did."

"An honor, a very singular honor. But I hear as how His Royal Highness is most partial to conjuring and the magic arts. Does a few card tricks himself, no doubt, eh?"

Moriarty nodded. It was time for him to take over the conversation.

"What are they paying you here, Bill?"

"Well, now, I don't think I—"

"I do, Bill. I have the controlling interest in a few halls myself—oh, not as grand as this, I admit, but I am willing to pay you three times as much as they're doing here."

Wotherspoon's head came up, an avaricious glint in his eyes.

"I'm not free until next month," he said quickly. Moriarty had struck the right chord.

"No matter. If you will agree to the proposition I am going to put to you—and I hardly think you will be able to spurn it—I shall begin payment as from Monday next."

"What, without my appearing? I would have to talk to my agent about—"

"What?" Moriarty laughed. "And lose ten percent? Your agent does not have to know, not until I put you into one of my halls anyway. In the meantime it would be a bit of business, something between the two of us and nobody else."

"Nobody? Not even Rosie? She's the girl I use—in the act, I mean."

Moriarty gave him a sly, conspiratorial smile. "Not in any other way, Bill?" he asked.

Wotherspoon chuckled. "Well, maybe once in a while. But nothing regular like some of them. Oh no, that's not for me, Prof. I can see you're a man of the world anyhow."

"You might say that, yes. You might say that I am a man of the world."

"Well, what's the proposition then? Fire away. I'm game for most things."

The Professor leaned back, a smile of pleasure playing around his mouth.

"I'll tell you what I want. . . ."

He spoke for half an hour or so, his voice soft, like that of a mesmerist, hardly believing that the great Dr. Night could be, offstage, so gullible.

When he left the theater and walked out into Leicester Square, Moriarty paused for a moment on the pavement to sniff the smells of smoke, grime and horses and look out across the square garden, with its shrubs and flowerbeds and the statue of Shakespeare, just beginning to lose its original whiteness.

He was lost for a while, his eyes taking in the bright posters, hurrying people, the rattling omnibuses and cabs. These folk, he thought, bustling and rushing along: What do they know of life? What do they really know of the world? Theirs was an existence so different from his own; their society far removed from the dark and secret ways he knew. It was like looking at two sides of a coin—and coin was the right image, for it was the one thing that bound the two worlds. One side had no experience of the other, and no stretch of the imagination could ever allow these honest, silly, people true access to his domain. When his time was over, thought Moriarty, not even the historians would really be able to reach into his world, untangle its many layers, or pick out the fabric.

For the next week Moriarty's lieutenants remarked on the fact that the Professor was absent for some three hours each afternoon. When they questioned Harkness about it, the man was dumb.

"It's the Professor's business," he said gruffly. "You know me. He pays me to drive him and not to talk. I know my orders."

They knew also that it was useless trying to press Harkness, he had been too long in the Professor's service to be led into temptation now.

Saturday, April 21, 1894

(THE HARROW ROBBERY)

IT WAS NOT much of a honeymoon for Paget and Fanny, what with Fanny's new responsibilities and Paget's normal work. Nor did Paget act at all like a carefree honeymooner. Certainly he did his duty, providing many pleasures in the marriage bed, but the rest of the time he seemed preoccupied.

Fanny became concerned and even confided in Bridget, who, being the girl she was, took the matter straight to Spear, who said there was a big caper coming up and Fanny should not be too worried.

Spear was back on his feet again, and although his hands still gave him pain he was beginning to use them a little. Indeed, on the night following the wedding—and all its attendant dramas—he and Bridget had their first taste of greens together. Paget's moroseness concerned him though, and he was not long in taking his worry to Moriarty, who put it down to the excesses of matrimony and left it at that.

If Moriarty had known, there was cause for him to be uneasy about Paget, for the events of the wedding night had plunged the man into extreme dolor, his newfound happiness with Fanny contrasting sharply with both his past and present life. The carnage of that night and the terrible deed he had been forced to perform on Kate Wright might well be described as practically the last straw. It was certainly the penultimate, for the final revulsion to his way of life was to come in connection with the robbery planned to take place on Saturday night.

The van was ready, with two good horses, and the arrangements were well rehearsed by all the participants. Paget was to go to Harrow on the Saturday morning, walk out to the Pinner estate, visit the public house, and generally sniff out the land.

In the early evening Bill Fisher was to come down with one of the

Jacobs brothers, and they would meet Paget at Harrow station to get the latest news.

Clark, Gay and the other Jacobs would make their way over with the van later that night; Paget, once he had passed on the lie of the land to Fisher, would return to Limehouse.

With luck they reckoned the whole thing would be over by two in the morning, and they would be back, disposing of the loot, by half-past four at the latest.

Although she did not know the details, Fanny was aware that something big was afoot, and when Paget told her he would be away for the whole day on Saturday she pleaded to be allowed to come with him. At first he pointed out that her own duties as housekeeper would prevent her, but she so persisted that Paget, more in self-defense than anything else, went to see the Professor.

"You know I'm not happy about showing myself down there anyway," he told Moriarty. "I might just escape suspicion if I take a woman with me. After all I posed as a man looking for a job on the estate last time; and I mentioned that I had a wife, anxious and willing to move out of the city."

Moriarty was now even more versed in the art of misdirection, having spent a few afternoons with Dr. Night, finding him a most able teacher and a great professional showman despite the seedy offstage appearance. He could see that Paget going down with Fanny might well be an extra piece of dressing that could throw any thought of suspicion away from his man. He finally agreed, making certain that Paget would relay only the most necessary facts to his wife.

So it came about that Fanny, all done up in her new bonnet and a new cloak, which she had made for herself, went arm in arm with her husband to pose as a couple looking for work on the Pinner estate at Beeches Hall.

While it could not be called the real countryside when compared with what Fanny had been used to, the environs of Harrow were the nearest she had been to open fields, woodlands and nature since arriving in London.

She behaved with all the excitement of a child during the railway journey, and Paget had to keep reminding her of the part she had to play once they reached their destination.

It was a fine day, not over warm, but clear, with a bright sky once they were a mile or so away from the grubby smoke of the congested areas. The walk through Harrow and out toward Sir Dudley Pinner's estate, Beeches Hall, was as carefree an hour as Paget had known, what with Fanny skipping along beside him, chattering about her own life in Warwickshire, naming birds and darting into hedges to pluck and identify the occasional wildflower.

It was almost noon when they came in sight of the few clustered houses, the shop and public house. At about twenty past the hour Paget opened the door to The Bird in the Hand and ushered Fanny inside.

Mace, the landlord, was engaged in conversation with a tall man, dark haired and dressed in tweeds and leggings, like a gamekeeper. The only other occupants of the bar parlor were an elderly couple, the man with a tankard, pulling at a clay pipe; the woman, gray haired and respectable looking, sitting quietly, with hands folded on her lap.

"Well now," said Mace, "this is the very fellow I was telling you about, Mr. Reeves. Come in. Jones, isn't it?"

Paget put on a sheepish grin. "You remembered then?"

"Out here we always remember new faces. What's it to be? This is Mr. Reeves, manages the estate."

The man nodded amiably enough, and Paget ordered a tankard for himself, while Fanny took a little port.

"Mace says you were over a while back, looking for work," Reeves' voice was rough, but not harsh, and Paget detected his eyes were making a thorough appraisal, as though he was looking over cattle to be bought for meat.

"My wife, Fanny," Paget said shyly.

Mace grinned and nodded. Reeves gave a quick smile.

"Looking for work," he repeated.

"Well, yes," Paget contrived to sound uncertain. "I work in the docks, and Fan, well, she's done a lot of things. For a while in the kitchens—domestic service, like. I took her from that and recently she's worked in a public house. But we're both tired of the life back there. It's long hours and dirty. Fan comes from the country, you see."

"This is hardly the country, but near enough," said Reeves. "And as for long hours, you'd get longer out here. Sometimes five in the morning till ten at night, harvest time."

"Yes, I know about that."

"And the wages wouldn't be what you'd be getting in the docks."

"We know, but there's perks, isn't there?" Fanny piped up.

Reeves laughed. "There's perks, yes. A cottage, vegetables in the spring and summer. It's not as bad as it was, not since the Prince of Wales set about improving the position of his tenants down in Norfolk; and I suppose the wages are better here than further out. You'd bring in about thirty shillings or two pounds between you."

Paget's heart sank. He knew people had to manage on this, and less, in the poverty-stricken East End, but he wondered how he would fare if it were really his intention to take a job on the estate.

"Well, you look strong enough." Reeves leaned over and felt the tight muscles of Paget's arms. "Long hours, hard work doing the outside jobs around the house, and helping the farm workers in summer. And you," he turned to Fanny, "would be peeling veg and washing up. At least until he got you with child—then you'd be no good to Sir Dudley. I don't know. What do you think, Mr. Burroughs?" He called to the elderly man sitting with his wife.

"Looks healthy, broad and tall enough." Burroughs took his pipe from his mouth. "Could do with a strong one instead of those whippety lads we've had in the past."

Mrs. Burroughs smiled. "Come and talk to me, my dear." She patted the bench beside her, motioning to Fanny, who, after looking questioningly at Paget, went over and began to talk quietly with the woman.

"Mr. and Mrs. Burroughs," explained Mace, nodding in the couple's direction. "They're really sort of caretakers, kept on out of Sir Dudley's kindness. They live up at the hall when the master and mistress are away, and there's no servants about. Look after the place. Mrs. Burroughs helps Cook when there's entertaining, and the old boy sometimes assists the butler. They're both up there at the hall now. The servants are all off, but for two of the young footmen, while the master and mistress are away."

"They're not back yet, then?" asked Paget trying to sound disappointed.

"Not for another couple of days. But I said they wouldn't return till after the twentieth."

"Yes. Yes, you did. But, well, we thought we'd come over just in case."

"You mean you'd like the job?" from Reeves.

Paget lowered his voice. "It's the missus," he confided. "Downright unhappy where we are. Doesn't like it at all, and I'm anxious to get her out."

Reeves was silent for a while, looking hard at him.

"Well, I can't make promises. In the long run it'll be up to Sir Dudley, but you might as well come over and see the cottage. There's plenty who would be glad of it, but, well, you seem a good enough couple, and if we don't find you suitable there's only a week's notice and out you'd go, bag and baggage."

Paget nodded uneasily. He had the information he required and was not anxious to stay overlong, but it was necessary for him to spin it out now. He looked over at Fanny, who was in animated converse with the Burroughses.

"What do you think, Mrs. Burroughs?" asked Reeves.

The elderly woman smiled. "She'd do real well, Mr. Reeves. Real well, I've no doubt."

Reeves gave a small sigh of doubt as though he still needed convincing. "Well, I'll take you up to the cottage if you like."

"Oh, please," chirped Fanny; and Paget again experienced the sinking feeling.

His bride's face was lit with a happiness which even surpassed that which he had already seen in their moments of ardour.

The cottage was tiny. One room and a scullery downstairs, a wooden door opening up to a small and narrow cramped stairway leading to the one upstairs room. But it was clean and in good repair and there was a small plot of garden at the back.

"It's all so clean and fresh," laughed Fanny. "Oh, Pip, we could be so happy here, don't you think?"

"Now, easy, Mrs. Jones." Reeves held up his hand. "I cannot give you the job until after Sir Dudley returns, but you will be first on the list, I can promise you that."

"Oh, sir, we'd be so grateful. I love it already."

They walked back to The Bird in the Hand and took some bread and cheese and another glass or two before setting out to walk back to Harrow.

"I meant it, Pip," said Fanny quietly after they had cleared the knot of houses. "I really meant it."

"I could see that." Paget sensed despair within himself, for he had also seen the vision of the pair of them, working and living in this place: a new and different life, hard but without the constant strain or the fear of discovery and arrest.

"You'd better put it out of your mind though, Fan. It'd never do."

"But, Pip, if we could. I know it would be hard, but my mother used to say that the harder life was the more rewarding."

"She didn't have to live in a couple of filthy rooms though, did she?"

"The cottage isn't filthy. It's clean and I'd keep it like a new pin."

"I wasn't talking of the cottage. I meant where I grew up."

"Was it that terrible?" Her hand rested on his arm, eyes shining up at him.

"No worse than many who've worked for the Professor. But I'd wager your mother never had to get out of a night to chase the rats from gnawing at her brothers and sisters."

They remained silent from then on as they walked toward the station, wrapped in their own private thoughts—Paget in a kind of despondency, for he knew beyond doubt that there was little hope of escape from the Professor. Had he not saved Moriarty's life but a few days ago? And had not the Professor saved his, in a manner of speaking? Yet you did not leave the Professor's employ alive. In some ways it was like being in prison. He remained in this state of gloom for the remainder of the evening.

Fisher and Bert Jacobs came off the railway train at eight o'clock, and they all went over to the nearest inn to talk.

Paget told them that apart from two young footmen and Mr. and Mrs. Burroughs, Beeches Hall was empty.

"It'll be a soft crack then." Fisher smiled. "Just like I told the gaffer it would be."

"Which way shall you go in?" asked Paget.

"Gay'll go in through the back and open the front door to us, like we had been invited."

"And you'll silence the footmen and the old people?"

"Tie 'em up and dump 'em in the cellar. Soft as butter. You can tell the Professor we'll be back in good time, provided the others get down here without trouble."

Still in the black mood, Fanny and Paget rode back to London, returning to the warehouse before ten o'clock.

Fanny went straight to the kitchen to get food for them, and, going up to their quarters, Paget met Ember dressed in his greatcoat, which flapped around his ankles.

"Have you seen him yet?" asked Ember.

"The Professor?"

"Who else?"

"No."

"There's been some pigs nosing about, asking questions. I don't like it but he doesn't seem to bother. Cold as bloody ice, our Professor."

Dr. Night had an early performance on the Saturday, but Moriarty was still able to spend two hours with him after luncheon. He then returned to the warehouse and, locking his door behind him, sat for a further two hours before the mirror with his disguise material. He cleaned his face several times during that period, reapplying the paint and false hair again and again until he was finally satisfied with the result. Being roughly the same build as Dr. Night helped, and Moriarty reckoned that as long as the magician's mother did not turn up, he would be able to deceive most people.

At about seven o'clock Bridget brought him a supper of cold meats, pickles and ale. He ate it in a distracted manner, his head still buzzing with his plot and its execution.

Parker arrived at eight, in some agitation.

"They're everywhere, Professor," he gasped.

"Who?" Moriarty well alert now.

"The coppers. All round the area: detectives, pigs. They don't think my lads are on to them, but they're in the public houses, all round and about, asking questions. Asking about you."

Moriarty felt his neck go cold, the short hairs rising.

"You're sure of this?"

"Certain. I've seen a pair of them myself. It's the questions I'm not happy about."

Moriarty turned down the corners of his mouth sourly. "What kind of answers are they getting?"

"None. You know that, Professor. There's nobody around here would blow on you."

"Kate Wright blew to Green. There could still be some of his cronies. . . ."

"Not a chance. They know what happened before."

Moriarty thought for a moment or two. "Keep your eyes and ears open then, and let me know of any developments."

Parker's lurkers had proved their worth during the week. They had let him down by allowing Green and Butler to creep into the warehouse during Paget's wedding, but since then their information had been exact. Moriarty had known for the past two days that Crow had pigs out in the streets, though this was the first time they had penetrated as near as this.

The Professor had been putting off the decision for too long. It was unlikely Crow's men would get to him for a while yet, but within the week he would have to get his closest people out to Berkshire. He would, himself, probably be required to move further afield for a while. But he had already proved that the organization could remain intact without his physical presence. Paget would see to things and Spear would soon be himself again.

He would talk to his most trusted lieutenant when he returned, and then, tomorrow, set full plans in motion for the move.

Paget came to him soon after ten with the news that the Harrow business was proceeding as arranged.

"I saw Ember on his way out," said Paget. "The coppers are sniffing, it seems."

"Let them sniff away." There was disdain in Moriarty's voice. "Let them sniff till snot blinds them. We'll talk tomorrow. If I think it necessary, then we'll all move down to the Berkshire house. They won't find us there, Paget, and we can return when things get tranquil again. I'll discuss it with Fanny and yourself in the morning."

None of this in any way quietened Paget's heart or mind. He was confused enough already, and now there was something new in the air, a brooding, however indifferent the Professor might appear to be. Paget had been told about Inspector Crow, and he sensed his master's concern. This uneasiness was to grow worse before the night was through.

Fanny, tired from her day in the unaccustomed open air, fell to sleep quickly, but Paget tossed and turned, restless as the hours wore on.

Finally he dozed off, only to wake with a start, imagining he had heard something moving. Fanny's soft breathing was all that came to his ears; then, far off in the warehouse, there were other sounds.

Softly he slipped from the blankets, striking a match to look at his watch. It was almost five in the morning. He pulled on his trousers and a shirt, slid his feet into his boots, picked up his old revolver, which was now always kept loaded by the bed, and went out into the passage.

At the top of the spiral staircase he stopped to listen again. There were voices, coming, it seemed, from the "waiting room." Quietly he moved down the iron stairs and along the ground-floor passage until he arrived at the kitchens. The voices were loud now—Fisher and Gay, he recognized, then Bert Jacobs, and lastly, Moriarty.

"Well, the stuff's good enough. You'd better get everything away," he heard Moriarty say. "Bert, you take the paintings as I told you. They have to be off on the morning tide and you've not got long."

"Right, and I'm sorry about the old folk, Professor."

"There was little else you could do. People have to be sacrificed. Off you go."

Paget could hear Bert Jacobs' boots clumping out and across the warehouse floor.

"What really happened?" he heard Moriarty ask.

"Just as he said," Fisher replied.

"Exactly." Paget thought that was Clark's voice.

"We got in all right," Fisher continued. "The footmen were no trouble at all. Cooperative, you might say."

"They knew what was good for them." Gay.

"Then we were going upstairs to do the safe, and the old boy and his missus came out screaming fit to wake the dead. Bert hit the old man and he went down the stairs. Then the woman went for him with a poker. She was shouting for help and the like. He took her by the throat to make her shut up. I don't think he meant more than that."

"You left them where they lay?" Moriarty asked.

"Where else? We didn't want to hang around."

Paget had heard enough. The Burroughses were dead done for, and he did not fancy either Fanny's chances or his own, if the coppers got onto them now. They were bound to be questioned once Reeves or Mace had been seen by the police—and it would be a Criminal Investigation Department job. Scotland Yard.

As he went back to his quarters Paget felt his mind leaping in a hundred different directions. The Harrow crack had been done, but botched with killing. Coppers were nosing around the East End—and the West no doubt—asking questions and bandying the Professor's name about. It was, Paget reasoned, only a matter of time. True they would probably get clear away into the country: to the Berkshire place. It was nice there and Fanny would like it, but it was only a matter of time also before Fanny would hear about Mr. and Mrs. Burroughs and how would she take that? Paget knew exactly how. Fanny had been in a state after the killings on their wedding night. This could well prove too much for her. And too much for him also? He wondered. Maybe they should take their chance now. He had served the Professor well and there was no need to blow the whole gaff. He wanted Fanny. He wanted her happiness, and that was worth the risk.

Once inside the room, Paget lit the lamp. They would have to move quickly, for the sky outside was already starting to lighten. He shook Fanny gently.

"Fan, love. Fan, wake up."

She slowly opened her eyes and smiled at him. "Time to get up already?"

"Time for us, Fan. You really want that cottage and life together in the country?"

She was awake now and sitting upright, her long hair tangled and eyes still doused with sleep.

"What's happened? What. . .?"

He put his hand gently across her mouth.

"Get dressed quickly. Try to make no noise, I'll explain later."

They could not take much—simply their most precious possessions: rings and pieces of jewelry, and the three hundred pounds that Paget had saved, which they stuffed into a cowhide Brighton bag he had actually purchased a year before to carry small stuff to fences (it was never safe to carry loot in a stolen bag).

There was nobody about in the kitchens or the "waiting room," and it was not until they got outside, into the area in front of the warehouse, that they were challenged by one of Parker's lurkers.

"It's only me," Paget said briskly when the man spoke.

The lurker stepped out of the darkness. "Oh, it's Mr. Paget. I wasn't told to expect anyone else yet."

"Something has just occurred. Nothing to worry about. But we have a small errand to perform before the Professor is up. Watch out for anyone else though; keep sharp eyes. And well done for challenging me."

The man touched his forelock, drifting back into the safety of the wall, while Paget and Fanny turned away, walking down the alley and through the archway, trying not to run or appear to be in any undue haste.

Now that he had set his mind to it, Paget knew exactly what he should do. There *was* no point in just running off, for someone would always be close behind—if not the coppers, then men sent from the Professor. It was a risk either way, but he was now faced with the most difficult and alien acts of his life. If things did not go right, then he would at least have the satisfaction of knowing he had made some effort to change his mode of living and bring happiness to Fanny.

They did not discover the Pagets had gone until amost half past seven, and it was eight o'clock before Ember and Parker realized the missing pair had taken their valuables with them. Parker questioned the lurker on duty at the front of the warehouse and was not long in discerning that something was exceedingly wrong.

At first the Professor could not believe there was anything the matter. He argued to himself that there had to be a simple explanation, that Paget and Fanny would be back in a short time, or at least would send some message. But when he heard nothing by noon, Moriarty became disturbed. He had always been wary, as he so often stated, of men who lost their souls to women. If Paget had been led astray, then the woman was responsible and a good man was lost.

However much he had relied on and trusted Paget, the Professor now knew that his thinking would have to be governed by the most pessimistic conclusions. Paget and Fanny were gone from the warehouse, so he could assume only one of three things: that the pair had gone into hiding, the girl, like some bleating salvationist, had convinced Paget to give up his present way of life; that Paget was bent on joining or even leading a rival faction; or—most dubious of all—they had blown everything to the police.

At ten minutes after noon Moriarty sat in his chambers with Spear, Ember, Lee Chow, Parker, Terremant, and the Jacobs brothers, It was undeniably a crisis meeting.

"You all know that the coppers are proving troublesome," he began. "That's bad enough, but now Pip Paget and Fanny have gone—where to I've no idea, but perhaps your men, Parker, will flush them. I have one particular job that has to be done this week, and by God, I'm going to do it, whatever else happens. After that is over we shall see. In the meantime, Spear, if you are up to it, I want you to take over Paget's duties."

"I'll manage," grunted Spear, "and I'll manage Pip Paget an' all if he's played the crooked cross."

"Enough time for that when we're safe." The Professor waved Spear's violent tone aside. "We're moving house, lads. Lock, stock and barrel. Everything out as quickly and as quietly as we can, without drawing any undue attention. Everyone and everything is to be taken to the Steventon house in Berkshire. Have you got that?"

They nodded approval.

"If there is trouble, you can all hole up there until it dies down." He cast his eyes around the assembled lieutenants. "Now, it is possible that some of you will not see me for a while; but I will be in touch with you, and things must continue as though I was still here. I shall return as soon as it is reasonably secure: Just go about moving the valuables and weapons. Spear will organize you. Start now."

He motioned for Parker and Ember to stay where they were for a moment and, when the others had gone, gave some brief and private instructions to them.

"Send Mary McNiel to me," he ordered as the two men were ready to leave, "and, Ember, take care of the painting." He indicated his beloved canvas by Jean-Baptiste Greuze. "I shall see you tomorrow afternoon as arranged."

When they had gone and their footsteps were out of earshot, Moriarty began to remove papers from the drawers of his desk, putting some in a briefcase, burning others in the hearth.

He unlocked another drawer, removed the Borchardt automatic pistol, checked that it was loaded, and placed it in his coat pocket, together with some extra ammunition. Lastly, he packed his disguise material: the sticks of paint, the brushes, powders and false hair would, he reflected, play a most important part in his life during the next few days.

Mary McNiel arrived as he was closing the briefcase.

"Is it true?" she asked. "True we're leaving?"

The Professor nodded. "We're all leaving. And, Mary, my dear, you and I have particular things to do."

He faced her, holding her eyes in his in that strange mesmeric way he had, as though the whole of his strength and will were pouring from his mind into hers.

"In the next few days you will be witness to many strange things. I shall call upon you to perform certain actions you might not wholly understand. But I need your loyalty, Mary, and your promise that whatever occurs, you will obey me instantly and without question."

Mary felt lightheaded, as though she were about to swoon, yet most aware of the importance of what the Professor was saying. Her will seemed hardly her own, and there was no resisting her master.

"I shall do whatever you ask," she said firmly.

"Good, then go down and get Harkness to bring the cab to the front. We go within the next five and twenty minutes."

Moriarty stood for a short while at the window, then turned to look around the room. It was frustrating to think that circumstances forced him to leave all this, but needs must. There would be other places, as well out of sight as the warehouse—maybe even better. He shrugged into his greatcoat, picked up his briefcase, jammed his hat on his head and walked with purpose from the room.

Sunday, April 22, to Friday, April 27, 1894

(THE REALMS OF NIGHT)

"IT'S ALL A risk." Paget looked thoughtfully into his mug of ale. "Everything we do—now we have left the warehouse—is a risk; so I have to do my best to see the Professor is as inconvenienced as possible—to hamper any search for us. If I can do that without bringing any harm to him, more the better."

"But then what?" Fanny looked close to crying.

They sat, close together in the corner of the refreshment rooms at the Great Western Station at Paddington, their eyes constantly moving and searching for any of Parker's lurkers who might be about.

"Then," said Paget, "we take the railway to the Midlands. Not a city, Fan. If we hid in a city he'd find us, sure as eggs are bloody eggs. But you know the country. I mean you know Warwickshire—"

"I can't go home, not now. You know that."

"No, not home, but somewhere in the country. Fanny, my love, I've three hundred pound in my pocket that'll keep us going for a while. We'll put up at some inn, out of the way, where neither the bobbies nor the Professor would ever think of looking. It'll give us time, and time's what we need." He looked at her hard, a loving and almost foolish smile crossing his face. "Fanny, I've done it for you, girl. You didn't want to stay chained there for the rest of our lives, did you?"

She sighed, a shallow breath. "No, Pip. Lord, you know I didn't want to stay there a minute longer." She put out her hand, covering his. "But, Pip, if anything happened now when you—"

"Nothing'll happen. You just get us tickets to . . . Where? Where's a good place that you know?"

"Warwick? Or there's Leamington Spa—Royal Leamington

Spa. There's plenty of villages around there with inns, and there'd be work.''

"Then get us tickets to Royal Leamington Spa, my girl. Just wait here. Look.'' He pushed the Brighton bag toward her with his foot. ''Everything's in there. Everything we have, including my three hundred pound. If I'm not back by four o'clock, take it and go to Leamington.''

"But if you get held up? If you're late?''

"If I'm not here by four o'clock, then you go without me, Fan. But I'll be back before then. Long before then.''

At least he hoped he would be. Just as he prayed none of Parker's men were already hunting. Getting away into the country was really the only hope they had, and a good distance from Steventon also, where Moriarty had the other house. There was nowhere Paget dared take Fanny in London; nobody he could even think of trusting. It was a case of going it alone and trying to put pressure on the Professor—at least enough to keep his head down until he and Fanny were clear. If it worked, then he reckoned a year would see them in a new life, settled and comfortable. He'd grow a beard, that would help, and they'd try and dodge all the old things. Time would inevitably cool the trail. In a year or so they would be safe.

But now it was a case of remaining safe for another few hours. Putting his head deep inside the lion's mouth before leaving London.

Paget took a hansom to Scotland Yard, screwing his courage to the limit and asking the cabbie to wait while he strode over to the porter's window, looking for all the world as if he had every right to walk into the place and give orders.

''Inspector Crow.'' Paget sounded urgent, as though authority were on his side—a ruse learned from watching the Professor in action.

The sergeant at the desk looked at him, suspicion grained into every line of his face through years of dealing with dubious characters.

''He won't be in today.'' The sergeant had a surly voice, as though he resented having to work on Sunday. ''You'll have to come back tomorrow.''

''I can't do that. This is an urgent matter; family business. I've traveled all night to get here.''

''Well, he's not in today.''

''Where can I find him? Any ideas?''

The sergeant looked him up and down, still uncertain. ''Urgent, you say?''

"Greatly so. Matter of life and death." It *was* as well, thought Paget.

The sergeant turned away to consult a ledger. "Well . . ." His frown was deep. "I'd rather you didn't tell him I said so, but you might find him at his lodgings: number sixty-three King Street. What did you say your name was?"

"I didn't, but I'm his cousin, Albert Rookes. With an E."

"Oh! Well, that would be all right, I'm sure, sir. You try sixty-three King Street."

It was a full ten minutes before the sergeant began to wonder about Inspector Crow's cousin being called Rookes, with an E.

"I'll pay you what I owe you now, and give you five shillings besides, if you'll wait," Paget told the cabbie when they pulled up in front of 63 King Street. "I have to take a message from here, so you'll have to drive like the devil when I come out. There'll be another five shillings in it."

The cabbie nodded, touching his hat. "I'll be here, guv'nor."

Paget descended from the cab and walked cleanly up to the door of Crow's lodgings. He put one hand inside his coat, wrapping his fingers around the butt of his revolver. With the other hand he pulled the bell.

Harkness drove Moriarty and Mary McNiel to a public house off Leicester Square that opened on Sundays and served roast luncheons. They ate in silence—beef and potatoes—Moriarty pausing to talk only when the food was cleared. He gave Mary a few simple yet precise instructions. Then, once the account was settled, took her outside, ordering Harkness to drive to the Alhambra, where he was already half an hour late for his daily appointment with Dr. Night.

The stage-door keeper, who appeared to live on the premises and had got to know the Professor well during the last few days, gave them a cheery smile.

"He's waiting for you up on the stage, sir. You've the run of the place this afternoon. Nobody else here on a Sunday."

Night, or Wotherspoon, or whatever else he wished to call himself, was on stage with the plump Rosie, who looked peeved at having to come in from her lodgings in Clapham on a Sunday afternoon. Moriarty noted the look and wondered at the ways of a woman who was quite willing to take the extra money Dr. Night was paying her, yet obviously begrudged the time she had to give for it.

Things had fallen out well though. Moriarty had not intended to put this part of his plan into action much before Thursday evening, but the change in matters made the moves essential now. Moriarty smiled. At least he would be able to disappear from police and public alike without a trace. A truly magical feat.

"Ah, there you are." Wotherspoon came forward with outstretched hand.

"I am sorry we have been delayed," Moriarty said pompously. "Business, even on a Sunday, you know, always business."

"And a lady as well." Wotherspoon raised an eyebrow, not quite happy about Mary McNiel's presence.

"Mary Malloney, my private secretary," Moriarty said, quite unconcerned by Wotherspoon's attitude. "I wanted to show off to somebody and thought she'd make a perfect audience."

Wotherspoon softened. "Of course, of course. You've let her into our little secret then?"

"Naturally. She is my *private* secretary."

"Well . . ." The magician rubbed his hands. "Well, my dear, your employer is very good, an apt pupil. Do you know that he can perform my act nearly as well as I can do it myself."

"Not the new one though." Moriarty indicated the two slim, almost coffinlike boxes that stood upended on the stage.

"Ah, well." Wotherspoon tapped his nose with a long forefinger. "I'm not sure that *I* can do that yet. Rosie and I have just been rehearsing it. I'm saving it for when we start at one of your halls." He beamed, and then addressed Mary. "It will be most spectacular, my dear." He became conspiratorial. "We shall get members of the audience to come up on the stage and examine the boxes—I call them the Transmogrification Cabinets. Then Rosie is placed in the one on the right, and it is roped up and tied. I am put into the one on the left, which is treated in a similar manner. The audience count to five after I have knocked on the inside of my box. Then the cabinets are untied and opened. I appear from the one in which Rosie was placed, and she steps from mine. What do you think of that?"

"Amazing!" gasped Mary. "How's it done?"

"Ha! That would be telling. I'll say one thing though, nobody could possibly get out of one of those boxes while the ropes are around it."

"Good gracious!"

Moriarty shushed her. Mary was overacting. "I wonder if Rosie could, perhaps, take Miss Malloney to . . . er . . . to wash her hands, while we talk for a moment. In private." He looked hard at Mary and then back at Wotherspoon.

"Of course." Wotherspoon smiled nervously, his dark beard

twitching. "Rosie, show the lady up to your dressing room."

When they had gone, Moriarty sat down on a wooden stand chair that was part of Dr. Night's equipment.

"You must be getting most excited about Friday," he said amiably.

"Yes, yes indeed. Getting stage fright, if you want to know— something I've never suffered from in my life."

"Do they take you down on a special train or anything?"

"Oh my, do they not. They've got another act to replace me here for Friday night—the Elliotts and Savonas musical act. Perhaps you've heard of them?"

Moriarty nodded. Heard of them? He had employed them at one of his own music halls.

"I have to be here, with all my apparatus at the stage door, for three o'clock. Special coaches to Shoreditch and then a train down to Wolferton. There'll be an equerry traveling with us."

He made it sound very grand, and it was all Moriarty needed to know.

The stage curtain was down and nobody else in the vicinity, but for the stage-door keeper. Dr. Night's time had come.

"I was practicing that cut-and-restored-rope trick you showed me yesterday." Moriarty rose, quiet and slow—there was no sense in causing alarm. "I don't think I've got the moves quite right. I wonder if you could show me again before the girls come back."

"Yes, of course. There is a knack to it." Wotherspoon went over to one of his many tables. "Here, you take one piece of rope and follow the moves as I do them with this one."

He tossed a three-foot length of soft rope to Moriarty and began to walk toward him. When he was only a couple of paces away, Moriarty pointed across the room.

"Is that cabinet all right?" He sounded concerned.

Wotherspoon turned. Quicker than any magician, Moriarty lifted his hands. The rope was grasped tightly in each, passing around the fists, while the wrists were crossed.

The noose fell, exact, over Dr. Night's head, and Moriarty pulled outward and hard. He had learned the garrotte long ago.

The magician gave one low gurgle, like an airlock clearing in a water tap, his hands scrabbling at the curtailing rope, legs threshing, his whole body heaving, but it took no more than a minute before he went limp, dropping to the floor like a pile of clothes put out for the rag-and-bone man.

Moriarty, breathing hard from the exertion, rested for a moment before walking slowly to one of the Transmogrification Cabinets and opening the lid.

He dragged the body across the stage and pushed it, all of a heap, into the cabinet, reaching in to clear out the keys, watch and wallet from the pockets before shutting the door. It took some five or six minutes to rope and secure the cabinet. Dr. Night was correct when he said nobody could get out once the box was roped. He won't anyway, thought the Professor.

He was sorry about the girl but there was no other way the matter could be acocomplished, and he consoled himself with the thought that she was running to fat, would have been out of a job soon anyway, and appeared to have a vulgar streak.

"There ain't half a pong down here," she said when she returned with Mary. "Where's the great doctor?"

"In the cabinet," smiled Moriarty. "He wants you in the other one."

When it was all done, Moriarty dragged both cabinets into the wings, piling them against a convenient wall. He then took a pair of large labels from among Wotherspoon's effects, spent a few moments writing in plain capitals, and affixed one to each cabinet. They read:

DR. NIGHT. ILLUSIONIST AND
PRESTIDIGITATOR EXTRAORDINARY.
NOT WANTED AT SANDRINGHAM.

Moriarty had no doubt that Mary was truly frightened, but his mesmeric influence was still upon her, and there would be ample time to reinforce it during the days ahead. In the meantime she helped him pile Dr. Night's equipment in its usual position off stage. Moriarty had an eye for detail, and during the previous week he had made certain of the correct manner in which the magician kept his apparatus.

Once it was done, Moriarty led the girl up to Wotherspoon's dressing room. He was approaching the most difficult phase.

On the previous afternoon, the Professor had espied one of Wotherspoon's atrocious check suits hanging in the dressing room. It was still there and with Mary's help Moriarty changed. As he had guessed, they were about the same size, and although the effect was far from immaculate, there were no unseemly bags or bulges. He then opened his briefcase, removed the disguise material, and sat down in front of the mirror to complete the already much-practiced transformation.

It took a little less than half an hour, and when he was finished, Moriarty turned to face Mary.

"I can hardly believe—"

"You have to believe it." He spoke sharply. "From now on you have to believe that I am Dr. Night. You understand?"

She nodded meekly.

"Good. And you know what to do next?"

"I know."

"Then go to it."

Mary left the dressing room, passing down toward the stage door. The keeper did not seem to be about, but she waited for a moment before leaving quickly to join Harkness in Leicester Square, whence they drove to an appointed rendezvous.

Moriarty allowed another half hour to elapse before following her, but this time he paused at the stage door—it was the first test of his disguise.

The old keeper was there, sitting in his cubbyhole, all snug with a cup of tea and a pipe.

"Anyone using the stage in the morning?" Moriarty inquired.

"Not so far as I know, Mr. Wotherspoon." The old boy hardly looked up.

"Well, will you tell the stage manager I may need to use it all day," he said sharply. "I'll be rehearsing a new girl."

"New girl?" This time he did look up. "What's happened to our Rosie?"

"Didn't she tell you before she left?"

"Haven't seen her."

"Well, you won't now. I've had to fire her. Getting a bit above her station, that one."

The keeper nodded his head. "I had noticed, so I'm not surprised. Right, I'll tell him. You got anyone in mind?"

"A girl that's worked for me before. I'll have her in temporary anyway."

Moriarty walked casually through the stage door. He felt safer now—a new man almost.

Mrs. Sylvia Cowles opened the door.

"Inspector Crow?" asked Paget, smiling comfortably while inside he trembled, aspenlike.

"Who wishes to see him?"

"Inspector Crow, is he in?" he repeated.

"He is in, but who wishes to see him?"

"Me."

Paget drew the revolver: a movement of the hand and wrist only, no flamboyance or dramatics as he stepped inside, Mrs. Cowles backing away, her mouth gaping open and eyes screwed up as though the scream she wanted to let loose had actually broken from her vocal chords.

Paget kicked the door closed behind him. Now he could afford to menace.

"Where is he? No shouting or you'll get this in your pretty belly."

Her mouth opened wider; she swallowed, closed the lips again, then gaped once more.

"Come on, come on," Paget said gruffly.

She was not to know that the last thing he would have done was pull the trigger. She kept looking to her left, toward the second door along the passage.

"In there, is he?"

The look in Mrs. Cowles' eyes told Paget the truth. He prodded the unhappy lady with the barrel of his revolver, easing her forward and into the room.

Crow was sitting in an easy chair, turning the pages of some catalogue—for the couple were in the process of choosing items for the refurbishing of their home: garnering for domestic bliss.

Paget had to admit the copper was a cool one. He turned, almost lazily, taking in the situation at a glance, his eyes resting first on the revolver and then on Paget.

"Mr. Paget, I think," said Crow.

Paget tried not to sound alarmed. "You know me?"

"I was at your wedding, Paget. What's the meaning of this?"

Paget gave Mrs. Cowles a slight push toward her intended husband. "Both of you get over there." He indicated the corner of the room. "I won't keep you long." Then, as they obeyed his command, "You looking for me, are you?"

"You and several others."

"Professor Moriarty?"

"Naturally." Crow showed no sign of fear. "I would advise you, Paget, to put the gun down. If you do anything foolish, you'll not get far; that I'll promise."

"I'm not doing anything foolish, Inspector. I've come to make an arrangement with you."

"We don't make arrangements—as you put it—you should know that."

"Not even to lay hands on the Professor?"

His eyes strayed for a second to the ornate timepiece on the mantel. It showed almost half-past two.

"Give me the gun," said Crow calmly. "Then you can tell me

what you know: turn Queen's evidence, and I'll do what I can for
you.''

"You think I was born on a Friday and brought up by can-
dlelight? No, Inspector. I want my liberty. My freedom—''

"And your bride's?''

"Hers also.''

"I see no way. We'll get Moriarty, you know. If not today, then
tomorrow, or next week, or next year. It makes little difference to
us. We'll get him.''

All this time, Inspector Crow held Mrs. Cowles, an arm crooked
around her shoulders, while she sobbed quietly from shock and
fear.

"I've never blown on anybody yet, Mr. Crow. But now I'm
forced to because I want to live for me—and Fanny. I want to get
away, out of it, without your crushers pounding after me.''

"And what of Moriarty's crushers? Will they not be pounding
after you also?''

"Not if we're fast.''

Crow gave a small shrug.

"I know coppers aren't gents,'' continued Paget. "But I have to
take the chance. There are men around the house, back and front.''
He lied with the ease of one long practiced in the art. "Here's my
offer: I'll direct you to Moriarty's hideout. Like you, I can't make
no promises, because he'll know by now that I've gone. He'll
probably have half London looking for me at this very moment, and
I've only got a handful that's loyal to me.''

"You're a damned traitor. A turncoat. A blower.'' Crow
sounded disgusted.

"I value my future and I'm bidding all on it. I'll tell you where the
Professor's headquarters are located, how to get in—everything.
I'll give you that, if you'll give me an hour's start.''

The possibilities whirled in Crow's head. This was a gift: unexpected manna from heaven. They could catch Paget later, for if the
man were offering Moriarty's den on a plate, all the police resources
would have to be directed toward scouring it out. There would not
be time even to start looking for Paget—not yet anyhow; and that
was exactly what Paget had wagered upon.

Slowly Crow nodded. "I'll give you an hour.'' He spoke evenly.

Paget's stomach turned over: a wave of hope so strong he nearly
relaxed the grip on his revolver.

"All right, Inspector. It's a mutual trust. We have to take each
other at face value.''

He paused for what seemed a long period; then quietly, lucidly,
and without any trace of guilt, Paget gave the policeman precise

instructions concerning the warehouse. He spun it out for as long as possible, telling how to get to the place, painting, in words, the way to breach the wicket, describing the locks and bolts on the big double doors, and then outlining how the interior was arranged. It took some ten minutes during which Crow's concentration never wavered.

"Is there anything more you need know?" Paget finally asked.

"How many men might I expect to find there?"

"I can't say. There was confusion when I left. As I said, your birds may have flown. If not, there could be up to twenty or thirty—more if he's going to stand and fight. The entrances will be covered also from the outside. Moriarty has an excellent system of spies and watchers."

"And you say it has to be approached by foot, unless one goes through the docks?"

"You can get vans up to the front if you go through the docks, yes."

"Tell me about that."

Paget described the route for getting through to the court in front of the warehouse with vans and carts, knowing well enough that by now there should be transport enough leaving from that very spot.

"All right," Crow said finally. "I won't thank you now, Paget, because I'm sure we'll meet again."

"There are men around the house, I've told you that." Paget again eyed the clock. It had taken more than twenty minutes: seventy-odd minutes before Fanny would leave Paddington. "They'll be watching you for the next ten minutes." He smiled wickedly. "Believe me, Inspector Crow, they'll shoot anyone who tries to leave, back or front, before that time is up." He met Crow's level gaze and knew, deep down, that the policeman was onto his bluff. "I need time to get clear. You understand?"

"You'll be allowed to get clear."

Sylvia Cowles still sobbed hysterically. Paget did not envy the copper stuck with this lady.

"You mind I do, then."

Paget backed carefully to the door, and in a fast movement he stepped into the hallway, pulling the door closed behind him, then running to the front entrance.

The hansom was there waiting; he ran down to it, swinging himself up and calling, softly, to the cabbie, "Take me up to the Marble Arch." He knew he could slip quickly through the back streets from there down to Paddington.

The cab pulled away at a trot almost before he was inside. As Paget plumped into his seat a voice sounded in his ear.

"Well, Pip. I thought I'd save you for myself. Lucky my lurkers have been watching Mr. Crow."

Parker was seated next to him, an evil smile on his face, and a revolver pointing steadily at Paget's belly.

William S. Wotherspoon—Dr. Night—had lodgings in a house near St. Martin's Lane, convenient for the Alhambra which, Moriarty presumed, made up for the expense.

The Professor had already furnished himself with the details of Dr. Night's surprisingly uncomplicated domestic arrangements, knowing that offstage, and out of the theater, he was a man who kept mainly to himself. He also knew that Wotherspoon's landlady, a Mrs. Harrington, had a small, spare attic room that was unlet.

On leaving the theater, Moriarty walked quickly around to Cranbourne Street, where Harkness was waiting with Mary and the cab. From thence they drove to the vicinity of St. Martin's Lane, where Mary and the Professor left Harkness—the Professor giving his driver quick instructions to meet him on the following afternoon. They then walked through to the house owned by Mrs. Harrington: a cheery, red-faced woman, much enamoured of the gin bottle.

The Professor had to make a guess at which key on Wotherspoon's chain belonged to the front door, an easy task, for he was experienced in the ways of locks and locksmiths. Once inside the hall, Moriarty faced the second test of his disguise.

Mrs. Harrington came out of her front parlor as the Professor closed the door behind them.

"Mr. Wotherspoon," the landlady began gushingly, then, seeing Mary, raised her eyebrows. "Oh, you have company. You'd like tea in your room, would you?"

"If we could, Mrs. Harrington." He lowered the pitch of his voice slightly, bringing it more in line with that of the late departed magician. "And I wondered if you could help me."

"Anything for you, Mr. Wotherspoon." She giggled, primping like a young girl.

"It's Rosie," the Professor said gravely.

"What, young Rosie in your show?"

"I've had to let her go."

"Oh. Given her the sack, have you?" Like the stage-door keepkeeper, she did not sound surprised.

"I try to avoid that phrase, Mrs. Harrington. Not a pleasant phrase. But, yes, she's had to go. This is Miss Mary Malloney, who'll be replacing her."

The landlady smiled, warm with spirits. "Pleased to meet you, I'm sure."

"Pleased to meet you," responded Mary.

"I was wondering," Moriarty hesitated. "Miss Malloney has no lodgings nearby, and we have much work to do if she's going to be an asset to the act."

"Yes?"

Any minute, he thought, Mrs. Harrington was going to say something about hers being a respectable house.

"I was wondering if, for a few days, Miss Malloney could have your attic room. You haven't let it, have you?"

"No," she said uncertainly. "No, it's not let."

"Then I'll pay you well above your normal price, as it is only for a short while and would be a great convenience to me."

Reluctant though she might be, Mrs. Harrington was not one for turning down quick and good money.

"Then she shall have it; but for how long?"

"Only until the end of the week. You see," Moriarty became pompous in the true Dr. Night fashion, "we have much to do before Friday when we appear before the Prince and Princess."

Mrs. Harrington had obviously allowed that small jewel to slip from her mind, and now almost bowed in vicarious respect.

"Oh, yes. Yes, of course, I was forgetting. Of course, she may have it."

"Then I'll come down and talk terms later."

The landlady bobbed. "I'll get your teas then. Give me just a few minutes."

After tea Moriarty bade Mary to be silent while he sat at the table in Wotherspoon's pleasant, if cluttered, rooms. The tea things were cleared and in their place Moriarty spread out a map, armed himself with a pair of compasses, a ruler, some paper, pen and a nautical almanac—all of which were handy in the briefcase he had brought from Limehouse.

For an hour he pored over the map, noting a section of sea coast, straddled with sandbanks, spits, bars and mudflats, bearing such names as Thief Sand, Peter Black, Middle Roads, Sal's Bay, Old Boat Knock and Vinegar Middle.

After an hour of calculations Moriarty picked up his pen and began to draft a long, coded, telegraph. It would be sent, first thing in the morning, to Jean Grisombre in Paris.

The cab was rumbling away, picking up speed as the driver lashed at the horse, and though they were being bounced and bumped in the cramped interior the smile of victory did not leave Parker's lips, nor did the gun tremble in his hand.

"I think I'll have your weapon," said the chief lurker smoothly.

"Where are we going?" Paget's voice was desperate with anguish.

"You'll see soon enough. Your weapon."

Paget glanced out the window to see that they were turning away from the direction he had first ordered, now heading to Kensington. From thence, he supposed, they would rattle out toward Berkshire, and once there he would stand no chance. If he did not act quickly, Paget would certainly be a dead man before morning.

"I can explain." He tried to smile. "It's not as black as it may seem, Parker."

"You can tell that to the Professor. Or to Spear. He wants a word with you as well."

The cab had begun to roll with an even rhythm. Paget shrugged, hoping that a nonchalant manner might put Parker off guard.

"Come on. Your weapon. Where is it, in your belt?"

So saying, he stretched out his left hand, keeping his right at his side, the revolver leveled.

Paget did not move quickly: undue haste in a captive made for quick work with the trigger. He dropped his hand to his belt, slowly reaching inside; then, as the cab rolled, Paget went with it, letting his weight fall across Parker. Slipping the gun from his belt, he cocked and fired in one motion, the muzzle jammed hard into his captor's guts.

He heard Parker's weapon fall to the floor and was conscious of wetness spreading from the man's body to his. Paget pulled away, glancing up to see if the driver was doing anything about the shot. But the man had all his time cut out controlling his horse, which was now almost at a gallop, weaving through the heavy traffic. On their right Paget saw the green of Kensington Gardens.

He moved as far away as he could from Parker's corpse, which now bumped and rolled around the interior with every sway and bounce. But they were slowing; the traffic was getting thicker all the time. Paget grasped the handle on his door, pushed open and leaned out. There was an omnibus ahead, and several cabs. Behind them a van and at least three carriages, all jamming together as they approached the High Street. But their positioning was in Paget's favor, his cab being far over to the left, quite near the pavement, dotted with folks out for their Sunday afternoon stroll, window shopping.

The driver was pulling the horse back now, slowing and glancing back into the cab. Pushing his gun back into his belt, Paget took a deep breath, threw open the cab door and leaped out, sprawling on the pavement to the accompanying cries and gasps of passersby.

He heard a loud shout from the cabbie and a yell from one of the drivers coming up behind, but he did not hesitate. Recovering as fast as possible, Paget took to his heels, handing off the few people who seemed bent on trying to stop him. He swerved, faltered, swerved again, then turned and dashed full tilt down a friendly alley.

It was ten minutes' hard running before Paget knew he was away for sure and able to slow down, gulp at the air and mop his face with his handkerchief. He could not tell where he was, but some five minutes later he hailed a passing cab, offering the driver double fare if he got him to Paddington station before four o'clock.

They were too late. Crow waited for only five minutes, paying scant attention to Sylvia's pleadings to do as Paget had ordered. He wanted to get the commissioner and assistant commissioner as quickly as possible. Time was not to be wasted now, for he had a duty to mount the largest police raid ever undertaken in the history of the force.

There were no mobsmen waiting with guns as he finally ran from King Street, nor was there any sign of Paget, and it was not until the following day, when the report of Parker's death in the hansom came in from T Division that Crow was able to put two and two together.

By five o'clock the commissioner had given his blessing and men from both the Metropolitan and City forces were assembling at their stations.

The raid took place at a little after twenty-five past six. Seven police vans galloped through the docks to pull up, with snorting, rearing, horses, in the open space before the warehouse. At the same time more police poured into the Limehouse area, trotting down through the archway, running in file the length of the alley to join with those who had come in by van.

They smashed the wicket and charged into the big, open, ground floor. From there detachments swarmed through to the "waiting room" and kitchens, along the passages, up the spiral stairs to the chambers and secure rooms, and speedily ascended the short flight of wooden stairs to Moriarty's private quarters.

But the warehouse was empty. Food was still in the kitchens and store rooms; numerous private possessions were left scattered about—rings, pictures, clothes and the like—but nothing of any real value.

In Moriarty's chambers, the books had been removed from the shelves, and all that remained were a few papers and a pile of ashes. Crow sifted through the burned cinders, retrieving the odd scrap of charred paper on which writing was still legible, and during the next

few days every item left by the former occupants was neatly labeled
and examined. Yet there were no hard clues, no hints of where
either the Professor or his gang had gone. It was as though they had
vanished in a puff of smoke.

It was almost ten past four when the hansom got Paget to the station.
He pushed money into the cabbie's hand and ran toward the refreshment rooms. But there was no sign of Fanny. In a panic he ran again
out onto the main hallway of the station, his eyes turning this way
and that, wild, like the eyes of a madman in his frantic search. But
still no sign, until at last he caught a startled porter by the waistcoat,
demanding if there was an engine to Leamington.

"Over there. Just going . . ." The porter raised a trembling hand
toward the platform.

Paget ran once more, the money in his hand. The ticket collector
at the gate tried to stop him but he pushed money at the man,
shouting he would pay at the other end if necessary. The ticket
collector—a portly officious menial—even attempted to halt him by
stretching out an arm, but Paget merely pushed him to one side as
though he were a flimsy bush.

The guard had already blown his whistle and the flag was up, but
Paget could see Fanny now, leaning from a window halfway down
the train, shouting to him. He called, all right and he was coming,
then forced the last ounces of speed from his leaden legs as the train
began to move.

Fanny had the door of her compartment open, assisted by a young
man with spectacles, who looked like some clerk but entered into
the spirit of the adventure suddenly thrust upon him.

As the engine screeched its departing whistle and let out a huge
whoof of white smoke, so Paget's foot hit the carriage floor and he
was hoisted up and into Fanny's arms—embracing her as though
there would never be another day for either of them.

There were those among the stage staff at the Alhambra Palace of
Varieties who said they had never seen Dr. Night work in such a
concentrated manner as he did on the Monday when taking his new
assistant through the act. Most of them, naturally, put it down to the
forthcoming engagement at Sandringham. But, whatever the
reason, the magical doctor put the young woman through the hoop
well and proper.

During the morning he led her, gently at first, through the routine
of his act: where she had to stand, when she was required to hand
things to him or show them to the audience. Then after a break for

lunch Dr. Night had the stage cleared, the safety curtain lowered, and ordered everyone out of the wings while he rehearsed the attractive Miss Malloney through her paces in the big illusions: how to position herself to make the secret entrance to the Egyptian sarcophagus; how to buckle on the special harness and metal rods hidden under her costume for the levitation, and then exactly how to use them in order to give the impression that she was floating in midair.

They spent much of the afternoon, once she had everything firmly in her head, running through the act again and again, except for a break of half an hour when the doctor received two visitors in his dressing room.

The two callers were, of course, Ember and Harkness, to whom the Professor was now able to impart further instruction, hear about how Spear was organizing matters in Berkshire, and the depressing news concerning the raid on the warehouse and Parker's untimely end.

Before they left, Moriarty reinforced his orders.

"You must be waiting from at least ten o'clock onward," he told Ember. "Just in case anything goes wrong. And you"—he turned to Harkness—"had better get down tonight. I want you to know those roads like the backs of your own hands, so that you could drive them fast and blindfold—as indeed you will have to do."

That evening Dr. Night appeared to be in exceptional form. The stage manager said later, "It could be a completely new act. He seems so fresh. Perhaps the girl's giving him something he's never had before."

"I just hope it ain't leprosy," rejoined the stage hand.

During the whole week, everyone at the Alhambra had to admit that Dr. Night had never been as good, though there were those who found him much less approachable offstage: getting swellheaded, they said, what with the royal command and all.

As for Inspector Crow, his job had rarely been so frustrating. They had gone over the few papers and scraps a dozen times, hoping some clue might be unearthed. But Moriarty's whereabouts remained a mystery that Crow despaired of solving.

Friday, April 27, 1894

(THE LAST TRICK)

AT PRECISELY THREE o'clock on the afternoon of Friday, April 27, 1894, two carriages and a van turned into Leicester Square and pulled up to one side of the Alhambra. Workmen began to bring heavy packing cases from the stage door and load them into the van. There was also a large trunk, bearing the painted legend DR NIGHT.

An equerry and two other gentlemen left the carriages and made their way to the stage door, where the manager of the theater was waiting to introduce them to Dr. Night and his charming assistant, Miss Mary Malloney.

At half-past three the whole party came out and boarded the carriages, which bore them away to the special train chartered to take the illusionist to Wolferton and thence by coach again to the royal house at Sandringham.

It was half-past seven when they finally steamed into Wolferton and boarded the carriages that were to carry them on the last fifteen minutes' journey to the Prince of Wales' country home. The road passed between bare commons and clumps of fir trees—a wild, flat and bleak part of the world.

On arrival Moriarty reflected that the old Queen, it was said, considered Sandringham an unlucky house, while others thought of it as the flashpoint of society. Perhaps, Moriarty thought grimly, both these things will truly be proved before the night is done.

More workmen appeared to unload Dr. Night's props, while the equerry ushered the doctor and his young woman through the portals, along corridors, and into the big Edis ballroom, which had been set up for the entertainment—some thirty or forty chairs arranged in neat rows facing the large bay windows on the east side, in front of which Dr. Night was to perform.

It was an impressive room, a room in which to make a crowning appearance, thought Moriarty. It was nearly seventy feet long, thirty wide and twenty-three high, with a smooth oak parquet floor, rich alcoves, panels and, so the equerry said, one hundred and twenty-six gas jets for illumination; the whole was embellished with Indian shields, tiger skins, elephant cloths and the like.

To one side of the eastern bay window, chairs and music stands were arranged for the orchestra, which already waited patiently for Dr. Night's arrival, and once the trunks and cases were unloaded, the doctor handed out his orchestra parts and went into quick consultation with both the conductor and leader.

Once the orchestra had run through the music and the conductor was certain of all the cues, Dr. Night asked the equerry if he might be left alone to unpack and prepare the act in front of the rich cream tapestry curtains that draped the large windows.

The equerry saw to it and told the illusionist that light refreshment was prepared for him in one of the nearby rooms—he would dine later, when the performance was done. Their Royal Highnesses and their guests were at dinner now, and it was thought they would be ready for the entertainment at about ten o'clock.

Outside a breeze was stiffening up the Wash, bringing with it the rain that had threatened all day. A few miles off, in a tavern at Wolferton, Harkness drank a glass of brandy, often taking out his watch to count off the slow-passing hours.

Back in London it had been an irritating, frustrating day for Angus Crow. He had looked through the papers and charred remains from the warehouse yet again, and he found himself strangely returning, for the umpteenth time, to one fragment: a piece of paper, scorched, burned off at an angle, and brown with heat, upon which a few words could be made out:

> If
> e in
> , that
> be most
> onvenient,
> time and date
> mply.
>
> ant,
> spoon.
> Night)

There was something there which Inspector Angus McCready Crow found disturbing. He could not put his finger on it, but the thought had nagged since he first saw the fragment. Night was right, no matter if it was spelled with a capital letter: all the logic in the world would not change that. The business became so downright irritating that by late afternoon Crow had reached the end of his tether. He should not, he thought, be cooped up here in an office, trying to use his own particular methods of logical deduction. He should be out and about, searching, raking over the middens and cesspits of the criminal world, hauling in every petty villain and sneak thief, every dipper and macer on the streets—beating information out of them if necessary.

He was tired. Maybe tomorrow he would go out with his men, make a few surprise raids, drag in known villains, and go through them like an overdose of the Duncan & Flockhart's Cascara Capsules Sylvia kept in her medicine chest. But today he would let it rest.

He left Scotland Yard at ten minutes to five and took a hansom back to King Street, surprising Sylvia Cowles, who was in the sitting room, in an absolute uproar, with writing materials, envelopes, scissors, and what seemed to be a huge pile of *The Times*.

"You've caught me properly on the hop, my darling," Mrs. Cowles said brightly. "I have been writing letters, and clipping out copies of our engagement announcement to send to a few friends and relatives."

"We could start a shop with all this," Crow said cheerfully, picking a hacked sheet of the newspaper from his favorite chair. His eye ran across the page still held in his hand. Then suddenly there it was, staring him in the face under the Court Circular:

. . . . There will be a dinner party on Friday, 27th, when the entertainment will be provided by the celebrated illusionist, Dr. Night.

The charred fragment? Night? Dr. Night? Crow scanned the whole paragraph in the Court Circular again. Sandringham? The Prince of Wales? Could it possibly be? No, he thought, too much of a long shot. But then again, what if it was? He would never forgive himself. Dr. Night and the Prince and Princess of Wales?

Crow leaped to his feet.

"Good God!" he exclaimed. "I have to rush. Don't know when I'll be back, but don't worry. I think I know where Moriarty's been hiding himself."

In the hansom on the way back to Scotland Yard Crow reasoned things out. He could not make an official issue of this, for the red tape would strangle matters; everybody would be havering, not knowing whether they should do this or that or the other thing. He would have to bank his whole career on it. If he were wrong, it could be that he would cause great displeasure with Albert Edward, Prince of Wales. It would be the end of him. But then if he were right . . .

Tanner was still in the office.

"Get your things together, sarn't, we're going for a wee' train ride."

The sergeant tried to ask questions, but Crow was having none of it. All he required was the time of the next train to Wolferton, or if necessary, King's Lynn. There was one, he discovered, at ten minutes past six, and if they hurried, they might just make it. Crow hastily scrawled out a telegraph message for the constabulary at Lynn and instructed a constable to get it off posthaste. He next unlocked his desk drawer, in which he kept a service revolver and fifty rounds of ammuniton, stowed the weapon in the pocket of his Inverness, which he wore because the weather looked threatening, and made for the street with Tanner close at his heels. With any luck they would be in King's Lynn at half-past nine, Wolferton by quarter to ten, and, if the constabulary at Lynn did as they were told, they could be galloping up through the Sandringham estate by just after ten.

Crow wondered what time their Royal Highnesses dined, and what time they gave their guests the special entertainment.

Harkness left the tavern soon after half-past nine. Five minutes later he was in the driving seat and had his horse trotting up the bleak road, made even more wild now by the rain which was becoming heavier, and seemed to have set in for the night.

Dr. Night and his assistant set up the many tables and pieces of apparatus. They then went to the rooms provided for changing into their dress for the performance. Moriarty took his briefcase with him.

Mary McNiel put on the special Egyptian princess costume, which was cleverly made so that it could be disguised and worn under the golden fringed outfit she wore for the first part of the act.

Moriarty arrayed himself in the full evening dress required, neatly brushing the coat and making sure his disguise was in perfect conditon. He then opened the briefcase and drew out the Borchardt automatic pistol, cocked it, set the safety catch, and placed it in one of the many easily accessible pockets of the magician's dress coat. When all was done, he left the room, called for Mary, and together they were taken for some light refreshment. Their Royal Highnesses and their guests, the equerry told them, were just finishing dinner. The ladies had withdrawn, and His Royal Highness the Prince of Wales had indicated that the gentlemen would not linger long over their port.

It was almost quarter to ten.

At the lodge the gates were open, but the porter came out and stopped Harkness just the same, inquiring his business. Harkness said what he had been told—that he was one of Dr. Night's people, carrying some important items for the performance. The porter thought nothing of it and Harkness drove quietly through the parkland, for the rumble of wheels and noise of his horse's hooves were now well drowned by the rain. The driver turned up his coat collar, finally bringing the cab to a halt in the shelter of a wall by the east window of the ballroom.

It was nearly ten o'clock.

The train was late. A good half hour late, for it was ten o'clock by the time they pulled into King's Lynn. Tanner looked and felt decidedly nervous, not having great faith in Inspector Crow's logical deductive theory. He felt, as he told his superior, that the name Dr. Night, scrawled on one scrap of burned paper found in the warehouse, did not constitute any real evidence. Not enough anyway to warrant their plunging in on the Prince of Wales' dinner party.

Crow became decidedly dour and sharp as the journey got later. At King's Lynn a somewhat abrupt-mannered inspector came aboard the train to talk with Crow. He had done as Scotland Yard had requested, said the inspector. The carriage and van load of constables were already waiting at Wolferton, though for the life of him, he did not see what all the fuss was about.

"Just trust me, Inspector," said Crow, somewhat mysteriously.

He was damned if more cold water was going to be poured on his theory by the new arrival.

"I'll take full responsibility," he added, looking at his sergeant. "That also applies to you."

It was twenty minutes past ten before the Prince and Princess entered the ballroom with their guests. Moriarty watched the arrival with some pleasure. The portly little Prince was beaming, at his most charming. Princess Alexandra looked as lovely as ever, though she limped badly from her rheumatism, a sad legacy of the cold and damp that silted in around Sandringham from the North Sea and the Wash. The young Duke and Duchess of York were also present, living as they did in York House in the grounds of the estate. And there were many other faces Moriarty recognized—the ladies elegant and dripping with rich jewels, which made the Professor's mouth water.

At last they were all settled and the master of ceremonies announced, "Your Royal Highnesses, my Lords, Ladies and Gentlemen. For your delectation, the great illusionist—Dr. Night."

At a signal the orchestra began Dr. Night's music. Moriarty's hand stole into the secret pocket, his fingers touching the butt of the Borchardt. He then withdrew the hand, straightened his shoulders and made an impressive entrance to regal applause.

The time was a quarter to eleven, and Crow's train was at a halt, held up by a signal some ten minutes from Wolferton station.

Dr. Night had never before performed like this. The act as presented at Sandringham included a number of small items—most suitable for the relative intimacy of the audience—not usually in his stage show. And by the time the Egyptian sarcophagus illusion had been performed and Mary, enchanting in her costume, completed her sinuous dance (which she did with much more style than Rosie), the audience was gasping with pleasure. Moriarty felt extreme elation. To perform like this was as enjoyable as any sensation he had yet experienced and he determined to savor it to the very end.

Dr. Night proceeded with the borrowing of the rings, even taking a signet ring proffered by the Prince himself, and mixing the magic omelette.

The time was ten minutes past eleven.

At a quarter-past eleven Crow's train drew into Wolferton station. It had hardly reached a halt before the detective was out and running, with his sergeant and the inspector from Lynn, toward the barrier and the waiting transport. He stopped for only a brief word with the drivers and constables before climbing into the coach and yelling to the driver, telling him, above the now steady hiss of rain, to "go like thunder."

The cavalcade set off at a dangerous gallop.

It was plain to see that the Prince and Princess, let alone their guests, were enjoying the performance enormously: Princess Alexandra had squealed with delight over the doves, and the Prince guffawed when the selected playing cards magically appeared on the points of the silver star. But now Dr. Night was reaching his apogee—the great feat of levitation.

With care he mesmerized his assistant into a trance; the music shivered softly as she was placed upon the couch, and, with deep concentration, the doctor made his mystic passes. Slowly she began to float into the air.

The police cavalcade was just turning into the main gateway, and Crow, already with one hand on the carriage door, curled his fingers around the butt of his revolver.

With snorting horses, pawing hooves, and much clatter, the carriage and van came to a halt. Crow leaped down with Tanner behind him. The constables tumbled from the van, a pair of them peeling off to go with Crow, the remainder running in an attempt to seal off all possible exits.

As the floating figure of Mary McNiel descended to the couch, so Crow hammered on the front door.

Moriarty, as Dr. Night, bowed to the enthusiastic applause that burst from the private audience. Amid the clapping he could hear the Prince of Wales cheering, "Bravo! Bravo!"

He made one deep bow, a sweeping act of obeisance, his eyes lifting toward the bearded and smiling Prince, and his right hand moving back to grasp the Borchardt, thumb pushing the catch off safety. Then, as he straightened, Moriarty drew out the weapon.

As the Professor's hand moved up, finger tightening on the trigger, there was a loud babble of voices from outside. For a second, Moriarty hesitated. Then the doors burst open.

The Prince turned, half coming to his feet, a confused grumble of words rolling across the audience. Moriarty brought his hand fully up, squinting aim down the barrel, but his eyes were drawn to the doorway where several dripping-wet men were pushing their way past three flunkeys. The leading man, tall, in a soaking Inverness, shouted, "Stop. Stop or I fire."

Moriarty paused, then, in expected retaliation, moved the pistol a few inches to the left of his aim, and squeezed the trigger.

Crow heard the wood and plaster splatter to his left as the bullet whined into the wall. He took quick aim and loosed off a shot with his service revolver; the bullet smashed through the windows behind the dark and bearded figure standing amid the magical apparatus.

There was screaming now, and Moriarty knew there was but one course to take. If he stayed, death was inevitable. To run was more prudent. Another bullet, closer this time, fragmenting the silver star used for the card trick. Somebody shouted, "Down. Get down." Then another voice again commanded, "Stop."

The Professor waited for no more. One bound and he was behind the east bay-window drapes, and with a leap, turning in the air, went crashing backward through the glass.

Crow was dashing pell-mell down the ballroom, pistol up and his wet boots slipping on the polished parquet. He stopped short for another shot at the fleeting figure, but the revolver bucked in his hand a second after the crunch and tinkle of glass signaled that Moriarty was through the window.

The Professor rolled as he hit the ground, feeling the shuddering jar, and then the enveloping dampness. He scrabbled to his feet, the sound of shouts and screams still coming from behind him, and the piercing shriek of a police whistle cleaving the darkness.

It took him only a second to get his bearings and run toward where he knew Harkness was waiting with the cab. He rounded the building, and heard the snort of the horse; then, out of the blackness, came a uniformed policeman. Automatically Moriarty brought his gun hand up and fired, smiling into the rain as he heard the gasp and saw the figure disappear, to go rolling onto the wet ground.

"Here. Quickly, Professor," Harkness called, and the next moment he was in the cab with the driver whipping up the horses just as another shot ripped into the woodwork.

Crow and Tanner had followed Moriarty through the window, and indeed it was Crow who loosed off the final shot at the fast-departing cab. Now he was running for the police carriage, shouting at the driver to turn the horses and get after the hansom.

Harkness peered through the heavy rain and murk that surrounded them, urging the horse forward with his whip. For him this was the most difficult part; the roads outside the boundaries of the estate he knew backward, having spent the whole week driving them night and day. Soaked to the bone, he hunched forward on his seat, watching for the gates ahead.

They came up quickly through the film of water, the porter running into the drive waving his arms, but Harkness flicked the whip over his horse's flanks and drove on so that the porter had to leap for his life. Behind him, Harkness heard a shot—the Professor potting hopefully at the sprawled porter.

Then they were out, turning and rumbling off toward Dersingham, eating up the road, with the wind and rain stinging the driver's face, roaring in his ears above the rattle of the cab and the metal hoofbeats of the horse.

The gatehouse porter was lying, drenched, beside the drive, part of his shoulder ripped away by the Professor's parting shot. But he was conscious enough to cry that the cab had taken the Dersingham road. Crow swore, shouting to him that there'd be others along in a moment.

The police driver called back that he did not think much of their chances on a black and wet night like this. But Crow, infuriated with failure, screamed at him to go on.

An hour or so later, going around in circles, riding back and forth through Dersingham and along the surrounding roads he knew it was no good. Tomorrow they would mount some kind of a search for the cab but Crow knew it would be useless. It was at this moment, standing by the side of the road, his clothes sticking to his body, hair plastered over his head and down his face, that Inspector Angus McCready Crow dedicated his life's work to the capture, imprisonment, and final execution of Professor James Moriarty, or any man who lived under that name.

At Dersingham they turned left, heading toward the sea. After a mile or so Harkness slowed, in order to cross the Hunstanton Railway at Dersingham station. It was a mile further on that they saw the light, held swinging by the roadside.

Ember came out of the darkness, holding the lamp high.

"You're all right, Professor?" he shouted through the wind and rain.

Moriarty swore, stepping down from the cab and wrapping around him the cloak Harkness had placed in the back of the cab.

"Did you—" started Ember.

"Crow," spat Moriarty. "Crow, by heaven. He was onto me."

"We got away though," chimed Harkness with relish.

"Aye, we did. But I'll be back."

Ember clutched at Moriarty's arm.

"We must go quickly. They'll not wait forever. It's nearly two miles, and heavy going at that."

Moriarty nodded, raising his hand in farewell to Harkness as Ember lifted the lamp and began the long trudge, guiding his master across the sand and mud flats to where the dinghy waited at the entrance between Wolferton Creek and the Inner Roads.

Snug in their bed in the small tavern some three miles out of Leamington Spa, Fanny Paget smiled in her sleep, rolled over and threw an arm across her husband's chest.

Tomorrow, she thought dimly within sleep. Tomorrow we can look for work. The new life is here, and we are free.

Saturday, April 28, 1894

(THE SECOND EXILE)

MORIARTY GAZED OUT on the shoreline as it receded into the morning mist. They had followed the coast through the early hours, hugging it and making good use of the stiff breeze, wallowing a little from the heavy swell. Now, *Le Conflit*, an old French-built fishing smack that Grisombre had sent for him was pointing her bows toward home. For Moriarty it meant safety.

Ember had been sick from the moment they had got into the dinghy to row out to *Le Conflit*, and was now propped, green, in one corner of the wheelhouse. Moriarty drew his eyes back from the dipping shoreline and smiled. In a few hours he would be in Belgium. Tomorrow Paris, next week Marseilles and a boat to America. He glanced back again. It would not be long before he would return.

He thought of the house and estate in Berkshire. Spear would be just waking, next to his Bridget. Today he would doubtless make arrangements for the cash carriers to pay their money to some house in London, convenient for it to be brought down to the country. With Parker gone there would have to be much rearranging among the lurkers; one of the Jacobs boys would perhaps take Parker's place. The lurkers would become more important now that the headquarters was moved out of London.

He felt a twinge of annoyance at last night's failure. But something like that would not go against him. If anything, the attempt would only serve to show him to good advantage—for who else but Moriarty could have walked into Sandringham and out again, with the police baying at his heels. He thought about that for a moment, wondering in passing what had become of Mary McNiel. She would live. Girls like Mary McNiel always survived.

In London they would be waking up also, the markets setting up stalls for Saturday's trading—in Lambeth and the Elephant and Castle; Petticoat Lane, Berwick Street and out at Shepherd's Bush. The costermongers would be carting their wares about, and the more fashionable shops—the drapers, grocers, haberdashers, tailors and dressmakers—taking down their shutters. The whores would still be sleeping, their turn to come at evening; and the public houses, taverns and inns would already be alive with people.

The dippers would be at it by now, and the macers and bullies: his dippers, his macers, his bullies.

Moriarty laughed aloud, for as he thought of all this trade and work beginning, he also reflected how, at some point during the day, pairs of hard young men—one of them always carrying a black bag—would pass among these people, stopping at stalls, in shops and restaurants, public houses and thieves' kitchens. They would smile quietly at the proprietors and stall holders, or at the whores' cash carriers, and say wherever they went, "We've come for the Professor's contribution."

Better still, it was not just happening in London, but also in other cities—among tradesfolk and criminals alike—in Manchester and Liverpool, Birmingham, Newcastle, Leeds, and soon further still, in Paris, Lyons, Marseilles, Rome, Naples, Milan, Berlin, Hamburg, right across the Continent—and maybe further, even to the new world of America.

As the spray came up over the ploughing bows of *Le Conflit*, Moriarty felt truly master of his world. For the fine mist that spread about the ship seemed to carry with it those words of comfort—"We've come. Come for the Professor's contribution."

Glossary

abbess	female brothel keeper
alderman	a half crown
barkers, barking irons	pistols, revolvers
blow, blower	inform, informant
bludger	violent criminal, apt to use a bludgeon
broadsman	a card sharper: hence, *broading*
buttoner	decoy
cash carrier	ponce, or whore's minder
caper	a criminal act, dodge or device
candle to the devil, to hold a	to be evil
Chapel, the	Whitechapel
chaunting	singing: more explicitly, criminal informing, or exposing
chiv	knife
cracksman	burglar, safecracker
crooked cross, to play the	betray, swindle, cheat
crow	a lookout
devil's claws	the broad arrows on a convict's uniform
don	a distinguished (expert, clever) person; a leader
dollymop	a whore—often an amateur or part-time street girl

287

drum	a building, house or lodging
dipper	pickpocket
duffer	a seller of supposed stolen goods
esclop	policeman: backslang. The *c* is not pronounced, and the *e* is often omitted
family, the	the criminal underworld
fawney	a ring
fawney-dropping	a ruse whereby the villain pretends to find a ring (which is worthless) and sells it as a possibly valuable article at a low price
flash	vulgar, showy, criminal
gen	a shilling
glim, to catch the	venereal disease
gonoph	minor thief, small-time criminal
gulpy	easily duped
hammered for life	to be married
holy water sprinkler	a cudgel spiked with nails
Huntley, to take the	take the cake, or biscuit: to be most excellent (Huntley & Palmers Biscuits)
irons	See *barking irons*
kinchen-lay	stealing from children
know life	knowledgeable of criminal ways
lackin	wife
ladybird	a whore
Laycock, Miss	female sexual organs
lurker	criminal man of all work, especially a beggar, or one who uses a beggar's disguise
lushery, lushing ken	low public house or drinking den
macer	a cheat
magsman	an inferior cheat
mandrake	a homosexual

mobsman	a swindler, pickpocket, usually well dressed and originally of the Swell Mob (early nineteenth-century high-grade thieves and pickpockets)
monkery	the country
mollisher	a woman, often a villain's mistress
mutcher	a thief who steals from drunks
nibbed	arrested
Nebuchadnezzar	the male sexual organs. Hence: *put Nebuchadnezzar out to grass*, to have sexual intercourse
netherskens	low lodging houses
nickey	simple (in the head)
nobblers	those who nobble, i.e., criminals used for the express purpose of inflicting grievous bodily harm
palmers	shoplifters
pig	policeman, usually a detective
punishers	superior *nobblers*, men employed to inflict severe beatings
racket	illicit criminal occupations and tricks
rampsman, rampers	a tearaway, hoodlum
ream	superior, good: as in *ream swag*, highly valued stolen property
Rothschild, to come the	to brag and pretend to be rich
salt box	the condemned cell
St. Peter's needle	severe discipline
sharp	a (card) swindler
servants lurk	lodging or public house used by shady, or dismissed, servants
shirkster	a layabout
shofulman	a coiner
snakesman	slightly built (boy) criminal used in burglary and housebreaking
sweeteners	decoys used by street traders and swindlers to push prices up or be seen to win

toffer	a superior whore
toolers	pickpockets
trasseno	an evil person